Honeymoon Diary

BOOKS BY JIM BISHOP

Honeymoon Diary
The Murder Trial of Judge Peel
Some of My Very Best
The Day Christ Was Born
Go with God
The Day Christ Died
The Golden Ham
The Day Lincoln Was Shot
The Making of a Priest
The Girl in Poison Cottage
Parish Priest
Mark Hellinger Story
The Glass Crutch

Honeymoon

HARPER & ROW, PUBLISHERS

Diary

by JIM BISHOP

NEW YORK, EVANSTON, AND LONDON

With enduring affection,
this book is dedicated
to my wife,
Kelly

FOR THE RECORD:

       THIS IS the story of the first thirty days of a marriage. It is, of course, an intimate document. For a brief moment, the world revolves around a man and a woman who feel that love insures happiness. During the same brief moment, the man and woman move around the world on a honeymoon and thus, in a twofold sense, they are adventurers. And perhaps fools.

The man is a middle-aged writer. The woman is twenty years younger. There is a psychological thesis that most humans, if given the opportunity, are prone to repeat their biggest mistakes. Both these people have been married before and feel that they know, and can avoid, the irreparable errors.

The word honeymoon is, in itself, an illusion of romance, which declines to acknowledge, in prefix, suffix or root, the possibility of shocking maladjustment, of failure to distinguish between whim and need, the rutted monotony on the face of the future, the end-over-end falls into valleys of doubt, the seal of shyness on blunt speech, the reaching and groping to comprehend and appreciate a world of two, rather than one.

Newlyweds exist in a cocoon of affection. For a brief time, they are insulated against almost all of the practicalities. They tell a rosary of ecstasy; they find poetry in the prosaic; faith in a glance; music in a vagrant touch; God in a wedding band; mutual idolatry at the altar of vanity. This is the false sunrise which will, in time, become a warm and enduring day, or, if it is stared at long and hard, cause blindness.

What is true love? I do not know, unless it is weighed against adversity. Even then, I could not say whether the little woman who suffers constant beatings and neglect at the hands of a cruel husband is in love or in a rut. How about the cuckolded husband who knows, and who forgives again and again and again? Is he in love? Or is he afraid to be alone in the dark? Love is an emotion unseen by all except one person. It usually is synonymous with the word forever.

How long is forever? Love is nourished on a reciprocal emotion. Can it starve to death? It can. It has. It will. Ergo: the word forever is an exaggeration. How many loves fill one heart? How many kinds? Love of self; love of the adored one; love of parents; children; brethren—how many? Love of self, it would seem, takes precedence over all the others because when self is threatened by any of the other loves, those loves wither.

So, if one is to measure love, it is necessary to start with the ego and ask it how much it will sacrifice of its sovereignty for someone else. The ego, unfortunately, is unresponsive to questions. It thrives only on the warmth of approval. Love, therefore, is difficult to measure.

The two people in this story have no excuse for failure. Each has loved before. Each has lost a marriage. They know the dark hours; they know the noble ones too. Each is certain that, this time, he is prepared to give more than to receive. The ego is slightly wrinkled.

The story opens on the day of the marriage, and closes on the thirtieth day, when they return from their around-the-world honeymoon. The man is a mosaic of all the writers I know. The woman is an average, fairly intelligent person, a bit too quick to pander to the man, a bit too afraid of another failure.

It is not my wish to detail a massive apology for marriage. I am in favor of the marital state, and I would not want the protagonists of my first novel to fail to attain the tranquillity to which they are entitled. On the other hand, I do not believe that permanent good can accrue to anyone who does not work for it. In the case of two people, it is twice as true.

JIM BISHOP

Sea Bright, New Jersey

THE FIRST DAY

THE outer office was warm. A male secretary sat at a desk, tapping the keys of a typewriter with one finger, his eyes glancing at the sheet of paper after each tap. The venetian blinds were open and, outside, fat snowflakes tumbled slowly to calcimine the skyscrapers and streets of New York. Far below, wintry gusts carried the flakes on opposing courses so that, from the high window, they appeared to be racing up one narrow street and down the next.

Small figures hurried through Foley Square, heads low in obeisance to the snow, collars up, hands in coat pockets. In separate streams they converged at the subway kiosk, and flowed dark and slow, disappearing like metropolitan miners.

A telephone rang. The secretary stopped his slow tapping. "Yes," he said. "Yes. They're here. No. Sure thing." He hung up and looked at the document he was typing. Without raising his eyes, he said, "The judge will be here in a minute. He had to talk to a lawyer in chambers."

This led to little jokes among the wedding party of four. There was still time to leave, to cancel, to change a mind, to divert the course of love into the safe channel of status quo. Still time. Well, no. Not really. It would be more embarrassing now to walk out than to stay. The man and the woman had had eight weeks in which to think, to ponder, to wonder, to worry, to love, to dream, to plan, to match whims and wishes and aspirations, to confess to weaknesses, vices, mistakes, to pledge all the forevers and, toward the end, when good sense elbowed romance out of the seat of reason, to assess the effect of their union on children of their former marriages. There were two children, one on each side of the impending marriage, and each child fretted about the change in status, about the effect on his little universe of a new planet shedding light and warmth, or darkness and cold, on his daily life. A factor. There had been many factors, almost as many, one might say, as snowflakes now covering the sill of the office window.

The clerk turned away from his work. "It's all made out," he said. "The blood tests, the three-day waiver, the license. Now, which one is the bridegroom?" The gray-haired man turned from the window. He was of medium size, with a hard, bulldog mouth and soft hazel eyes. The eyes were important, in his case, because they revealed a compassion and a sensitivity that sharply contradicted his mouth. The gray hair, swept back along the sides of his head, made him look authoritative—like a police inspector or a reformed hoodlum.

He grinned at his bride, and said, "Me." The clerk assumed the monotone of officialdom and said, "Lon Michaels, age fifty-two, residing at Clark's Landing, Point Pleasant, New Jersey, born Newburgh, New York, September third, 1909, of Patrick Michaels and Helen McIntyre Michaels, both native-born Americans. Religion: Roman Catholic. Occupation: Author. Marital status: Married to Elspeth Russell, June first, 1932. Wife died of natural causes April thirteenth, 1956. Certificate of death attached to this marriage certificate."

The clerk looked up. "That right?" Lon Michaels nodded. "Do I pay you?" he said. The clerk moved the sheet of paper up in his typewriter. "You don't pay anybody," he said. "The judge doesn't want your money." He turned to the bride. "You the bride?" She was sitting. She stood. "Yes," she said.

The clerk shook his head mockingly. "You're too good for him,"
he said. It was an old quip, dusted carefully and thrown from an
expressionless face. "Now," he said, "let us see if I have the facts
straight in your case." He consulted the sheet and mumbled a few
items to himself. The bride stood almost at attention. She was as
tall as the bridegroom, a honey-haired blonde with a bun high over
the nape of the neck, a young woman with a face delicate enough
to be almost spiritual; the china blue eyes serious, the profile remi-
niscent of a Greek coin, the figure strong and the more pronounced
because the carriage was so erect.

". . . and we have here," the clerk said, running a finger along
the proper line, "one Katherine Ann Block, spelled with a K, not
a C, age thirty-two, residence at 231 Third Street, Hollywood,
Florida, born Homestead, Florida, March seventh, 1930, of Robert
Clark and Catherine Murphy Clark, both native-born Americans.
Religion: Roman Catholic. Occupation: secretary. Marital Status:
Divorced on October fourteenth, 1961, in Dade County, Florida,
from one Francis Block, a certified copy of which decree is attached
hereto."

Kay nodded dumbly. The clerk made a slight erasure. "Do you
both," he said, "without reservation swear that these statements are
true to the best of your knowledge, so help you God?" They looked
at each other. He said, "I do." She said, "Yes, I swear." The clerk
yanked the paper from the typewriter, and ironed it flat with his
hand. "Sign here," he said. They signed.

The other woman spoke. "It's a lot to go through," she said. She
was a tiny woman, a dark hoyden who was willing to trade all the
tears of life for just one of the laughs. "I'm nervous," she said,
"and I'm only the bridesmaid. No, the matron of honor." The clerk
blotted the signatures. "In a civil ceremony, madam," he said,
"you are a witness." Her husband blinked through thick lenses. "So
I'm a witness too," he said. "I was asked to be best man and I'm a
witness."

Margie Murray had the appearance of a sleek burro. There was strength in her small body, an ability to shoulder big burdens and make little jokes. She had been married to Harry for seventeen years and he had never been a good husband, lover, father or wage earner. She was happy with him and often said she wouldn't trade him for the best in the world. It is possible that Harry and his mediocrity were exactly what Margie needed. She was planner, aggressor, decision-maker and applicator of kisses and Band-Aids.

Lon held Kay's hand and made an elaborate study of the law diplomas on the wall. "Nervous?" he asked. She untwined her fingers and retwined them in a more comfortable manner. "If you want a proper answer," she said, "yes. You're going to hate me for this, but the ceremony seems anticlimactic."

"It's the waiting," he assured her. The one attribute they shared was a pretended serenity at all times. His was an old mask he had donned when his father used to beat him for infractions of the rules of boyhood. When he grew up, he forgot to remove the mask, and now he couldn't. Lon Michaels had a lot of warmth—maudlin sentimentality would be more accurate—but it was tucked under the lines of a hard face.

Kay Block's attitude was one of smiling assurance. This too was veneer. She was beset by the bad dreams of an insecure child. In sleep, she often moaned and wept. The dreams fell into a pattern of helplessness, the most recurrent one being three men without faces chasing her down a dead-end alley. She ran at top speed, knees high, eyes popping with panic, knowing that the men were gaining, knowing that her strength was ebbing, knowing that sooner or later she would fall to the pavement.

Awake, Kay also had strong feelings of insecurity, and in exchange for protectiveness in a man she offered too much love, too much passivity, too much service, too much jealousy. She had a clawing need to be loved, and she saw all other women as threats. For years, she had offered treasures of sentiment, but most of the men who sorted through them were searching only for a memento.

What Kay wanted was someone who would take them all. She wanted to be possessed more than she wanted to possess. She was so feminine as to be almost a caricature of womanhood. Her mouth was pretty, with never too much lipstick, but sweet and mobile; her smiles were expressive and easily drawn; her neck was slender and a little too long for her face. Her figure was neither plump nor thin, but it too was feminine and rounded, with long legs that tapered slowly to thin ankles and long feet.

"Sometimes," Lon once told her, "you remind me of a two-year-old filly. Beautiful and graceful, young and full of spirit, but liable to run straight through a fence or a barn door." "Thanks," she had said. "Let me think it over."

On another occasion, she had shown him a book. The story did not interest her. She wanted him to see the author's dedication: "To my wife, who is every bit of me, as I am every bit of her." He had read it and said: "That's the way you want us to be?" She had nodded. "Every bit of you, and every bit of me. In you, on you, under you, living with you, dying with you." "I've got you by twenty years," he had said. She had shown her irritation. "That's becoming a little sickening," she had said. "You are more man, more courage, than I've ever known, and if there were fifty years difference I'd still want to go when you go."

"We'll talk about it some time." "No we won't. There's nothing to talk about." "Okay." "Okay then."

The outer door swung open. They were still reading the diplomas when a tall man of dignified bearing came in. The clerk got up and took the judge's coat as he walked out of it with his arms behind him. He rubbed his fingers together and glanced into the eyes of each person in the room. "Mr. Michaels?" he said, making the correct guess. He shook hands. Michaels introduced the rest of the group. The judge pointed to the bride and said: "Ohhhh—pretty."

"Come," he said, and opened a door to the inner office. The

others followed slowly, glancing around the big room at the photos of celebrities, the carved walnut desk, the deep pile rug, and the desk photos of a woman and children.

The judge stood behind the desk, studying messages. Some he crumpled between his fingers and tossed under the desk; others he read and smiled at; one brought a frown. "Everything in order?" he said to the clerk. "Then what are we waiting for?" He was a dark man with headstone teeth and he showed them. "These writers are always working up a new plot; changing their minds. . . ."

He arranged the wedding party to suit himself, got a book from a desk drawer, glanced at the sheet that the clerk had typed and, in a moment, was saying: ". . . and with the power vested in me by the State of New York, I hereby pronounce you man and wife." Lon looked expectant, as though more were coming. Kay looked stricken. The judge reached out, shook hands with Lon, and said: "Don't mind me. Kiss her."

Lon did. It was a mechanical thing, with no response. Margie looked at her husband and said: "That's the fastest . . ." The judge shook hands with the bride. The clerk said: "I get something for all the work I did," and kissed her on the cheek. Kay looked long and searchingly at her husband, and then smiled. Lon thanked the judge, and asked him please to keep the matter secret. "She has a mother who doesn't know yet."

The judge promised. He looked at his clerk. "This stays in the four walls," he said. The clerk said: "Not a word." Lon thanked the judge again. Then everyone started saying thank you, and they left. In the hall, Kay reached a gloved hand for his. "Romantic?" she said. He laughed. "I think the whole thing is the poorest excuse for a wedding I ever heard. It's about as romantic as depositing money in a bank."

Harry walked ahead. He shoved his glasses higher on his nose— an habitual gesture—and looked back. "I never crack dirty jokes," he said, "but that's the new broad jump record."

"Harry!" Margie said. They waited for an elevator, but, because it was Saturday, only a few were in operation. They walked down the steps slowly. The conversation was perfunctory, the parting with the Murrays cordial but brief. On the street, Lon squinted up into the swirls of snow, and said: "How about lunch?"

"Lunch and a drink first," Kay said. They walked across the busy cobbled streets and found a little place up a side street. Lon hung up his coat and Kay's, then pulled a chair out and said: "Mrs. Michaels?" She grinned, and sat. "Say it again," she whispered. He shook his head and took a chair beside her. "No, you say it. When I say it I feel that I'm bragging." "Please brag," she said. "Please."

Her pale blonde face was deep in the thin mink collar, her nose was pink, her eyes watery from the cold. She walked beside him in the late afternoon, hesitating to say that her whole body was shivering. He walked through Radio City, expatiating on whatever occurred to him, smiling a little at the snow hat on the gold statue of Prometheus, noting the deep saffron of the sun as it declined behind the Hudson, the blue shadows of the tall buildings inching across the crusty snow and up sheer walls.

It was not his kind of afternoon. Lon Michaels was a summertime man. His hands were cold and he did not like to wear gloves. He carried a briefcase and a typewriter. His knuckles were numb, but he wore an amused expression, happy to explain what he knew of midtown Manhattan. He knew much because he had worked in New York for thirty years. His recollections, gilded ever so slightly by the storyteller's art, were sharp and interesting. Kay enjoyed listening, and enjoyed being taught by him. For his part, he loved to teach, but was irritated by his own pedanticism. Also by inattention.

"I'm killing time," he said, walking down Fifth Avenue. "We don't have to be at Idlewild until six thirty." Her eyes were on the passing women, assessing the coats and shoes and hats, the coiffures

and the make-up, all in a crosswise brush of the eyes in passing.
"Maybe," she said, "we could stop for a cup of coffee."

"I'm coffeed to the ears," he said. He might have said: I'll sit
while you have one. But he didn't. "I'm a pretty poor lover," he
said. "We should have gone directly to a hotel after the wedding.
We could have killed the whole afternoon."

"I love the way you phrase it," she said. "The bed is a great time
killer." "Oh come on," he said. "You come on," she said. He
shoved her with his elbow. "I was making fun of myself as a lover.
I should be eager." She did not smile. "We have lots of time," she
said. He stopped smiling. "You don't seem so eager yourself." "A
lady," she said, "never does." "Even when she is?" "Even when
she is." "I'm eager." Her face broke into planes of laughter. "After
all the women you've had?" "Oh, it's going to be that kind of
marriage." She stopped to look in a window. "Do you like figured
silk ties?" He shook his head. "Solid colors. Grays and blues."
"You don't like that one?" He looked. "I don't like that one," he
said.

At Fifty-seventh Street they got into a taxi. "Idlewild Airport,"
Lon said. The driver knocked the flag down. "Pan American
overseas." They settled back in the bumpy seat. "Now the butterflies begin," said Kay. "You afraid?" he asked. She thought it over
for a moment. "It isn't fear," she said. "It is and it isn't. I've always been afraid of airplanes. But there's another thing. I never
count on anything until it's ready to happen." He looked at her.

"I've been had too many times," she said. "All the way from
childhood, someone has always been promising something—a doll
that speaks, a vacation in the country, a dance, an opening night—
a lot of things that never happened. Once my mother promised me
a plaid dress and she got mad at something I did and I didn't get
the dress. I cried in bed two whole nights."

"So you didn't think the wedding would take place until today?"
"Oh," she said, "I wouldn't say—" "And the flight around the

world was phony too?" "You don't understand," she said. "We should have gone to a hotel," he said. "The bed is a great persuader."

Traffic crosstown was slow, and Lon looked frequently at his watch. It was dusk when they moved through the Midtown Tunnel and out along the choked elevated highway. They had fallen into thinking silences, but they weren't aware of it. She was secretly supremely happy to be Mrs. Lon Michaels, wife of a popular, though not too profound, author. He was wondering whether he had made the right move.

The coffee shop was like a jar of honey beside an ant hill. Streams of people, many laden with luggage, came through the door as others wiped their mouths, dropped a coin at the cashier's desk, and left. Kay watched the traffic from a window table, surprised that the counter was always full but that enough people departed to accommodate those on the way in.

"I should have been a columnist," said Lon. He flipped the newspaper closed, folded it small, and dropped it between his chair and the wall. She looked away from the crowd. "The waiting is killing me," she said. "Have a drink," he suggested. "I'm going to have one on the plane." "Have one now." "Are you?" "I had three at lunch," he said. "It gave me the courage to say I love you."

"Didn't you have an appointment with the doctor this morning?" "Who told you that?" "Harry." "Good old bucket mouth. I went to Doctor Clemson's for a cholera shot. The final one. Then to Robertson's for a throat examination." "What did you say about a columnist?" "Doc Robertson did a biopsy. He says I smoke too much." "That's a piece of tissue, isn't it? Does it hurt?" "He said it would, but all I felt was a pinch." "Did you want to be a columnist?"

"I didn't say that," he said. "I said I should have been one. Years

ago I did a lot of newspaper work." She spread jelly on a small
piece of toast. "I was on the *Trib* when Stanley Walker was there."
"Was he a columnist?" He shook his head and smiled at the table.
"Stanley Walker was a great city editor." "Well, you said something—"

"It's an insured income. A newspaper columnist should average
twenty-five thousand or better. It's a strange thing, but in my span
of time I remember the early columnists like Karl Kitchen and
Don Marquis and F.P.A. and Broun. They didn't make much.
They were a little bit ahead of the fad. Then Winchell came along,
and Hellinger and Louis Sobol and Bob Considine and Wilson.
They were syndicated widely. A good one could earn fifty thousand
or more. Suddenly a lot of rewrite men wanted to be syndicated.
The newspapers were glutted with columnists. Once the reader
got beyond page three there was very little news, just opinions."

"Then why would you want to do it?" "As I said, honey doll,
insurance. Insurance. A man could rap out a thousand words a day
on the life of a silkworm in a lamasery and the paycheck comes in.
But books—well, you've heard that story." "I think you sell yourself short." "No I don't. There is no modesty in me. First, last
and all the time I'm a confident character. But I've been bitten by
a few of my own books." She said nothing. "It's like rolling dice,"
he went on, "except that you're doing it in interminable slow
motion. You research and you write and there go a couple of years.
Then the book comes out and either someone else has one exactly
like it—published three months ago—or your book is lousy and
everyone knows it except the author."

"You like writing." "No I don't. I work hard because I don't
know anything else. I'm a pretty good second-rate man. I mean it.
There are a fistful of first-rate inspired writers. I'm a crafts-
man. I fashion the boat in my mind and go out and find the planks
and cut and saw to fit and then drop it in the water to see if it has
integrity. The first-rate man is inspired to build a boat that no one

ever saw before and he does it with love, knowing all the time what it's going to look like before he drops it in the water."

He finished the cold coffee. "That's a lousy figure of speech." "The whole thing," she said, "is more like a painting than building a ship." "How long you been writing?" he said, standing and dropping a quarter on the table. He picked up his check, left the newspaper, and helped Kay with her coat. That was another thing he had to become accustomed to—helping her with coats, holding a match for a cigarette, holding doors open, permitting her to go first. He had been alone for a long time and the sweet solicitudes had to be studied again.

"What do we have to do now?" she said, as they left. "Just wait for somebody to announce that they're boarding Flight One Fourteen. Our baggage is checked—incidentally, I hope you brought very little with you because you'll be buying stuff in different countries—and they've checked us in. I'm hungry." "The food on the plane is by Maxim's of Paris." "Oh come on." "Yes. I saw it on the Pan American brochure." "Maybe so. But I'll bet Maxim never saw the cheese sandwich I'm going to have." "I'm going to try Maxim's roast beef." "How do you know they'll—" "They will. All good menus have prime ribs. But why a cheese sandwich for you?"

He thought about it as though analyzing an old truth for the first time. Lon couldn't eat because he was tense. Not afraid. Just wound tight. There was a tremendous excitement for him in flight, but there was also an understanding of flight. He knew that the basis of all flight is a momentary victory over gravity. Each time he went aloft, this victory had to be complete and controlled for a certain length of time at a certain speed. The victory could not be lost momentarily and then regained. Once lost, all was lost.

Lon had written many magazine articles on aviation, as well as on military affairs, and both had led him into research on flight and the elements of air frames, propulsion and the components of the air ocean above. He loved and respected flight as he loved and respected the sea. Sometimes, when he took guests aboard his cabin cruiser, he wondered why they always asked "How many does it sleep?" instead of "What safety devices do you have? What are you going to do if your engines die, or catch fire?"

No one ever asked. On planes, he always consulted a flight map and, quite often, could predict landfalls and scenic attractions and even tell which side of the plane a given city should be on. He had flown in open-cockpit planes before Kay was born. He had seen American aviation grow, and had been a discerning observer. He knew so many line captains that quite often he was invited to the flight deck even though this is forbidden by the Federal Aviation Agency.

Still, he felt tense—not only at take-off, but throughout the flight.

Once, he had been in a DC-7 eastbound from Los Angeles to New York and he had looked out his window at the number three and four engines. There was no reason for this. As always, he was checking. The blades spun like bright coins in the sun, and Oklahoma, chocolate as a cracked layer cake, lay 21,000 feet below.

As he watched, the hubcap on the number four propeller began to make eccentric turns. It wobbled. Lon Michaels, the gray-haired man with the mask, sat up straight and beckoned to a passing stewardess. Even as she responded, he knew how ridiculous this was going to sound to her.

"I know that passengers are always seeing things that aren't there," he said, "but that number four propeller is off center." She bent low from the aisle to look. It was obvious that she could see nothing wrong. "Look," he said, "just tell the captain." There was a rough edge of authority in his tone, and she nodded. She started toward the flight desk and Lon, irritated, wondered why it had not shown up on the engine analyzer? Why didn't the engineer know that number four was out of kilter? He was still thinking when the loudspeaker boomed open.

"Ladies and gentlemen," said a deep, soothing voice, "this is your captain. We've having a little trouble with the outside engine on the right side so I have feathered the propeller. There is no danger whatsoever. This airplane is good on three engines, even on two. So I've killed it and we're going to head into Tulsa, which is—let me see—about twenty minutes—yes, just about twenty, away. There, with any luck, we'll pick up another DC-7 and be on our way. In any case, ladies and gentlemen, there is nothing to worry about."

Well, yes. The victory over gravity can be maintained on seventy-five per cent of power, or even, as the pilot said, on fifty. But a hundred is a lovely round figure. On another occasion, he had flown out of Mexico City for Havana and, sitting aft on a DC-6, had watched the hydraulic fluid pop up on the starboard wing and cascade sparkling into the slip stream. Nothing terrible happened, but it would have been nice if one of the Mexican mechanics had thought to check the hydraulic hose connections. An old piece of hose had split under pressure.

There had been the time, out of Dallas bound for New York, when the captain had cut in to say: "Ladies and gentlemen, there is a cold front dead ahead—about five minutes away—and it is spread over so many hundreds of miles and is so high that we are going to head straight through it. There is no danger, ladies and gentlemen. If there were, we'd turn right back to Dallas. So, if you will please buckle your seat belts and get secure, we'll take you through it as slowly as possible."

He did. That DC-6 had leaped and plunged so hard that a stewardess fell to the deck and couldn't get up. Something in the midships galley boiled over and a fire started. Lon could hear the wing spars snap as the second pilot tried to make his way aft with a fire extinguisher. There was no danger. There had been no danger.

The galley was built of fire-resistant material and the flames would have died of lack of fuel in another minute. Still, the violence of the cold front unnerved him so badly that Lon had promised God that if only he were delivered safely back to earth he would remain there for the rest of his days.

The air ocean had beckoned to him again, and he had responded. He could not ignore the clean configuration of flight and he knew that each of the so-called "close shaves" had not been a close shave at all. He had been in B-47 bombers, B-36's with their giant nineteen-foot propellers and jet assists, old Dumbos, Constellations, Electras, DC-8's, 707's, a B-34 which no one seemed to remember, DC-3's, Curtiss Condors, Ford Tri-motors, Fokkers, helicopters, Bonanzas, Pipers, and, once, an OX-5.

"Tense," he said, pushing Kay ahead of him as they boarded the Boeing 707. "Not fear. Fear jellies the mind. Maybe excited is a better word. Remember when you were a kid and you knew that you were going somewhere on vacation tomorrow and you couldn't sleep? You tried hard, but your thoughts skipped from cloud to cloud? Like that."

"I feel that way sometimes," she said, "when I'm making a dress." He was getting out of his black chesterfield. "Holy mackerel," he said softly. "What a comparison. You want the window seat?" Kay thought about it. "No," she said slowly, "from all I've heard the pilot can't fly without your assistance. You sit at the window." "Don't be sarcastic," he said sharply. "Just say you want it or you don't." "Okay. I don't." "Good. But don't be sarcastic, hon. You just married a master of sarcasm. It's probably the only thing I do without strain."

She looked stricken. He sat, buckled the belt, and she stood, half in the aisle, staring at him, her mouth partly open. Kay knew that this man, sometimes under small provocation, could heap vituperation on his victims mercilessly, often with a smile. But there had been no provocation. She had made what she called a "funny ha-ha." Now, as she stood, with passengers trying to get by, she could feel the tears coming and she tried to swallow the feeling and turn her mind elsewhere.

The flight steward stood behind her and said: "Let me hang this for you." She gave him the hat too, a dark doughnut of mink. Kay sat and stared stonily at the front of the plane, still trying to stop the tears from starting. She knew that if one escaped, she would really cry. Lon said something to her, but she did not hear it and she kept looking ahead. She curled her fingers around the fronts of the armrests and kept fighting that first tear. If he said one more word, just one more . . .

He looked out the window. The night was black and dirty. New York was clouds at seven hundred feet; visibility one mile; rain on snow; blue runway lights; a man with huge rubber earphones and luminescent bats, waving the giant Pan American airliner on its way; a crisp voice talking to the first office: "Pan American One Fourteen proceed to runway thirty-one L and wait"; it was the rising whine of four engines crying for air and it was, in a small sense, and bride and groom with their faces averted.

The white giant lumbered slowly down the taxi strips, pausing to look carefully before crossing over to others, conscious of the flickering Christmas lights of other aircraft coming down out of the low swirling clouds to appear suddenly, like bats with huge lighted eyes, racing toward the nest. Others, dead ahead, queued up in a ponderous shuffle toward thirty-one L, waiting for the word which would send them off into the vast blackness of the night, blinking brightly as they fought for altitude, each one making a tremendous noise and longing to be heard though not seen, each one disappearing like a small tick in a bale of cotton.

Lon kept looking out the window as his hand reached for hers. He found it, touched it lightly. She had her fight almost won, until she felt his fingers, and then she almost lost it. She opened her black

bag with her free hand, pulled out a handkerchief, and blew her
nose. He turned, as though aware of her for the first time.

"I have Lindbergh's log in my briefcase," he said softly. "You
know, he flew this leg of our trip in 1927." She nodded, and ran
the edge of the handkerchief under her eyes. "I was a kid at the
time, but I remember it—well, I can even recite parts of his trip."
"He flew alone?" Lon nodded, and squeezed her hand. "Alone.
Some people called him the Lone Eagle. Anyway, he flew in a small
single-engine Ryan monoplane. We're using a Boeing 707 jet. He
averaged around a hundred and three miles an hour; we'll average
better than six hundred in the jetstream. He took thirty-three and a
half hours to fly from New York to Paris; we'll do it in about six
and a half. His altitude at times was less than fifty feet above the
ocean; we'll probably be assigned thirty-one thousand feet or better.
Unless my memory is cockeyed, he needed four hundred and sixty
gallons of gasoline to make the trip; we'll waste that much kerosene moving this dragon out to the runway."

"Yes," she said. She freed her left hand from his to tuck loose
ends of hair back into the bun. She could feel them brushing her
neck. He started to retract his hand, but Kay got it back and held on.
He was sorry that he had hurt her. She knew that. But she also
knew lots of things that he didn't. One was that this was his regular
attitude toward all people, and that he was now mute because he
had not intended to hurt and he was worried. Was she going to
turn out to be one of those wives who weeps over every disagreement; over every blunt criticism? If so, he was in for one hell of a
life.

Lon had seen her weep before. Their courtship had lasted only
eight weeks, but now that he thought of it, she had wept the night
he asked her to marry him; she had cried when her little girl would
not eat dinner; she had shed bitter tears when her ex-husband had
told her, after signing a divorce stipulation: "I'll wait for you.
No matter how long it takes. I'll be waiting."

Flight One Fourteen waited a few minutes at the head of the runway, then emitted a rising screech and started slowly down the long path. The runway lights went past, slowly at first, then faster and faster. The run seemed, to Kay, endless. Lon knew it was planned, almost to the foot. He understood that the weight of the plane would be about 170 tons, and that the weight factor, pushed by close to 60,000 horsepower on take-off, plus the barometric pressure at Idlewild, would determine how many feet of roll this clipper would require to attain the 150 knots or so to lift clear.

The plane turned her nose to the sky, tucked her big rubber feet into her belly and in thirty seconds was out of sight. Kay glanced at her husband for reassurance. He patted her hand. "You're practically in Paris," he said. She felt the plane lift her a little, then drop abruptly. It lifted again, and she could hear the engines hum to themselves, outside in a world of swirling fog.

Kay knew that her confidence was not in the plane. It was in Lon. She believed in him, in everything he told her. She had the same faith in him that a little girl has in her father. This thought was repugnant to her, and she tried to put it from her. Lon was not a father image. Definitely . . . not . . . a . . . father . . . image. She loved him for what he was: an aggressive male. She liked to have him think for himself, and for her too. She enjoyed being obedient to his wishes, within limits. He was rough at times, almost sadistic, and she would not admit, even to herself, that she took pleasure from this too.

In some ways, he reminded her of her father. She remembered him clearly, but the things she recalled did not amount in the aggregate to much. He had left home for an Arizona sanitarium when she was ten. Her mother, a big blonde woman who sold real estate on the Florida west coast, received two letters. That was all. Kay's father never arrived at the sanitarium. He was tubercular in one lung, and was too ill to make a living. For a while, the police

used to come to the house with "leads" (always from some small
western community), but her father was never found.

Kay recalled that he had not looked sick. He had thick brown
hair, a strong, broad body, and his avocation was drinking and
playing cards. Kay was an only child, so her father had found it
easy to surprise her with little presents, grab her unexpectedly and
swing her, screaming, over his head, take her on walks on the
sunny days, down the long hill on the west side of town—sometimes to a saloon, sometimes to a ball game, sometimes to the home
of a friend where the men talked of big deals.

No, there was nothing of her father in Lon, except the easy way
in which he could lift her to the highest pinnacle or, with a phrase,
drop her off a cliff. ". . . coming out on top now," Lon was saying.
"You can feel him making the big turn. He'll swing east over Long
Island, then east by northeast."

She leaned close to him, her chin on his shoulder as she looked
out the window. The tops of the clouds moved fast underneath and
Lon pointed back toward the engine nacelles. "There's a moon
out," he said. "See the reflection? Must be overhead." She could see
the rim of silver light. Overhead, the stars spun slowly clockwise.
It was a beautiful, clear night. The plane was climbing, and would
continue to climb, for the next twenty minutes. They watched the
steward roll a tea wagon, laden with liquors and ice, down the
aisle. He had trouble stopping at each row of seats; the tea wagon
wanted to race to the back of the plane, so he toed it in toward
each seat.

They had a drink and consulted a huge dinner menu. "See?"
she said, pointing. "I see," he said. The captain opened the inter-
com and spoke to the passengers. "Welcome aboard Flight One
Fourteen," he said. We are climbing to an assigned altitude of
twenty-nine thousand feet. Reports have reached us that there is
a sizable jetstream at latitude fifty-six, so we will be somewhat
north of the usual track. . . . We estimate Paris six hours and

twenty minutes out of New York. . . . There may be a little turbulence moving into the jetstream, but if it persists, we will ask permission to go to thirty-three thousand feet. . . . Right now, off on our left is Nantucket Island. It is hidden under clouds, but we can expect clearing weather at Nova Scotia. . . . Reports from Paris indicate clear weather and a morning temperature of about forty degrees. . . . Enjoy your dinner and your flight."

"Order your prime ribs," Lon said. She wanted to get some for him, but he stuck to the cheese sandwich. This embarrassed a tall, leggy blonde stewardess who kept repeating: "Only a cheese sandwich? Don't you want to have dinner? How about some hors d'oeuvres? We also have lovely chicken and wild rice? No? A little later, maybe? All right. What kind of cheese?" "Plain." "Just plain cheese?" "Just plain cheese. A cup of coffee too. Later on, if I may, I'd like to have an apple."

The first-class section was in darkness. One passenger, reading under the beam of a small spotlight, diluted the blackness to pale gloom. The others slept. Three hours ago they had left Idlewild, bright-eyed, well-dressed, glowing with well-being and self-assurance. Now they lay crumpled, some tilted back in the seat like Kay, some curled up across two seats. All slept to the lullaby of a D-flat note from the jet engines, and they slept while moving east at six hundred miles per hour. A little boy managed to get his head and entire body on one seat between arm rests, and slept with his knees up. An old man with a white mustache that curled upward blew the loose ends of it with each breath and slept leaning on his fist, his elbow on the armrest, like a caricature of Rodin's "The Thinker."

Lon was awake. He had seen the lights of St. John's move under the plane, and had wanted to show Kay, but she was sleeping. The Atlantic Ocean was below, and there were no lights. No world. No life. He felt as though he were in a warm capsule, a bullet

with a filter, flying through the night. Still, when he looked out at
the stars, there was noise but no motion. Pan American Flight One
Fourteen was a white moth pinned to the stars. It thundered and
blustered six miles above the sea, but all around it the horizon
stood still, the world of suns and planets stared, unmoving, unblinking; below, far below, was the black silent well down which
one might drop a round stone, and never hear it splash.

Lon removed two black notebooks from the briefcase. They were
fat with hundreds of pages of notes and with information scissored
from travel brochures and books pasted in under the proper cities.
The index to the first book read: "Idlewild," "Paris," "Beirut,"
"Jerusalem," "New Delhi," "Bangkok." The second one, which
he returned to the briefcase at once, had index ears which read:
"Hong Kong," "Tokyo," "Honolulu," "Los Angeles." This was
the trip around the world and he wanted to study some of the
Idlewild notes.

It wasn't easy to step past Kay's crossed knees, especially with
the seat in front in a reclining position, but he did it and took his
notebook into the bridge-table lounge. A four-stripe line captain
was sitting, facing forward, smoking a small cigar. Lon took the
seat opposite him, and introduced himself. The officer said he was
aboard to check the flight. He was a man with hair running white
above the ears and dark and curly on top. His features reminded
Lon of a well-broken-in valise.

"You the writer?" the captain said. Lon nodded. The captain
stuck his hand out again. "I have one of your articles on my locker
door. It's about the F.A.A." Lon grinned. "That one. The only
people who liked it were the A.L.P.A." "No," the pilot said, "I
think you did a little better than that. The Air Line Pilots are
opposed to the Federal Aviation Agency in some respects, but
you made sense to my wife, for instance. And her brother, who has
never flown." "Well," said Lon, "Let's say I don't believe in over-
regulation. It was wrong in my judgment to order co-pilots to look

out the window for other aircraft when the jets move at five hundred and forty knots. What can a man see, especially if it's another craft moving at five hundred and forty knots in his direction? No one in authority pays any attention to what I write, but I think that the greatest dangers in airline travel are assigned altitudes and changes in flight plans, holding patterns, and private aircraft."

The captain looked out the window at the dark well. In any field of endeavor, he knew, there is nothing worse than the intelligent layman. One can smile at the dicta of the ignorant layman, but the man with some knowledge of law or medicine or engineering or flight is, by his knowledge, bound to be half right on everything. The captain was sorry that he had started this conversation, because now he would be forced to listen to a man who almost knew what he was talking about. Nor could the captain afford to set him straight, because that might turn out to be an offensive gesture, and it might appear in a new magazine article. He said nothing. He stopped looking out the window and began to roll a yellow pencil on the table.

"I was coming into Miami International one time," said Lon, "with Tom Ferris and a couple of kids. We had been fishing at Key Marathon and we came back in a Piper Apache. It's a good airplane. We were on the final leg and I was wearing a headset and I heard the tower say: 'National Flight Seven Four, can you see him?' Then National said: 'We got him dead ahead one mile.' Miami tower said: 'Hotel One Seven Nine Four'—that was us— 'would you please make a one hundred and eighty turn left out of the pattern and come back in behind the Electra?' Our pilot turned in his seat, and by swinging left, could see the Electra climbing up our tail. We got out of line, and back in behind him. That Electra couldn't go as slow as we could, on final approach, and still maintain flight. There wasn't any danger. The tower had both of us under control, but why mess around with a hundred lives because two men are coming home from a fishing trip?"

The captain picked his pencil up. "You plan to write something about this trip, Mr. Michaels?" Lon shook his head. "Not me. I'm on a honeymoon." "Well," said the captain, and the hand came across the table for the third time, "congratulations. That's wonderful. Is this your first marriage?" Lon frowned. "No. The second. My first wife died five years ago." "Oh." "It happens in a lot of families. We had twenty-five years together and one kid." He opened his hands in the mercy-of-the-court gesture. "It was a good thing, I guess. A lot of love and a lot of battles. Frankly, I put it all behind me when she died. Hung up the gloves. But then, eight weeks ago, I asked a young woman if she'd like to go out to dinner. I plan to ask her for the rest of my life."

They talked a while about other matters. The captain was interested in going over the original flight log of Charles Lindbergh. There was silence for a long while, as he read it. "I go back to this time," he said. "I remember May 1927 very well. It's hard to believe that I was only a kid, but I was. You read a thing like this, and you realize how far man has progressed. Lindbergh had a radio. We have twenty-one of them, not counting automatic navigational aids and the Doppler. He must have been afraid his engine might catch fire. We're afraid ours will go out. I was just figuring —let me see now—we will be landing at Orly at a time when Lindbergh was still over Nova Scotia." "In one way," said Lon, "he was a better pilot. He did everything the hard way." "Agreed." said the captain. "He was, in effect, sailing a small bark alone across uncharted waters. Today, we fly the big ocean liners. If someone could make the 707 think, it would do the work better without a flight crew."

Outside, the inkwell seemed to be turning gray. "Here comes dawn," the check captain said. "The sun races toward us at a thousand miles per hour, and we race toward it at six hundred. Result? Quicker sunrise." Lon took his notebook and got up. "Are we going to see Ireland?" The captain glanced at his watch.

"Roughly in a half hour we should be over Shannon. We've been on a northerly circle course and we're coming down toward Shannon. We'll leave there and head for Bristol, then on to London. We should pass right over London International, then a turn to the right and over the channel and into France."

Lon held out his hand. "I can't imagine spending the first night of my marriage with you, but there you are." They both laughed. "I wish I could take you up front," the captain said, "but you know the rules." "Thanks. I understand," Lon said.

The work he had in mind required only a few minutes. He removed a fat leather diary from the briefcase by leaning across Kay, who was still asleep, took it forward to the lounge, and sat at his portable and wrote the usual terse entry.

Married N.Y. Felt depressed at ceremony. Bride wonderful, beautiful—My Kay for life, I'm convinced. Worried about unhappy feeling at post time. Tried to think of happy life ahead . . . trip around the globe . . . someone to share the lean victories. No dice. Killed afternoon freezing her in Manhattan. Stupid approach to sex. More I'm with her, more convinced I am that she's intelligent, sympathetic, completely feminine. Has a hard streak for those she no longer needs. As sun went down, felt happier. Or, less unhappy. Don't know cause. Can't be Elspeth. Gone five years. Can't be Sonny. Kid urged me to remarry. Begged. Very frank: "I can't stand you alone." Had first little brush with Kay on plane. She'll learn. So will I. Must curb tongue. Me, that is. Gifted with the reaction of a rattlesnake. Always strike first, with fangs bared— so stupid. Lose friends. Lose respect for self. Spent night on plane to Paris. Dawn coming up now. Great love affair. We held hands. Know from experience that she warms up over light touch of finger here and there. Glad her motto is: "No wedding ring, no sex." But then, would not have married. I know me. Maybe depression

was over Robertson and his throat biopsy. Doubt it. Must shake it.
Best way to shake it is to do nothing about it. Feel as if I'm living
in a noisy corridor of a monastery. More later.

"Darling, the sun is coming up. Darling. You want to see it?
Come on, sleepy-head." Kay's head rolled to one side. She wiped
her mouth with the back of her hand. The eyes opened, looked at
him for an instant, and closed again. The mouth made a smile. He
shook her gently and she opened her eyes, squinted toward the
window, and said: "The sun?" He helped her into the window seat
and sat beside her.

"See those clouds down there?" She turned away from the window and kissed him on the mouth. "Good morning," she whispered. "Happy good morning to my husband." "Those clouds are
fifteen thousand feet below us." They looked like slate-blue fleece.
The sun was about to come up almost directly ahead of Flight One
Fourteen. It transmuted all the darkness into changing hues; the
vault of the sky selected indigo, so that the stars could still show
through; the rim of the horizon behind the plane picked pale green
and yellow; below, the highest clouds were tipped with peach; the
valley's shades were a military gray or slate. The first rays whipped
across the world of silence and caromed yellow off the plane windows and the wings. Kay could watch the sun by pressing her cheek
against the window.

"I don't believe it," she murmured. "It's beautiful, beautiful."
There was sleep in her eyes, but she kissed him again. "Thank
you, dear, for waking me up." The colors changed quickly; the
cloud tips were white and there was a world of violet in the valleys.
He rested his chin on the top of her head. "It maketh the eyes
drunk," he said. She nodded. "Beautiful. Beautiful. Could you
write about this? I mean, describe it?" "I doubt it. Who would
believe it?"

She turned in time to catch the steward's eye. He was standing up in the front. She made the word coffee in silence, and raised her eyebrows as a question. The steward nodded and disappeared. Lon sat. He thrust his sealed and locked diary into the briefcase. "I love you," he said. "But you know that." She held his face in both her hands. "Say it, Lon." "Again?" he said. "Again." "Okay. I love you. I love you with all my heart. I said this the night I proposed. It gets monotonous."

Kay smiled. "Monotonous, he says. Oh God! Monotonous. Lon, if you say it every waking hour on the hour for the next twenty years . . ." "I won't be around that long." Her happy expression died. "You're not going to start that again." "No. I just like to face the actuarial facts. And the fact is that I will not be here. Oh, come on. Let's not talk about it. We're happy. We're in love. That covers all bases." She did not smile. "Are we still over the Atlantic?" He pointed toward the front of the plane. "Look that way. If you see land, it's a little point outside Shannon Airport." She looked. "That would be Ireland?" "Right." "There is a lot of blue between the clouds. Ocean, I guess. Oh, I see it!" she exclaimed. "Now I see it. It's far down—like a piece of chocolate." "Shannon," he said. She shook her head. "I'm mixed up. I thought Ireland was green."

THE SECOND DAY

THE sun was still low and faint-hearted. The cobbles of the Place de la Concorde picked up the flecks and tossed them into the taxi. It pulled to a bucking stop in front of the Hotel Crillon, "Tired?" she asked. She was always solicitous and he wondered if she had been like that with her first husband. It is not difficult, he thought, to take a second wife or a second husband if one is not too deeply committed, but the firmer the love, the more ineradicable the first husband and first wife become. Would he live with a ghost? Would she?

"Tired," he said. "Tired and excited." "I'm not tired," she said. "You had no sleep. Did I tell you I studied French in high school?" He got out and reached for her arm. "No," he said, "and I wish you hadn't."

The doorman's face was pinched with cold. He crouched in his gold-and-blue greatcoat and held the door handle to the taxi as he readorned his face with his welcome smile. He had been doing this for twenty-five years. For a time, he had to do it for German officers and their French girls, and this had been most difficult. Today, the cold face thawed for tourists.

A bellboy ran out and back through the double glass doors to get a handtruck. Kay shaded her eyes and squinted into the sunlight. "Where are we? What part of Paris?" Lon paid the driver. "About

26

dead center, I'd say." He pointed across the huge square where many cars and motorcycles and bicycles formed several separate streams of traffic. "See the building with the flag on the far side?" he asked. "That's the Chamber of Deputies. Congress. The big granite needle in the middle of the square is an obelisk. I'm not sure, but I think Napoleon brought it from Egypt. The Seine runs under the middle of the square. Now look over the trees to the right. See the Eiffel Tower?"

"Oh, yes," she said with pleasure. "Oh, yes. I can see it."

He drew a joy from her enjoyment. The pleasure was in her eyes and all over her face. Last night, she had been in New York. This morning, she was in Paris. The farthest she had ever been from her home before, he knew, was New Orleans, on a honeymoon. Another honeymoon. She had married a red-headed soldier named Francis Block for no other reason than that he had seduced her, and she had been afraid to tell her mother.

"Around the corner in the opposite direction," he said, pointing, "is Maxim's. You know, where the cancan started. Further up the street, blocking it as a matter of fact, is the Church of the Madeleine. Right here, next to the hotel—no, over on this side—is the American Embassy." She marveled. "Is that where our ambassador lives?" "Lives and works. It is also where Ambassador Myron Herrick took Lindbergh on that first night after he landed at Le Bourget." She looked closely and saw the American flag on a staff, and a gleaming Marine, in white gloves, at the door.

They followed the handtruck into the Crillon. Lon held her arm. He was delighted at her attitude. His own view of Paris was dismal. The last time he had been here, he had made the trip alone. Elspeth had remained home. At that time, she was walking the high edge of sanity and kept looking down. "I have nerves," she had said. "Nothing but nerves. You go. Have fun. I'll be fine when you get back. All I have to do is learn to relax." She had died. Now, he saw Paris with uneasiness. The five-year span kaleidoscoped to

yesterday. The city had been big and cold. It was peopled with
short men in blue uniforms, men with bristling mustaches who
comprehended only when it pleased them; with women in cheap
print dresses and kerchiefs riding on the backs of motorcycles. It
was filled with sidewalk cafés and bookstalls and coffee shops and
museums, and garish night clubs. France had appeared to him then
to be possessed of an unreality, a nation of losers embittered and
materialistic. The body, the mind, the wit, the beauty were all
there, but France was playing Pompadour in an era of Polly Adler.

He signed the register: "Mr. and Mrs. Lon Michaels, Point
Pleasant, New Jersey, USA" and left the passports with the clerk.
Everything he did seemed to strike a familiar chord. The signing of
the register led him to wonder how many hotel registers he had
signed that way with how many attractive women. Most of the
time, the women had had aspirations to make the signature valid.
He remembered how they looked, standing back from the desk a
few paces staring with careful unconcern into space, or busy with
something in their handbags, or studying another woman in the
lobby. Now it was legal, and he felt certain, as he saw the clerk
glance at Kay, that he did not believe that this attractive young
blonde could be truly married to this tough-looking man.

He tossed the keys to the bellboy and asked the concierge for
mail or messages. There were none. They got into the little bonbon
box of an elevator and went to the second floor. Kay was smiling
a small smile to herself. She felt no embarrassment, but she sensed
that Lon did. The room was on the right side of the hotel opposite
the Embassy. It had a foyer and, like most French rooms, big keys,
big locks, a high ceiling and a bathtub large enough for two. The
bathroom also had a bidet. He wondered if Kay knew what it was
for. Some American women did. Many did not.

He tipped the boy and set the valises on the bed. Kay stood in
the center of the room, looking about. Good. She liked it. The little
dressing table with its three mirrors and tiny side lamps looked so

French. So did the service buttons with their drawings of a maid beside one, and a valet beside the other. She pulled the heavy draperies and the gossamer curtains aside to look out on the street below and the Embassy across the way. She examined the two closets, and picked the larger. She bounced on the bed and kicked her shoes off.

"Nice," she said softly, watching Lon yank suits and shirts from the suitcases and put them away. She didn't like the green bedspread, but who would be looking at it? She reminded herself that she must not make any overtures to her husband, knowing from past experience that he could be brusque when she made the advances. She preferred it his way but she was afraid of lapsing into habits that had worked with her previous husband. Francis had never made a move unless she did something to arouse him. Also, he had deep disgusts about certain functions of his body and his fears and inhibitions had been nailed to her consciousness until she wasn't sure she could be uninhibited with anybody. She loved her new husband as she had never loved anyone, but she wasn't sure he could remove the nails of restraint without leaving big round scars.

"Nice," she said again, getting off the bed and tiptoeing into the bathroom. She closed the door and looked around. She smelled the soap in the trays and tried to identify the scent. She felt the towels and marveled at how big and thick they were. Then she saw the bidet. Kay recognized it at once, and stooped to try the mixing faucet. The stream, instead of running around the shallow bowl in a vortex, popped straight up, almost to the ceiling, and came down on her head.

She gasped. He heard it and ran in. "Oh," he said. "I'm sorry. I could have explained that to you." She sat on the tile floor, shaking her hair. "Don't bother," she said. "I know what it's for. I just wanted to mix the water. Anyway, get out." He went back to unpacking and she got up from the floor and turned the catch on the door.

Unpacking was always a chore, and he did his own. Her bags remained unfastened and open on luggage racks. When he had finished smoothing the last tie, he lit a cigarette, undressed slowly, and put on a terry-cloth robe. He pulled the green bedspread down until it fell off the foot of the bed. Then he folded the sheets down halfway, turned the four pillows lengthwise, and lay down flat, puffing and thinking.

He was still puffing and thinking when he heard small noises, like mice with dance taps on their feet. He got up and went to the bathroom door. "Kay?" he said. "You all right?" The door knob turned. "I'm all right," she said, "but I'm sort of locked in." He smashed the cigarette in a tray. "You're sort of what?" "Locked in. I can't open the door." His thoughts of love-making were extinguished. "Do you mean to tell me," he said, "that you locked this door and cannot get it open?" "Yes," she said. "Now don't get mad. I think there's something wrong with the lock."

He tried the door. He turned the handle as far as it would go in each direction. He pressed hard enough to bend the handle, but the door remained locked. "Is there a catch on the inside?" he said with his face to the door. "There must be a catch or a bolt." She began to laugh. "Nothing," she said. "Just the key and the doorknob. The key turns all the way"—her laughter was becoming more helpless —"but nothing happens. The knob turns and the door stays locked. Can you call the manager, darling?"

"What the hell do I want him for?" he said. "What can he do? Call a locksmith? Why did you have to lock the door in the first place? You're in a room with your husband." "I don't know," she said, swallowing her laughter. "Force of habit." He was angry now. "Force of habit, my ass," he said. "Do you know how ridiculous this is? I have to ask for help—I should let you spend the day in there—and how am I going to explain the locked door?"

"As you say," she said sweetly, "the hell with them. Just call them and get me out of here. Tell them you have a bride waiting to fly to your arms." His sarcasm was coming to the surface. "If I phone for help, do you think you can tear yourself away from that bidet so that these wise idiots will understand that this mess occurred before, not after?" This struck her as so funny that she sank to the floor laughing. "Only you," she retorted, "would think of that."

"I'll call," he said. Her voice became frantic. "Wait a minute, Lon. Not yet." "What now, dear?" "Give me time to change back?" He looked puzzled. "May I ask," he said sweetly, "from what to what?" "I wanted to look attractive, so I showered and put on a filmy pink negligee." "How filmy?" "Anybody can look through it." He groaned. "Oh fine." "I can change back into my dress," she said. "It's in here." "Change. Please." "Give me two minutes and then ask for help." "Okay, but you don't know the French. I could phone now and nobody would show up for an hour."

"Two minutes," she said. "Just to make sure." He waited. Then he phoned. The operator understood a little limping English. "Yes?" she kept saying. "What 'as 'appen in de bathwhoom?" "My wife. Madame. She is locked in. The door is closed. She is inside. I am outside. *Comprenez?*" "Just a minute, please. I will call the engineer." It took a little time. Then the engineer got on the phone.

"My wife," said Lon, pronouncing each word slowly and distinctly, "my wife she is lock in the bathroom. She is lock in. No key. I am outside in room two two nine. She is inside with much heartbreak. You will hurry, please?" The man listened, and asked questions beginning from the start: "How she do this?" Lon lost his wandering temper again. "How the hell do I know?" he shouted. "Get someone up here, buddy. Get her out. Break the door down. Bring a key. Do something." There was silence on the phone. "In good time, M'sieu," the voice said.

Lon slammed the receiver down and went back to the door. "Don't worry," he said. "The plane doesn't leave until Monday."

"Is somebody coming?" "I hope so," he said. "I can't wait to see their expressions when the French learn that the bride is locked in the bathroom." He went back to the bed and slammed himself onto it. "A lovely day," he said to the ceiling. "Married yesterday. Paris this morning. The bride spends the honeymoon in the can." He propped himself on one elbow and shouted. "Do you know anybody who will believe this story? Can you hear me?" "Yes," she said. "I hear you. Just get me out, dear, and I'll make it up to you." "Ha!" he said and plopped back onto the bed.

Two men, obviously janitors or helpers, appeared at the door. The little one was the boss. Both nodded a greeting to Lon and the bridegroom tried to explain what had happened. They understood almost nothing. "Open door," he said, pointing. "Take lock off. Do something." He leaned against the door and changed his tone to the solicitous. "You dressed, dear? The men are here." She said yes. The tall man listened to the feminine voice from the far side of the door. "Madame?" he said. Lon nodded. The tall one studied the man in his bathrobe, then the locked door. He looked at the small one. "Ah-ha," he said.

"Ah-ha what?" said Lon. The man glanced at him and knelt beside the doorknob to begin his work. None of it was simple. There appeared to be complications in removing the lock without chipping the paint around the big flange. Lon phoned room service and asked for two pots of coffee. He went back to where the men were working and he said: "You know what?" through the door. "This honeymoon is becoming comical." His tone of asperity registered on the workers, who began to whisper in French and shake their heads. Their conclusions were clear. The husband had forced his attentions on the lady in mid-morning and the woman had fled to the bathroom.

When they got the door open, they packed their tools and refused his tip. They lifted their caps to Kay. She sat on the bed beside Lon, in silence, and began to peel stockings. She moved over to the closet and her dress, a plain blue wool, came up over her head. Lon was still irritated, but not too much so to appreciate that Kay was the most exciting woman he had ever seen. Her face, her body had a pale, almost snowy, assortment of curves, indentations and lines which made him think of Diana in flesh tints. He knew that she did not have a mathematically perfect figure, that there were models and candidates in beauty contests who had the right numbers at breast, waist and hips, but none of them could move him. Sometimes, all she had to do was turn her head sideways and smile a certain way and, at once, his thoughts were diverted from whatever mental archives they had been wandering in to the earthiest of the he-and-she philosophies.

She stepped into the closet to remove the rest of her clothing. Lon sat back and reflected momentarily on the feminine virtue of modesty. Almost all women had it in greater measure than men, he thought; even a prostitute would clutch her bathrobe tight around her neck when the milkman called. Still, he was not convinced that there wasn't more to it than modesty. Some of what was called modesty must be prompted by a fear of being less attractive without clothes than with them. Some of it must be intended to tease. The average woman, he had learned long ago, felt more alluring in a revealing gown than nude.

He saw a hand come out of the closet and reach for the filmy pink gown. This had gone far enough. He stood up, threw his bathrobe on the floor, walked into the closet, and grabbed her hand. "Wait a minute," she objected. "What are you doing?" She wore nothing. She needed nothing. He said nothing. He yanked her to the big bed and he pushed her onto it.

She tried to sit up, half laughing, half protesting. "Lon, dear," she said. "A lady has some rights." He pushed her back down. "We'll talk about your rights later." She pretended to be surprised and hurt. "I didn't know you were rough," she said. He kissed her, managed to get both arms behind her shoulders, and held her so tightly she couldn't breathe. "You knew it," he said. "You knew it all right."

He felt the coolness of the sheet under his knees and he felt her body, under his hands, lose its rigidity and become pliant. Her fingertips were behind his shoulders. When he wasn't kissing her, exciting her, lifting her from ground zero up to his level he noticed that her mouth was open, as though breathing was difficult, and her eyes closed.

Most of all, he wanted to avoid the signs of hurry. Anticipation was all. Actuality could be a disappointment. There would be no disappointment here because he knew, with every passing moment, that his inner fear that a man cannot fall in love twice in a lifetime was wrong. He had known, when he proposed marriage, that he was irrevocably in love, but so many of his friends warned him that it might be plain loneliness that, for a time, he had doubted his true feelings. Now he knew, more surely than ever. He felt no inhibitions, as he had with some women. He was immersed in Kay's breathless loveliness when she said suddenly: "Lon, someone is at the door." He murmured something. She heard the key turning. "Lon!" He sat up in bed quickly, and turned toward the door.

"For God's sake!" he shouted. "Go away!" The door opened slightly and a waiter stuck his head around the corner. "Your coffee, M'sieu."

"Should I wear a coat?" she asked. Lon was in the bathroom, scraping the last of the lather from his face. "Yes," he said. "If you look in the guidebook you'll find that the temperature averages about forty." She was peering between the draperies at the people below. Shop clerks were returning from lunch. They looked cold, hunched in their coats. Always she had imagined Paris as a female, pirouetting saucily among fragrant blossoms. It was a schoolgirl image. Paris is cold in March. The wind swept the clouds over the egg cup of the Cathedral of the Sacré Coeur and down across the boulevards and the flat plain of the city to the Eiffel Tower, where the girders set up a baritone roar, a steady, unremitting tone of resistance.

She stared down at the sidewalk, her face framed in the velvet maroon of the draperies as she gathered them under her chin, and she was thinking of her own happiness. Until now, she had been occupied with making him happy, at least with pleasing him, with making herself more attractive to him, with deciphering his moods, decoding his wishes, divining his intentions.

It was not easy, she had found, for a woman to express her innermost feelings to a man. She had the feelings, sensitized to the slightest touch, but, until now, no one had seemed interested in exploring the depths and heights of which she was capable. For some years, she had been ashamed of these extremes. She was different from other women. Now, she had found, less than an hour ago, that her husband was delighted with her sensitivity; that he could demand and command with a tenderness she had not known existed. He was a complete aggressor; he seemed to take some cruel pleasure in dominating every move.

Before their marriage, she had been serene and content with him; now she was on a pinnacle of ecstasy. Was this a momentary thing, she wondered—or would he be like this all the time? She wished. She hoped. She did not know that happiness, in large doses, carries its own side reactions of anxiety. It is not good to look down but, from a pinnacle, there is no other direction.

Kay turned from the street scene. She sat at the dressing-table mirror and tucked a hanging wisp of hair over her ear. "May I say something immodest?" she said. Lon was still in the bathroom. He had brushed his gray hair back along the sides and, in the mirror, could see Kay at the table. "Say it," he said. She smiled. "I'll never say it again." He put the brushes down, and came out of the bathroom to get a fresh shirt. "You are in every way three times the man I expected."

"I could have told you that," he said facetiously. "No," she said.
"I'm serious." He thrust his arms into the shirt and kissed her on
the back of the neck. "I'm glad you're serious," he said. "I didn't
think I could be happy ever again." He began to button the shirt.
"And I am. You know what?" he went on. "This is third time I've
been in love. Truly." She wasn't interested. "I won't say it again,"
she said. "I said it once." He looked over the rack of suits and
picked one which was not badly wrinkled.

"Once," he said, half to himself, half to her, "I was in love
with the fair Honora. She had hair as dark as a raven's wing. It
had sheen, even in the movie house. She used to look at the picture,
and I looked at her. She was sixteen and I was seventeen and I had
it so bad that all I hoped for was a chance to die protecting her
from something. She was the smartest girl in high school. Majored
in chemistry and made her own clothes. Ah, that Honora. Five
dates before I dared to kiss her. Love? My dear girl, you don't
know what the word means. Once, a sexy thought crept into my
mind and I wanted to kill myself."

Kay appeared to be hurt, for a moment. Then she caught the
spirit of his inner happiness, his gaiety, and she began to smile and
listen. "Unfortunately, she met an older man," said Lon, "and I
lost her. He was twenty and he shaved. I told her that she'd be
sorry, but she just shook her head. Pity, I guess. I said that older
men only had one idea in mind, and she said, as I recall: 'I hope
so,' and this wrecked my faith in young ladies."

"Did she marry the older man?" Kay asked. Lon sat on the bed
in his shorts and shirt and pulled his shoes on. "I never found out,"
he said. "The last I heard of her she was teaching school. Then I
met Elspeth on a blind date and I began to learn something about
love. Truly. I dated her every night. It was the fiercest, most pos-
sessive affection possible."

"I'd prefer not to hear about it," Kay said. He stood, working the
back of the shoe over his heel. "You want to hear about it," he

said. "We have discussed this thing before." He wasn't smiling. "I want you to know everything about me, the good things and the bad, and I want to know every last thing about you. I'm not kidding. When this honeymoon is over, I don't want anyone ever to come to me with any story about you that I don't already know." She stood a moment, smoothing her skirt, and went back to the window. "I've told you everything."

"The bad things," he said. "The wrong things. Sure. You know all the bad things about me too. That is, unless I can think of more. But I want to know the good things, the happy things, the silly things, the—"

"Like the bell outside the window," she said. He stopped. "Bell?" he said. "I don't remember that story." She shrugged. "It's a silly thing. When I was sixteen, I used to go to bed and tie a cord to my big toe and hang a bell on the end of it outside the window."

"What window?" "We lived on the ground floor. The boy who lived upstairs used to come home late and pull it." "The cord?" "Of course. Then I would feel it in my big toe and I'd wake up and go to the window." He selected a tie and tossed it around his neck. "At sixteen?" "At sixteen," she said. "Was this the kid's idea?" "No," she said. "Mine."

"You played some pretty good games for a kid." "Nothing happened." "I hope not." "I would go to the window and he would pull himself up to the windowsill and kiss me good night." "You were in pajamas?" "I never wore pajamas." "Okay, then. A nightgown." "I never wore anything in bed." "You're kidding." "Even in the dead of winter. I used to put a heavy robe on when he pulled the cord, and I went to the window and he used to whisper to me and kiss me. That's all."

"That's pretty good for openers." He pulled on his trousers and tried to adjust a safety pin inside the belt lining. Something heavy fell on the rug and bounced. Lon looked startled. Kay

stooped and picked it up. Her expression was puzzled. "What do
you need a gun for?" she said. She turned it over in her hand. It
was the smallest she had ever seen. It was all silver, an automatic,
she presumed. "Give it," he said, and took it, checked the safety
catch and then pinned it inside the waistband of his trousers. "You
never know on a trip like this." She stared. When she spoke, she
spoke slowly. "I don't like this," she said. He ran his belt through
the keepers and cinched it over the small revolver. "Neither do I,"
he said.

"Then throw it away." "I'll do nothing of the sort." "Why do
you need it?" "We may get in a jam with natives in some country."
"What country?" "Who knows?" "What is the real purpose of
the gun?" "Don't be so inquisitive. And don't try to tell me what
I can do." "Lon, we don't need guns. Ever." He went on talking
as though she hadn't spoken. "I don't have a permit for it. That's
why it's kept under my belt. Look. You can hardly see a bulge."

"I hope the police catch you." "You don't." "Yes I do. I'm
afraid of guns. I don't even go to cowboy movies." Lon burst into
laughter. "Touché," he said. Her lips were compressed. She looked
like a little girl trying to work up a tantrum. The nostrils dilated.
"You're going to throw that gun in the river," she said. "You'll
throw it in the river or else—"

He put his jacket on. "No or else," he said. "There is no or else
ever in this family. You are not going to leave me or even threaten
it. Never play bluff, my dear. If you ante up a chip I'll be forced
to ante two and call you. I played this game with Elspeth and it
leads to misery." "Throw the gun away." "The gun stays with
me." He patted his belt. "Right here. You wearing a hat?" She
shook her head. "Then let's go." "Answer one question," she said.
"Have you ever carried a gun before?" "No." "Then why this
time?" "We might get in a jam somewhere." "When did you
start to carry it?" "Yesterday." "Our wedding day?" "Our wedding
day."

"Let us get one thing straight," Kay said, as she adjusted her coat collar. "That gun goes or I go." "I tried to warn you not to play that game," he said. "You must think you married some weakling who is going to drop to his knees every time you threaten to walk out. Now you listen to me for a moment: Go. You want your ticket home? I'll get it for you." He went to his briefcase and flung it open. "You have to be taught that you can't win by threatening to leave, by threatening to sulk, by threatening not to cook dinner, or by threatening to withhold your favors, or by running home to momma."

The tears began to come. She made no effort to hold them back. "Must you," she wailed, "always be such a tough son-of-a-bitch?" "Oh-no," he said, still looking for the ticket. "Listen to the language of the lady. Go on. Don't mind me." She sat on the bed, staring at the rug as the tears fell onto the dark fur collar. "All right," she said softly. "Okay. You win. Keep the gun. Keep me too." He kept rummaging in the briefcase. "For goodness' sake stop looking," she said. "What must I do now? Beg to be allowed to stay?"

He closed the bag and took her face in his hands and kissed her. She stood, turning half away, and he swung her around. "This is no way to start a marriage," he said. He unbuttoned her coat and took it from her. He threw it on the floor. Then he turned her back to him and kissed her again and again. "The museums will be closed," she said. He said, "Our marriage comes first and I can't leave a dispute hanging in air." He kissed her again. Kay smiled through the tears. "All right, Boss," she said. "Let's talk."

They walked out of the hotel swinging laced fingers. He was happy again. On the street, he caught the glances of a few women passing by. They thought he was a middle-aged roué with an attractive young woman. He unlaced the fingers and straightened his carriage. Lon was defensive about age. He knew he was defensive. He felt young when he was with her, but the morning mirror was remorseless. He was older. Much older. The mirror did not lie. He saw the pouches, the lines from nostrils to edge of mouth, the dewlapped throat, the gray hair, the blue highways on the hands.

He had other problems. He had forgotten how to show affection. All he could show was domination. He could not approach her with the tiny bouquet of violets. He could not make pretty compliments. He could not hold his love in his eyes for her to see. He could perform at making love, but a performance is not enough. It was something, he felt, that could never merit more than applause. He needed more. Much more. His problem was to keep what he already had—Kay's love.

Two blue-uniformed gendarmes stood in the shadows on the far side of the Rue Royale, the edges of their capes, and their short night sticks, swinging in the breeze. Lon and Kay walked past Maxim's and up toward the Madeleine, talking a little, absorbing the sights with their eyes. Kay drank Paris. Lon drank Kay, admiring her as she admired the shops, the signs, the people, the famous places about which she had read.

She was disappointed, she said, in the appearance of the Crillon. "It is square in front," she said. "I imagined it as old and quaint, with courtyards and fountains." Lon said he knew two stories about the Crillon. One concerned a German major who had been quartered, in the war, in a front room facing the Place de la Concorde. He was stout and pleasant, and he tried to make friends, but the warmer his attitude toward the personnel at the Crillon, the colder they were to him.

Having no desire for French women and not being much of a drinker, he was reduced, for entertainment of an evening, to inviting waiters to his room to play cards. No one accepted. His loneliness was so apparent that studying him was one of the few pleasures enjoyed by the help. When General Le Clerc's Second

Division approached Paris, the major, like all Germans, packed to leave. After the retreat, a box of cigars was found on the major's desk. Clipped to it was a note: "To my American successor: I hope you are happier here than I was. Major Hans Fliegers."

The other story, Lon said, was about the coffee shop on the ground floor. For years, a fiftyish woman with a big nose and a lipless mouth sat behind the glass counter as cashier. All day, waiters slid checks and money in front of her. Without looking up, she would slap her hand over both, spike the check, read the total, hit the proper keys on the register and slip the money into a drawer, counting out the change in francs and centimes, and sliding them back to the waiter. There was never a greeting, a word, or a smile.

One morning, she arrived for work with two blackened eyes. She perched on her stool, and did not look up or talk to the waiters, who speculated among themselves, and to the headwaiter's pleasantries she replied with a grunt. There was a mood of sympathy in the coffee shop, even among the customers, but no one dared to ask her about her eyes. Beyond her ugliness, the woman was forbidding.

An official of the American Embassy who came in at noon for some potato soup and bread was fascinated by the black eyes. He called the captain of the waiters and asked curiously what had happened to the cashier. The captain shrugged. "M'sieu," he said softly, "we do not know and we do not ask for fear it will turn out to be only that she fell or was hit by a door. This way, all of us can think it was caused by a romantic disagreement."

They walked to the Madeleine, and back down the opposite side of the street. Lon suggested that Kay stop in a perfume shop and buy a good scent. "I still have the Shalimar you sent," she said. He urged her to buy something else. She didn't think so. He said she was pretending to be economical to impress him, and led her by the hand into the shop. There was a small counter and, behind it, a bar of perfumes. The air reeked of sweetness. Kay walked toward the back, looking at the bottles in a desultory manner, squeezing the atomizers on the sample bottles, and sniffing. The clerk smiled up at Lon. "Does your daughter have a preference?" she said.

"No," he said. He went back and taking Kay's hand walked toward the door. He smiled at the clerk. "She's too young to know what she wants." Lon hailed a cab. "Take us to the Louvre," he said. Kay got in. She looked upset. "Where to?" the driver said in English. "The Louvre. Louvre." Lon sat, removed his black hat, and slammed it on his thighs. "I'm so sorry," Kay said. "She had no right to say that."

"I know a funny story about the musuem," Lon said rapidly. "It's about two retired British schoolteachers. They met in a second-class pension and one said to the other: 'I've been here three days and I haven't been to the Louvre yet.' The other said: 'Neither have I. Must be something in the water.'" Kay said: "She had no right. She said it on purpose." "Get it?" he said, trying to synchronize his bouncing with that of the taxi.

"That woman knew better," Kay said. He stared at the back of the driver's head. "It doesn't matter," he said. He was lying. Kay understood. "Of course not," she said. "But I don't look like your daughter. I'm not that young." Lon grunted. "You are and you do," he said. "I'm fiftyish and I look it. I'm no mirror-mirror-on-the-wall man. I don't kid myself that I look younger, or even older than I am. I'm gray and middle-aged and you're thirtyish and you look younger. That clerk isn't trying to alienate customers. She made an honest mistake. You understand?"

He was talking louder than he wished. "This is a situation I must live with and I knew it the first time I thought of marriage." "It doesn't bother me," she said. "When you get there," he said to the driver, "main entrance." He half turned toward Kay. "It doesn't bother me that much. The wonder is that, so far, most people have been tactful. I could have a daughter your age, you know. I saw the slight surprise in faces when I introduced you to some of the Pan American people. Why not? If you change your hair-do and make it into a long pony tail, you'll look like my granddaughter. When we get home, I'll buy you a case of bubble gum."

"Oh," she said. "Now it's my fault." "You think this is the first time I've thought of this?" he said. "It's been a carrousel in my mind since we met. If only you were ten years older and I were ten younger, do you know how ideal that would be? Have you ever given it a thought?" She shook her head as the taxi stopped. "No," she said. "It's perfect just the way it is."

He paid the driver. "Like hell it is," he said. "Nothing is perfect. There is a price on everything." He steered her into the main hall and turned left, toward the Egyptian collection. "The price for this marriage is time. We are never going to be happy until we learn to face some of the ugly truths. You have some kiddish idea that we are going to be in a cocoon of ecstasy." He looked at her. "Don't cry, for goodness' sake, don't cry."

"Do you mind," she said, "if we stand here a minute? I can't appreciate this statuary and listen to you." "Okay," he said, "I'll stop." "No," she said. "I'm listening. I'm willing to learn. But I'd like to remind you of one thing. If it is true that I pay too little attention to the difference in ages, then it is also true that you pay too much attention to it."

He leaned against the wall. He thought it over. "Maybe," he said. "Maybe it's a raw spot with me. But I'm not going to pretend it isn't there. In fifteen years, I'll be close to seventy. You will be under fifty. If I'm crotchety now, what do you think I'll be then? What's it going to be like when I'm sixty, and you're still attractive? Am I going to turn out to be one of those wrinkled characters who is forever spying on his wife?"

Kay had determined to permit him to talk it out. He said nothing. They stood, facing each other, looking away for a moment.

Then she sighed and leaned forward and brushed her lips against his. "I think," she murmured, "that you must truly love me." He took her arm and they walked up the stairs toward the heroic statue of Winged Victory. "I don't like to see you hurt," she said. "I'm not," he said. "Forget it." "I don't like to see you hurt," she said, "but it does a great deal for my feelings of insecurity. Now, show me Mona Lisa."

The cherrywood paneling at Maxim's is more compelling than the music. It is old and burnished and it has craftsmanship and character. It has the look of mahogany with a rose tint. One can imagine, while ignoring the orchestra sitting like animated wax figures in a wall niche sawing out old arrangements of "Tea for Two" and "Good News," that once upon a time this cherrywood reflected the distorted image of Toulouse-Lautrec, and perhaps the dimpled legs of Mistinguette. The panels surely mirrored the fierce mustaches of Georges Clemenceau being wiped with a large dinner napkin, and the young well-muscled face of Hemingway in a Teddy Roosevelt grin. It must have picked up the brooding features of von Runstedt and the feverishly bright eyes of Picasso and, beyond doubt, the proud old lady who talked with her eyes, Sarah Bernhardt.

The couples danced across the small floor, and around the edges close to the white tables. How many, Lon wondered, knew or cared that this room had heard the original lilt of the cancan, had seen the kicking legs, the saucy garters and the white panties. Who recalled that once, years later, there had been young men in uniform, young men on leave—men whose names were Lufberry and Rickenbacker and Knight and Kilmer, and older men who bent intently over their soup—Sir Edward Grey, Edward VII, David Lloyd George, and, later, the handsome loser, Georges Carpentier?

Kay sat back against the wall at her table, smiling to herself and breathing the atmosphere of Maxim's. "If anyone had told me, a year ago—" He sat beside her, holding her hand under the table. "It isn't the same," he said. "The old headwaiter—Albert? I forget—he's gone. The stout lady in the hatcheck compartment looks familiar; the food is as good as ever, but the restaurant itself smells American." "I love it," she said. "Don't spoil it."

Lon liked to watch what the French could do to food. He felt that man had a restricted variety of edibles from which to obtain sustenance and anyone who could enhance their flavor or appearance was a benefactor of mankind. There were about a dozen common vegetables, a dozen common meats and fowl, a dozen common types of fish and perhaps two dozen farinaceous foods and cheeses. It was, to his way of thinking, a treat to watch all the things a French chef could do with two eggs; or a captain of waiters working over raw vegetables in a salad; or a waiter boning a fish or preparing a sauce.

Lon ordered dessert and coffee. They had *pêche Melba*. This had always been a favorite of his, and one of the comic-tragic aspects of a honeymoon is the desire to foist one's small passions onto the new heart. Kay suffered through the ice cream, the half peach, and the thick strawberry jam. "Good," she said. "It's different." She lingered over coffee, studying the glass ceiling panels and the colored leaves. Her eyes darted, drinking in a little there, sipping the scene somewhere else, noting the old paintings of lush nudes, the tiny peach-colored lamps on the tables, the silvery wine buckets, the busy waiters in black jackets and long white aprons. She missed little, noting even the white shirred Austrian draperies in the front window.

"Any time you're ready," she said. He paid the bill. They left and, on the Rue Royale, the moon was high and strong enough to spread the dark shadows to the center of the street. The metal covers were down over the shopwindows, in a steady wink. They walked around the corner to the hotel slowly, even though the cold was piercing.

The concierge gave Lon the room key and a cablegram. They rode up in the elevator in silence and, in the room, Kay began to undress. She had a leisurely, aimless way of disrobing, first kicking her shoes off anywhere, then shedding her coat, then wandering around the room as her double-jointed arms probed between her shoulder blades for buttons or zippers, garters were unsnapped and sheer stockings started to collapse.

Lon went to the bathroom, saying: "I won't lock it," and, when he got inside, he opened the cablegram, trembling inside—always inside—and read it. "Bat. Kate." He read it twice, then tore it up and flushed it down the lavatory. He washed his face and hands, brushed his teeth, and went back into the bedroom. Kay was propped up in bed reading. Her husband pointed to the pink nightgown. "I thought you never wore anything to bed," he said.

"I don't, but when a woman gets married, she's entitled to put on a little show." He began to undress. "It's a better show," he said, "without that thing." She closed her book, with a finger stuck between the pages. "That's what I like about men," she said. "You know one and you know them all." "Wrong again," he said, stepping out of his trousers and trying to keep the cuffs from dragging on the floor. "I have no ambition tonight. You rate three brief kisses, then I say my prayers and fare thee well."

"What was the message?" she asked. She opened the book again. "What was what message?" "The one you got downstairs." "Message?" "Yep. Message. You put it in your pocket." "Oh, that message." "If I'm intruding in your private business, say so." "You are," he said, "and you're entitled to." "So?" "So it was from Kate, the housekeeper." She held out a hand. "Let me see."

"I flushed it." "You what?" "Flushed it in the bathroom." He sat on the bed and removed his shoes and socks, then his shorts, and scratched the indentations the belt had made on his belly. "You didn't want me to see it?" "That's right." "Then forget it." "No. You asked." She looked up from the book. "I can tell by your eyes that it isn't good news." "Hardly. Sonny is drinking." "Sonny? O my God." "Two-word cablegram. 'Bat. Kate.' I told her to let me know if the kid went off the wagon. We haven't been gone twenty-four hours, have we?" "I forget the difference in time," she said. "What are we going to do?"

He looked full into her eyes. "You don't know how warm that word 'we' sounds." "Everything is we," she said. He nodded. "I know, but it sounds good." It was as difficult for him to express gratitude as it was to pay little compliments. "Thanks," he said. "If I get a cablegram," Kay asked, "can I tear it up?" "Okay," he said. "You win." "That's not good enough," she said so softly that it sounded like a hoarse whisper. "Not good enough. I have to know where I stand. If there are parts of you private from me, I want to know now."

"I said I was sorry." "You did not. You told me I win." "Same thing." He tumbled into bed beside her and flounced two big pillows. "I want to know," she said. He settled back, pulled the blanket up under his arms, and breathed deeply. "You're right," he said. "First of all, I apologize. I didn't want you to start a marriage with my problems. Secondly, you are right when you say that everything in this life is us—or did you say we? Whichever, I want this marriage to be as intimate as possible. I mean, everything. No secrets, no separations, no private conferences with my relatives, no independent thinking." She learned over and kissed his cheek. "The kid drinks," Lon said.

"He doesn't need you," she said, and the casual words made the crack of the whip on his flesh louder. "He wants a mother. His mother died and he can't take it." Lon turned on his pillow to stare at her. "So you're going to be his new mommy?" "I didn't say that. When we get home, Sonny is going to start off hating me. What are you going to do now? Go home?"

Lon turned away from her, threw one pillow on the floor, and pulled the bedclothes over his shoulders. "I'm going to sleep."

"I only asked," she said. "I mean, I'm willing—" "Don't bother me," he said. "I'm on a big happy honeymoon." She waited a moment. Then she said: "You mean, we are." Lon popped up in bed. "There I go again," he said. "I, I, I. Anyway, we're on this trip to stay." He got a cigarette from the night table and lit it. "I was just thinking, he must have started right after we left. You know the circular bar in the living room?" She nodded. "He hits that first. I've had heavy locks on it and he breaks them. It always starts at night, and by midnight he has enough of a load to become brave. Then he takes my car and drives into Point Pleasant and hits the bars.

"When he runs out of money,"—Lon shrugged—"he signs my name. He signs it to anything, for any amount. I make good, or he goes to jail. After all, Sonny is twenty-three and is supposed to know right—" "Why do you call him Sonny?" she asked. "Isn't that babyish?" "Oh," he said, "indeed it is. It was his ever-loving sainted mother who hung that on him. Now it's an old habit. If I refer to him as John, he thinks I'm angry."

"Are you going to phone?" "Nope. Kate knows what to do." Kay threw her book on the floor. She was worried. She had to play a role in this situation, but she wasn't sure what it should be. If she made any suggestions, she risked the sting of being told to mind her own business. If she didn't, he might think she wasn't interested. Kay had been aware that the boy was a periodic drinker, a moody, red-headed replica of his mother, a boy so inadequate, so insecure, that he could be offended by a greeting which sounded too casual.

Lon crushed the cigarette. "No more children," he said. "I've had it." The topic was unexpected. "Don't you think," Kay said, "that I should have something to say?" "I'm sorry," he said. Suddenly, he grinned and hugged her. "If you think I'm going to spend my life telling you I'm sorry, you're wrong." Lon began to kiss her with more interest, but she pulled away. "One of the reasons I married you," she said, "was that I wanted to have your baby."

"What? My baby? I have now heard everything." "Listen a minute," Kay said. "I happen to love you, deeply and permanently, and isn't it natural for a woman to want to have babies?" Lon sat up again, yawning. His eyes were red from lack of sleep; he looked like a hairy Buddha. "Let's get one thing straight right now. No babies. No babies ever. I am in no condition to start the infancy thing all over again; the colic, the middle-of-the-night fevers, the school days with the report cards and the homework—"

"My feelings don't matter?" she said. "Your feelings do matter," he said. "They are most important to me. I have only two goals left: to live in peace with you, and to earn enough money to keep us from starving. But you are going to have to learn to think of some things from my standpoint as well as your own. This afternoon we had a little conversation about ages. I'm not having a baby whose old man is in a wheelchair when the child wants to play baseball."

Kay was going to lose this debate. She knew it, and still she was impelled to continue. "Want some tea?" she asked. "They have room service all night." He shook his head. She sighed. "Is everything a matter of difference in ages?" He said no. Part of the adjustment of this marriage was a matter of middle age versus youth. This caused her to laugh. "I'm a youth?" He nodded gravely. "From where I sit, you are." She made a deprecating gesture. "You'll never change." "Thanks," he said. "But do not ever come to me with the happy tidings that you are pregnant. I won't ask much, but this is important." She started to speak. "Wait a minute," he said. "Let me finish. I love children. All children. All colors, all kinds. In my opinion, it is an act of selfishness and cruelty for a man of my years to have babies, and not be around to bring them up, to be able to capture joy from their games, their excitement in opening a birthday present, or their first look at the tree on Christmas morning. I am out of the baby phase. I'm even beginning to think that maybe I wasn't a good father to the child I once had."

She worked a chip of nail polish off her little finger. "All right," she said. "All right. Let's drop it." But she didn't. She told him that, when she had married the first time, she wanted to have four babies. Her heart had been set on it. After the first, she had quit. "Francis was no father. He was a good husband, but he had no understanding of children at all. It isn't easy to put into words, but he was cold, disinterested. When he came in the house, he kissed her, called her Daddy's girl, but even she knew that it was—"

"Perfunctory," he said. "Yes," she said. "Francis went through the motions, but his heart wasn't in it. As Lucy grew, he became more annoyed with her, because she was naturally sensitive and nervous, and she asked too many questions. He would kiss her and hug her one minute, and the next minute he'd order her to her room. 'Daddy wants to talk to Mommy,' he would say. Later, he would forget that he had sent her to her room. Like a good kid, she'd stay upstairs with the door closed, waiting for the word. But it never came. Sometimes, I'd go upstairs and find her sound asleep, crouched on her bed with her doll in her arms."

Kay lit another cigarette. "That closed the book on children. I didn't have four. One was too many. This time, I thought—well, as you say, let's drop it." He turned his face into the pillow, and his words were muffled and lazy. "Happiness," he murmured, "is a thing called greed. A man grabs for success, for a woman, for money, a drink—he thinks only of his own needs. I'm like that. I reached for you, thinking of me. Now I find that you are a person, a separate entity with needs of your own. So you start grabbing. The things you reach for affect me. Or," he said sleepily, "vice versa. You feel a need for a baby, and you reach. I place it beyond your reach. Conflict. Contention. Still, my heart's desire is to make you happy. How can this be if I keep pulling your hand back every time you reach?"

He was slipping off the high edge of consciousness. Kay drew on her cigarette and said: "What will Kate do with Sonny?" Lon roused himself for a moment, opened the eye that wasn't buried in the pillow, and said: "Sanitarium. He's been there before. Third day he'll be so sick. So sick. So very sick . . ."

THE THIRD DAY

THE room was dark. Lon looked at his watch. The time was one P.M. He slipped out of bed quietly, rubbed the soles of his bare feet against the rug, and stood. He fumbled in the closet for a robe, and wondered why he never put the robe across the foot of the bed at night. He went to the bathroom, closed the door softly, and stared in the mirror at the pouches in his face. They were always worse when he woke up. He pressed both hands against the high bones on his cheeks and pulled upward.

At once, the face smoothed. He looked ten years younger; he also looked slightly Oriental. He puttered around the bathroom for a while, mixing the shower water, looking for something bigger than the small cakes of soap furnished by the hotel, shampooing his hair, and returned to the bedroom. Kay was still sleeping, the sheet over her head. He watched her rhythmic breathing for a moment, then got his diary.

He snapped a small desk light on, and began to write:

This is a day late. Too tired last night. Matinee chinga with Kay. More and more in love, although that is impossible because the cup was full weeks ago and the extras are just pouring down over the sides. In effect, she's too good for me. Senses the right thing to do

*in this newborn marriage. Instinct or something; whatever it is
that women have. Embarrassed when she said she liked the smell
of my chest. Didn't know it had one.*

*Had to tell her Sonny is off on another one. Don't like it. Refuse
to feel ashamed of son, no matter what. She tried to pry; told her
what I pleased. She doesn't know he's manic-depressive. Can't tell
her, yet. Don't know enough about it myself. Kid had one cycle
after Elspeth went; may be ready for second now. Kate will let me
know. Kate also takes care of Lucy. Beautiful child, but also confused. Harsh father. Divorce. At eight, feels same lack of father
she felt when she had one. Never knew kids need one so badly.
Always thought it was mother love that they missed. This one is
rattled.*

*Kay loves Paris. So happy for her. Never cared for it. I'm a
Rome man. On this trip, no Rome. Just refueling stop. Kay strange
woman. Doesn't shop. Probably a sham. Have to urge her. Don't
care. She's rare jewel. Has beauty, personality, intellect and lovely
vices. Yesterday, Louvre, Eiffel Tower, Maxim's. Today, if she ever
gets out of bed, Versailles. In winter?*

The cab bounded up the Champs Élysées to the Arc de Triomphe
and under it, always heeding the traffic lights, always starting up
from a red one as though the rear end were grinding itself to bits.
The driver was a kind man with an unkind face. He wore a black
peaked cap, and had tiny pale eyes no bigger than blouse buttons,
a narrow mustache which gave the appearance of a forest of hairs
coming down from his nostrils, and a chin too timid to join his
face. His name was Michel and his English was confined to the
halting hybrids of two languages.

He was a happy man. He made it known to the Michaelses that
he was happy that their name was close to his, that they wanted
to drive to the gardens of Versailles, and that he was lucky enough,
on a day as gray and cold as this, to be dozing in front of the

Crillon when the doorman hailed him. Occasionally he pointed out places of historical interest, but could not find the words. Kay leaned forward, listening and frowning, and trying out her high-school French, but she had little success and once he turned almost completely around to say: "Please to speak English."

The cab moved out of Paris and through the little villages to the west and southwest. The trees were dark and sturdy and bare, with crusts of old snow or new frost on the east side of the trunks. In the parks, men pushed perambulators, and women walked behind, holding the hands of the older children; old ladies, looking elegant and slightly stooped, fed the birds. Everywhere on the roads were small cars, small trucks, some with but a single wheel in front, noisy motorcycles, and the customary coveys of cyclists, moving lazily like steel swans through the traffic.

Kay and Lon sat holding hands, nodding toward special sights to the left and right. Kay wore her coat open, over a black wool dress with a gray monk's cord sash. The hem kept creeping up over her crossed knees; she kept pulling it down with her free hand, and Lon kept pulling it higher with his other hand. She showed mock shock, and said: "Haven't you had enough of me?" "If I said yes," he answered, "it would ruin your day. And mine too."

"But don't men have a letdown after making love?" She was whispering. He knew what she meant, but he said: "Letdown how?" "Don't their emotions die for a time? Like yours should be dead now?" "Are you like that?" he asked. She giggled. "No woman is like that. Women in love are always ready. All the man has to do is to supply a match." "Not now," he said. "Maybe not later either."

"Shhhh," she said. He looked away. "I'm not talking loudly. Even if the driver could hear, what could he understand?" She looked her husband over, this time trying not to be a bride, but rather a stranger. She liked the solid gray tie, the plain blue suit, the Italian loafers and the blue shirt with the rounded collar and gold collar pin. Best of all, she loved his hair. There was still a little black in it, where the wave on the left was deep. Along the sides, it was as white as a bow wave. She wondered what he would look like with a mustache, but decided not to mention it.

The driver slowed down in the old seventeenth-century town of Versailles. They saw the coffee shops, the little TABAC signs, the small hotels and, off in the distance, the Palace of Versailles itself. Originally, Lon told Kay, most of the twenty thousand men who built the palace and the formal gardens had lived there in the town. It was a postilion stop to and from Paris and was noted for its grand stables.

At the palace, Michel parked outside the gold-topped gates and said that he would wait for them. Lon studied the hundreds of parked cars. "How will I find you?" he said. Michel tamped the hot tobacco deep into his pipe. "When you come, M'sieu," he said, "I will find you."

They walked for an hour. Lon bought a guidebook and explained that this was the wrong time to see the famous gardens. "I imagine they're bedded down for the winter. We'll see." Lon was not a museum man, but he had a broad cosmopolitan interest in history—not only as a seeker of knowledge, but as one who believed that almost all of man's works were vain and futile. Few men, he felt, from the dawn of history onward had ever progressed beyond love of self. The exquisite palaces and the ornate tombs were designed to resist time (the builder's mortal enemy) and to stand as monuments to the memory of those who no longer had a memory. Once, he had driven out of Cairo to see the pyramids, and he had stood on the sand of the desert and studied three of them. "Folly," he had said. "Folly. The pharaohs took the living sweat of thousands of men to make tombs for themselves, and other living men took the bodies of the pharaohs away. The winds, the sand, the sea and plant life can obliterate anything man can build." In Germany, he had smiled ruefully at the equestrian statues that

Bismarck and Wilhelm II used to build to each other. Napoleon
was one of the great warrior-statesmen and his memory was evoked
by a piece of pastry. Other men, with an eye to the spiritual life to
follow, built huge and costly temples to God, and counted themselves His partners for having taxed the poor and spent more on
an edifice than other men.

"Be good," an elderly woman had once written. "All else is
vanity." Lon Michaels understood this eternal truth, but could not
follow it. It was the answer, the sole solution to his life, but he
could not live it. He was quick to see the faults in others, and he
pinpointed them with deadly accuracy, but, throughout his life,
he had worn the cloak of the homely philosopher while carrying
the pistol of vengeance inside his belt.

Kay marveled at the formal gardens, executed in swirls and
loops of plants that would soon be in flower, bordered by broad
bands of dwarf hedges. There were formal forests with long
straight avenues or lanes for the princely hunters to ride through
with their dogs. There were lakes, fountains, the broad front of
the palace itself, hugged closely by buildings for government
officials on one side and an ornate chapel on the other.

"Marie Antoinette was married in that chapel," he said. "The
floor is a marble mosaic of intricate designs in reds and blues." Kay
was impressed. "Louis XV?" she said. "No," he said. "She bowed
her head in this chapel to accept the crown as Louis XVI's queen.
I'll show you the spot, in front of the Crillon, where she bowed
her head to the guillotine." "Oh," she said, "that's awful." "No,"
he said. "It's a tribute to the childishness of man. In large masses,
he is mute when he's well fed. He finds his voice only in anger.
Then he kills without mercy, tears down the very monuments
which were built to old heroes, and builds new ones to the villains
who led him to the murders."

"You make it sound terrible," Kay said. "I'm sorry I came here."
"No, you aren't," he said. "You must learn something of history,

and it isn't all dates and laws and wars. It has only the barest resemblance to what Metro-Goldwyn-Mayer has been drumming into your eyeballs. It is a long pathetic march to nowhere. Nothing points up the futility of man's progress better than his scientists. First they fashioned an atom bomb. Then they signed a petition begging the warriors not to use it."

"She must have been pretty," Kay said. She was studying a small original painting of Marie Antoinette. "Ah," he said, "you pay no attention to me." "I heard you. Let me think pretty thoughts." "Of course," he said. "But before you begin, let me tell you about Marie Antoinette's last words, because you will be touched by them. As she knelt before the guillotine, her dainty foot accidentally touched the shoe of the executioner. Just before the blade came down, she murmured: 'Monsieur, I beg your pardon.' "

It was no wonder, Kay said, that Versailles was one of the beauty spots of the world, since three kings had worked on it. Louis XIII bought the grounds and put a hunting lodge on it. Louis XIV built the palace and courtyard and had a small marble apron built in front of his bedroom windows solely for the use of the royal coach and the horses of a few highly placed friends. Louis XV expanded the Grand Trianon and the Petit Trianon, and bought additional property so that, at one time, the castle wall measured twenty-nine miles in length.

"You've been reading the guidebook," Lon said. Kay laughed and shook her head. "The hotel has a lot of free literature." "Frankly," he said, "I don't think Versailles today is anything like it once was. The grand canal, down to the left from where we are now, once measured over a mile in length. It wasn't a canal. It was a pool. Louis XV had a theater built in the back and had troupes of performers brought out by stage from Paris. He had fourteen hundred fountains here and yet his engineers had trouble finding water for the place. Sometimes, on summer evenings, the king invited Cardinal Richelieu and the Duc d'Orléans

and Madame du Barry and a few friends for a musicale. You see
the tier of marble steps over there? The ones with the ivy and grass
growing through the cracks? Well, that's where they sat. The
musicians were hidden behind a screen of flowers, and in front of
the benches there was a marble floor, and there the king held his
cotillions."

"I'm thinking pretty thoughts again," Kay said. He shrugged.
"Think them, my pet. But I see no Louis sitting there, and I hear
no music. Just ivy and grass growing through marble cracks."
"That's where you're wrong," she said. "At least, once upon a
time, they had it." They walked back up the broad gravel paths
and a little girl, barely able to walk, turned toward Kay and held
out a wild flower and a rich smile. "She has it now," Lon said.
Kay stooped and tried to speak a few words in French to the
child. They both smiled—so did the parents—at the international
language of a baby and a woman.

The day died before they were halfway back to Paris. For the
first few minutes of the ride, Michel had spoken of his children.
Lon tried to understand, but gave up and looked out the window as
if he were seeing nothing at all. Kay tried harder, and managed
to learn that he had four children, one in high school, and that
he lived in a fourth-floor apartment in Montmartre.

"Kay," Lon said abruptly, cutting in on the conversation,
"there are so many things I have to tell you about—things that
concern our life when we get home." Kay turned to face him.
"Begin," she said quietly. Lon said it wasn't that simple. "I'm
anxious for you to know everything," he said, "but I can't think
of everything at once. It may take a long time. You'll forget half
of them, but, when we get home, the place won't seem strange."
"I know the house pretty well right now," she said. "You only
think you do," he said. "There are wheels within wheels in that
place."

"It's an old house," he went on. "As you know, it sits between Clark's Landing and the canal leading to Barnegat Bay. I bought it right after Elspeth died. She was a city girl. I'm a seaside sailor. She wouldn't have lived in it, so I waited. It cost sixteen five originally. I had all the guts ripped out and put in knotty pine throughout. Then I improved the landscaping, retrimmed the outside with California redwood. I had inside walls and ceilings pulled down, put a big sitting room on the back, built an office and so forth, with library shelves for research, and the house now costs $52,000."

"You owe the difference?" she asked. "Paid off," he said. "Completely. I owed money almost all of my adult life. This house has no mortgage. I also own a house in northern New Jersey. It was sold to a kid cousin of mine but he and his wife broke up and he turned the house back to me. I'm selling it at a loss." "How much?" Kay said. "Seventeen, I think," he said. "It cost twenty." "Why don't you hang on to it for a while?" "I did. Then the bills started to come in for cracked ceilings, a leaning garage wall, a new oil burner, and I said the hell with it. In any case, it's going, and good riddance.

"All checking accounts are being made out in your name and mine, so you don't have to come to me for money. I'm not going to preach economy, Kay, because I know you're economical to start with. Maybe too much so. In any case, you'll have charge of the house and all that's in it—the people, the food, the entertaining, the services. Me, I'm in charge of all work in my office and all mail and all checks that come in from publishers." "I'll go along with that." she said. Lon glanced at her, and Kay wondered uneasily if there was a hint of mockery in that look, but all he said was "Good. You know, my housekeeper Kate has been with me four years and, though she's getting on in years, she's the cleanest, most honest woman you'll find. She comes from a town called Linz, in Austria, and, as you know, she has an accent straight out of Tann-

häuser but she knows that house inside out and she has a good hold
on Sonny."

"She must have lost her grip yesterday," Kay said. "Maybe,"
Lon said. "It's possible. However, I know that you like to cook
and sew, and so does Kate. Instead of dividing you two, I hope it
brings you closer together. She'll probably end up trying to mother
you, but take it. She means well. My secretary you've met too."
"Louise is tops," Kay said. He nodded. "She knows more about
my business, my deadlines, my so-called fan mail, contracts and so
forth, than I do. If she left, I wouldn't know how to look up my
insurance in the filing system."

"We'll get along, if that's what you're driving at," Kay said.
"No. It isn't. I would assume it. She's a competent woman with a
fine family. They live in Brielle, right across the river, and she
doesn't need the job. Now and then, she gets fits of the blues and
wants to quit. So far, I've talked her out of it. I won't mind if
you ask her questions about the routine of the house, but don't ask
her to do anything that isn't part of her work." "Like what?" Kay
said. "Like anything," he said. "I don't want her telephoning
the grocer or butcher or any department stores for you. Do your
own phoning. In other words, her work is secretarial. Hell, you
were a secretary when I met you."

"So far," she said, "you've told me practically nothing that I
don't know." He nodded. "That's fine. I'm delighted to hear it.
Now, what else? Incidentally, please don't be angry if I tell you
things which you already know, because if I stop to ask myself
whether you're acquainted with this fact or that one, I'll end up
telling you nothing. Oh, yes. I know another thing. Burge. He's
the handy man." She nodded. "He's the third employee around
the place," Lon said. "Burge does a lot more than rake leaves. He
can fix anything. He can repair a roof, plant flowers, build a
desk, set flagstones, take care of an automobile and fix a boat
engine.

"He's a cripple. Lost one leg in the war. It slows him up. Don't try to rush him. Let him take his time. He's the only one around the place who gets paid by the hour. He gets two dollars. He does everything deliberately, much slower than he has to, because he's a crook at heart." "You don't mean that, of course." "Yes, I do. Burge is a thief. He stretches the work out, lies about the number of hours he works each week, makes every job sound complicated and almost impossible—except for his genius to accomplish the impossible—and isn't above stealing books or other small objects from the house."

"I'm sorry you told me this," Kay said. "I liked Burge." Lon gave her a smile. "I like him too," he said, "or I wouldn't keep him. He's worth more to me than I pay him, plus what he steals. So he and I come out even. He has deep feelings of inferiority, and it makes him feel smarter than me when he's able to put something over on me. On a few occasions, when he goes too far, I stop him. Last summer, for instance, I found out that he was blackmailing the butcher. Burge told Mr. Preston that unless he gave him some meat free now and then he would get Mr. Michaels to switch to another butcher. Preston was giving him chops and steaks, and adding it to my bill. Kate found it out and I told Burge I was going to take it out of his pay."

"If I find a handier man, will you get rid of Burge?" Kay asked. Lon waved her off. "Not a chance. This man is about my age and he has been defeated in everything he has tried. Being a handy man isn't much, but he can't lose at this too." She smiled and tossed her head back. "Ah-ha," she said. "You see a little bit of you in him." "Exactly. I made it and he didn't. So, as long as I'm around, Burge stays."

"Is the boat paid for?" "That too," he said. "It's a good boat, and you know that I love the water, but it was a stupid way to spend thirty thousand dollars." "Sell it. Get your money back." "You don't know the boat business, hon. But you'll learn, because you're going to be first mate on this tub. It's a Richardson 1960 sedan. It's a thirty-five footer, with twin 225's in it. That doesn't mean anything to you, I'm sure, but it's a solid sea boat and it's fast. When we clear Manasquan Inlet on the good days, with the fair southeasters coming up deep green, the Irish Mist will make for Shrewsbury Rocks at 15.2 knots an hour without any strain at all. I hope you'll like the water, Kay. I hope it very much."

"You don't have to sell me," she said. "I love the sea. I don't know anything about wind and tides, but you'll teach me." "Before the summer is out," he said, "I'll have you docking the boat." As an afterthought, he said: "I talk and talk and I get nothing but anemic syllables coming back." "You have a faculty," Kay said, "for saying everything I want to hear, and then sort of closing the book." "Oh, nuts," he said. "Lon, my dear," she said. "I didn't mean it that way. I mean most men wouldn't even volunteer this kind of information, but I can't think of anything offhand to ask."

"That's a lie." "No, it isn't. My concern is with something else. I'm concerned about moving to a house already established." "Is this bad?" he asked. "Yes," she said. "Yes, it is. It wouldn't occur to a man, but a woman has a nesting instinct. She wants to build and furnish her own place. She wants to have something to say about the furniture and the color of the rugs and where the mirrors go and the closet space. Your house is already arranged." "Our house." "All right. Ours. But it's a going concern and I am going to have to adjust to it." "Oh," he said, "too bad." "Don't be like that," she said tartly. "It does require some understanding on my part, and some adjusting to things that don't reflect my particular taste, so give me a little credit."

"You don't like the house?" he said with exaggerated patience. She closed and unclosed the clasp on her pocketbook a few times. "I like the house," she said. "I . . . like . . it. I like Kate and your secretary. I don't like Burge. I like the boat and I'm sure that I'll learn something about it. Enough to be of some help to you. I like the fact that we can get to New York from Point Pleasant in two hours or less, if we want to see a show. I like most of the furniture. The leather couches in your dining room—excuse me, our dining room—make it look like a dentist's waiting room, but I just don't feel godawful enough about anything to argue. I'll get used to it."

"As long as you like the place as a unit," he said, "we can always correct the couches or whatever it is that you don't like. I happen to like those couches." "Obviously," she said. "You bought them." "We're back in Paris," he said, looking out the taxi window. She kicked her shoes off and rubbed her feet. "My toes are frozen." "When we get to the Crillon," he said, "I'll draw a warm bath for you." This, she thought, must be a new way of apologizing.

"Anyway," Kay said, "I'm getting a fast, superficial look at Paris. I have a thing I must tell you about." It was night, and they were walking the streets of Montmartre toward the Folies Bergères. "When a man speaks in a foreign language, I think it's romantic. Isn't that silly?" Lon thought it was silly. "I knew you wouldn't understand," she said. "It's the sound. Sound. It doesn't matter what he's really saying, it sounds romantic in my ears." "Sexy?" Lon asked. She thought about it. "Yes," she said slowly. "Ah," said Lon, "you've seen too many movies."

Kay laughed, but insisted, "French is the sexiest language, don't you think?" He didn't think so. He said it sounded sexy to her because like the rest of the world she liked to think of the French as a romantic race. "They aren't, really," he said. "Their population decreases, and their preoccupation with money keeps them busy. What makes the Frenchman seem sexy, I think, is that he places such little value on the act itself that he looks like a libertine to everyone else. If he kisses a lady, he feels that the bed will follow in due time. I think he is jaded. Once he is accustomed to the compliance of his wife, his desire dies. He needs a mistress at once, if he can afford one."

Kay looked up at the dark night sky. "Heaven protect me from this man," she said. "He kills all my nice illusions." Lon smiled. "I'm sorry," he said. "I'm sure that there are very romantic Frenchmen. I just want you to get out of the habit of imbuing whole races of people with set characteristics. It is not true that Hungarians make the best goulash, for example. There are French chefs who can spot any Hungarian four noodles and a box of thyme and still make a better goulash. It is equally untrue that all American tourists are crashing bores, or that all Texans are millionaires, or that all Latins are lousy lovers, or, to get back to the topic, that all Frenchmen are good ones." "I understand," Kay said, "but do you understand what I was saying?" "Certainly," he said. "I grew up thinking that all Chinese laundrymen were members of tongs and had hatchets in the back room for cutting off pigtails and heads. In my neighborhood, all Italians had barbershops, fruit stands or repaired shoes. As I grew, I realized that the only thing more important than learning was unlearning."

They walked on in silence, past the little shops with the paintings under lights, the dress shops with aloof models holding their waxen noses high, along the streets with sidewalks so narrow that Lon had to walk behind Kay when anyone approached.

"Paris has always been one of the places I've wanted to see most," Kay said. "I'm glad I've had a chance to." Lon's hand tightened on hers but all he said was, "Plane time is nine in the morning, which means arriving at Orly at eight." "Eight?" she said with dismay. Lon said they would need that much time to clear customs. She didn't like it; she was a good solid sleeper. "We'll have to leave a call for six thirty," she said.

"Six," he said. "I like a little loafing time. I'm no good when I first wake up. I need some cigarettes and time to get the hair out of my eyes." "That," she said, "makes two of us. But six?" He didn't answer. It had to be six. He was not going to miss a plane because of traffic, or because of some hitch in customs. "Okay, six," she said, as though she were making a concession.

The Folies Bergères was well lighted. Groups of people pressed toward it; some on foot, some in taxis. A gendarme in the middle of the street kept the cabs moving and another, outside the box office, kept those with no tickets in motion. The lobby, a burgundy red, was huge, big enough for a bar, a painting exhibit, and some souvenir stands where stout Parisian women held rubber nudes and made them wiggle.

"I've never been here," Lon said. "It's going to be one big striptease." Two painters were selling small originals of the Basilica of the Sacré Coeur and the windmills of the Moulin Rouge. There were wall photos of former Folies stars, mostly statuesque blondes in the nude posing beside muscled young men in silver loincloths.

Lon produced the tickets, which he had bought through the hotel concierge, and was surprised to find that they were for aisle seats in the second row. The seats were red plush, each one wide enough to be a small lounge, each one furnished with a separate red plush pillow. "All the comforts of the boudoir," he said. Kay was looking around the theater. She had expected that it would be a cheap tourist trap, but she was impressed. The mezzanine boxes were edged with thousands of tiny electric bulbs which gave the effect of a huge inverted rhinestone bracelet. From the ceiling, a birdcage of lights hung, surrounded by four concentric rows of lights. The theater was almost full when the lights dimmed. Lady ushers hurried up and down the aisles with small flashlights, showing last-minute arrivals to their seats.

The opening number was a cancan of the year 1900 at Maxim's. On the program, the dancers were listed as "Les Cancaneuses" and "Les Cancaneurs." The dancing seemed to Lon, who had seen many cancans in America, to be more spirited and naughty and less dirty and suggestive. Still, neither he nor Kay was ready to admit admiration for the Folies Bergères until the tableaux were presented. The court scenes of Louis XIII and Louis XV were so vivid, the costumes and lighting so beautiful that the audience repeatedly burst into applause. In one scene, a nude man and woman stood waist deep in a fountain, posing in marble stillness as the waters, made gold by colored lights, spouted high over the stage and cascaded down over their bodies.

Some scenes were funny, but the amusing lines, the gay songs, the lyrics were lost on Kay and Lon, entranced with the spectacle—the sets, the mounting, the choreography, the orchestral arrangements. Lon was prepared to admit, before the end of the first act, that this was one of the finest musical extravaganzas he had seen. His earlier opinion, that the Folies Bergères was merely French flesh as the Americans wanted to see it, was replaced by respect. When the show was over, and he helped Kay into a taxi, he said that he would have to go back to the last of the Ziegfeld Follies and the Vanities to think of a musical review that could match this one.

"In one sense," he said, as they bounced over the cobblestones, "this is the best of its type, El." Kay was looking out the window. She turned to frown at her husband. "What did you call me?" His heart seemed to falter. "El?" he said. "That's funny. I wasn't thinking of Elspeth." "Yes," Kay said, "it is funny." "I'm sorry," he said quietly. "The name slipped out accidentally. Who knows what the tongue will say, five years after?"

"Forget it," she said. "It does nothing for my morale." She turned away, and he took her arm and tried to turn her toward him. She kept her head doggedly toward the window. "Jealous of a dead woman?" he asked. She shrugged. "Maybe." "Ridiculous." "Maybe." "She was the kind of a woman who would be tickled if she knew she could make you miserable from the grave." "Then she's happy." "You ought to be ashamed." "No, no. You ought to be." He dropped her arm and hunched back in the seat. "I'm tired of apologizing," he said. "So don't," she said.

The operator said she would be sure to call the Michaelses at six A.M. Lon hung up and told Kay curtly that he would shave now. "I'll pack," said Kay. She began to pull the suitcases from the closet. It was going to be like this, she knew, all the way around the world. They would spend two or three days in each city, and then the packing would start, the tickets would be rechecked, the customs would be a hurdle, and then the rush to board a cold jet, dozing on concrete with its doors open. It would be nicer if they could spend more time in each place, but Lon obviously felt that the burden of their absence from home would be on the children: Lucy and Sonny.

Her thoughts reverted to his use of Elspeth's name. She could not accept his explanation that it was accidental. Does he miss her? Kay asked herself. If he doesn't, how can the name pop from his lips in a happy moment five years after? He's had dates with other women; he's had affairs too, since Elspeth died. Did he call those women "El"? If not, why me? Do I represent the past—maybe the happy part of the past?

Why am I so jealous? Why is it that I die when he gives a second glance to a strange woman on the street? A few months ago, he was nothing to me. Now he and my next breath are equal in importance. I want to love this man, and I do love him, but at what point do I go down the drain in selflessness? I want to be an entity; somebody. I almost beg for his approval, and I dread the cut of his words—what am I? A self-made slave? At what other times does he think of Elspeth? He says, only in his prayers. That's enough. That's plenty. That can start a train of thought at bedtime. I'm unreasonable, but I don't want to be generous. I want all of him all the time. She's been dead a long time; why can't she stay dead? She had him and didn't know what to do with him. It's my turn, and if this is greed let me face it squarely and call myself greedy.

At one A.M. Kay was sleeping. The room was dark. In the deep bowl of nothingness, Lon found that he could see things by staring up from his pillow. Tiny comets burst across his vision and he tracked the little stars through the blackness to the place where they died on the edge of his eyes, and a new one burst, like the tail of a white rooster, in the center of the ceiling. Or rather, where the ceiling would be if the lights were on. He closed his eyes and, by looking, he could see disjointed, translucent worms wiggle across his field of sight. He wasn't sure whether he preferred the little comets to the glassy worms, or vice versa.

The ache in his feet was a nice ache. He was walking more, on this trip, than he usually did, and he felt no fatigue until he removed the shoes and socks at night. Then, as he scissored his toes against each other, he could feel the ache come to life. He could feel it sitting or standing and, if he walked to the bathroom, the bones in the balls of his feet hurt and the ache transmitted itself to the bones of his toes, and sometimes even his heels felt hot and sensitive.

Now, in bed, with his feet between fresh cold sheets, the ache was sweet. When his feet warmed the sheets, he moved them to a new, and cooler, place. With his hands clasped across his chest, outside the sheets, he felt like a person who was dead but whose brain was a whirling centrifuge with the power off, the momentum carrying it on at decreasing speed.

Diminuendo, he said to himself. Sleep will not come to me until the carrousel of thought stops, with its plunging horses and loud music. The carrousel spins and spins, and the brass ring is unconsciousness, but I cannot reach that far. It is slowing, but the rate is imperceptible. She sleeps at my side and she sleeps without snoring or grinding her teeth—like a lady, perhaps—or as a lady should—but I detect a callousness in this. The little contretemps did not bother her. It bothers me. She rests. I trace rooster tails and glass worms in the dark. If sleep does not come soon, I am going to be one fine first-rate bastard in the morning.

She could have passed the thing off for what it was: a name to which I became accustomed over twenty-five years. For five years afterward, I hardly ever used it, and seldom heard it. Now it has to skid off my lips as though it were part of daily living. It isn't. She knows it isn't. She tries to pretend that she thinks I am living with a ghost. She knows better. Oh, she knows, all right. Maybe all of her other emotions have been wrung out and she needed a good cry.

Women live on deception. They feel that it is feminine to pretend to be what one is not, to play a role, be a haughty queen or an innocent child, to comprehend or not to comprehend as the mood suits them, to please, to tease, to thwart, to sorrow, to love, to hate, to reject or supplicate—and they can do it all to one man. The young brunettes must have a streak of gray; the old gray ones must have blonde hair; the fingernails must look like bloody talons; the lips must be reddened, the necks whitened, the eyes blued.

The waist is pinched, the bust padded, the rump smoothed, the belly flattened, the heels raised, the fingers ringed, the wrists jeweled, the ears perfumed, the eyelashes put on one at a time, the dress tightened, the neck lowered, the hem raised, the legs lengthened and, with all of this, they must react with shock if a man suggests that he'd like to go to bed with them.

Oh, that bed. The key. The slave block. All the drama of all the families takes place in bed—birth, death, love, sickness, rest and unmitigated boredom—all occur on a pile of padded springs. I would write an ode to it if it would bring sleep now. But it won't. I should get up and write an entry in my diary, but I am not in a mood for it. The diary: a schoolgirl's confessional. You write your innermost thoughts, being careful to scrub them a little on their way through the pen. The thought that is good and clear and true tonight will be a lie in the morning. I can write: "I hate Kay" and I will find it to be valid and blunt but, in the morning, she will be the happy bride, the one and only love, and then I will read "I

hate Kay" and throw the diary in the basket. A diary is a wandering minstrel of moods; many dispositions in one mind; written
proof that the keeper belongs in the cell; that no opinion remains
fixed except the one that says: "I want to be loved."

Elspeth. Elspeth. Please keep your name off my lips. What's
done is done and it was all a long time ago. I did not want you to
go. Live, I said. For goodness' sake, live on. You could have had
such a ball. Such a perfectly lovely ball if you'd only learned to
relax. But no. You started married life as a red-headed vixen, to
whom the dance, the drink and the delights of defiance were all.

Flapper. You were a flapper when the real ones had walked
offstage. You wanted to Charleston when the world had moved on
to the Varsity Drag; home-made gin was your drink when your
friends were sipping legal Scotch; you pirouetted through the
time-payment plan when our friends were buying houses; babies,
ah yes, babies. You wanted babies, but only as book ends. Girls,
preferably, because, as you said: "You can do so much with a girl."
So you had a boy, a nice, handsome image-of-mother boy, and you
lost interest in him except when he was on parade.

He never lost interest in you. His affection never dropped a
notch, even when you swore at him and called it discipline, even
when you were drunk. Oh, no. All he had was love. No brains.
No opinions. He saw everything in the world in varying shades
of gray, except you. You came up in Technicolor. Now he is a first-
class alcoholic, a nervous, fretful boy who is still looking for his
mother, and who is afraid to turn the night light off for fear that
he might see her.

Well, I'm not afraid to look at you, even in the dark. After five
years, your image should dim a little, but I can conjure you in a
trice. Like now. There. Let me paste your face against the black
ceiling. You were a great wife in the early years. You were tall
and slender, almost regal in your bearing. There was a great deal of
love in your heart for people. You never dreamed that the day

would come when you would fear them all and hide in a closet when the doorbell rang. You wear your mantle of tragedy well, my dear. You look good, smiling in silence on a dark ceiling. You are young again and, wherever you are, the calm, sweet light of the early serenity is back in your eyes.

May I tell you something funny? Promise you won't laugh? I felt unfaithful to you in getting married again. Your expression doesn't change. Isn't that funny? Me? I should feel unfaithful for turning my back on your headstone? Ridiculous. I didn't feel unfaithful to you when I was being unfaithful—when you were alive and suspicious. You guessed, you divined, you suspected, but you never knew. Not really. Let me tell you something about cheating. Spurious love carries its own punishment. There is a tingling thrill in getting away with something and, for an hour or two, it is a remarkably good imitation of love, but, please believe me, remorse sets in almost at once and it remains. Your idiot husband never learned. If he could not get true affection at home, he was always ready to accept the imitation.

I despised myself for loving you to the end. You turned out to be habit forming. I knew that you were through with me at least a year before you knew it. You changed from the big happy outgoing laughing girl, year by year, into the emotional cripple. First, you alienated your old friends. This required time and spitting contempt, because some of them were loyal. Then you turned away from Sonny and you stood in the shadows and watched his confidence disintegrate.

Your father was next. He was all you had left, but he had to go. So you watched him for the small mistakes, the little errors in judgment or in words, and your beak picked at him and picked at him until he had a thousand small wounds. You made him ashamed to leave his room. He, who had once dominated everyone—including you—was reduced to begging mutely for approval. He tried hard to please you; tried to anticipate your wishes. Mixed drinks for you, sneaked them to you when I was in another room, gave you sleeping pills when even your doctor denied them. But he had to go, and you kept cutting and cutting until the old man, unshaved and in utter weariness, took to his bed and died of God knows what.

Still, you rate a bow. You did not weep at his funeral. The pills and the liquor kept you under control, and everyone remarked how well you looked. It was after the funeral that you turned your attention to me. I was the next to be disintegrated, to be erased from your mind, the man most likely to disappear. First came the bedroom divorce, and with it the deep loneliness of knowing that a marriage is dead although the sponsors are living. Each night was a private funeral service. "Can I help you unzipper that dress?" "No, thank you. I can manage." "Would you like a cigarette?" "I have my own." "How about a little friendly chat?" "Are you kidding? What would we have to talk about?"

The irony, my pet, was that the marriage was dead but love was alive. Love on both sides. You never cared for another man, and I tried, and couldn't love any other woman. Next, you stopped reading anything I wrote. I can see how my words, my thoughts, would have been anathema, but there is no rule in the marital book which says that you have to tell, and retell, the victim. "That new book," you said one evening, "the one about the opium wars of China—I tried it twice, Lon, and couldn't get beyond page forty." Now wasn't it tough that you couldn't bear to read page forty-one? On the other hand, what gallantry for you to don your jungle boots and wade through the swamps of the first forty, I said. "Too bad," and Sonny giggled.

Inch by inch, I was erased from your consciousness. I was consulted less and less, even about such mundane matters as whether I wanted onions with the calves' liver, or bacon. I took what you offered, because to question you about anything, even a trivial matter, was to risk vituperation. I learned not to comment adversely about anything. But you miscalculated a bit. While you were erasing my name, you were erasing the "Mrs." too. You were not aware that you were planning your own destruction. How old were you when you died? Forty-two? You had a lot of time left, if you had wanted to use it. A lot of time.

Two years before the end, you realized that your new self was erasing all the others. Oh, it hit you hard. All in one day you knew. You looked at yourself and saw a bloated old lady, a woman with pouched cheeks, like Queen Victoria, a woman with weeping eyes, a woman frightened, a woman who did not want to wash, to comb her hair, a woman who would not answer the phone or the door-bell, a woman sitting at a dining room table alone, dreaming into the depths of the shot glass before her. You knew all right. Once, when you had a lucid moment and I was dressing to go out, I said: "What the hell are you afraid of?" And you shrugged and said: "I don't know. Dying, I guess."

THE FOURTH DAY

ORLY was in a bowl of milk. The mists floated like veils around the airport. Two Air France Constellations took off, one bound for Algiers, one for Brussels. They were thundering ghosts racing down the runway, lifting off to disappear at once, though the thunder played a game of diminishing returns for a minute or more. An Alitalia DC-8 came down through the world of sunshine, through the fleecy blanket, its electronic nose feeling for the concrete ribbon below, and, bursting out underneath, touched its many wheels to the surface as though the landing were never in doubt.

Pan American Flight One Fourteen would be a few minutes late, the announcer said. Inside the airport, Kay and Lon studied the glass shelves of the souvenir shops. He bought a *New York Times,* two days old, and tossed it in the briefcase. "I wish the plane would come," he said. "I'm tired." She bought a bronze replica of the Eiffel Tower. "You're not used to going to bed so late," she said. "I'm not used to getting up this early," he said.

The hurt of yesterday was beginning to heal. Kay smiled at her husband. "I don't know of anything funnier than you getting out of bed this morning." "I can name ten," he said. "When the operator called us," she said, "you went out of bed flying." "I slept on starting blocks," he said. She giggled, and held her gloved hand over her mouth. "The phone . . . the bounce . . . then the waiter with the breakfast before you could get into a robe . . . the crois-sants . . . coffee . . . washing . . . snapping the suit cases . . . " Lon began to smile. "The elevator . . . " he said, picking up the cadence, "the bellboys . . . the cashier . . . the bill . . . the concierge . . . the doorman . . . the taxi . . . the airport . . . the tickets . . . the passports . . . the customs . . . and now, I'm ready for bed."

"Oh?" she said. "This kind of bed," he said, "rhymes with dead. *Alles kaput. Todt. Finite la musica.*" "Excuse me," a voice said, "you're American, aren't you?" Both looked around. "Yes," said Lon. They faced a tall man with snow-white hair, stout and polished and reeking of cologne. He wore a plaid beret and there were diamonds on his fingers, in his cuff links, and a blazing one in the dark tie glared like a distant fire.

"My name is Cointreaux," he said, offering his hand. "It's spelled c, o, i, n, t, r, e, a, u, x. Cointreaux, almost like the liqueur. Grandpa was Swiss, but I'm from New York and I need a little advice. Do you know how to read these damn tickets?"

Lon took the top ticket and looked at it. "I think so," he said. "What's the problem?"

"Well," Mr. Cointreaux said, "the missus and I are going around the world. We're supposed to be on Flight Two all the way. I haven't heard it called and it's due." Lon flipped the pages, then looked up. "By the way," he said, offering his hand, "my name is Michaels." He smiled at Kay. "My wife," he said. The fat man bowed. "Oh, brother," he said, staring at Kay. "Ain't you some-thing?" Lon, irritated, handed the ticket back to him. "Flight Two will be your flight most of the way around," he said, "but it goes to Frankfurt instead of Paris and you'll pick it up again at Beirut."

"So what do I do here?" asked Mr. Cointreaux. Lon showed him. "Flight One Fourteen," he said. "We're taking it too. It's a little late on account of the fog." Cointreaux, who had a face most easily described as a summer sunset said: "Let me get this. One Fourteen

out of here to where? Rome?" "No," Lon said, suppressing his
annoyance, "Rome is a fueling stop. You go on through Rome to
Beirut, according to your ticket." "So we get on here and stay on?"
"Yes, sir." With a grunt of relief, the fat man thanked him, then
said, "Wait a minute. I want you to meet my wife. What'd you
say your name—?" "Michaels. Lon Michaels."

"Don't move." The man waddled away and was back in a moment with a mountainous woman with a rhinestone cigarette holder
jutting up from between her teeth.

"Mrs. Cointreaux," he said, beaming. Kay and Lon nodded
pleasantly. The big woman wore four strands of pearls which lived
on a perpetually warm earthquake. Lon studied her without appearing to. "My wife's a doll," Cointreaux said. "Some people think
she looks like F.D.R. in drag, but they're just jealous." He jabbed
Lon with his elbow. Mrs. Cointreaux towered over the little party,
beaming at one and all. "Have you ever," she said, through locked
teeth, "seen so many goddamn foreigners?"

Kay began to cough. Lon didn't think it was funny. "We are the
foreigners," he said. "These people are natives." Cointreaux looked
puzzled. Then he brightened. "Gotcha," he said. "They're French,
this is France, we're Americans, right?" Kay nodded, still coughing, still trying to stifle her amusement. "Peg," Cointreaux said,
"the man has got a point. We're just ugly Americanos."

Flight One Fourteen was called, and the four walked to the
proper gate, and boarded the jet. "I hope," said Cointreaux to a
stewardess, "that we're going to have breakfast. I'm dead for bacon
and eggs." She told him that breakfast would be served after take-
off. "When he isn't eating," Mrs. Cointreaux said to Kay, "he's
drinking. He just eats and drinks and reads the stock market." Kay
smiled, and said nothing. "He's no drunk," said Mrs. Cointreaux,
as she slid into her seat. "He just appreciates a little boozeroo."
She laughed heartily. "Never hurt anyone, I always say. Where you
from, honey?" Kay said New Jersey. "Larry," said Mrs. Cointreaux

loudly, "they're from across the river." He grinned. "Brooklyn? We're from Sutton Place, Manhattan. This is the small world department."

There is a world which is neither real nor unreal, neither sleep nor wakefulness, and Lon was in it. He dozed across Switzerland, through the fueling at Rome, down the boot of Italy, across the Dodecanese, all the way to Cyprus. He was aware, at all times, that he was in a plane, and yet his fatigued mind passed in and out of dream states. Sometimes he heard people talking around him; at other times, he imagined he was in a vacuum of silence. He could hear the four big jet engines, but he wasn't aware of them. When the plane turned, he could feel the tilt in his body, but he wasn't sure whether he was floating alone in space inside the plane, or whether his body and space were synchronized.

At Cyprus, the captain spoke. He said that he expected to land in Beirut in a half hour. Lon heard the voice, and opened his eyes. He felt tired. He looked out of the window, and there was darkness, except for the blinking of a red light on the edge of the wing, and the reflection of another red light from under the plane. He sat up. Kay was reading the *Times*. "You slept," she said. He nodded. "Somewhat," he said. "In and out."

"I've been talking to Mrs. Cointreaux," she said. Lon reached into his briefcase and drew out his diary. "Mrs. who?" "Cointreaux. She's sitting behind us with her husband." "Oh," he said. Kay smiled. "She's very funny," she whispered. Lon shrugged. "I can become hysterical thinking of him." Kay went forward for the final powdering before landing. Lon unlocked his diary and wrote:

Another entry one day late. This one is written over island of Cyprus. I am learning anew about marriage. Women are women are women. Left Paris cool to Kay, and vice versa. The name just stricken from my vocabulary is Elspeth. Must not, ever. Kay doesn't like. Don't blame her. If, in a tender moment, she moaned "Oh, Francis!" I would strangle her. Could happen. Left Paris in fog, actual and mental. Not enough sleep. The itinerary is beginning to cut in on my love life. Kay does not realize how much I love her. Strange. It seems so apparent to me. I can tell she feels that all the deep affection is on her side, and she is not at all sure of me. I want her to be sure. Do not believe in this keep-'em-guessing game. Do not believe in any type of game in marriage. Kay was once a prime flirt. Gave every man the lowered lids, the faint smile.

All of them got the message. Guess all of them thought it was going to be a cheap conquest in bed. Says she did it because she felt neglected. Lie. Did it because she is unsure of self. Doesn't believe what mirror tells her, has to see hungry look from strange men. No more. Warned her before marriage that only way in which this marriage can be broken is by idle flirtation on her part. Would walk out. Mean it. No threat. Just couldn't stand other men thinking my wife is available. Told her it doesn't matter at what early point she stops the game, I don't want it started. We used to have a phrase describing such women. Told her. Kay was shocked. Said she had heard it once before. Told her the only way she could have heard it is if someone called her that name.

Denied. Then admitted it. Told me men used to phone her when Francis was not home; sometimes, when he was. Scared. Always trying to put out fire she had started. Asked her if all right if I played a little; especially if innocent. She said no. Said she didn't believe I could be innocent about anything. Told her I felt that way about her. Must close now. She's coming back to seat.

The room had a small sheltered porch. Kay was on it in the early evening, looking down at the beach, the freighters in the harbor, and the mountains to the north. Even in the dark, she could see snow on the peaks. Still, Beirut itself was tropically warm and, between the crashing sound of green combers against the sea wall, she could hear the swish of the palm leaves in the street below. The wind was strong from the west, and when she stuck her head outside the sheltered area, it whipped her hair around her face and spanked her eyes.

For a few minutes she would be alone. Lon was in the lobby, arranging for a car to take them to the casino. She had never cared about gambling, but he wanted to go and said she should try roulette once. He didn't understand enough about chemin de fer, or any of the other games, to risk his luck, he'd said, but roulette was a matter of mathematics and luck. She was willing to try, but she was not particularly excited about it. My mind has been geared too long to the dollar-ninety-eight-cent bargain, she thought. I don't like to risk money, even to win more.

That had been one reason for her dismay when she'd asked him if it was all right to buy a doll for Lucy at Orly Airport, and he had replied snappishly, she thought: "If you're going to buy a doll, okay. But if you plan to buy one in every country around the world, no. They take up too much room in the luggage." She hadn't been angry, but she had felt hurt. And after the dispute over Elspeth the day before, she was darned if she was going to start a second one over a toy.

Now the hurt was gone, or almost gone. Twice on the plane Lon had said: "What are thinking about, Mrs. M?" and she had replied: "Just thoughts." Both times he had gone back to dozing, murmuring: "Save a pretty one for me." Now, alone on the little porch high above Beirut, she found all the thoughts returning, and they were not good ones. Somewhere along the road, she thought, I've lost myself. He's still there, but I'm gone. I'm something that has melted into him—a small, perhaps integral, part of his life, like the writing of a book, or horseraces, or big game fishing, or Sonny. An appendage.

I must be more than this, she thought. I've got to be an equal partner, without being one of those insufferable women who

smother their men. I won't mind being the junior partner, even the
silent partner, but I've got to have more status than something he
talks into. Why did I have to ask him about the doll? I could have
bought it. Who needs a husband's permission to buy a trinket? But
no. I had to ask. I couldn't wait to be turned down.

I cry inside for you, Lon, she wanted to tell him. Now, I barely
have you and I'm afraid of losing you. Afraid of your frown, afraid
that I may do something you'd call "stupid," afraid I won't respond
to your needs quickly enough, and that you'll find me slow.

It was when the bruises were inflicted, she thought unhappily,
that she started thinking, and that was no time for it. Why couldn't
she think before it happened? Why had she had to make a big
thing out of the "Elspeth" matter? It hadn't been that important,
but she had risen to what she thought was the challenge of a ghost,
and oh what a mistake. She shivered suddenly, feeling again the
recoiling chill in the taxi, and was swept by a sense of loneliness,
of rejection. It's as though I were his traveling companion, she
thought, rather than his wife. Not even a mistress. Just someone
who jumps when he says: "It's in my briefcase" or "Pick up the
phone and order some tea and toast." A secretary with bed
privileges.

Ah, but when you're happy with me, Lon, everything changes.
I cannot remember the unhappy thoughts. I am all woman; all
wanted; all loved; all necessary. I am important. Mrs. Lon Michaels
—the permanent Mrs. Lon Michaels. I feel tall and straight and—
yes, pretty. It isn't nice to think that, but I do. When you make love
to me, I am reduced to the point of death. There is no one else in
the world; there is, indeed, nothing else in the world. You keep
telling me that love-making, no matter how good it is, is not love,
but if it is not then it is an amazing forgery because I am utterly
overwhelmed. But I don't dare tell you this, Lon, because you'll
ask if it hasn't happened before, and if I say no, you'll turn sarcastic.

She moved restlessly about the balcony, wondering what was

keeping him, already missing him, though really, she supposed, he hadn't been gone so very long.

She was happy much more of the time than she was miserable, she acknowledged honestly. The same was true of him, she was certain, but the difference between them was that his irritation faded in a few minutes; hers dropped her to the fourth subcellar and left her there. Perhaps it was natural for a woman to be more emotional than a man, but something had happened to her self-confidence when she fell in love with him. But, whatever the early tests of a marriage, she thought that they had passed them. Also, both had had experience in marriage, and at least weren't making the childish mistake of constantly challenging each other's love.

In this, she felt, she was probably much more mature than he, more conscious of the fact that they would be adjusting to each other for a year or so. Whatever was irreconcilable between them after that would probably remain that way.

In the darkness she peered at her watch, trying to make out the time, wondering how it could take so long to arrange for a car, wishing he'd come back. He made her feel safe, she thought. Flying with him, she lost even her fear of planes. When they'd landed in Beirut, she'd had a queasy feeling that she was in a land of mystery; of Turks or something. Not Turks, Arabs. When they'd arrived at the hotel, the doorman in his fez and droopy trousers, and in the lobby the Arab bellhops serving small cups of Turkish coffee had increased her sense of strangeness. But watching him, dignified, aloof, cool, telling the clerks what kind of room he wanted, ordering the bellhops to pick up the luggage, asking for mail and messages, bringing everything under control, she had relaxed, her uneasiness had disappeared; with Lon nothing bad could happen to her.

I just wish though, she thought, that he would say "we" now and then, instead of "I." Then she twitched her shoulders impatiently, reminding herself that he had been a bachelor for a long time and it couldn't be easy to change his manner of making decisions. It was up to her to be patient, and she would be. But—well, it was another small item. "I can't go now"; "I don't want to have lunch right now; I'm not hungry." Even this thing tonight; it was another "I." He didn't really care whether she learned to play roulette. He wanted to play. She understood, she thought, but was she so far ahead of him that she could see the motivations, and he couldn't?

What will it be like when we get home to "his" place, she wondered. Was he the kind who would say: "Don't hang that pot there. It belongs over here"? How about Lucy? Would he be a true father to her? They had talked about this in the early days of their engagement, and now she experienced again her pang of dismay when he had told her he wasn't even going to try; he'd settle for being an uncle. "Her father," he had said flatly, "has prior rights to Lucy's heart, and I'm not going to usurp his place or sabotage him to please you." Well, she'd have to accept this for the present; there was no arguing with him. But after Lucy had lived with Lon for a while, wouldn't it be natural for her to yearn for a full-time father? If Lon hung back, what was she to do? Lucy was going to need a lot of love, after what she had been through.

And what about Sonny? Was she to try to mother him, baby him, and take a chance of earning his contempt? She couldn't replace his mother; she'd be afraid to try. She didn't agree with Lon that the boy—boy?—needed mothering. That was precisely what he didn't need. That's what he'd got until it ran out of his ears. And how was she to explain Sonny to Lucy? Say that he was sick? The child would know better. She'd seen her father drunk. Suppose Sonny during one of his drunks . . .

I'm borrowing trouble again, Kay told herself firmly. Sonny wouldn't hurt Lucy for a million dollars. But why was Lon afraid to admit that his son was an alcoholic and needed treatment? Each time the boy went off the wagon, Lon acted as though it were the final fling. He knew better. She knew better. The best thing was to go along with . . .

"Going to jump off?" Kay looked up, startled. "I didn't know you were back." He smiled and kissed the back of her neck. "And I didn't know you weren't dressed." He turned back into the room. "Got a car, finally. And a good driver. His name is George and he speaks better English than I. Than we."

The car moved through the night along the beach, the lights flicking off and on at the curves, a firefly with a purpose. The sky had cleared, though the road still glistened with the spray of the sea. The mountains, dark and sheer, stood back from the road, a permanent picket fence between Beirut and Damascus.

"Soldiers," the driver said. He dimmed his lights and pulled to a stop. Uniformed Lebanese, with rifles hanging on their shoulders, approached. They flashed a light on the driver and spoke in Arabic. He answered. The flashlight focused on the back seat, picking up Lon's scowling face and gray hair, then moving to the frightened-looking woman beside him, sitting very straight in a high hair-do, the choker chain of her black velvet cape loose about her throat, her hands snapping and unsnapping the small black purse.

"Go," a soldier said in English. The driver went. Lon leaned forward. "What was that?" he asked. The driver thought it over. "They look for two men," he said. "Come on," Lon said. "You can do better." The driver smiled dimly in the rear-view mirror. "A few months ago," he said, "there was a plot. You know, the government. Some crazy men. They have caught the big ones. Except two."

"Do they expect to find them with one roadblock?" "Ah, no, mister. You will see other soldiers." "How far is the casino?" "About eight miles, twelve kilometers." "How many more roadblocks?" "I'm sorry." "No you're not. How many more?" "Two,

I think." Lon sat back in the seat. He lit a cigarette and glowered at the dead match. "Trouble?" asked Kay. "Should we go back?"

He shook his head. "I don't recall any revolutionary plot in Lebanon," he said, "and I read the papers pretty thoroughly." "No revolution," the driver said. "Is dead." "Are you of the army?" Lon asked. The driver said no. "I was captain of the president's guard. The old president. But that is no more." "You like the new president?" "A very good man. Too quiet maybe. Sits home and says nothing. But he is good for the people."

"Lebanon," Lon said softly, "is a small country. Small and dependent on others. It runs—I'll take a guess—not much more than a hundred miles along the edge of the Mediterranean. There are a couple of million people, mostly Syrians or of Syrian extraction, and they're known as peaceable people. The only time they made trouble was after World War One when they tried to throw the French out. The French had a mandate over Lebanon, and the people—about half Christian, the rest Moslem and Druse—fought to become an independent nation."

"Now they have trouble," Kay said. Lon shrugged. "I don't think so. My suspicion is that the government uncovered a plot. They have arrested some people and, from these, they have the names of the others. I think they're looking for more than two or three people. You don't maintain three roadblocks in eight or ten miles for a few political plotters. If these roadblocks are here, then there are others south of Beirut toward Sidon. There are others on the road to Damascus too."

Lon had been speaking quietly, almost in a whisper, and he was surprised when the driver said: "You have right." After a few minutes, he said: "President house." The car passed a wall. Some distance behind it was a house. There were sentry boxes out front, and some soldiers lounged in the road, blinking in the headlights. They moved on, and were stopped twice. At the first stop, a soldier asked for passports, examined them, page by page, and handed them back, waving the driver on. A little later, they were on the far side of the saucer of beach around Beirut, climbed a steep hill, and turned and stopped in front of an ornate building. The chauffeur yanked the parking brake, jumped out, and trotted around the car in time to open the door for Kay.

"You know a lot about history," she said to Lon. He grinned as they walked through the big lobby and checked their coats. "No," he said. "But I like to hear you say it. History is an old love, but I have never been able to remember more than five per cent of what I want." They started up the grand staircase. "You're so funny," she said, "when you're modest." "Right," he said. "But this isn't modesty. If you're talking about my knowledge of Lebanon, let me assure you I brought research notes on every country, every city we're going to see.

"Sometimes," he went on, "when you're knotting your hair in back, or whatever it is you do with it, I'm studying notes. In matters of history I'm a slow student. I'm pretty good on this century and the last of the Roman Empire, but there are some big blank spots between. I know something about the Crusades of the twelfth century, if anybody should sneak up and ask me." Kay laughed. "Nobody does, I'll bet." "Right," he said.

He stopped and bought a membership in the Le Bain Casino, and at the cashier's desk he bought $100 worth of chips. The Lebanese pound was worth thirty cents, he explained to Kay, so he got 333 in chips of varying denominations. "I still think you know a lot about history," Kay said, "even mine." The room was large and square; attendants cleaned ash trays, brought drinks, found chairs for ladies who wanted to sit, and ran errands. The croupiers, the dealers, the house managers, all sat around the many tables, the upper parts of their faces shaded by the shielded lights so that, from the nose up, they wore the masks of bandits.

Most of the big Arabian oil players were still in the dining room across the hall, watching the girlie show through sunglasses, waiting for a chance to make a play, either on the chorus line or the baize table. The Arabians were mostly in their late thirties, molasses skinned and inclined to be paunchy. All of them had fat, impatient fingers which seemed always to be in motion. Later, they would be around the roulette tables, placing castles of square chips on a number, and doubling the amount if the number failed to win. Always, they won or lost without expression, the sunglasses reflecting the smooth spin of the wheel, the jogging of the white pill, or the open bodice of a woman sitting in front.

Lon gave half the pile of chips to Kay, as an attendant edged a chair under her. He explained that she could play odd numbers or even, the first twelve numbers, the second or third twelve, or even red or black. The play and the odds appeared to be complex, but were simple. She could play a number, and get paid thirty-five chips for a chip if it won, or she could play a half chip on each of two numbers, or a quarter on four and so forth.

The Lebanese croupiers spoke French. The play was slow and heavy, with much conversation between croupiers on who played what and who should be paid and how much. The operation imitated the casinos in the south of France, the way ketchup on an egg imitates a tropical sunset. Lon watched and played. Once in a while, he won. When he lost, and his chips ran low, he played red or black until he had brought his winnings back up. Kay played a chip on number twenty-one, and a chip on the middle twelve numbers. She won many times on the middle twelve, but never on twenty-one.

At midnight, Lon's chips were running low. He dropped one on the floor, and picked it up. "I split my pants," he whispered. Kay looked up, smiling. "You what?" she whispered back. "Split my pants," he said. Her expression changed to one of amused horror. "Your pants? Really?" she asked. "Don't look as though you were about to have a stroke," he said softly. "It's been done before. When I picked up the chip, I heard the pants go. Why do you play number twenty-one? You've been at it all night." "It doesn't win," she said. "Also you told me that twenty-one was your house number. And the necklace you gave me has twenty-one gems." "Keep playing it," he said.

An attendant appeared beside him. "Pardon, M'sieu," he said. "Your pantaloons . . . " Kay heard it and burst into laughter and a fit of coughing. The croupiers stared; the players around the table turned their karat-sized eyes on her. "Can you see it?" asked Lon. "Oui, M'sieu." "Oh fine," Lon said. He gave the attendant a couple of chips and a hat check. "Please go to the cloakroom downstairs," he said, "and get my coat."

"We can go," said Kay. Lon shook his head. "Get the coat," he said to the attendant. The young man left. Lon clasped both hands behind his back, and said: "I only have a few chips. Put all of mine on number seventeen. Put all of yours on twenty-one." "I don't want to play it all," Kay said. "Put them all on," Lon whispered. "I may be thrown out any minute. Or arrested. Get those chips down."

She was convulsed. Even as she was putting the chips on the proper numbers, tears sprang to her eyes and her face contorted with laughter. The croupiers began to smile. Then one of them laughed, almost tentatively, as though he wasn't certain whether he should. A fat Arab in sunglasses showed Kay three gold teeth.

The wheel spun. All the chips were down. Someone hurriedly put a few chips on double zero. An elderly lady inched two toward the even-numbered blank. The white pill spun in a direction opposite to the wheel and, as it slowed its flight, it spun down, hit the edge of a number, bounced out and up the mahogany side of the wheel, came down again, bounced crazily over several numbers, and fell into number twenty-one, taking the rest of the ride in its nest.

Two croupiers stopped laughing. They stared at Kay and said something to each other. The losing chips were raked off the baize,

including Lon's on number seventeen. "My dove," he said, between
his teeth, "you have won." Kay raised herself from her chair to
look, then sat down slowly. "How much do I get?" she asked.

"You don't have to count it. They will treat you honestly. See
the slot in front of the croupier? It's the custom to throw a few
chips in there, for them. It's a tip. Whatever they give you, divide it
by three and you have a rough idea of how much you have won."
She was being paid off when the attendant came back with Lon's
trench coat. "This is it?" he said. Lon thanked him and put it on.
Then he felt under it, in back. "The trousers," he said to Kay, "are
split from belt to crotch." "No," she said. He nodded. "All the
way. No wonder the kid saw it. My shorts must have been hanging
out."

When Kay left, she had $178. "You must tell me about this
game sometime," Lon said.

She came out of the bathroom nude, toweling the back of her
neck, but halted when she saw her husband sitting on the rug
tailor fashion, the knuckles of his hands pressed together across his
belly, his cheeks puffed out. "What am I?" he said. She stopped
toweling. "Nuts. If someone walked in here and saw you sitting
like that with no clothes on, they'd call the wagon." "You're evad-
ing," he said, trying to keep his cheeks puffed.

"You're supposed to be something?" she said. He nodded.
"Buddha," she said. He exploded the air. "Right," he said. "Which
one?" She paused. "There are more than one?" "There are more
than one." "You've got me." Lon looked pleased. "I'm the Great
Buddha of Kamakura without the seed pearls," he said. She tossed
her hair away from her neck and walked past him. He grabbed her
ankle and she fell to the rug. She looked surprised and she kicked
at him with her free foot. He grabbed that one too, and dragged
her toward him. "You see," he said, as she struggled, "when Buddha
calls, you are powerless." "All you have," she said, "is the belly."

He stood, took a deep breath, and pulled in his stomach. Through the half-open bathroom door he could see himself in the full-length mirror.

"Know what?" he said. "I have a shape like a Japanese wrestler. All torso. No arms, no legs." "Don't jump off the porch," she said. "You have to meet Cointreaux in the morning." "Yeah," he said, expelling his breath noisily, "how do you like that?" She sat up slowly. "You didn't have to say yes." He went into the bathroom, and mixed the shower water, and came out in the semi-gloom of the room.

"Admitted," he said. "No contest." Kay asked, "You didn't know he was at the hotel?" "How the hell would I know?" Lon said. "I had trouble remembering his name when we ran into him downstairs." "He knew all about you," she said. "Where's the nail clipper?" Lon asked. "Oh, he knew all about me because someone told him. When we met at the Paris airport he didn't know who I was. He was busy trying to find out who he was. But once they begin to pull the author bit, the good writer is lost. He needs the food that Cointreaux furnishes. This one," he said, pointing to his chest and tapping, "is a sucker for any crashing bore, so long as he has read something I've written. It's like listening for echoes of self-esteem. A horrible business."

He rummaged in the brown bag and found the nail clipper. "That wife of his," he said, "looks like an old showgirl." "Not too old, my friend. She has big eyes for you." "Fat chance," he said, moving toward the bathroom. "You think all women are after your husband." He peeked around the door as he started to close it. "Until you came along," he said, "I had no offers at all."

Kay got up and drew the curtains, turned the desk lamp on and got a pen from her handbag. For a while, she sat and wrote post-cards. Someone had to do it, and her husband wouldn't. He said he dreaded writing of any kind and wouldn't write a letter or a postcard or, unless urgent, a telegram. Kay stacked them, and wrote having-a-wonderful-honeymoon messages to relatives, to friends like the Jack Sullivans in Spring Lake and the Allan Witwers in California and a special one to Sonny, telling him how much they missed him, one to Lucy and one to an old boss in Florida who had given her many an afternoon off when he knew that her little girl was home alone.

She had almost finished when Lon came out. "May I?" he asked. He riffled through the cards. "Send one to my literary agent," he said, then added: "No, better not. She knows my handwriting. I'll do it, even though it kills me."

He parted the curtains and she snapped off the desk light. "Are you going out on the balcony like that?" she asked. "Why?" he said. "It's warm." "I married a nut," she said. He didn't think it was funny. "This porch," he said, "is enclosed on three sides. It is eight stories off the ground. There isn't a building near here more than three stories high. The light is out and the room and porch are in darkness. How am I a nut?"

"Put a robe on," she urged. He opened the sliding glass partition and stepped out into the cool of the night. "I was a big boy," he said, "before you were born." "Excuse me," she said, walking out behind him. "May I join you?" It was an early morning hour and they stood together looking out at a scene that had to be sipped again and again until the mind remembered every detail—the foaming white crests crashing against the rocks below, the big curving scimitar of the harbor with its toy ships rocking under ghostly lights, the tall mountains with their snowy passes, the lights from the unseen lobby below spreading a white fan over the dark, dead streets.

"This is part of the Middle East," she said. Lon nodded. "It has several names," he said. "The Middle East, Asia Minor, it is part of old Arabia and was once Persia. It is here," he went on, "that East really meets West. This is the crossroads." He pointed out over the Mediterranean. "Over there are ancient Greece, Italy, and all of Western Europe. In the opposite direction are Iran, Israel, India, the mysteries of the East and, further on, China and Japan."

"Interesting," she murmured. "So another world begins here."

"Another world. A world of Moslems, Buddhists, Shintoists, Sikhs —I don't know them all. But what fascinates me is that the crossroads used to be Suez. In a way, it still is. Now the air ocean is beginning to come into its own. Soon, shipping will be in a decline, as the planes become bigger, the airports longer, the freight hauls heavier. Beirut will someday be the Suez of the air." There was a little silence and she shivered. "Is this the short cut to India? The one that Columbus sought?" "Ah, yes. This is it. The proof is that this is the second airport Beirut has had in five years. The traffic keeps outgrowing the facilities. You cold?" She said she was.

"Let's go in," he said. He closed the glass partition and drew the curtains. "All over the hills," she said, "the Arabs are now repacking their binoculars." Lon laughed. "You should write comedy material," he told her. "You're so funny. Go to bed." She raised her chin in defiance. "When I'm ready," she said. Lon shook his head. "No," he said. "You go when I'm ready."

I could write one word, "Happy," and go to bed. I should, because anything which attempts to define happiness tends to dilute it. Kay seems to be learning that she has married a man far from perfect, and I sense that she is trying to accommodate her life to mine. There are little things, like meeting a couple named Cointreaux in the lobby, Kay does not like. She hides it so that it can be seen. Still, when they asked could they share our car tomorrow, and expenses, I said yes, and my bride gulped and accepted it with grace.

Had this situation been turned the other way, there would have been a private war in our room. Proving what? Proving that she is a better person than I, in so many ways. That's one of the reasons I married her. Underneath all her shivering romanticism, she is practical and selfless and that I need. Maybe it's realization of her superior qualities which makes me want to dominate, to make her look small, insignificant. Must keep in the driver's seat. Whenever there is dissension.

Flight to Beirut was routine except for black thunder shower in final thirty minutes. Never saw such thick rain in sky. Pilot put big landing lights on, slowed engines, and rain poured across the beams thickly. Engines sucked in tons of water, but jet furnaces kept burning. Like Beirut. Going to Jerusalem day after tomorrow. Anxious to see the holy places, almost all of which, I find, are on Jordan side rather than in Israel. Travel director in hotel says we cannot cross border into Israel. Or, if going to Israel, cannot cross street into Jordan side of Jerusalem. Prince of Peace must weep at this situation.

THE FIFTH DAY

THE car stopped for a moment. It was a rainy, gusty day. The driver got out. The wind from the sea almost whipped his eyes shut. "You want to see the Dog River?" he shouted above the cold roar. Cointreaux smiled from behind the closed window. "Not me," he said. "We'll wait here. Maybe Mr. Michaels." He was right. Mr. Michaels wanted to see the Dog River. So did Mrs. Michaels. They got out, and walked toward the little bridge.

Below, a muddy stream raced like cold cocoa toward the sea. It came down out of the mountains. They were green and had the soft look of deep velvet. On a small peak stood a big concrete statue of Christ, facing the sea. "What's the iron thing sticking out of His head?" asked Lon. "Lightning rod," the driver said. Kay smiled. "Oh ye of little faith," she said. The driver took them a little way up the south bank of the river and showed them marble plaques set in the side of the hill. There were the names and dates of many generals, many armies. The last was French. There was one with General Allenby's name, another with Napoleon's.

On the opposite bank of the river, a man with a black umbrella was trying to fish. He was attempting something impossible: tying a fly and steadying an umbrella in the wind. His trousers whipped around him and once he almost lost the umbrella. From the high bank, he looked small and dark against the sand and mud on the opposite side, but it was obvious that he would not quit.

Back in the car, the driver moved on toward Jebeil. "What are we gonna see when we get there?" Cointreaux said. He was wedged in the back seat with his wife and Kay, hanging on to the strap beside the door to give them an extra inch of room. "Ruins," said Lon. Cointreaux squeezed his wife's chin. "I married one, didn't I, dear?" he said. She pressed the plunger on her long cigarette holder and ejected a butt. "Who the hell wants to see ruins?" she said, almost mockingly. "You see one fallen arch you've seen them all. Where do they hide the beach boys?" "Oh," said Cointreaux, "she's a great kidder, this one." Kay studied the back of her husband's head. She was watching for signs of steam.

"Very old ruins," said the driver. "I'm looking for a star sapphire," said Mr. Cointreaux, "but I'm not doing myself any good. In Paris, I must have made seven or eight jewelry shops. The wife, she wants a topaz and she's busting a garter to get a big one." "They go back seven thousand years," said the driver. "To Phoenicia." "This place," said Lon, from the front seat, "is called Jebeil today, but once it was Byblos. Someone was telling me that we get the word biblio, and bibliography, the study of books, from byblos. Also Bible."

"You know a good jewelry store?" Peg Cointreaux asked the driver. He nodded. Larry Cointreaux said: "You get a rake-off?" The driver half turned, smiling. "What is this, a rake-off?" he said. "He gets a cut," said Lon. "They all do. It's part of their bread and butter." "I like to know these things," said Larry stiffly. "If it's a bum steer—"

"It's not," Lon assured him. "All the guides have tie-ins with certain shops. Whatever you buy, they get a little kickback. Still, the merchandise is good and the price is low." "No rake-off," said the driver, who now understood the phrase. "Nothing for me." Lon said: "The probing questions force them to fib—if you follow my slang." Cointreaux nodded. "Gotcha," he said.

The car passed the gambling casino, and went on around the big rocky promontory. Cointreaux was, it seemed, almost always ebullient, almost always willing to talk about himself. "I made a pot for myself in Wall Street and I managed to arrange a little keeping money," he said. "So Peg and me, we travel. We have no kids so we have no problems. Just a fourteen-room duplex on East Sixty-third Street, two television sets—both color, of course—a maid and a valet, and two Boston terriers. You know anything about dogs, Mr. Michaels?" Lon, half-turned toward the back seat, said, "No, very little." "Well," said Cointreaux, "these are champions and the sons of champions. They sort of run the house, don't they, Peg?"

Mrs. Cointreaux was busy injecting a fresh DuMaurier cigarette into the holder. "Yes indeed," she said. "Where the hell are these falling-down ruins? We've been on the road an hour." The driver pointed. "Where the Coca-Cola sign is." They looked, as he pulled to the left off the road, toward a small Arab shop. "Here," the driver said, "I am not allowed to tell you. Byblos has own guides."

They got out and found that the Coca-Cola shop was a curio and gift shop. The Cointreaux began to brighten. They looked over trays of jewelry and, after a few minutes, Peg Cointreaux smiled at Kay. "Junk," she said. "Pure unmitigated junk." The man behind the counter shook his head. "Is not junk," he said softly, but firmly. "Real stones. Guaranteed." On the shelves were bolts of cloth, which the clerks offered "cheap." There were Arab daggers, flogging whips of black braid, rosaries, silver cuff links, gold cuff links, and, while the customers browsed, young attendants brought in small cups of Turkish coffee, and soft drinks.

Kay bought a braided whip. She handed it to Lon. "This is for you—in case I get out of line." She showed how the handle unscrewed, divulging a knife with a blade chased with hieroglyphics. "In case," he said. "Yes," she said, "now you can throw the gun away. I'd rather go by knife." "Who has a gun?" Mrs. Cointreaux asked. "You?" "My wife," said Lon boldly, "is talking of quite another matter. She doesn't mean a gun that shoots. She's talking of a hypodermic. I take a little heroin for my asthma."

Mrs. Cointreaux waved the holder at him. "You're tough, aren't you? I mean, you say things right out." "It depends on how much I want to divulge," Lon said. "In your case—I'm sure you will excuse me—nothing." "Larry," Peg Cointreaux said, "I like this man. I . . . like . . . this . . . man." Mr. Cointreaux was studying an Arab girl who was studying the rings on Mrs. Cointreaux' fingers. "What the hell," he said, without altering the focus of his eyes, "he's a writer. They get away with murder." Mrs. Cointreaux nodded. Lon remarked to himself that she was the only woman he had ever seen whose throat bobbed. "I should have married a writer," she said. "I do so love the Bohemians."

Lon had taken Kay by the hand. They moved out of the little building toward the ruins. An old Lebanese bowed curtly. "I am the guide," he said slowly. "I can tell you much about this." Lon called the other couple. Cointreaux yelled that he would join them in a few minutes. "Study a stone," he shouted. "I'm doing a little studying on my own."

They followed the old man over the sod and stones toward the sea, which broke below an eminence. The guide hunched his bearded head into an old overcoat. His voice was deep, and dripping with the gravy of an ancient accent. Lon stayed close to him, and asked him to repeat parts of the talk several times. The guide responded perfunctorily, as though he had been tried often by the dull ears of the Christians. Sometimes, the old watery eyes tossed a momentary indictment of stupidity at Lon, but, as the tour of the old excavations continued, he appeared to appreciate the genuine interest of these particular tourists.

When Cointreaux joined the party, he stared at the old walls exposed below ground level, at the huge square stones lying like dead dice on the hillocks, at the fluted colonnades and the remains of a fort. "The U. S. should have charge of this," he said to the guide. "We'd have it repaired in no time." It was difficult to tell, in the face of the almost perpetual smile on Cointreaux' face, when he was joking and when he was serious. "Ruins are all right," he said to Lon. "But who can sell ruins? What they need here is an attraction. Maybe a replica of what this joint was like years ago— Arabs and a slave market, a few veiled babes." Peg Cointreaux stood behind him, grinning, the omnipresent holder jutting almost straight up, past her nose. "Put a few male slaves in that production," she said, "and the lady tourists will pay a dollar just to feel the muscles."

Kay and Lon moving a few feet away, exchanged impressions in whispers. The whole place didn't amount to more than a few acres, but it was a rare place which had spawned and survived three civilizations. One of the tombs below the surface, the guide told them, proved that the Phoenicians had used Byblos as a port 6,000 years ago. In time, the Phoenicians lost it and, 4,300 years ago, the Syrians had built a city of Egyptian culture there. Their kings, in fact, were vassals of the Pharaohs, and sold wood and resin to Egypt. Still later, the Romans arrived, reduced the city in battle, and Roman temples were erected over the old ruins. Both Alexander and Pompey found the place important enough to defeat, and rule. The last civilization, built astride the old walls, was a fort erected by the Crusaders in the twelfth century. On their way to Jerusalem, they had paused at Byblos to build a depot of communication with Europe.

The guide showed them down a narrow circular walk to the tomb, far below, of King Ahiram, who had ruled this small promontory in the thirteenth century before Christ. His casket had weighed, by modern standards, about 450 pounds. The grave, dug by the household servants of the king, was a twelve-foot circle, running straight down about twenty-five feet. There, an alcove had been dug to the south, the final resting place of his majesty.

So far as was known, the guide continued, there were no mechanical instruments such as a block and fall, or winch, in the thirteenth century B.C. Still, the grave diggers were able to get the casket, encrusted with precious stones, down to the alcove without trouble. They dug the well and the alcove, then filled both with sand taken from the sea. The casket was placed on top of the circular grave, and the workers began to dig the sand from under it. Inch by inch, it was lowered to the bottom. Then, as they dug the alcove out, the king in all his glory slid slowly into the niche. Altogether, nine ancient kings were buried in Byblos and the tops of the graves were made to look like the rest of the terrain. Still, if there was cleverness in the burial, there was adroitness in the thieves of later centuries because, by the time modern archaeologists got to Byblos, only three tombs were left intact.

"All," said Kay, "is vanity." "All," Lon agreed. Vanity and irony. Irony that each of the ancient civilizations had come, with might and arms, to bring what it thought was enlightenment, that each, in turn, had been defeated by time and a fresher adversary, bringing enlightenment. The Crusaders, for example, built a fort in 1103, and used old Phoenician stones and Roman arches to do it. Within eighty years, the fort had been reduced by a victorious army, which smashed most of the fort back into the rubble from which it had been built. "I am convinced," he said, "that anything man does is temporary. Nothing stands forever."

"A little Scotcheroo would brighten this place," said Peg Cointreaux, joining them. "Stones depress me. Unless they come in topaz form." Kay bought some guidebooks for reading on planes, and the party left for Beirut. On the way, Lon fell into a silence. "Did I say something wrong?" Cointreaux asked. Lon roused himself. "No, no. I was just thinking of how archaeologists trace the history of these places. In the oldest part—remember those small walls underground?—the people had one-room apartments and they buried their dead under the gravel floor. Skeletons have been found, and all are in the fetal position, with knees under chin and arms folded across chest. Those who lived there a thousand years later are buried with copper knives which have riveted handles. So you can see how much man learned in a thousand years. He learned to use metal and he knew something about riveting."

"This proves something?" said Larry. "I'm not up on these things. Ask me about General Motors or Jones and Laughlin and I'll break your ear." "Nothing, really, but I'm kind of surprised that, in the short span of a thousand years, these people moved from the use of stone to the fashioning of metal." "Can we invite you to dinner?" Peg said. Kay opened her mouth to answer, but Lon cut in. "We were planning to have dinner at the Phoenicia," he said.

"We were?" Kay asked. Cointreaux said: "If you two want to be alone . . ." "No," Kay said. "We'd be delighted." Lon gave in: "What time?" The driver said: "You will not use the car tonight?" "Ten in the morning," Lon told him: "We're going to the airport. I will pay you and you can pick us up when we come back from Jerusalem." "Eight o'clock be all right?" Cointreaux said. "We'd like to have a few belts at the bar. In fact, if you please, we'll meet you at the Phoenicia Bar at eight."

Lon said fine. He began to feel that these people were around his neck, and that there was no way out of the friendly embrace. He sneaked a look at Kay. She was staring at the road and smiling. Well, as it didn't bother her, it wouldn't annoy him. Much. "This leads to a second question, Lon," said Cointreaux. "You don't mind if I call you Lon." "Not at all." "Well, I'm Larry to everybody. Even the newsboys." He turned to his wife, who had sud-

denly stopped smiling. "Shall I tell him?" he said. She shrugged.
"You are on your own, dear boy," she said. "I had hoped we'd
be nearer the hotel before the explosion, but do go ahead."

"Well," said Cointreaux, lamely and haltingly, "when we met
at Paris, I didn't know who you were, frankly. I'm not much of
a reader. The *Times* in the morning; the *Journal-American* in the
afternoon. The last book I read was *Lolita*. So, on the plane, the
steward is up front and I'm talking to him and he starts to give me
a rundown on you. You know, what a hell of an author you are,
and a book you wrote about how history shows that man progresses
scientifically but regresses—that the right word?—emotionally. In
other words, he learns lots of things, like how to make an atom
bomb, but he can't understand himself. So we're blabbing away and
I get to thinking how little I know, and how Peggy here, if you
steer her out of the beauty shop, she acts like she don't know what
she's doing, so anyway, I got a friend in Pan American real estate
who just happens to be here in Beirut right now."

Larry paused to light a cigar. "Go ahead," said Peg. "Give it to
him right between the horns." "Well," said Larry, puffing, "I
asked this friend if Pan American could change our itinerary to
conform to yours. You know—the same planes, the same hotels and
so forth. This is a lot of nerve, but I know that you know a lot
more than I do."

"Did he change it?" Lon asked casually. "Working on it,"
said Larry." "It's a free country," Lon said. Kay compressed her
lips to hold back her laughter. "Maybe it's even a free world,"
Lon added. "In any case, nobody can stop you from changing your
trip to conform to someone else's. I suppose, in a way, it's flattering."

"Most of all," said Larry swiftly, "I don't want to be a leech.
You and Kay go wherever you please and deal us out. We'll be
on our own. But now and then, when you want a little company,
we'll be around. That okay?" Lon nodded. "A lovely arrangement,"

he said, facetiously. "I guess we'll see you when we get back from Jerusalem." "We're going," said Peg. "Middle East Airways eleven A.M." "Oh," said Kay.

"We're staying at the National Hotel too," said Larry hastily, "but don't let it throw you. I mean, you're under no obligation—"

"Think nothing of it," said Lon. "I was just thinking of the inevitability of rape and the proper attitude of repose."

The dinner was good. The spirit was Arabic, the cooking was French and the food was American. Kay said she was beginning to understand that Beirut was truly a crossroads, a midway point between ideologies. She and Lon had shared a chateaubriand with Lyonnaise potatoes and string beans, pointed up with a mixed salad of romaine and tomatoes and sliced onions weighted by Roquefort dressing. It was, as Larry Cointreaux pointed out, "just like home, except dig them crazy fezzes."

"For dessert," Peg said, "I want a B and B." "Make it two," said Larry. "It will sit good on those three Scotches." "Five," said Peg. "Ice cream for me," said Kay, "with chocolate sauce." Lon motioned to the waiter, who came over and took the orders.

Lon kept stealing looks at Kay. When he noticed that she observed him, he turned away. She had always seemed pretty to him, but now she seemed lovely. She had a decorative comb in the back of her hair, a blue dress which fell into soft folds, a single strand of pearls and blue shoes with heels a little bit high and a little bit thin. There was a blue flash to her eyes, and more of it in the wedding ring she wore.

Larry was telling a joke about New York when there was the noise of music and the captain of waiters came into the dining room, leading a parade of waiters and a guitarist. The captain had a big birthday cake decorated with a single lighted candle, which he shielded with a cupped hand.

"Happy birthday to you," they sang, "Happy birthday to you,

Happy birthday, dear Mrs. Michaels, Happy birthday to you." The
cake was placed before Kay, who looked startled and put her hand
to her mouth. The waiters sang a second chorus, and this time,
most of the other diners joined in. "Oh," she whispered, smiling
happily and bowing around the room, "you bastard." He told her to
blow the candle out and make a wish. She blew. "Nice talk," he
said, "from a demure bride." "Oh," she whispered breathlessly,
"you bastard. You knew all the time." "I should hope so," he
said. "How many men celebrate your birthday?"

"You never told us," Peg Cointreaux wailed. "It's Kay's birthday and he never said a word." "Pal," said Larry unctuously, "this
is embarrassing." "Cut the cake," Lon said. He stood and walked
off with the guitarist and slid some bills into the man's hand. When
he came back to the table, he kissed his bride and said: "Happy
thirty-third birthday." "Judas!" she said loudly. Lon looked around.
"Don't mind him, honey," Peg said. "We didn't hear him. Besides,
thirty-three looks pretty good from where we are." "I'm just
jealous," said Lon.

Kay was cutting the cake when the captain brought the ice
cream. "See?" she said. "See how well this sneak planned it?
He let me order ice cream knowing he had ordered a birthday
cake." "If I gave Larry a cake," Peg said, "he'd expect a file in
it." Lon slipped a small package onto Kay's lap while she was
cutting. She looked at him and smiled. Then, impulsively, she
kissed him. "That's for remembering," she said.

The package became the center of interest. Kay unwrapped
it slowly, trying to remove the pretty blue ribbon without ruining
the bow. Inside was a gray cardboard box. Inside that was a small
lavender box made of plush, and inside that was a white lining
from which two lavender earrings sparkled at her. It wasn't often
that Kay reacted like a little girl, but this was one of the times.
She set the box down on the table, pressed the palms of her hands
together before her mouth, and made a big "Oh" sound. The

amethysts were flanked by diamonds. She stared at them, then reached down and raised the box. Her eyes were blinking mist away as she passed the gift around the table. "They're cute," said Peg, with a patronizing smile. "Nice rocks," said Larry. "You get 'em here?" No, Lon said. The name on the box said Tiffany, New York. "I didn't want to say anything," said Larry, "but I wouldn't blow that kind of dough here." He called for the check, but Lon talked him out of it because he had arranged this dinner as a birthday treat for his wife.

"Well," said Larry, "at least let us buy a birthday drink for the happy bride." Lon looked at Kay. She said no, thanks. It had been a big day. She wanted to read up on Jerusalem before she went to sleep. "We're Lutherans," Larry said. Kay smiled. "We're Catholic." "That so?" Peg said. "How interesting. Didn't you say you divorced a husband?" Lon was beginning to look bored. Kay picked up her gloves and bag from the table. "I mean," said Peg, "it's none of my damned business, but your church is worse than ours on that stuff."

"I'm divorced," Kay said. "Shall we go?"

Room service thought that the kitchen was closed, but would see. In a moment, the voice came back. Yes, two pots of tea and cinnamon toast could be sent up. Some butter, perhaps? Jelly too. Very good. Kay hung up. "I've been reading so long," she said, "I forgot what time it is." She parted the curtains, pulled her robe tightly about her, and looked out. "The storm has died," she said. "The stars are out."

"Jerusalem is about three hundred miles southwest," Lon said. He was using a map and a ruler. "Middle East uses Viscounts on this run, so it should be an hour or under." "How long would it be by car?" "Who knows? We'd have to go back through the mountains to Syria. Otherwise, we'd be driving into Israel, and those people won't permit anyone to drive across into Jordan."

She sat on the edge of the bed, staring at him as he measured the map. "Are you anti-Semitic?" she asked. "I'm not anti anything," he said. She said: "People are funny about Jews." "How, funny?" "Either violently opposed or violently pro." "Well," Lon said without looking up, "shake hands with a Christian who has been a Zionist for years and is still opposed to David Ben-Gurion." Kay looked puzzled. "I don't understand." "That's just it," he said. "Nobody does. But it makes sense to me. No nation is big enough to afford Mr. Ben-Gurion's militant whims."

"But you're in favor of Israel?" "And Ireland and Lebanon and Iran and Pakistan and lots of other lands," Lon replied. "Sure. The Jews are a people. They're entitled to this country. It's just too bad that they are gifted with a weak Knesset and a strong ruler. In my opinion, Ben-Gurion isn't even a good Jew. Another thing: no race of people is more sensitive than Jews. They want no criticism, just love and money." "Isn't that anti?" Lon looked up from his map. "No," he said, "Not unless we have just discarded the age of facts. My forebears are Irish. The Irish and the Hindus are the only people who starve with pride. Is that anti-Irish? The Germans are always deluding themselves with ambition. Is this anti-German? The British, a third-rate power, like to pretend that they are first-rate. So I'm anti-British? The Americans feel that they can stop the Soviet Union by throwing dollar bills in its path. Am I a traitor to my own country?"

Kay took off her robe, and slipped between the sheets, pulling the blanket up high under her chin. "Sometimes I feel as though I dropped a nickel in you," she said. He nodded. "Sometimes you do."

"Come on to bed," Kay said. "It's my birthday." "In a minute. I have to make an entry in the diary." She removed two pearl earrings and placed them on a night table. "Just write weather clear, track fast and come to bed." He unlocked the diary and began to write. "Don't be the aggressor," he said. "Every time you try,

I'm going to double-cross you." "Me?" she said. "I'm just a dutiful wife who obeys her husband's little whims."

Learned a lot in Beirut. Would like to drive south to Sidon before we leave. There is much to see there. Couple named Cointreaux have latched on with flattery. Have mentality of good-natured oxen. Nothing we can do without being rude. Kay seems not to mind. Maybe female company will be good for her. Too much me around all the time.

Kay has cosmopolitan interests. Gratifying to me. Elspeth interested only in gossip columns, P.T.A., television and Sonny. New life for me. Watched close at Byblos, loved the questions she asked. She's bright, not learned. Like something permitted out from under glass bell first time. Has spiritual face, earthy yen. Enjoyed birthday dinner, seemed more than pleased with earrings. I'm such a slob. Almost showed them to her on plane trip from Idlewild to Paris. Like boy who can't keep secret.

Know she worries about gun. Needles me. Must remember, in dressing and undressing, not to show it. With God's help, will not have to use it the way I plan. Something hilarious about sinner calling on God for help. Try hard to be better Christian, succeed only in having less patience with people, less tolerance, less charity —all signs of crotchety aging man.

Must cut this short. Kay is waiting. So am I.

THE SIXTH DAY

RESTLESSNESS is a concomitant to travel, Lon reflected. The voyager is never content. He drinks scenery and people with his senses, never pausing to digest or savor. He arrives and is gone. He interprets with his eyes, his ears, his tongue. He is armed with passport and shoulder-strap camera and his reward is a snapshot of his wife posing before a bed of flowers. He tastes without swallowing. Life is an endless necklace of airports—the rosary of the restless.

Lon feared the stigma of superficiality. He saw it in others; he feared to look at himself. "Sometimes," he said, hunching over a sandwich at Pigeon Rock restaurant, "I am overcome by the feeling that I'm a heel." Kay sipped soup. "A heel?" "Yes," he said, "a real heel. A failure as a person. A second-rate hypocrite."

"It's a mood," she said. "Everybody gets moods." He chewed absent-mindedly, looking out the window at the Mediterranean far below the cliff on which the restaurant sat. Little fingers of foamy waves scratched the sand; out farther an island of stone, marked down its sides with the terraced erosion of the centuries, stood alone against the sea. The center had been hollowed by time, and the green combers rolled through unimpeded, to meet defeat on the sandy shore.

He pointed to the barren cliff beside the restaurant. "That area," he said, "is famous for lovers and suicides." Kay's eyes followed his fingers. "You mean that people jump?" "Yes," he said. The driver of the car had told him that, two nights ago, a German girl—a singer in a Beirut cabaret—had quarreled with an Arab lover and had come here and jumped to her death.

Kay looked shocked. "Oh, Lon, how awful." Lon drank the small Turkish coffee in one gulp. "The police got here a moment late," he said. "They took the names of all the lovers along the cliff top as witnesses." Kay stopped drinking the soup and rubbed her bare arms as though chilled. She wore a black sleeveless dress with a thick gold belt. The knit jersey enhanced her figure and the blondeness of her hair.

"We got away from your feeling that you're a heel," she said. Lon summoned the waiter and held up two fingers. "More coffee," he said. He looked deep into her eyes. "It is not just a mood," he said. "It's an assessment I've made many times. I'm just not the person I want to be. I'm short of every goal—as a writer; as a father; as a husband; as a Christian. I know what I want to be, but I'm not it.

"Sometimes, when things are going well, I feel I've got it made. The image begins to form, almost like a piece of blown glass, and then I do something wrong and the glass shatters." He made a fluttery motion with his fingers. Kay's face was warm with sympathy. Her special quality, Lon thought, was that even when she could not, she tried to understand.

"What would you like to be?" she asked. He smiled, and, for a moment, was happy again. "I'd like to be the kid my mother thought she had: the boy who was polite and good; the youngster who could be trusted; the boy who never took money for going to the store for a neighborhood woman; the boy who took his beatings quietly, sometimes without rancor."

"Is that it?" she asked. "That's it." "You want to be a sort of altar boy?" He didn't smile. "Not at all," he said. "I would like to be a normal, wholesome human being. I want to be very good at something—just one thing. The clod doesn't aspire. He's content being what he is. But me—I'm no clod. I know that there are fine and noble people in the world, so I'm sort of—permanently dissatisfied. It leaves a bruise on the soul when you find that there is a difference between the you that some people admire and that you that you know so well. It is like—" he paused and shrugged. "I talk too much."

The coffee was set before them. They drank in silence, looking out at Pigeon Rock. The thoughts were now labeled "his" and "hers." Kay saw the sandy beach and wondered what had made the German girl jump. What manner of woman was she? What was *he* like? How deeply must a woman feel to be moved to end her life because of the words of a man? How did he feel, now that he realized that his power over her had been unlimited? And what good was having the power, once it was tested and used?

Lon dreamed through the window. The sea and the beach were serene. There was a quality of jade in the ocean and it appeared to be sharpest where it met the beige of sand and the bottom of the big cliff. Oh yes, serene. But not always. The water's edge had often reminded him of the human mind, capable of the most beautiful patterns, the wildest fury, the dullest grays, sprightly, threatening, sleepy, monotonous, violent, romantic, capricious, thunderous, destructive, energetic, listless.

Absent-mindedly, he paid the check. He stood and pulled Kay's chair out. The waiter bowed. They walked out under the awning and then into the sudden searing of sun, and into the car. "Sidon?" the driver inquired. "Sidon," Lon said, He mopped his cheeks. "Hot," she said. "But only in the sun."

"Did you ever feel like suicide?" he asked. She thought about it, as the car swung away from the curb, and south along the beach, passing the bright new checkered apartment houses, with their individual porches, the hummocks of trees huddled in the sandy soil like stacked beach umbrellas, the Lebanese shepherds, inching their flocks to the sides of the road as traffic passed. "No," she said finally. "No, I don't think so."

He looked out the window, not seeing the scenery, thinking, No. She wouldn't. She was moved quickly to despair or exhilaration, but in her they weren't far apart. She wore some kind of shield on her face; a plastic thing for deflecting bullets. When the going was bad, she put the shield on.

"Did you?" she asked. He inched toward her in the jarring automobile and felt for her hand. "Once," he said softly. "Just once. I have never told anyone and I'll never mention it again. All I know is that it was in 1952. One night I gave up. Surrendered. Just quit. I was in bed and I lay there with my hands behind my head, just staring into the dark and trying to figure a way to end my life without the insurance company finding out. It's an interesting problem. I worked on it until—oh, maybe three o'clock in the morning."

"So?" she said. He shrugged. "No dice. I didn't want to do it unless Elspeth and the kid would have a few dollars out of it, and there wasn't any guaranteed way. It was interesting for a time, like working out a plot. The nearest I came to an idea was to go down in the driveway with a box of tools, take the brake off the car—the driveway sloped downhill; and let it run over my head. Two things argued against it. One was that the car would be moving slowly and the weight of the wheels might maim without killing. The other was that everyone in the neighborhood knew that I knew nothing about an automobile, and never lifted the hood in my life. Besides, when my body was found early in the morning, everyone would ask what was he doing out there at night fixing a car with no light?"

"You decided to live on," she said. She squeezed his fingers. "It's so strange," he said. "In the morning, I recollected the whole thing and it shook me. I shuddered. The mood had passed. I'd never had it before; I've never had it since."

"I always thought that anyone who takes his life is crazy," she
said. "I mean, for that moment. A combination of unbearable loneliness and despair can do it." He stuck his tongue out at her.
"Okay," he said. "I was nuts." Kay protested. "No," he said.
"I understand. I agree. I never read about a well-known person
committing suicide that I do not think of that one night. I felt
ultra-sane at the time. I was surprised at my own calmness. Death
had always been a fearsome goblin. But not that one night in 1952.
It was a permanent pill for a headache; a way out; like leaving the
hot sun and walking alone into the shade."

"Was it a fight with Elspeth? she said. Then, hastily: "Not that
it really matters. . . ." He said he couldn't tell what led up to it.
"I can recall the night," he said, "and the thinking on the pillow,
but I can't remember anything about the day. I don't think it was
an argument. There was nothing new about disputes anyway. They
were habitual. No, it must have been something else. I may have
been writing and I may have been displeased with the work. It
could have been an accumulation of distress.

"All I know for certain is that I woke up refreshed and, when
I thought of the night before and the serious thinking I had done
about suicide, I was shocked. Later, I was going to tell it to a
psychiatrist friend at dinner, but then I thought, 'What the hell
can he do? Explain it to me? He may explain it so neatly that the
idea will come back again.' So I said nothing."

"How are you doing with your diary?" He removed his hand.
She reached for it and found it. "I'm keeping one too," she said.
"Want a look?" Lon shook his head. She reminded him that she
had no secrets from him. "Meaning," he said, "that, by keeping
my own thoughts under lock and key, I hold secrets from you?"

"Oh, come on," she said disengaging the hand and opening her
purse. "I want you to know me—what I'm like inside." She thrust
a few folded sheets of paper into his hand. He held them, crumpled,

for a moment, as though deciding the consequences of reading. "Read it," she said, pleading. "I'm not much at telling you how I feel, but I'm pretty good at putting it on paper." Lon settled back, adjusted his glasses, and read:

This morning, when Lon permitted me to get up on my side of the bed and walk around to answer the phone on his side, I felt that I was in an old echo chamber. My first husband was pretty good at permitting me to do those little things. At first, I did them because I wanted to do them. Soon, he was unable to make a sandwich at lunch. He was too busy to type his reports. He couldn't find a shirt or a pair of shorts.

What was given freely was quickly demanded. A woman gives only when she is given to. When the words "I love you" sound as empty as the words "Good morning," when the bed lacks spontaneity and becomes mechanical, the giving gives out. When pleasure outside the house becomes greater than the simplest evening at home, the woman is no longer a necessity to the man.

A woman must feel, among other things, wanted. Desperately needed. This one must. One of the small hurts of this honeymoon is that my husband wants to be alone when he writes, or when he is working out a problem. He invites me to go shopping, or wait in another room. But I am permitted to get up and walk around the bed to answer a phone. It just isn't enough.

Lon's eyes went back over parts of it. Then he handed it to her. "That all?" he asked. Kay was a little stiff-lipped as she stuffed the papers back in her pocketbook. "Yes," she said. "That's all." He noticed the stiffness, and put an arm around her shoulders and brought her face close to his. The chauffeur reached up and swung the rear-view mirror so that he could not use it.

"May I make a few observations?" Lon said. "Without interruption?" He could feel her head nod against his cheek. "Okay,"

he said. "In the first place, I love you completely and unequivo-
cally. No reservations. For me, it's you or nobody. Okay? Maybe
I'm dull at saying it, but it comes from the heart. In the second
place, my darling, you wound easily. Just because I asked you to
walk around the bed to pick up the phone, it led to all this searching of the soul.

"It's not worth it. One must start with love, or there is no marriage. You told me that your husband seduced you. That's why
you married him. It's a pretty lousy reason, but okay. You didn't
love him. In my estimation, this makes you a little on the unstable
side." She tried to speak. "Now wait a minute," he said, placing a
finger over her lips. "Without interruption, we agreed.

"You and I are in love. We know this. All right. Love is an
insulated emotion. If it is real, it is almost indestructible. I mean
this. Hurt is a part of love. No couple ever understood each other
perfectly, and lack of understanding breeds injury. So hurt and
love go together, but love survives. It always survives. If it doesn't,
one of the parties to it was not in love, or else one was hurt beyond
the ability of love to live. It bled to death.

"In this little document, you make a mistake in speaking about
what a woman wants; what a woman needs; what a woman will
do, or not do. You can't speak for all womankind, honey. I don't
know why it is, but most women firmly believe that all women
are alike. They are not. Some are much more feminine than others.
Some are brighter than others. Some have taste. Some do not.
Some love children. Some can't stand them. Many are masochists
and are attracted to sadists. Others are domineering, and marry
effeminate men. No woman can tell you about women."

"Finished?" she asked. He smiled. "Not quite. You may be
speaking for yourself when you say that a woman must be desperately needed, but I just can't show desperation. I need you now,
today, every moment of my life. How do I show it desperately?
By biting my fingernails? By bursting into tears when you go out

for a loaf of bread? Get on my knees if you threaten to leave me?
Oh, no, honey doll. You have a different man. I'm not the type
you must reassure every morning. I assume that you are an adult
woman and that you love me. And always assume—even at my
worst—that I love you."

She thought about it for a moment. Then she rubbed her cheek
against his. "Okay," she said. "If that's the way it's going to be."
He kissed her softly, tenderly. "Any other way would be fakery,"
he said. "I can't act." Vaguely, he had noticed that the car had
stopped twice.

"More check points?" Lon asked the driver. The man took a
hand from the wheel and made a deprecating motion. "No more,"
he said. "They still looking." Kay opened her purse and, against
the mirror inside, tilted her face this way and that. "It's a strange
country," she said. "A million and a half Lebanese here; a million
and a half overseas. Reminds me of the Irish."

Lon sat up, watching the road ahead. It curved against the dunes
of the sea, then went inland for a way, then snaked out along the
edge of the Mediterranean again. "You like to eat?" the driver
said. "Good place," he pointed to a hotel. They decided to keep
going. "Nice garden in back," the driver said.

"I feel secure when I'm with you," Kay said. "You should."
"Then why is it that I feel so shaky when you're not around—or
when you get angry?" He thought about it for a moment. "You
are a chronically insecure person," he said. "So is Lucy. I am
going to do everything possible to strengthen you. Lucy kisses me
interminably," he said, "not because she loves me, but because she's
scared that I won't love her. Both of you need a little hard
veneer."

They watched a woman, clothed in a long heavy dress, cross the
road with a basket on her head. Behind her was a city street with
houses. "Sidon," the driver said. They sat up in the back seat,
watching him thread the narrow streets, with the open shops on

each side; tailors, with mouthfuls of pins, staring at the car; boatwrights steaming timbers and bending them to camber a hull; fruit merchants, plucking at hanging strings of figs; here and there a beige minaret pointing a finger at God; veiled women in white gowns, the seductive nuns of the East; now and then a touch of modernity, a soldier leaning on a rifle.

Sun-washed walls standing on the edge of the sea; Sidon is one of the most ancient cities in the world, but the history of the city is the history of man's rapacity. It has been sacked and pillaged so many times that it does not want to grow. It remains a place of ten thousand Muslims, most of whom are unaware of Sidon's history. The smallness of the city protects it in times of strife. The ancient harbor of the Phoenicians to the south lies dormant under old stones; the modern harbor on the north side is shallow with silt. Between, a fort built by the Crusaders in the twelfth century stands, a pale monument to man's viciousness in the name of God. There is moss on the lower stones and the westerly winds purse their lips on the old ramparts and whistle.

Jesus visited the neighborhod of Sidon and the city was old then. St. Paul, on a sailing vessel, landed there and refreshed himself. Sidon was the mother of Tyre, and both inspired the Greeks to Homeric poetry. Once, the Philistines burned Sidon to ashes. Assyria, Babylonia, Egypt and Persia led assaults against Sidon. When Alexander the Great approached, Sidon submitted without a struggle. In one sixty-eight-year period in the thirteenth century the city was occupied by the Muslims, sacked and taken by the Franks. The Franks rebuilt it and Sidon was besieged and set to the torch by the Saracens. King Louis restored it in 1253, only to have it ravaged by the Mongols seven years later. The Templars rebuilt the city, then abandoned it.

This Kay and Lon learned as they walked hand in hand through the ruins of the fort, studying a booklet they purchased from a guide. They stopped in a small restaurant for lunch. The flies on the tablecloth were fat and lazy. They stretched their hind legs in a bowl of sugar and walked up the side of a small cup of coffee and, near the top, turned from the heat and walked down again. The flirt of a hand did not discourage them. They came up off the table in an angry cloud, a dark and brazen umbrella against the sun slanting through the open front.

Across the street was a foundry, completely open at the front as all shops were, and two men could be seen in the cool dark bending a piece of metal and hammering it to hold the proper curve. They poured foamy beer from a pitcher, and rested frequently. The smaller of the two had big biceps; his muscles jumped even when he lifted the glass.

"Christians," Kay said. Lon looked up from a sandwich made of goat cheese. "Yes?" he asked. "How do you know?" Kay shrugged. "Just guessing. Moslems don't drink. Anyway, Lebanon is over fifty per cent Christian." He took a solid bite of the sandwich, chewed manfully, tried to speak, chewed a little more, and said: "This is like eating a sink sponge loaded with sour milk."

Kay laughed and shook her head. "All right," she said. "That ends my sandwich." She put it down and left it on the plate. He said he was sorry. Kay was still giggling. "Don't feel badly," she said. "That's what it tasted like to me, except I couldn't think of the words."

The room was dark. Early in the evening, the moon was up over the edge of the snowy mountains, looking down the long deep green ravines to the sea. It caught the swinging anchor lights of the ships in the harbor, but it was too weak to light the mountains on the far side of the harbor. Below, the voice of the doorman could be heard bellowing for a taxicab.

The moon crept a little higher, and picked up the dark wings of a British plane coming in from Cyprus. Lights were on in homes all over the hillsides, most of them ugly flats built when the French had a mandate over Lebanon. Kay stirred. "What time is it?" she asked. There was no answer. She felt for Lon. "Is it late?" she asked. "I think it's dark out." Lon sat up. He fumbled for the chain on the lamp. Both of them fought the light with squinted eyes.

"Seven thirty-five," he said, falling back. "Time to get up." He turned toward Kay, put an arm around her and pulled her to him. "You," he said sleepily, "are a likely story. Either you are not really here, or I'm somewhere else." He kissed her. She snuggled closer. He held her tight and felt the seeping warmth of contentment suffuse his body. It was not an exciting feeling; it was as though he wanted to remain this way with her forever. Never to stir, never to get up, never to hear a sound except the rhythmic breathing of two persons as one. The feeling had hardly possessed him when his mind raced back to ask if he had experienced this with Elspeth. He could not remember; still he was sure he must have had this feeling before. It could not be a new emotion, or sensation.

Kay's face was buried in his chest. "What are you thinking of?" she asked. The voice was muffled. He said, "Elspeth." There was a moment of silence. Then Kay broke away and sat up on the far side of the bed. "If we're going out," she said, "we had better get started." He sat up and scratched his head vigorously.

"It never occurs to you," he said, "that I could lie. I could say you. You ask me what's on my mind and I tell you. Right away, the freeze is on." She got up, put on a robe and pulled the sash cord tight. "Do you want the bathroom first?" she asked politely. "Go ahead," he said. "Take your time."

He went out on the little balcony and studied the night sky and the swinging lights in the harbor. It was a soft, cool evening but he wanted none of it. He was aware only that this woman— in common with millions of others—was unjust. Couldn't she have been patient for a moment? Just long enough to ask wha he had been thinking about Elspeth? Did she have to make it so obvious that she was afraid of a ghost?

He was sure that some women, in certain situations, desired to be hurt. They could not bear the monotony of happiness. Like animals who act with instinct rather than reason, they deserted the secure lair for the risk of battle . . . and wounds. She's probably crying in the bathroom, he thought. She wants to feel defensive; what other reason is there for not even asking what I was thinking about a dead wife?

He looked around at the sky. The snow on the mountains was now luminescent, deep gray against the black of the near hills and the onyx of the sea. He took a long deep breath, and thought what a fool he was. He was newly married; he was reasonably happy and more than reasonably happy. He was being childish when he let small misunderstandings infect his thinking, dilute his happiness with doubt. That was true of Kay too. Nothing so far in their marriage had occurred that could be called a crisis; nothing hung over their heads to make them wonder if it would have been wiser to remain unmarried.

Then why, he wanted to know, do both of us attach such importance to minor disagreements? I know why. We're a pair of losers. Losing is a habit, a frame of mind. We're afraid to believe that this is going to be a victorious struggle. Now why did I use the word struggle?

He turned and went back into the room. He telephoned the headwaiter and left a few instructions. Then Kay came out of the bathroom, a towel half draped before her, one hand peeling a blue bathing cap from her head. "Listen," he said. She stopped. "What I was thinking about Elspeth was that it was never as good as this, and I was wondering why. I know how hard she tried to make it go. She failed and I failed. Okay. Now why is this marriage so lovely?"

"Is it?" she said. He yanked the towel from her and put a tight arm around her back. "This is no time to be funny," he said. "I'm getting tired of the little things." Kay tried to back away. She was held fast. "What little things?" she asked. He loosened the arm. "Oh," he said, "what the hell is the use? I'll be old and decrepit before we learn to trust each other. It's just no damned use."

The main dining room was a big square of good rugs and poor lighting, a place of intimate tables with ornate screen blocking the view of the lobby, little lamp shades, and waiters who whispered. Lon and Kay looked around the screen for the Cointreaux, but they weren't there. Kay wore a severely simple pale blue gown. Her hair was piled high on her head and, with the high heels, she looked taller than Lon, in his dinner jacket and black pumps. His face wore the frown of an English bulldog. "They're at the bar, I guess," Kay said. They turned and walked to the front of the hotel. The Cointreaux were sitting at the bar, a pair of Alexanders before them, popping peanuts into their mouths. They asked the Michaelses to have a drink and Kay said no thanks, and Lon said: "Make mine a triple Black and White."

"Ho, ho," said Cointreaux, "there's going to be some action in the hotel tonight." The bartender didn't seem to understand the order and Lon explained it. He downed it in two gulps. Kay smiled at Peg and the women lied to each other perfunctorily. Lon said: "Let me buy one for you," but everyone declined. "Okay," he said, "I'll have a single Scotch just to be sociable."

He had it. "I don't know where you've been," Larry said, "but that should get you off the ground." Larry signed the bar check and they walked to the dining room, the women still talking about gowns and jewelry and hemlines; the men talking about the trip to Jerusalem.

THE SEVENTH DAY

JERUSALEM was cold and clear. An edge of watery snow lined the roads. A few clouds crossed unchallenged between Israel and Jordan. To the west of Nablus Road, there were signs marked NO MAN'S LAND U.N. Arabs, with faces muffled behind woolen scarves, rode small donkeys down the Way of the Cross. The hills of Judaea, rounded and wrinkled, held the ancient city in the palm of the Valley of Cedron.

In mid-century, Jerusalem was an argument against religious faith. The city was split between Arabs and Jews, with pious Christians beseeching entry from both sides. Rolls of barbed wire were coiled, ironically, like crowns of thorns over tank traps along the border, and no one, except possibly the pilgrims, cared to recall that it was here that the Twelve Tribes came to find a home pleasing to God. It was here that Solomon built his temple; here that Jesus preached and was crucified; here that Mohammed came in a magical flight from Mecca in one night. It was here also that Christian sects fought among themselves for parts of the Holy Sepulcher, much as Roman soldiers once fought over Christ's garments; here, indeed, that one of the perpetrators of the greatest mass murders of all time—Adolf Eichmann—was tried, convicted and hanged for the deaths of five million European Jews; it was here too, and at Bethlehem, six miles south, that shepherds watched their peaceful flocks at night; here, indeed, that men sought the favor of the Almighty for forty-five centuries, a sacred place.

Kay was in the travel agency next door to the little Arab hotel when Larry Cointreaux walked in. "You going to Bethlehem?" he said. "Maybe we can split a car." Kay said no. She was waiting for Lon. He wanted to see Jerusalem. Larry shook his head. "We took a gander," he said. "Went through the Damascus Gate and around to the Wailing Wall and so forth. It's pretty dismal, I can tell you."

The agency manager was a small man with a big fierce mustache. He spoke precise, lipless English. "Do you," he said, "wish to see the Christian shrines?" "At Bethlehem?" Cointreaux said. "Yes. I guess so. My wife is a good Lutheran. I'm nothing. I don't believe in anything." He smiled. "My wife says I'm lost, but I claim that it is God who is lost. I don't know where he is, but I sure know where I am."

Lon came in. He nodded to Cointreaux and made arrangements for a guide. "We'd like to see the Way of the Cross," he said. "Gethsemane, the Mount of Olives, Bethany, the Tomb of Lazarus, the Holy Sepulcher—how about the room where the last supper was held?" The manager shook his head. "Sorry, that's on the Jewish occupied side. Besides, it's traditional."

"What's that?" Kay asked. The manager explained. "Whatever is historically accurate is—well, factual. It can be proved in one way or another. But no one can prove, for example, that the last supper was held in the room on the other side of the border. So it's called church tradition. It is church tradition that there was a Mary Magdalene. No one knows for sure. It is church tradition that Jesus met his mother while carrying the cross. No one can prove it."

"Are you Christian?" Larry asked. No, the man said, Moslem. He went about his task of making entries in his ledgers, jotting prices for guides and automobiles and signing chits for gasoline.

It was obvious that he did not like to answer questions about religion. He kept busy at his desk, speaking to the clerks in Arabic, and accepting payment from the two parties.

Lon and Kay got in the back seat of a shiny old Chrysler sedan. A chauffeur sat up front. So did a guide. "How is it," Lon asked, "that we need a guide *and* a chauffeur?" The guide was short and dark and sad of eye. He was accustomed to addressing pilgrims over his left shoulder. "Regulations," he said. "The government."

Kay added the charges. She pointed to a figure in American money. "It only comes to a few dollars," she whispered to her husband, "even if you have both." The car moved down past the National Hotel and back to Nablus Road and south around the old walled city.

Jerusalem sat inside walls on a small table of limestone. Around it, except on the north side near the Gate of Damascus, were deep ditches which, in Biblical times, had been called valleys. "There will not be too much to see today," the guide said, pointing to the afternoon sun. "We will see a little, and then tomorrow we shall start early."

"No we won't," said Lon. He was taking notes as the guide spoke. Someday, he thought, he might need an authentic background of Jerusalem and he might as well jot down his observations now. "We are late risers," he said. "Make it eleven o'clock tomorrow."

The guide smiled. "All right. Late," he said. "All right. Ten, maybe?" Lon looked up from his pad. "We'll haggle," he said. "Ten thirty."

The city lived up to all of its publicity, beginning with the Bible and the Mishnah all the way down to the Jordanian brochures Lon had on his lap. "I get a feeling," Kay said as the car inched through one of the gates of the city, "that this is the farthest away from home."

"About seven thousand miles from New York," the guide

said. Kay meant the farthest in feeling, in customs, people, culture and time. The car nosed between donkeys and groups of sheep and turned into an alley. From that point, the pilgrims walked.

It was an unattractive city full of stone houses shouldering each other over narrow alleys; people ragged and resentful; souvenir shops with Arabs playing chess outside the doors; coffee shops; Coca-Cola signs; the gold-domed Temple of the Rock standing heretically on ground once occupied by Solomon's temple; dampness; the smells of open shops with bluish-skinned sheep hanging in the doorways; an ugly stone church, obviously added to and detracted from, covering Calvary, where Christ died and was buried. Inside, the Greek priests, the Armenian Catholics and the Roman Catholics had divided the most precious treasures of christendom, so that one group had a hole in the floor where, reputedly, the true cross once stood; another had a sepulcher where it was believed the body had reposed for three days; a third had a piece of the cross on which, some believed, Jesus had died.

"Do you believe all this?" Kay asked. Lon continued to make notes. He nodded. "I believe that the archaeologists have done excellent work in locating the precise place of Golgotha. That hole in the floor may not be exactly where the cross stood, but I would like to bet that it is within a few feet of the place of execution. On the other side of the city, where they think Pontius Pilate's palace stood, some nuns had a cellar dug in a convent and the workmen uncovered huge flagstones with Roman markings on them."

"You know this?" the guide said. "It is true. It is now established that these stones were the courtyard of Pilate's praetorium." He folded his fist and made shaking motions. "The soldiers played dice for Jesus' clothes on these stones."

"Does it strengthen your faith in God?" Kay said. Lon looked up. He regarded her gravely. "I never doubted that Jesus lived here and preached here. It's an historical fact. If you mean, do I believe that he is God and the Son of God, I never doubted that either. Except," he said, "when I was very young and very wise. Then I doubted. The older I get, the more firmly I believe. And you?"

Kay did not smile at this. "I never doubted. The whole concept of Christianity and the Roman Catholic Church is so deep in me that I'm going straight to hell when I die. It scares me." The guide grinned. So did Lon. "Christ had more mercy," Lon said, "than most of his priests." The guide walked away to talk to the chauffeur. Kay appeared to be close to tears. "Look at our marriage," she said. "In the eyes of the church, I'm still married to Francis." "You're not going to cry?" he asked in alarm. She shook her head.

"How does Jerusalem impress you?" he said. He took her arm and walked through the gloom of the Holy Sepulcher toward the door. Kay said he was changing the subject. "Somehow," he said, "I'm getting the notion that we are the most self-centered people in the world. Even in the place of the crucifixion, we talk about our problems."

"I like Jerusalem," she said. "No, I don't. I'm impressed by it. Tremendously. But it's sort of old and gloomy. Run down, I'd say." "Yes," he said. That was the word for Jerusalem. They stopped near the Gate of David to watch the Jordanian soldiers, rifles slung across their backs and red polka-dot bandannas around their heads, guarding the little drawbridge fronting on Israel. On the opposite side, Jewish soldiers stood watching.

"Peace on earth," Kay said. This struck the guide as being funny. He saw Lon unlimber his camera. "Please," he said. "Not to take the photos here." They got in the car and went down and outside the east wall to Gethsemane. There, in an old olive grove, Jesus was said to have prayed as his apostles slept nearby. It was a small, fenced-in garden flanking a church. Both stood at the base of a hill on which slender cypresses grew. The hill was the Mount of Olives.

"On top," said Lon, asking rather than stating, "is where Jesus taught the Lord's prayer to his disciples." Yes, the guide answered, and it was also the place where Christ ascended into heaven in the presence of his chosen followers.

"Let's go up," said Lon. The drive was short and winding. At the top, they were shocked to find a tiny Moslem temple on the spot where Jesus rose from the earth to heaven. The guide was becoming clever at mind reading. "Nothing wrong," he said. "Moslems believe that Jesus was a great prophet. Not God himself; but a prophet, like Mohammed."

Lon was not mollified. He said so. "But we treat the Christian holy places with respect," the guide said. "Ask your church fathers. They will tell you. Down at the bottom, there is a second garden of Gethsemane. Two hundred feet to the right." He pointed. "It is administered by the Greeks. We official guides do not acknowledge it. We take the tourists to the Catholic Garden of Gethsemane."

"That's nice," Kay said. The guide detected acidity. "The Greeks also have the tomb of the Blessed Mother, but we take no one there unless they ask, because God took His mother to heaven bodily, so what is in the place? Nothing. They call it Mary's tomb. Who knows?"

Lon looked out at the setting sun and across the walled city— as it must have looked to Jesus—toward the modern Jerusalem in Israel. Over there were buses and glass-bricked buildings and sects still fighting to define the law of God among themselves; over here, Arabs and donkeys and village wells and women wearing pointed veils.

"I'm tired," Kay said.

The dining room was an oblong, with printed cotton curtains on the windows. Most of the tables were unoccupied. On the far side from where Kay and Lon sat, there were eight or ten young women, mostly in tweed suits. Their jollity made Kay think of British schoolteachers. Two waiters, with soiled napkins on their arms, stood near the doorway.

"This is it," said Lon, studying the small menu card. Kay had managed a nap before dinner. She looked bright and beautiful— well, a shade this side of beautiful—and Lon noticed that the English teachers kept glancing at her and whispering. The Arab waiters also had a sullen eye for blondeness. "This is what?" asked Kay.

"This? Dinner. The night life of Jerusalem. I asked the manager what one does in the evening and he said eat. There is an Arab motion-picture house a few blocks away—up near the American Colony—but the manager says that the movies are not American and we would not understand. There are no night clubs, no drinking places, no radio in the room, so this is it. Eat slowly because, after this, there is nothing."

"We can play cards," she said. The Cointreaux came in like scented cyclones. Peg, as big as the Statue of Liberty, was radiant in gems, golden sheath dress with gathered pleats on the side, and Larry bubbled inside a dinner jacket. They came over to the table like Lord and Taylor mannequins. Larry did a little time step en route, and said: "You just got to see Bethlehem. Jesus."

They sat and had much to say. Bethlehem, in sum, was the "wildest." They told about the church where an inn once stood and, far below, the manger where the Christ child was born. "Believe me," said Larry, "I'm not impressed with this stuff usually, but honest, there are still shepherds down in the valley and the priests have this crib fixed up with a red light hanging over it and the baby in it—not real, of course—well, you just have to see it."

"How about those Arabs and the call to prayer?" Peg said. She was twining and untwining her strings of pearls with her fingers. "A man with a beard comes out on a minaret and sings something flat, and all the people start to hurry to the temple. It must be a feast day, I guess."

"I feel," said Kay, "that the Moslems have more religion than we have." There was a little silence. "How?" asked Lon. Kay gestured helplessly. "It's hard to explain," she said. "But from what I've seen, religion is with these people all the time. They go to prayer several times a day, every day. Maybe I'm wrong, but I'm strictly a Sunday religionist." Lon shrugged. "So say we all of us. The Moslems, the Hindus, the Buddhists, they all practice their faith every day."

"I say a prayer every day," said Peg. It seemed shockingly sweet to hear this shallow creature speak of prayer. Larry pointed delicately to his own chest. "The best I can say for myself is I'm no hypocrite." "Meaning—" said Peg.

"Oh no," said Larry. "Meaning nothing. I'm not taking dead aim at anybody. I speak for myself. I wish I could believe this stuff about God but it's a blank spot. Your church," he said, talking directly to Lon, "your church, meaning no offense, preaches the humility and forgiveness of Christ, and your Pope gets himself carried around on some kind of a pallet like an oriental king."

"Faith is one thing," said Lon. "Religious form is merely a manifestation of secularism. My feeling is that the Catholic Church —or any other, for that matter—is bigger than any of its proponents. If a Baptist minister runs off with the choir singer, I don't think less of the Baptist Church. That minister wasn't big enough for his calling, that's all. The church is all right. Some of the people are wrong."

"Still," said Kay, "he's right about the pomp." "And the Pope," said Peg. Lon called the waiter. "I agree," he said to Larry, "that there is too much pomp in my church, all under the guise of tradition and liturgy, but I have a feeling that it was done originally to impress the ignorant."

"What are you going to eat?" Larry said. Lon tossed the menu down. "There are two choices, both bad. Fish or mutton." "Who's having a drink?" asked Peg, hopefully. She was told that there were no drinks. "Oh," said Lon, "this is going to be lovely."

"Just get a load of the rooms," Larry said morosely. "A creaky bed. One chair. A Grand Rapids chest of drawers and a bathroom with two faucets with the same kind of water." "I'm having lamb," Kay said. "You mean mutton," said Lon. "I'm calling it lamb," said Kay. Peg grunted. "I'm with you, Kay."

They ordered mutton. Larry ordered fish. Lon said he'd have some plain cheese and some bread. The schoolteachers finished eating and left, chatting and glancing at the table where an American sat in a dinner jacket and black tie. The table conversation had a recurring theme: that Americans regard all other peoples as backward, or retarded, and are shocked when they find that others are far ahead of America in philosophy or building or art.

The dinner was almost atrocious. Mutton came in big fatty cubes, steeped in hot grease. There was a green vegetable which somehow became soaked in the mutton grease. Lon looked at the other plates, and smiled. He placed the whitish cheese on a slice of bread, and placed another over it. "I'll bet that's goat cheese," Larry said. Lon smiled forgivingly. "You're sore because you have to eat that fish," he said. "Waiter? What kind of cheese?"

The waiter grinned. "Cheese," he said, nodding. "No," said Lon, "what kind? Not goat?" The waiter laughed triumphantly. "Yes," he said. "From good goat." The sandwich went back onto the plate. "Okay," said Lon. "I can eat the bread."

"Did you see the tomb of Absalom today?" asked Larry. Lon nodded. "Our guide passed it below the Jerusalem wall," Larry said, "and he was telling us that it was five hundred years old when Christ was here." Lon said he had seen it. They hadn't stopped, though. It was alongside the Cedron, between the wall of Jerusalem and Gethsemane. "Jesus must have passed it many times," he said.

Peg was trying to chew the mutton, and making a poor thing of it. "I recall something about it," she said. "Jesus condemned the tomb, or said something condemning about it. He said, 'Ye build monuments to the dead when ye should be something something something for the living.' I forget how it goes."

Lon said he was impressed by Gethsemane because, while standing among the olive trees, he looked up toward the Golden Gate in the wall of Jerusalem. "It was only about eight hundred feet away, and when Judas came through there with the Jewish guards and the Roman soldiers, Jesus knew that his time was up. I think I remember the quote: he went to the sleeping apostles and said: 'Arise, he who would betray me is at hand.' It was easy for him to spot a party coming through that gate with torches. It would be just as easy today because there are no lights at night."

"I give up," said Peg and placed her knife and fork on the plate. "How is the bread?" She tried some. Kay said that Jerusalem was a great place to lose weight. Lon said he was going out afterward and buy some chocolate bars. Larry said it was impossible. "I got news, pal. All the stores were closing when we came in to dinner. You couldn't get a prescription now for a heart attack."

They called the waiter and asked if there was any pie for dessert. He did not understand the word. They asked if there was any cake. He smiled brightly and said yes, there was cake, but the English ladies had eaten all of it.

Lon took two additional slices of bread to his room. "I have an unhappy feeling," he said to Kay, "that the waiters here speak English but do not understand it."

In the room, there was no real privacy. There was no shade, and the filmy curtain lifted in the evening breeze. Other guests around the courtyard stood at their windows, looking. Next door, the Michaelses could hear the conversation of the Cointreaux without trying to listen. At one point, they heard Larry say: "I got a half dozen oranges. Get me an English language newspaper in the lobby, honey, I'm about to start to eat." "Here," they heard Peg say, "give that orange to me. I'll peel it. I don't want you working on vacation."

Lon and Kay were playing cards across the bed, but as the Cointreaux' conversation continued, they started to laugh. "Did they go to the tomb of the Blessed Mother?" Peg asked. Larry grunted something they couldn't hear. Then, "All I know," he said, "is that when I saw those stairs, I was so bushed that if the Blessed Mother appeared and asked me to make it, I'd have had to turn her down."

Eventually they became hysterical; Lon laughed until tears stood in his eyes. Then he went next door and told the Cointreaux that everything they said could be heard up and down the hall. Larry picked up a small black banana and handed it to Lon with a bow of deep mockery. "My card," he said.

It was a long, dull evening and sleep did not come easily. The conscious mind was reluctant to quit. The only elation Lon felt was in thinking: "We're in Jerusalem. We're in the city where it all started. I hope we can put up with the lousy food long enough to see Jericho and the Dead Sea and maybe the River Jordan."

THE EIGHTH DAY

THERE was no sound from next door. The Michaelses, sleepy-eyed and slow, ordered breakfast. A floorman in a tarboosh responded. "What kind of breakfast may we order?" The man was old. His mustache was almost white. He pondered the words. "Here eat?" he said, pointing. Lon came out of the bathroom in a blue silk bathrobe and a white skivvy shirt. "Here eat," he said to the waiter. "What can we eat?"

The man struggled with the word. "Breakfast," he said. Lon gave him a faint one-sided smile. "Sure breakfast," he said. "What kind breakfast?" The man thought about it. "Breakfast," he said. Kay was moving a trunk rack from under the room window to a position between the beds where it would serve as a table. "Let me try," she said, patiently.

"Bring breakfast," Lon said to the waiter. "Nice, good breakfast." He held up two fingers and pointed to his wife and himself. "Two. Eat for two." The old man smiled and bowed his fezzed head. "Oh brother," Lon said, "I can't wait to see what this is going to be."

He washed and shaved and came back to the room looking haggard. "Why didn't we ask him to bring a newspaper?" His wife shrugged. She disappeared into the bathroom. "The whole world could be falling apart," he said, "and we don't know a thing."

"That's the trouble with civilization," Kay yelled back, "too many nosy people."

He went out into the hall and knocked on the door of the room next door. There was no response. Lon knew that Cointreaux was an early riser. He was amazed at how much he had learned about this man and his wife in a few days. Well, the Cointreaux knew a lot now about him and about Kay. The veneer of respect for the so-called great writer had degenerated to "Now listen, pal . . . ."

The breakfast arrived. Kay and Lon stood, like expectant children, watching the waiter set it on a bed of slats. It consisted of a pot of black tea, a pot of boiling water, some thick slices of white bread toasted lightly, two cups and saucers, butter in square tiles, and a saucer of dark jam. "Sort of continental," said Kay. She was laughing at the obvious irritation on Lon's face. He pushed her onto the bed. "Very funny," he said.

He fell on top of her and she tried to squirm out from under. "Very funny," he said. He held both of her wrists in one hand, then, with the free hand, took a dab of black jam and painted her nose with it. Freeing her wrists, she flailed at him with both hands. This led to a breathless rumpus, which led to more breathlessness, and more breathlessness, and then the most complete breathlessness.

Lon got out of bed, and felt the side of the white crockery. Cold. "We can order more," he said. Kay arose, adjusting her hair. "No," she said. "It's like giving them a running account of our private lives. No. Forget the breakfast. I'll tear up some of the pieces of bread and flush them in the bathroom."

"I want breakfast," he said. "Who the hell is the star around here?" "All right, master," she said. "But we're having a cup of coffee on the road. How about getting dressed?"

There is a road which hooks around the Mount of Olives and the Mount of Offense, where Solomon kept his five hundred concubines, and it runs east, always rolling and pitching a little between the rocky hills, in an easterly direction to Jericho, twenty-three miles away. It is a road that gives the tourist an illusion of driving between towering mountains.

He is, in reality, headed downhill almost all the way. The city of Jerusalem is at an altitude of about 2,300 feet. Jericho is below sea level. Between the two, there is a great deal of history. At Bethany, two miles out of Jerusalem, they saw the ancient tomb where Lazarus was raised from the dead by Jesus, and a few hundred feet away the church where Mary and Martha, sisters of Lazarus, fed the Messiah and the twelve, and where Judas, treasurer of the group, criticized Martha for anointing the feet of Jesus with an expensive unguent. At the halfway point there was an Arab police station, almost in ruins, and it is said that here the Good Samaritan saw an injured stranger and tended to his needs.

Along the left were precipitous valleys, tawny with erosion, and there they saw something one will not see anywhere else in the world. There were holes dug in the sides of the cliff, where ascetics lived withdrawn from the world, emerging only to care for their sheep. They do not speak and, when something must be transmitted, they whistle.

Further on was the huge mountain overlooking Jericho, a large patch of verdant green in a desert. It is said that Jesus fasted for forty days and nights on this mountain and that the Devil tempted him, pointing to the lushness of Jericho below, and promising "the whole world" if Christ would but bend his knee. Between the mountain and the city they passed a large camp of refugee Arabs, dispossessed from their homes and farms in Israel.

Jericho, where once in the Old Testament the walls came tumbling down because of a blast from a horn, has become a shopping center for Moslems. It has paved streets, traffic policemen with white pith helmets, summer heat when Jerusalem is cold, and the muddy swirl of the Jordan.

The guide turned the car south five miles to where the Jordan empties into the Dead Sea. Lon was interested because he had read it was the lowest place on earth (1,290 feet below sea level); the sea appeared to be as blue as any other lake, but contained twenty-five per cent salt—several times the salinity of the oceans of the world. On the eastern shore were the saw-toothed mountains of Moab, to which Moses led the Jews, en route to the Promised Land of Judaea. There, Moses died.

There also, Lon bought a bottle of water from the River Jordan ("After all, honey, John the Baptist baptized the Saviour with this water") and learned from the husky Arab that the cost was one dollar—"filtered, boiled and blessed." There was a monastery off the edge of the sea and, on the beach, a motel with an outdoor café.

The sun was staring hot, and some children were wading in the Dead Sea. The Michaelses watched as they ate with their guide and chauffeur. One of the children fell into the water. It was a little girl and she screamed, not because her frock was ruined, but because the water of the Dead Sea was in her eyes.

Kay found that the restaurant served liquor, so she ordered a bloody Mary. Lon, astonished to find that the waiter knew what it was, ordered a screw driver. "Well," he said, as the waiter disappeared, "if the Essenes could only see this." The guide found this amusing. Kay asked who the Essenes were, and Lon pointed to a small empty place of sandy cliffs on the west shore of the Dead Sea. "They lived over there"—he glanced at the guide for confirmation—"and they stored the Dead Sea scrolls in old jars and hid them in caves."

"Did they write them?" "Wrote them." Kay sipped her drink and ordered a sandwich. "I've been thinking," she said. He waited. When a woman said "I've been thinking" it could mean anything from the detonation of a marital mine to a suggestion for dinner. "Yes?" he said.

"A lot of my thoughts about man have been changed in a week," she said. "This place, for instance. This and Jerusalem and all the rest. It is much smaller than I thought. Sort of dirty and run-down. Neglected. It is ancient and impressive, but what I'm trying to say is that there is no peace here." The guide coughed behind his hand. The chauffeur excused himself and said he had to get some gasoline for the car.

"If you can't find it here," Kay went on, "then it is nowhere. I find it—" "Discouraging," Lon said. He sipped the thick Turkish coffee, and stared at the blue of the Dead Sea. "I disagree with your reaction. Most women like to think pretty thoughts. They pretend that this is a pretty world full of pretty—perhaps slightly misguided—people. It's a rougher, tougher, meaner world than that. So, when the ladies travel, and they learn that there is much more suffering, much more selfishness than they thought, they react with shock. But, by the same token, honey, they become smarter."

"May I finish my thought?" Kay said. "I am not a psychologist, but I am sure that most of us get our lasting impressions when we're young. Very young. God, the Bible, family life, the world, the hereafter, war, peace—the child's mind is a blotter. Very few of us, it seems to me, are prepared for the realities when we grow up. I felt that Jerusalem was exempt from the universal hatreds. Maybe universal is not the word, but the general dislikes and disapprovals is what I mean."

She chewed the sandwich as she spoke, and she asked for another bloody Mary. "All of this," her hand swept the horizon, "is pretty shocking. Say Jerusalem to me, and to millions like me, and I think of a beautiful temple and Jesus preaching on the steps. Say Bethlehem and I can smell Christmas boughs and see a fat little baby and animals. You know what Peg told me last night? She said that there is a big tizzy going on in Bethlehem because the Greeks who control the lower church broke a filigreed altar railing owned by some other sect upstairs in the church."

"On purpose?" Lon asked. "It was deliberate, from what she told me," Kay answered. "Well, my point is that if these ministers of God can't get along with each other in the name of God, then in God's name where is the hope for the rest of us?" Lon lifted both palms and applauded. "Bravo," he said. "Bravo. My bride's horizons are broadening."

She shook her head in sorrow. "The Arabs hate the Jews. The Jews fear the Arabs. At home, the whites hate the Negroes, the Negroes fear the whites. England distrusts Germany; Germany fears Russia; France thinks it can live alone; Spain wants to get back into the community of nations; the Chinese have nothing and want to fight with everybody. You call this a world?"

Lon was tempted to mock new knowledge. He thought better of it. He decided to treat her thesis seriously. "One of our vices," he said, "is that we can forgive man all his mistakes of the past, but when we mature, we cannot forgive the rest of the world for not maturing with us. It's a form of personal pedanticism."

The guide coughed. He had finished his second coffee and he was ready to go. "Patience," he said. "Jordan, for example, is so young that our nation is an infant in a cradle." "Oh, no," Lon said, feeling in his jacket for money and placing it on the table. "Oh, no, mister. You are not young. Your king is young. Your form of government is young. Your people are old, and so is the land. You did not come out of caves to form this country."

The guide shrugged and smiled. He knew that a philosophical disagreement with foreigners could cost him a tip. The tourist agency paid him half of what it charged. "Yes," he said, smiling a big smile. "I see what you mean. I had not thought of it that way."

"There is no point in talking about man," Kay said. "It's a complex subject. He thinks big in medicine and engineering, and he thinks small in philosophy and the arts." Lon had to smile.

"Let's get started," he said. "We have an appointment with those excruciating cooks at the hotel."

The guide was curious. "Excruciating?" he said. "What does this mean in English?" Kay walked beside him. She did not smile. "It means the same, in a way, as atypical. And you know what atypical means." Of course, the guide said. Of course.

They got into the car and started back. The ride required an hour and it was dark as they pulled over the top of the hill out of Bethany and could discern the silhouetted walls of Jerusalem. "I love being here," Kay said in one more obvious attempt to explain her feelings, "but it depresses me. Why didn't men listen to him when he preached? He was here and he handed down the rules, but they weren't listening."

"My feet hurt," Lon said, "though I don't know why. We've done more riding than walking." The guide asked if they would see Bethlehem tomorrow. No, Lon said, they were leaving for Beirut on the noon plane. He wanted to see Bethlehem, but there wasn't enough time. He would also have liked to walk the streets of Nazareth, but that was a hundred and fifty miles north—too far for a short visit to the Holy Land.

"We will take you to the airport," said the guide. He was slavishly anxious to please, while, at the same time, trying to maintain the dignity of a licensed guide. Lon said he would pay the bill tonight, and would make arrangements to be picked up at ten thirty A.M. for the airport. "Yes," the guide said agreeably, "you will need time for the customs."

"My feet feel all right," Kay said, kicking off her shoes and rubbing the soles of her feet against each other. "It's my head that hurts."

THE NINTH DAY

AT the airport, Lon stood shivering in a trench coat. Beside him was the guide. Kay and Peg were buying postcards, and writing them quickly, so that they would bear the cancellation mark of Jerusalem. Lon folded a twenty-dollar bill into a small square, and handed it to the guide. The man stuffed it into his pocket without looking at it, murmuring "Thank you. Thank you very much."

"We're all cleared now?" Lon asked. "Customs and all?" The guide shrugged. "Everything," he said. "I told them special handling in your case." Lon nodded. "That's nice," he said. He was watching the runway. It ran flat for about half its length, then it moved uphill and ended suddenly at the top. In the middle were crossing gates.

"What are those for?" he asked, pointing. The guide laughed. "You would not believe me," he said. "That's a sheep crossing. The shepherds are permitted to cross the airport." Lon showed disbelief. "Suppose," he said, "an airliner is coming in?"

"Well," the guide said, "it depends. If there is time, the gates go down and the shepherd must keep his animals off the runway. If there is not time, the tower radioes the pilot to make an extra turn around the airport." Larry Cointreaux was standing a few feet away. "Lovely," he said, as he adjusted his camera for another picture.

The women finished writing their postcards and used the remaining foreign currency buying stamps. Peg Cointreaux looked not only big, but imposing, as she stood in the transient room watching the Arab families waiting to board the Middle East Airways plane.

"I have done a lot of traveling," she said to Kay, "and one of the things that disturbs me is the meekness of people in the face of authority." Kay said she hadn't noticed. "Look," Peg said. The families sat on long benches, uniformly poorly clad, sad of eye, babies squirming and crying on laps, a soldier with a Bren gun with his back to the door.

"You won't see this meekness in the progressive countries," she said. "The English, the Americans, the French and Germans stand up to authority and ask questions and expect answers. But in Italy, in Greece, the Middle East and Far East, the people do as they're told without question. If they're told to sit, they sit. No one asks why. If the plane is an hour late, no one will ask why."

Kay looked. A few of the Moslem women glanced at her briefly. "Most of the time," Peg said, "Larry and I are busy having fun. I don't like to see tragic things and I don't like to hear about them. But sometimes—"

"You can't help noticing," said Kay. "I know. Maybe we shouldn't look at the things we can't do anything about." They walked out to join the men. The Arab soldier studied the rich Western-style attire of the women, and permitted them to pass. Outside, they were told to board the Viscount. Lon said goodbye to the guide. "We'll be back." he said. "There is much more to see." "Yes," the guide said. "You must."

In a few minutes, the plane was loaded and it ran down the runway, past the crossing gates, and on up the hill and into the sky. In a few minutes, the rocky rills of Judaea floated slowly under the wings and the pilot made a slow climbing turn toward

Damascus and Beirut. The stewardess was a stout Moslem girl with huge dark eyes. She was soon busy serving coffee. When passengers said: "What's that city down there?" she said "Jericho" throughout most of the flight.

"Are you happy?" Lon asked. Kay turned away from the small circular window. "Of course," she said. "Are you?" "Yes," he said, softly. "Most." She thought for a moment. "I'm getting to know you," she said. Lon looked shocked. "That's nice," he said. "I appreciate the effort." "No," she said. "I knew you before, and I knew I was in love with you, but now I am getting to know the inner you."

"Tell me about me," he said, making a small joke. She had learned to ignore these remarks. Sometimes, she knew, he made them because he did not want the conversation to become serious, or because he was afraid that, in the seriousness, a problem would arise to threaten the serenity of the honeymoon. "Perhaps," she said, assuming a mocking tone of her own, "I'm doing a mind-reading act. I'm learning to anticipate your wishes. Sometimes, when you want something from the briefcase, I find myself moving toward it while you're still fumbling at the typewriter."

"You're a girl who requires a lot of love," he said. "I don't mean in the sexual sense, although there is that too. You need constant reassurance." Kay turned to the window again. "Don't be offended," he said. "I'm serious. Our only chance in this marriage is to look matters in the eye."

"I'm listening," she said. She fumbled in her purse for a cigarette. "For example," he said, "I love you and no matter how many times I say it I do not love you a bit more than the first time I said it. And still, you expect me to say it all the time." She nodded sagely. "A woman expects to hear it. There isn't any monotony to it, for her. She wants to renew the same vows every day."

"Every hour," he said. "It smacks of hypocrisy or insecurity

or something. I love you. Then sixty minutes later, I love you.
Then, from the bathroom, I love you. When you're hurt, I
love you. When you're happy, I love you. In bed, I love you.
In the morning, half dead with sleep, I love you. In the theater,
in a bus, at dinner, walking, waking, sleeping, I love you. It
doesn't make me love you more just to keep saying it. In fact,
you say it more than I. And yet, I don't need it. I'm sure that
you love me. I'm positive."

Kay said that the conversation was now in a field where the
sexes did not understand each other. She believed that most
women would agree with her, just as she was certain that most
men would side with him. Lon said that perhaps his opinions
were masculine, but that he felt that love was a deep irrevo-
cable emotion. "One cannot fall in and out of love," he said. "One
can fall in and out of an affair, or in and out of admiration,
or even affection to a degree, but love should be as permanent
as death."

"How about Elspeth?" Kay said. "You were in love with her.
Now you're in love with me." That, he said, was the big surprise to him. He hadn't thought that it could happen twice in
a lifetime. "If you want me to say that I now realize that I
was not in love with Elspeth—that this is the real thing—
you're mistaken," he said.

"It's impossible to talk rationally with you," she said. "Besides, we're coming into Beirut now." "Who mentioned Elspeth?" he said. "Who brought that name into the conversation?
Do I ask you how you felt about your precious Francis? Do i
ask how you could have gone to bed with him before marriage.
Do I ever ask you about your other mistakes? Oh no. I'm no
the one consumed by jealousy. You are."

"The sign is on," she said. "Put your safety belt on." H
did. In a moment, the conversation had changed from a happ
thing about a new and wonderful marriage to an assortmer
of accusatory ghosts. The Viscount made a deep close tur

downwind, and the engines thrummed down until the craft appeared to be barely floating over the city and down toward the airport on the edge of the sea.

"How long do we wait here?" she asked. He snapped his briefcase shut. "Early evening," he said. "We have hours to kill. We can go back to Pigeon Rock and I'll push you off."

There is mysticism in tossing a large arrow into the black night with the expectation that it will come down safely. Flight Two Pan American, a huge silver arrow with 137 persons inside, disappeared in the dark sky beyond Beirut with a sound like summer thunder. The magic, the mystique, the engineering combined forces to aim the 137-ton vehicle at Teheran, near the Caspian Sea in Iran. Six miles below there was land, but it could not be seen, except once in a while when a vague cluster of lights appeared to slide dimly under a wing. There was the constant whine of the big engines, sucking freezing air, heating it instantaneously, and expelling it to provide propulsion.

Other than the infrequent lights, there was nothing to show forward motion. Once the plane was on its course, north by east, the visible stars remained motionless and unwinking, and the passengers, who sipped highballs or munched hors d'oeuvres, looked out and felt as though everything were standing still in a noisy tunnel.

Lon was up front, sitting in the curving lounge, waiting for an unoccupied rest room, when the captain came off the flight deck. They exchanged greetings and Lon asked their position. "We're directly over the desert," the captain said. He was a big man with lumpy fisherman's hands. "What desert?" The captain shrugged. "Damned if I know. The only one I remember from school is the Sahara."

It was said to be funny. It was. The most incongruous part of flight in mid-century was that pilots did not have to know geography. They flew, by an assortment of radios and homing devices, from one point to another without much knowledge of the terrain between, other than alternate airports. In the days of visual flight regulations, it was necessary to know every river, the height of every obstacle, how to navigate by fixed stars, cities, dams, even railroads and general highways. Now the soaring arrow thought its way to its destination, and did it with less error and much faster trimming of the craft in turbulence.

Lon went back to his seat for dinner. He waved to the Cointreaux, on the opposite side, and noticed that most of the passengers had finished their cocktails. The male steward, assisted by two pretty girls, was busy pulling trays down from the backs of seats and setting small tablecloths and napkins and knives and forks and spoons in place. The menu consisted of an appetizer, a salad, beef Stroganoff, fruit, rolls, coffee and ice cream. There was table wine, brandy, Benedictine, Scotch, rye, bourbon and gin.

The dinner was barely completed when the big ship began to soften its whine to a whimper and aimed its nose at a glow on the horizon. This was Teheran. It was twenty-five minutes away. "We are 907 miles from Beirut," he told Kay. She was not truly impressed by speeds or distances, but she knew that he was, so she always affected an interest.

"Why," she said, "we just barely got comfortable." He said that they would get off and look around the airport, but there would be no chance to see the city. "Next stop is New Delhi, India, and that is, let me see—" he studied a flight map—"1,67 miles from Teheran. If Flight Two is on time, we should ge into New Delhi with the rising sun."

Kay didn't understand. "Will the next leg take all night?" No, he said, not truly. "As we fly east, we're flying toward th morning sun and picking up three hours. The sun is going aroun the world in the opposite direction." She nodded. She wasn quite sure she understood, but she understood his impatienc and a nod ended the matter.

Within an hour, the big plane was roaring down the runway and climbing toward the stars. Lon waited until the seat-belt light went off, and then pulled out a tray and set his typewriter on it. Kay curled up in a blanket beside him. Across the aisle, Peg was curled up with her head on Larry's shoulder. Lon began to type and at once it was obvious that a woman sitting in front of him was displeased. She rose in her seat to stare back at him. He looked up, smiled briefly, and kept typing. The steward dimmed the lights in the main cabin and Lon turned on the little spotlight so that he could see what he was doing.

The woman in front remained quiet for about five minutes. Then she stood, glared at him, and said: "Must you type?" Lon showed no apologetic smile. "Yes," he said. "I must. It's a tribute to the soundproofing in this plane that you can hear me at all." The lady, a middle-aged spinster type, who may not have been a spinster at all, made an elaborate to-do about picking up her purse, her magazine, and her blanket and walking to the rear, where she plumped into an empty seat.

The loudspeaker opened and the captain announced that the plane had been flying at 33,000 feet, but had received permission to climb to 37,000. Kay slept through it. Her attractive face was in repose, her lips parted slightly, small bluish pouches showing under both eyes. Lon wished that he could sleep in an airplane. If only he weren't so curious . . . or so nosy . . . or so quick to indict . . .

He took the diary from the briefcase, unlocked it and took a few fresh sheets of paper out. He began to write, slowly, pickingly, at first, then at increased tempo, pausing now and then to glance at Kay.

This is written en route to New Delhi. Entries have been neg-lected for a few days because time and travel tend to kaleidoscope each other. I could write: "Very happy" and be done with it. The two words are capsule truth. I am most happy. Happiest. But that too has a telescoping effect. On this, the ninth day of marriage, I know that I have joined hands forever with the finest woman I've ever known. Many years ago, I felt reasonably happy and I did not miss, nor aspire to, this new happiness because I was not aware of it.

It is difficult to comprehend how good Kay is—how sweet, how feminine, how pretty, how intelligent, how easily she can humiliate me by subordinating her desires to mine; how exalted she can make me feel about my work; how much she wants to share. "Whither thou goest . . ." is a phrase she repeats. Yesterday we passed an old Jewish cemetery outside the east wall of Jerusalem and, from nothing, she asked me whether I would be buried with Elspeth or with her.

This is hardly a honeymoon topic. It was a new thought to me. An ugly one. Still, I realized from the tone that it was a somewhat old one to her. Kay had waited until something in the form of death presented itself. Then she asked the question. I told her that I would prefer to rest for all eternity with her, but again the damned age factor came into the conversation and I reminded her that I am twenty years older, that it is possible that I might go twenty years before she does and that, with much time on her hands, she might remarry.

This induced angry tears. Angry tears are different from the others. She did not want to weep and, when the tears came, she exploded. There were words she used that I haven't heard since the last time I used them. "——your age!" she said. I had to laugh. This made her madder. Before the dust subsided from the explosion, she had managed to complete whole sentences consisting only of four-letter words.

Later, she said that she was sorry that she had lost her temper. I wasn't. It was a revelation to learn that she had one. Until now she has been repressed and secretive when something displease her. I asked her why burial was so important on a honeymoon. She said that she loves me so deeply that it has crossed her mind many times that someday we will be apart.

The body, once dead, is of no consequence. This thought did not appeal to her. "I want to know now that we shall be together forever," she said. "Alive or dead, it makes no difference, just so long as I know that we will be together." Once again, I was touched and humbled by the depth of her affection. I promised. She wiped her eyes and smiled and the next sentence stunned me. "All right," she said. "When we get home, we can look for plots."

It was my turn to become short-tempered. "We'll do nothing of the kind," I said. "I'm not decrepit. I don't feel that I'm dying, and I don't think you're about to kill me. Plots my eye! What's the reason for the sudden morbidity?" Kay said it was neither sudden (which I suspected) nor morbid. "Do you feel morbid when you pray to God to forgive your sins?" she said. "You're asking him for a free pass to heaven, aren't you? Well, you can't get there unless you die. How about insurance? Do you have any? Do you feel morbid about it? The policy isn't worth anything unless you're dead. Have you ever written a will? I suppose that's morbid too. Me, I'm morbid about planes. I'm scared to death of them. But because you're beside me, I'm afraid of nothing. I can even fall asleep in a plane. It's not that I fear them less, but that I trust you more. Is this understandable?

"Well," she said, "if it is, then the rest ought to be under-standable. I don't want to die and lie somewhere alone. I want to have it settled now that I will definitely be with you—unless, of course, you have other plans." I told her that I had no plans. "When we get home, I promised, we would look for a place, a sweet little headstone in the hills somewhere. She accused me of being funny. Far from funny, I said. "I'm shocked. Truly."

She said that she had given the matter a lot of thought, al-

most from the time I had proposed marriage. "You see," she said, with almost macabre sweetness, "I'm afraid of planes and snakes and lots of other things, but I'm not afraid of death. If you go first, I've got it all arranged in my mind to take an over-dose of pills, so that we can be buried together. If I go first, all I ask of you is that you not bother with any other woman. I couldn't take it."

If her opening was shocking, her peroration was, to me, stunning. I told her that I had had no intention of "bothering" (if that is the sorry word to be used) with any other woman even before I met her. I had had enough of love, enough of disappointment, enough of tragedy—my emotions had been drained, and had been replaced by suspicion and cynicism. Both of these were pretty good crutches for a man of middle years. He needed nothing else except books, a quest for knowledge, and a zest for life. However, I had met her and, sliding against my will, fallen in love. If she was still around when I died, I wanted no heroic hara-kiri, no pills, no last notes.

What I would prefer, I said, was a little less cowardice. If I died, I would like her to replace me as the caretaker for Lucy and Sonny. "I don't expect you to love Sonny as much as you do Lucy. But I do expect that you will stick around and bail out his mind every time he starts to sink. He likes you. He needs you. Lucy, I feel, would crack up without you. This stuff of 'Whither thou goest . . .' is great; it's flattering to me, but you're carrying it too far. I'm half in hope that you aren't serious about this; that you're sort of joking; or playing a bit from Joan of Arc."

The discussion became most serious for a time; almost dangerous. We have had disagreements before marriage, and since, and some of them have been sharp. But this was dangerous inasmuch as it threatened the emotional balance of our marriage Inwardly, I had felt flattered up to the point where she discussed the pills. Then I began to feel that there was a sickness in this union. Before we closed the topic, I forced her to promise that she would not try to follow me in case I died first; whichever of us remains will take care of the children; frankly, I don't know two children who need a parent more than Sonny and Lucy.

Afterward, I feared that she might be promising blankly and blindly, to placate me and to stop me from asking further questions. I went back over the matter with her, trying to express sympathy so that she would not feel belittled, and she convinced me that the idea of following me off to the Great Perhaps is gone. The children are more important than our petty ecstasies.

She sleeps beside me, half sitting, half hunched against the back of the seat. The coverlet is over her shoulder, and the breathing is deep. In sleep, she wings toward India at better than six hundred miles per hour—no strain, no effort—and she loves a man in a similar way.

THE TENTH DAY

THERE is a moment in time when the night dies and dawn is not yet born. Blackness is still over the earth, but it is weakened and diluted with deep grays so that a full moon glows like a Japanese lantern, but objects on the ground are thrown into silhouette and can be seen as charcoal drawings, and lights in farm windows appear yellow and radiant. It is a moment when the night wind stands still, leaning on the helpless leaves of a million trees, just before the first stirring of birds and just after the street lamps have been extinguished.

The big bird, still shrieking, crept up to the New Delhi Air port at that moment—the symbolic precursor of a plague o giant locusts such as India had never seen—and died. A few customs officials stood behind the hedges and flowerbeds framin the awkward buildings, and watched. The bird had flown hig and far in the night and now, when the sky was about to dre in attractive colors, its work was done and it was grounded.

The passengers filed down the steps in pairs, carrying sma shoulder bags and cameras, looking about in the gloom for guide to show the way. The officials, men with mahogany fac and licorice-drop eyes, beckoned and the passengers went in a long room with counters to await their luggage, declare t amount of cigarettes and cash they had, and to be welcomed, in t precise diction of Hindus trained to speak Oxford English, to an enormous land which excites pity.

— The trip to the Ashoka Hotel was short and exciting. The streets of New Delhi were broad and tree-lined. The first pink rays of the sun erased all the deep indefinite grays and put hunter green on the leaves of small umbrella trees and cast long shadows and beribboned the sky with pinks and pastel greens and, here and there, a knot of yellow on a fluffy white cloud. The weather was summery—in February and March, Lon told Kay, it averaged better than eighty degrees—and the four passengers in the car saw a few Indians sleeping under trees, the white loincloths folded loose around the thighs, the upper garment of white cotton as ill-fitting as a comfortable pajama top.

A huge vulture, sitting on a topmost branch, attracted attention by spreading his broad wings, then folding them again to watch sleepily as the lone automobile moved by. A few men rode by on bicycles; they wore white "overseas" caps, gray tunics with stand-up collars, and tight-fitting white pants. "They dress like Nehru," said Cointreaux. He was in front with the driver.

— The chauffeur's name was Joga. He wore a brilliant orange turban with little hints of white in it, a replica of an orange ice sherbet. It had a puffy loose end sticking up in front like a small peacock tail. He was "twenty and a half" in years, he said, and he had a thick jet beard which, at night, he pressed close to the skin with a net harness tied from chin to top of head.

"You see," he said in his British brand of English, "these men dress like Nehru only because they come from the same province. In India, one studies the attire and one knows at once, you see, where the person is from. You will see many types of dress here. You have been in India before?"

"Isn't he cute?" Peg said to Kay. "In Switzerland, Larry's father left us a big marble house—eighteen rooms—can you imagine this one as the doorman?" Joga could not help but hear, but it did not affect his disposition. He had, as the tourists would learn, an old philosophy in a young head.

The car moved north, then east past the Soviet Embassy, the Brazilian and the United States embassies. At the intersections were small elevated stands for traffic policemen; around them were empty oil drums. Ahead was a huge pale building stretching over an enormous part of a low hill. It looked like a Tibetan lamasery. Joga pointed. "Ashoka," he said. "That," said Kay, "is the biggest hotel I've ever seen. It looks like a medical center."

Lon made arrangements with Joga to be their regular driver, on call each morning. The price was reasonable. "One of the reasons I am here," he said, "is to see the Taj Mahal." Joga had a way of bowing agreement that amounted to more than a nod and less than a curtsy. He was not subservient, nor was he snobbish. "Agra is one hundred twenty-five miles south," he said. "It is important, you see, to start early. One does not drive one hundred twenty-five miles easily in India. There are many villages and many people. Some animals. We will leave at seven o'clock and be in Agra at eleven. You will see the Taj and all the other things and still be back here in the early evening." "We will leave at ten," said Lon firmly, "and get there when we can." Joga smiled, his teeth snowy against the rich deep color of his skin. "As you wish, sir." "Right now," Lon added, "we are going to check into the hotel, unpack, and get some sleep. Please be at the door at three P.M. We will want to see something of New Delhi."

"Sunday is not one's best day," said Joga. Lon was not going to fence with him. "Be here at three," he said. "And thank you, Joga."

The car drove through the streets slowly. Once, it paused to permit an untethered gray cow to cross, and Lon remembered that the cow was sacred in India. "Not sacred, if you please," said Joga. "It is possibly the reincarnation of someone who once lived as a human and now, you see, he must do it all over again as a cow because there was some error in his previous life."

"Suppose there was no error?" asked Lon. Joga said: "In that case, he would not be forced to return as a cow, or a reptile. He would go straight to Nirvana, you see. If one leads a blameless life, it is not necessary to come back and do it again. One attains spiritual rest and happiness. If one falls into deliberate error, then one keeps coming back again and again in different forms until perfection is achieved."

He turned the car around a corner near a university building and they saw a big crowd of men standing in an empty space. "Cobras," Joga said. "The Hindu fakirs." Cointreaux sat up. "The snake charmers?" he said. "Stop the car. I have to see the snake charmers."

Joga, who hid disgust under the thickness of his beard, said: "If you give them a few rupees, they will do the whole act for you. One may make motion pictures too." Everyone except Joga left the car and pushed through the mob. In the center, with a discreet area of space around them, were two filthy-looking men playing bulbous flutes while squatting in front of baskets. The snakes appeared to be lethargic, and needed a touch of fingers on the side of the head to bring them swelling and swaying from the reeds.

They had with them a young boy, with a red and blue turban set rakishly on his head. The boy too was in rags, but he seemed happy. When one snake got loose and squirmed out of the circle, the crowd of men ran in panic and the boy laughed heartily, picked the snake up by the tail and returned it to the basket. Cointreaux tossed some money to the men and took pictures as the leader stood and the boy took a dozen or so snakes and flung them writhing around the older man's neck.

Kay said: "I'll meet you back in the car." Peg Cointreaux joined her, saying: "It's a funny thing, but almost all of these men look like Mahatma Gandhi to me." The men rejoined the ladies and Joga drove them up and down the streets, apologizing for the closing of so many shops on Sunday. He took them to the Lakshmi Narayan Temple, a garish pink-and-white edifice, almost gay, where thousands of pilgrims had left their shoes in neat rows on a marble walk. There were vendors of orange flowers—like small zinnias—at the temple gates and the supplicants bought them and went inside to one or another of many holy rooms where statues of Hindu "saints" abounded, and the flowers were tossed at the marble statue as the pilgrims recited their petitions—for a sick child, a job, a new baby or an old parent. The marble floors around the statues were covered with orange petals.

Outside were statues of elephants, terraced gardens, and an aura of happiness, as though it were a privilege, rather than an obligation, to visit the home of God. More than a privilege, a joy, as if the people had received an invitation to a party. The family faces wore smiles as though some happy surprise were due. Those who had worshiped reclined on the grassy sod around the temple, conversing softly in little groups, eating, watching the children frolic, and lying back to feel the hot sun.

Across the street, where the taxis waited, a holy man in loin cloth, with orange and white lines on his forehead, stared unblinking at the sun as though trying to blind his eyes in one day. A mother in veil, looking hardly more than thirteen or fourteen, carried a baby with belly swollen from malnutrition. Wherever she was going, her bare feet moved swiftly, silently and surely. She did not appear to be worried about the imminent death of the baby who, for certain, had committed no error and would soon be in Nirvana.

India is the pendulous breast of Asia, but it hasn't enough nourishment to feed itself. There are 420,000,000 people within its borders, and most of them are philosophical, purposeless, unhygienic, compassionate, religious, ignorant, poverty-stricken and free. It is a place of stupendous mountains, insufferable heat, tigers, maharajahs, elephants, lepers, crocodiles, banyan trees, scorpions, rice paddies, locusts, tea, and the world's most beautiful butterflies. It is a land of more contrasts, more intranational confusion, than any other in the world, including China. India is flanked on two sides by Pakistan, each part of which has no means of communicating with its other half, except across India. There are thirteen major languages within India, starting with popular tongues like Hindi and Panjabi, and ranging down to Oriya and Assamese, spoken by less than four per cent of the people.

Religion is most important in India, in many cases taking precedence over the will to live, but the spiritual goals are not the same. About 250,000,000 Indians practice Hinduism; 95,000,000 are Moslems; 6,000,000 are Christians of several sects; 6,000,000 are Jains and only 1,500,000 are Buddhists. The Sikhs hold their adherents under such tight rein that young men do not meet women socially, preferring to wait until parents select a mate for them. It is a temptation to oversimplify, but the difference in faiths is best exemplified in the aphorism that the Moslem feels that in killing a nonbeliever he does a service for God, whereas the Hindu believes that if he permits himself to die he is more pleasing to the eyes of his God.

Certain rivers are sacred to Hindus; others are not. Certain animals are holy; others are not. The Hindu thinks of himself as a lonely individualist, but he travels in mobs, on foot, in coveys of cyclists, jammed on ancient buses or trains. The subject of sex, even among groups of men, induces abashed silence, but the population swells beyond the ability of the nation to feed its people. Personal modesty is a fetish, but Indians on foot squat in public beside the roads to have bowel movements, or to urinate. A camel making slow circular turns around a well as he pumps water gets more food and better care than the children of his owner. The cheapest commodity of all is human life, which is something God's children must endure as a trial until they are ready for the eternal ecstasy of Nirvana.

In the evening, Lon and Kay dressed for dinner. On the main floor of the hotel there was an avenue of shops selling saris and shoes and books and gowns. Near the end of it was the entrance to the dining room. As they entered, Lon said: "Now I am touched. Truly touched." They found themselves in a vast dining room filled with impeccably white cloth-covered tables. Each one held a small lighted orange lamp and a small bouquet of fresh flowers. Between the tables, tall bearded Hindu waiters in bright orange turbans carried trays of food. In the front of the room was a long wall mural depicting acts of the gods and goddesses of India. Below the mural stood a long stage. On it, squatting, were seventeen Indian musicians playing Kandyan music. Their faces were all grave and motionless, and the instruments were strange —some looked like washtub-sized mandolins. The music had a minor key lilt, a lively Oriental quality akin, in a way, to Grieg's "Anitra's Dance."

"This," said Kay, "is beautiful." Yes, he agreed. Beautiful and colonial. It looked like something out of Kipling: the stiff-backed British women and their mustached consorts eating with forks reversed, in silence; the native waiters bringing ruddy beef and Yorkshire pudding and kidney pie, all in silence except for the music.

They sat entranced. Fatigue and hunger were almost, not quite forgotten, in the magic of the Ashoka dining room. The food was placed before them, but the eating was automatic. The musicians, in tight gray tunics and white jodhpurs, plucked their instruments without appearing to move, or to hear.

Over dessert Lon asked Kay if she wanted to retire early. "I want to write a note to the Sullivans in Spring Lake," she said. "I owe one to Margie Murray too. How about you?" He grimaced. "I'm a poor letter writer," he said. He owed a note to Sonny, she reminded him. "Maybe," he said. "But who's to know whether he is in the sanitarium or home?" Kay thought he should write in any case.

"Ah," he said, "you're going to be my conscience too." His impulse, if he wrote to his son, would be to ask him why he had to ruin a honeymoon with liquor. The letter would berate rather than be solicitous. He could not write having-a-fine-time-wish-you-were-here when he knew that the boy was sick, hurt, warped or, in some emotional manner, crippled.

Nevertheless, before they went to their room, he sent a cable to Sonny. MISS YOU MUCH. BE HOME SOON. LOVE, MOTHER AND DAD. He studied it a moment, then crossed out the words MOTHER AND.

THE ELEVENTH DAY

THE breeze was cool and it billowed the filmy curtains on the big French windows. Lon came out of the shower naked and stood for a moment, feeling the cool touch on his skin. Kay was dressed. She telephoned the front desk for mail. The clerk said it was too early. There had been no word from Lucy, and Kay felt upset without wanting to discuss it. Lon was aware of the problem, but he did not comment because he had learned that, when Kay had a personal problem, nothing could unlock it, not even a sympathetic approach.

Her response in such situations was to shrug, study the floor and murmur: "It's nothing. Nothing, really." She was worried, and she was half inclined to phone home, but she dreaded the expense. Kate had promised to cable if there was any news. Maybe everything was fine. Maybe there was no news. Still, she heard all the inner alarm bells ringing. Lucy, until this marriage, had been her world. She was doubly precious because she was a hysteric; she needed her mother all the time.

Lucy's world, Kay had explained to Lon, was a simple place in which all things were either very good or very bad. A cross word was very bad. A kiss was very good. All schoolteachers were bad because they smiled and said: "You can do better." Or "Stop daydreaming and pay attention." Or "Your work is sloppy." In fact, the whole world of big people was bad because they had the power to tell her to stop talking, to leave the room, to fetch a newspaper, to go to the store, to stop singing, to go to bed.

She had a hypersensitivity which was tuned to adversity. Even when she watched television, she felt that something terrible would happen to the "nice lady" or the "nice man." Kay said that, on the average, Lucy wept at least three times a day for a variety of reasons, ranging from finding that her pencil had no eraser to the discovery that she had left her arithmetic book in her school desk.

To a stranger, the child looked short, chubby and belligerent. Sometimes she kept her lower lip thrust out for long periods of time, just to show the world that she hated it as much as it hated her. And yet, a considerate word, a kind gesture, a casual kiss melted her at once and she would cling to the person desperately and defiantly—hugging, holding, kissing and sometimes, if she truly liked the person, weeping.

"You'll catch cold," Kay said. Lon said that the cool breeze felt good, like a hundred fingertips. "What were you thinking of?" he asked. "Nothing," she said. "Oh, come now." "Okay, I was thinking of you." "What about me?" "What a funny figure you have." He turned from the window. "I can remember times when you didn't laugh."

"I'm not talking about that," Kay said. She gave a snort of repressed laughter. "I must be comical," he said, studying himself in the vanity mirror. "Not comical," she said. "You have a build like a hammered-down bull. Look at your legs. Like clubs. The chest belongs to a taller man. The arms are too short and too thick. Too much hair. Sort of Neanderthal type."

"Any more dimensions?" There was a knock on the door and, simultaneously, it opened. Two Hindu waiters came in bowing and smiling, carrying breakfast trays and saying "Good morning, sir"; "Good morning, madam." Lon fled to the bathroom. Kay rocked with laughter as the waiters impassively laid out the food on the coffee table.

Lon came out of the bathroom in a robe. He was cinching the knot and he looked angry. "Listen," he said. "Knock. Then wait. I'll open the door. Don't walk in here like that." The waiters managed to look astonished and contrite at the same time. "Yes, sir," they said. "We did knock." "But you didn't wait," he said. "Don't come in here unless we open the door. Understand? And pass the word around."

Kay tried to pour the coffee when the men had left, and kept breaking down. "All right, Tarzan," she said. "Sit." Lon sat, but his mood was grouchy. He picked up the morning newspaper and read the headlines and flipped the pages, while dipping edges of toast into the yolks of fried eggs. "It isn't funny," he said, and she began to laugh all over again. Tears stood in her eyes and her face contorted, as though in pain. "It could have been you," he said sternly.

Kay wiped her eyes. "I know it," she said. "They have some sort of free-and-easy system here. Last night when you were shaving, I ordered a pot of tea and I was standing here in my slip when the knock came. I got the robe on so quickly that I didn't know whether it was inside out or not. It took two waiters to bring one pot of tea and they trouped in without waiting for an answer."

He looked at his watch. "We have to hurry if we're going to meet the Cointreaux and get to Agra."

There was a repellent magnetism to misery compounded, Lon thought. Human beings could fall to a state of squalor and sickness and filth beyond which there was no further descent. It shocked the mind and intrigued the eyes. Along the macadam road between New Delhi and Agra the trees were few. Under them, camels rocked and elephants swayed as merchants carried their produce to market. The villages had long stretches of road emptiness between them, flanked by tilled fields and local ghats, where the dead were burned in open amphitheaters and left to cool for the vultures. The villages consisted of a well, sometimes open, sometimes pumped by a camel harnessed to a circular yoke, surrounded by small huts and big odors. Old men in loose white diapers walked back and forth before the huts, their heads bent forward, their mahogany hands clasped behind their backs. Little girls in dirty saris, wearing tiny bits of gold in pierced nostrils, carried sick babies on their hips. Many of the infants had lumps under the skin of their faces and dull tearless eyes.

"This," said Kay, "is the worst." Joga, sitting up front resplendent in his orange turban, listened. "It is not so bad, I tell you. In some places, it is bad, you understand. Really bad." The taxi bounded on and on, moving southward over a thin dark scar on a big brown plain. It moved in and out of villages so fast that Cointreaux, who sat in front with his motion-picture camera poised, seldom had a chance to shoot a few feet. "I never thought the Taj Mahal was so far away," Peg said.

"From what?" Lon asked. Peg shrugged. "From New Delhi, I guess." Lon lit a cigarette and found he was puffing on a filter. He made a face and threw the cigarette out the window. "What's worse than this, Joga?" he asked. Joga always had a broad smile. "Many places," he said. "In some, the rivers dry and there are no crops, you understand. The people are hungry and the government cannot feed them. Indians sometimes die in the streets, thousands in a single day. No one can help and no one feels very bad about it. In the poor places, you can tell by the vultures which of the bodies are dead, you know."

"Okay," Cointreaux said. "You made your point, kid." The taxi passed through a large town and there were many Hindus walking beside hundreds of bicycles. Among them cattle moved freely, threading through the people and the vehicles. For a time, the taxi crept and it was almost inundated by people, all wearing

the same impassive, staring expressions. There was no rancor, no
friendliness. In the doorways, women crouched on their haunches
in semicircles, the hems of their dirty saris stretched out so that
they looked like filthy fans. Holy men, with orange paint dotting
their foreheads and their noses, held their hands out begging alms
from those who had nothing to give.

"How much further?" Kay asked. Joga said a few miles. He
asked if they would like to refresh themselves at a little place
which had tea and a water closet. They stopped. It was a tourist
place with a big veranda and Hindu pitchmen hurrying to the
table to display feats of magic which could be purchased for a
few rupees. There were imitation mother-of-pearl replicas of the
Taj Mahal at a souvenir stand and photos of Mohandas Gandhi.

Lon, like the others, had seen so many photos and newsreels
of the Taj that he referred to it as a "big lacy valentine." Kay
and Peg would have none of that; they refused to listen to him.
However, when they walked through the brownstone and marble
entrance to the mausoleum, it was Lon who sighed as he took a
long look through all the arches to the snowy onion and the four
stalks of marble asparagus.

"I don't believe it," he said. Kay put a hand on his. "Don't
speak," she said. "Just look." Larry shook his head in disbelief.
"It reminds me of a barber friend of mine who got up enough
money to go to Rome. He walked inside St. Peter's, took one look
and said: 'Jesus Christ!' He didn't mean anything wrong."

A guide took them along the walk beside the reflecting pools
to the Taj itself. At the bottom of the steps, they tied the required
cloth slippers over their shoes, and ascended the staircase to the
plaza. The guide said that the hieroglyphics around the main door
of the mausoleum were words from the sacred Koran, and were
set in onyx against the white marble background. The words increased in size around the perimeter of the huge arch so that, no
matter where the pilgrim stood, they appeared to be the same size.

The Taj Mahal is a place for thinking, rather than speaking, and as the four walked the marble plaza around the four sides, staring up at the slender minarets, and then going inside to see the octagonal room where the sarcophagus of the queen reposed, they listened to the monotonous knowledge of the guide, and formed thought exercises of their own.

Larry Cointreaux thought: The king must have been real nuts about this broad. It must have cost zillions. I love Peg—God knows —but I can't see myself building a headstone like this. Crazy. It must have taken fifteen or twenty years to put together. Ah, maybe labor was cheap. Maybe the king just told the army to build it. In those days, everybody had to do what the king said. It probably cost him nothing. Time, that's all. They had no radio or television, so they had time. So he built a Taj or two. My people, they made watches and booze. I wonder if the gems in these flowers are real? They make a border all around the inside of this joint and they look real. Probably phony. The visitors would be chipping them out with nail files if they were real. What did the guide say? The queen's body isn't in this coffin? She's down in the cellar? That's nice. I wonder where they put the king?

Kay thought: Devotion. Devotion. Devotion. What an enormous love the Shah Jahan had for his queen. Almost religious. A form of adoration. Everywhere I look, I keep thinking the word lovely. How beautiful, how dominating, a love can be. Why does it surprise me that love is deeper in strange lands than in my own country? Or why is it that I am surprised that love, three hundred years ago, could be this sentimental? The women of India practiced suttee until the British stopped them. When the husband died, and his body was on the flaming logs, the widow sat with the body and burned to death so that their ashes would mingle in flight to heaven. How beautiful; how awful. How is it that a man can be so deeply moved that he will spend a treasure and so many years of work to display his grief for his dead wife? Just look at this marble screen. Incredible. It must be three inches thick and it has been scalloped with thousands of holes so that it looks like starched lace standing around the whole interior. How many hands worked on this marble? For how many years? Suppose a mistake was made—and some must have been made. Did the king order another octagonal wall of marble so that the men would start drilling holes again?

Would Lon love me this much? I'm being vain again. But I'd like to know. If he went before I did, I'd build a Taj for him, if I had the money. Would he do it for me? I doubt it. It isn't lack of love. He just doesn't like ostentation. He can admire something like this, but he wouldn't build one. Come to think of it, I don't think he has ever kissed me in public. If only he weren't so damned serious about everything. What was it his mother said about him? "He couldn't wheel a garbage can to the curb without analyzing how it was made, how much it cost, and why the contents had to be thrown away." Something like that.

The guide says that the Shah Jahan also built the big red fort in Delhi. He built in many places. I guess this was his crowning achievement. He even diverted the river behind the tomb. His wife had fourteen children and died in childbirth. Male conscience? Could be, but it's sweeter to think of it as love. He cared deeply. Still, the guide says that the Shah did not want to be buried with his wife. He wanted a tomb built on the other side of the river. Why? Why not at her side? An act of unworthiness, perhaps? A deeper love than all others—or the shallow sentiment of the perpetual builder? No, it must have been an act of humility. He wanted his tomb to be smaller, and he expressed a desire for it to be behind this one, on the other side of the river. I can't read ego into a man like that. Devotion is the word.

Lon was thinking: The Shah must have been fascinated by mathematics. Everything is lined up exactly on a center line. There are six arches leading to this tomb and I can stand in the center of the one farthest away and see the exact center of the doorway of the Taj. The reflecting pools are lined up precisely with everything else; even the formal gardens and flowers can be measured down to the inch on one side or the other of center. The queen's tomb is on the center line too, so much so that if you stare over the middle of it you can look through the arch straight through all the gates.

Mathematicians are perfectionists. She must have been *some* woman. Or else the Shah hurt her in some way, some way that required a gigantic reparation. No, I'm wrong. Once the woman dies, reparations are out of order unless guilt disturbs the sleep. No, he was a man in love. He also happened to be a mathematician and a builder. So he combined his hobbies and his love and made this thing.

He certainly wanted it to endure. I don't think I've ever seen so much marble. The pharaohs made their pyramids of ugly rocks which cracked in the heat of day and the chill of night. This man made a delicate, precise home of love. Funny, in all the reading on this place, I don't recall any writer telling about that huge, onion-domed guest house and the temple on either side of the Taj. The guide says that the Shah built them so that old friends could come here and stay awhile, paying their respects to his dead love, and praying for her in the temple.

Even so, nothing turned out the way the Shah expected, except this building. One of the sons of his great love grew up to kick him off the throne and toss him into prison. He spent many years in the filth of a lonely cell. And though he pleaded not to be buried with his queen, that the Taj was meant for her alone, the son buried his father in here. The queen's sarcophagus was left in dead center, but the Shah's was set slightly off center, which made the king less important than his queen.

It's all vanity, anyway. Even the Indians do not believe that a body is worth anything. They leave it to the vultures, who must also live. The Taj Mahal is basically a tragic story. I can tell that Kay is touched and thinks it's all a beautiful love story. It's wonderful to see things through her eyes; I live all over again, just listening to her. I've been around too long. I see things, not necessarily as they are, but reduced in size. Nothing is as it seems. Once, the Empire State Building was the biggest object I knew. Then I flew over the Rocky Mountains and they looked like small wrinkled hills. Later, a mechanical object named Tiros flew around the world and was ordered by men to take a picture of its home: Cape Canaveral. The picture was transmitted back from space and there was all of Florida, a swollen finger, most of the east coast, the gulf ports, and, on the rounded horizon, Oklahoma and Illinois. All of it looked like an old sand pile at the beach.

I have lost the romantic values of what is big, what is beautiful. They're gone. Once, my father was big. He died long ago and he was a little man with a rosary entwined between his fingers. Once, calla lilies on an Easter altar were beautiful. Then I learned that, on Easter, He came out of a sepulcher with wounds in His hands and feet and blood on His winding sheet and no one offered Him a flower; no one even offered a drink of water.

Kay is beautiful. Let me stand still with this thought forever. Kay . . . is . . . beautiful. Do not ever let me see anything more attractive, more intriguing, more important to my life. Maybe the Taj Mahal is the most gorgeous structure in the world, and perhaps, as they say, it is priceless, but I would rather study Kay looking at the Taj than look at the place. Once, a long time ago, I saw a rodeo through Sonny's eyes. Now why did I say a long time ago? It wasn't so far back. Fifteen years, maybe a little more. Before that time I didn't like cowboys. Since then I've felt no interest.

Now I see new places through new blue eyes. Still, I must admit that, even without Kay, this place is worth the long ride. It would have been better if I had not known what happened to the king. And by the way, how does the government of India feel about having both bodies in the cellar of this place? How does it justify its lack of sentiment? The Shah has been dead about three hundred years, but his mausoleum attracts millions of dollars from tourists. It's an almost unbeatable attraction, and yet the government doesn't even follow the wishes of the Shah Jahan. He wanted his queen upstairs in the main room and he would have liked his bones to repose across the river.

Peg Cointreaux thought: My feet hurt. These people are like a bunch of goddamn tourists, walking, walking, walking. If they're not walking, they're on their asses, riding. This Michaels may be a good writer, but he has a gift for making me look stupid. All I have to do is point at something and say "What's that?" and his fangs start dripping. It's all right to be clever, but it's better to be happy. I'm going to tell Larry I need some shoes. Maybe if I tried eight-and-a-half my feet could breathe a little. Being with the Michaelses is like doing a hitch in the army. I must admit that this Taj is adorable. I'll send some cards back to Larry's people in Switzerland and one to Elsa. Who knows? If I think of something bright to write, it may make the column. But what the hell can I write that's bright? Send a picture of the Taj Mahal and say: "How do you like our new can?" I wonder what's up in those minarets?

I wish I knew what Larry sees in these people. She's cute, but he's one of those pains. Larry thinks he'll get more out of the trip hanging around the Michaelses. My feeling is that Larry has a beady eye on Kay. I know my guy. He never gives up. He gave up on me, but that's different. He's now in the young woman stage. He thinks a new body will cure what's wrong with him. There isn't anything wrong with him, really. One of these days he's going to sneak off with some young thing and come home sick.

Oh God, haven't we seen enough of this place? Even the guide looks tired. But that Michaels—the son of a bitch will milk this place for every bit of information. The worst part of it is he'll

remember it. We'll be getting it at dinner from here to Honolulu.
If they ever split his head open, an encyclopedia will fall out.

Kay had a habit of handing things to Lon in silence. He was
in bed, ready to sleep. She pushed a sheaf of papers over. "What?"
he said. She smiled. "My diary, of course." He was about to say,
"I'll read it tomorrow," but didn't. She probably had some pride
of authorship or at least would be hurt if he refused. So he propped
his head on one hand and read:

*Airport: Defleaing before deplaning—ugh. Foolish to be fright-
ened. But the mass of people milling around and the lack of personal cleanliness. The roadsides are used as privies. But New Delhi
is truly beautiful—pink and white. Draped saris in fantastically
beautiful hues highlighted by the most beautiful hair I have ever
seen. The ladies have black silken hair—straight—worn in buns
or twists—without the look of hair pomades—as though brushed
not 100 times a day but 500.*

*The people surprise me. The people turned out to be most
pleasant, and sang as they talked. Maybe it's a musical lilt in the
speech. But outside the city, poverty makes the people desperate.
One old lady ran after our car begging for just a rupee. She must
have been 90; at least she looked 90. A track star in filthy feet.*

*First afternoon stopped at La Bohème. Disappointment. It tries
to be American. I like the unusual, but this isn't it. However, like
a newly married couple, we ordered the Honeymoon Special.
Pleased me. Don't think my husband likes to do as others do. A
condescension? I don't either, normally. We both grew up "too old
for our years." But now and then, especially in the foolishly romantic things, it is pleasing to conform. I wish we could capture some
of the time we didn't have together. Lon has much more sentimentality than his wooden face would indicate.*

First evening: Dining room at Ashoka. Could have stayed all night, listening to the almost mystical music. Talked of trying to buy l.p. records of this music.

Taj Mahal: Belgian lace. So very beautiful. So poignant. It lays a heavy hand on the throat. Purple azaleas—hmmmmmmm. Amazed by the thought put into everything there. The Koran, placement of words. Nothing detracts from anything else. Mostly it is love, as though in Braille. (He'll make fun of this.)

More love. He must bedeck me. When we left the Taj Mahal, the guide showed us a government-licensed jewelry shop. No tourist trap. At this place, Lon asked the manager to show him a tray of amethysts—my birthstone. He chose the finest, deepest-colored one and asked to have it set into a ring at once. Manager protested. Lon insisted. Had to have finger measured; manager had to hunt white-gold mounting. Lon said it must match my earrings.

Later: I die at sight of the fabrics in this country. Love to sew. Always did. But am not nearly a professional seamstress. Could stay here and buy and buy and buy. Sewing is a joy to me—not a chore. Had to do it for Lucy; like making dresses for doll. Like to make her look lovely. There is much serenity to be courted in sewing. Much satisfaction when something comes out as visualized. In India, I can stop in a yard-goods store and stare as the clerk serves small cups of mocha and unwinds great bolts of gossamer material in colors like orange ice, sky blue, bottle green, pale canary, antique white, gun-metal gray—I wish I had the nerve to buy and take a chance on making some dresses for myself.

"It's good," Lon said, handing the sheets back to his wife. She said he was trying to be kind. "No," he said. "I'm not. I'm always surprised at the things that impress a woman, things that escape the notice of a man. Anyway, this man."

THE TWELFTH DAY

THE big square room was quiet, except
for the pecking sound of the typewriter. Kay was in bed reading
a Pan American guidebook. She wore an ice-blue nightgown so
thin that Lon said it would keep her neither warm nor concealed,
and she said that that was the general idea. He sipped tea as he
wrote, concentrating not so much on individual words as on complete thoughts. The orange lamp shade made his hair look whiter
and his skin darker.

"Slant your eyes," Kay said, "and you'll look like a Chinese."
"A little more tea," he said, "and they'll slant by themselves." The
time was only ten. They wanted to get to bed early because Flight
Two was scheduled for 6:20 A.M. heading for Bangkok, Thailand.
The desk clerk had told them that they would have to be at the
airport no later than 5:20, and a call was in to get them up at 4:30.

Lon was a good sleeper, but Kay was a better one. She hated
to go to sleep; she hated to get up. Both, on arising, were wan-
derers—that is, they shuffled past each other on their appointed
rounds without much knowledge or consciousness of what they
were doing or where they were going. Sometimes, both headed
for the bath at the same time, cigarette smoke curling up into
blinking eyes, and he would stand aside and say: "Please. Be my
guest."

He wrote quickly and superficially:

A very dull day. Wrote part of a magazine article in the morning. Poor stuff. It sounds like an old movie travelogue: "As we say farewell to the friendly natives . . ." Will not submit it. This trip has, so far, taught a valuable lesson in writing. It isn't easy to depict faraway places without falling into the old clichés. Perhaps the material reads badly because I don't like to read travel material. There is a mandatory pedanticism in what the literary traveler has to write about natives, customs, credos, flora and fauna. He spends a few days in each country and is at once an expert on local politics, economics, theology and, to cap it neatly, can solve all problems in six or seven paragraphs. I do not pretend to understand India, nor its problems. It is impossible to write about that which you do not understand.

I look at this country and I think of beauty and sickness in one body. All the eyes I see are onyx pools of sorrow. No one appears to be happy, even Joga when he is laughing. He told us today that, under the laws of his sect—the Sikhs—he is not permitted to date a girl, or take one to a dance, or even to entertain romantic thoughts about one.

He must wait until, in his village, the mother and father of an eligible girl call upon his parents and ask them to produce their sons. When that time comes, Joga will be called home with his brother, and they will be "shown" in their home to the parents of the girl. If all goes well, one will be selected. He will offer no objection to the marriage, even though he may recall the particular girl from childhood days, and not like her. Obedience to parents is everything. I asked him if he would be permitted to court the young lady and he said no.

The question amused him. He flashed his big white teeth and said, "There is time to become acquainted after marriage, you see. That is what a wedding trip is for." If he married without parental

*selection, or if he declined the girl his parents wished him to marry,
his mother and father would be permanently mocked by the people
of their village. Face and caste would be lost and Joga would be
publicly declared dead by his parents and would be ineligible to
inherit part of their farm or their possessions.*

*Kay asked how many unwed mothers there are in India. Joga
Singh said he never heard of one. Perhaps the price of morality is
insufferable filial devotion. All of this conversation took place en
route to the Alankar Shop on Connaught Street. There I saw some
of the dress material that Kay wrote about in her diary yesterday.
This is, I fear, another subject about which I must confess ignorance. The store had fixed stools before long counters. Clerks served
the usual Turkish coffee as Kay looked at the many materials, always with her index finger tapping her lips. She said that rare silks
could be bought at $7 a yard, and that the width was 45 inches
instead of the usual 36. She bought some black sheer material
with silver threads fashioned into ornate designs. There were other
purchases, but I paid little attention, although she kept sliding a
hand under the cloth and asking if I liked it.*

*I felt a deeper interest in driving a few miles to Delhi, or Old
Delhi, as some call it. The skies darkened momentarily as we
started and the rain came in large slanting veils, splattering noisily
on windshield and roof. Lightning flashed across the skies and lit
up coveys of cyclists, all pedaling manfully with heads down, all
close to the edge of the road.*

*Two baboons sat on a low tree branch, staring at the honking
traffic, watching with interest man's progress. Fat green parrots
picked dung from the road, taking wing barely in time to escape
the automobile bumpers. The storm dissipated quickly and the sun
was sharp and colorful on the pools of water. An elephant plodded
behind a slow truck, its trunk tucked under the chin to escape the
gasoline fumes.*

Delhi is old. It is encrusted with moldy antiquity. Many Moslem women wear white from head to toe, with squares of glass in the veil through which the wearer looks. In the center of the city is the largest mosque in the East, an edifice of many stone steps, like a huge layer cake a thousand feet in diameter. Around the mosque, at street level, are open shops by the hundreds, stretching around the temple like a dark necklace of pots and pans, shoe stalls, fly-flecked meat, old bicycles, clothing, all accompanied by a stench which seems to assail the nostrils of foreigners only.

We must get up very early to make the flight to Bangkok, so I am going to cut this entry short. There are some things which should go into the diary because they may be forgotten. Kay has a great capacity for commiseration. This is common to women, I suppose, but she is genuinely (and permanently) touched at the sight of people or animals who are hurt. She also has a great capacity for joy. When I placed the amethyst ring on her finger, she jumped straight up and down, clapping her hands like a little girl. Somewhere along the line—I forget the city—I bought her a small nose-gay and she held it and her blue eyes misted over and she smiled and squeezed my arm.

She is so good for me that I find myself being repetitious. She doesn't realize it, but in the short week and a half she has massaged a lot of the roughness from me. It is as though we have been married forever. No. Not quite. It is as though I cannot remember back to what it was like before I married her. She wanted to see the ghat in Old Delhi where Gandhi was cremated and, ironically, she seemed to know little about the man. She remembered the phrase "passive resistance" as belonging to the spectacled lawyer, but other than this, and the fact that he lived with a Christlike humility, she knew nothing.

The place is called Rajghat and it is a squarish amphitheater with a sloping walk leading up to the inside. There, Hindu men sat on slabs of stone, chipping. There were scores of them, some holding huge stones upright as others chipped letters or designs onto them.

I asked Joga about it. "Gandhi," he said, "asked that no memorial be made for him. The government has decided to make this place a library for all his works and for a history of his particular time."

The ghat itself is a smooth slab of concrete, with wreaths of orange flowers placed on it each day. As Kay listened, I tried to imagine the vultures standing on the perimeter of the wall—like dignified undertakers in swallow-tail coats. Normally, people like to stand at a place like this to feel close to the person it repre-sents. I cannot achieve this. I could not achieve it at the grave of my father, whom I cherished. The closest I came to this feeling was at Gettysburg, where, by squinting my eyes, I could see the 6th Infantry of North Carolina racing up the slope, vaulting the little farm walls, and being cut to ribbons. For a moment, I could see the young faces, exultant and breathless, and then just breath-less.

The packing is complete except for a few items, like this portable typewriter, and some linen which cannot be laundered and returned quickly enough to suit the restless tourists. Of one thing I am sure: the more I dwell upon the fact that I must arise at 4:30 A.M. the less I will sleep.

THE THIRTEENTH DAY

THERE were four big valises and a brief-case. They were spread across the arms of four chairs, open. Kay was unpacking again with hands now practiced and swift. Dresses, suits of clothes went onto hangers at once. Some were shaken out; others went into the bathroom and hung in clouds of steam; still others were tossed on the floor with soiled linen and socks.

"Which is your chest of drawers?" she said. Lon sat on a small stairway, leading up from the main part of the room to a curtained area which held two beds. He said it looked like an opium den. The lower part of the room had a big window, looking out on the Chao Phrya River, a broad muddy stream laden with fast junks and slow freighters and many craft which looked like floating quonset huts but which, in reality, were houseboats.

"Doesn't make any difference," he said. "Want some help?" She declined. "I do better when you stay out of it." When the laundry was ready, Lon pressed the button for a houseboy. "I wonder," she said, "why Peg and Larry aren't speaking?"

"Aren't they?" he asked, surprised. She straightened up and her shoulders dropped a little in despair. "Don't men ever notice any-thing?" she said. "They sat directly across from us on the whole flight. There wasn't a word."

"I spoke to them," Lon said. He was bewildered. "They seemed all right." "Sure," she said. "They spoke to you. They may even

173

have said something to each other when you were standing there."
He shrugged. "I was pointing out something the steward told me,"
he said. "We were at thirty-eight thousand feet and he said it was
rare to be able to see the Himalayas. Remember? They looked like
clouds hundreds of miles north."

"Not a word," Kay said. "They didn't even speak to each other
on the way to the airport."

There was a knock. Lon got up off the little stairway and
opened the door. Two boys stood outside; they were kicking their
shoes off. Both were grinning. Both had gold teeth in front.

"Hello," said one. "Me Dong. This one Wong. You understand?" Lon nodded. "Yes," he said gravely. "You Dong. He
Wong." He pointed at each one in turn. Kay left the room and
hurried up the steps. "Me Mister Michaels," he said pointing at
his chest. "She number one woman. Okay?" Both boys grinned
even more broadly. "We not Thai. We Chinese."

"Good," Lon said, with no interest. He picked up the laundry.
"Wash," he said, handing it over. "Press," he said, handing suits
and dresses. Dong stopped smiling. "No dry crean?" Lon shook
his head. "No dry crean," he said. "You Chinese? You talk like
Japanese." This struck both boys as very funny. They laughed
heartily.

"Where you come from," Lon said, "people say dry crean?"
Dong was still laughing. "You know Hainan?" he asked. "Yes.
It's an island somewhere in the South China Sea." The boys
nodded as they bunched the laundry. "Hainan," they said, pointing
to themselves. Lon pointed to a door directly across the hall. "You
knock," he said, still speaking pidgin English. "More laundry."
They nodded happily and Lon closed the door.

At the top of the little stairs, Kay came out from behind the
curtain chuckling. "You're too much," she said. "No savvy melican
talk?" he asked. He looked out the window. Below was a tea garden
with neat tables, a swimming pool, and the river with its Siamese
boats. "The Oriental Hotel is straight out of Somerset Maugham,"

he said. "Not Kipling. Maugham." Some naked little Siamese boys were running down the edge of the muddy river and he watched them jump in.

Kay walked down the stairs, smiling and dabbing at her eyes. "Which is proper?" she said. "Thailand or Siam?" "Thailand," he said. "Pronounced without an h. But it is still Siam to the romantics. Most melicans think of Rogers and Hammerstein, *The King and I,* temple bells and Buddhist priests. Others, I suppose, think of Siamese cats."

He put his arm around Kay and they stood looking out at the river. "There is a tourist bureau in the lobby," he said. "An old Siamese with big flat feet runs it. He says he'll take us around for about seven dollars our money." "Apiece?" "Apiece." "Is there much to see?" she said.

"I'm surprised at you," Lon said. "You read the guidebook." "The temples," she said. "And some kind of boxing with the feet." "No," he said. "There is more to Thailand than that. Bangkok itself should turn out to be a gold mine of interest. The half of the city behind us is modern. All the way to the airport. But this half, according to the guide, is built on klongs. I think that's the word, klongs. Anyway, klongs are canals and this half of Bangkok lives in houseboats on the klongs or in houses on stilts on the edge of the klongs."

"Let's rent a boat," she said. He said the guide promised to take them out on the klongs to see something called the Floating Market, but the starting time would be seven A.M. "Let's do it," she said. moving closer. "Even if it kills us to get out of bed."

The door opened behind them. Without turning from the window, Lon said: "Dong, you must learn to knock." There was no reply. Both turned slowly. In the doorway, leaning against the jamb, was Larry. His eyes and mouth were wide open with fright. His hand was pressed against the left side of his neck. Blood seeped between his fingers and ran down over his shirt collar. He stared at the Michaelses without expression.

"Quick," he muttered. "Call a doctor." Kay recoiled, knuckling a fist and sticking it between her teeth; she seemed to be trying to back out the window. Lon stood stupefied, then he said: "Jesus! What the hell happened?" Larry, a big man, began to sag against the side of the door. "Please," he said softly. Lon moved. He ran to a telephone, jiggled the hook, but there was no response. "Oh, come on!" he shouted. "Come on!" Kay tried to help Cointreaux to a chair. When he removed his left hand from his neck, she saw a huge open wound, with raw flesh hanging over it and below it in strings.

She felt faint. She was not the kind of woman who would fail in an emergency, but the sight of lacerated flesh and the spreading stain of dark blood on the collar of the shirt made her dizzy; the room seemed to darken. She fought the feeling and got Cointreaux into an armchair and, as Lon kept jiggling the telephone, she pressed a hand over her mouth and climbed the little steps up to the bathroom.

Lon was sick. His spirits sagged. As far as he was concerned, the honeymoon had come to a dead stop on the opposite side of the world from home. The room seemed to be full of strange faces, coming and going. The manager, a short man of impeccable manners, had been one of them. "It is not easy to say this," he said, "but under the circumstances we should like to have you leave as soon as possible."

Kay sat on a small leather sofa next to him, watching the people and the excitement and telling herself that this was just one more of those bad dreams which often terrified her sleep. Wakefulness would come soon and they would be on a plane, or in a hotel somewhere, and Lon would take her in his arms and hold her close and tell her that she had been mumbling in her sleep. None of this could be real.

"Does anyone know how Larry is doing?" Kay asked. The question was directed to Lon, but intended for the ears of the police who kept moving from their room across the hall to the room where Peg sat. "He may need blood," Lon said. "May I offer a transfusion?" He pointed to his inner elbow. A policeman standing near the window motioned for him to remain seated. Behind him, the final struggle of the sun to remain alight tinged the sky with lavenders and greens and blues.

After a while, the three main policemen—as least they seemed to have more authority than the other people—finished questioning Peg Cointreaux and came back into the room and ordered everyone else out. Then they closed the door. A short one, with slick hair, made a sign to the one against the window to leave.

He drew up a chair for a big stout man with puffy Oriental eyelids, then motioned to the other man, obviously a stenographer with book and pen, to sit on the far side of the coffee table. Then the short man found a place on the big sofa. Kay moved away from him toward her husband.

"Now," the short one said in precise English, "we will begin." He pointed at the stout, impassive man, and mentioned a name. Lon inclined his head. "He is our superintendent," the short one said, "and he understands English very well, but speaks it weakly. Therefore, I will interpret for both sides. Now this one with the book understands and speaks English, and will take a statement."

"We know nothing," said Lon, half angrily, "except that we met these people on our wedding trip. Period. No new paragraph."

The stout man said something under his breath to the stenographer, who reached into his pocket and presented a sheaf of papers. The superintendent riffled through them, pointing out various points to the short man. They were still whispering when Lon said: "Is it against the law here to ask if Mr. Cointreaux is going to live?"

The short one smiled. "He will live," he said. "Does this anger you, Mr. Michaels?" Lon started to get to his feet, and sat down.

"Oh," he said wearily, "what the hell is the use?" The stout one waved his hand for Lon to remain seated. For the first time, he spoke in English. "Sit," he said. "We ask questions. You—you—"

"—reply the truth," the short one said. The big one nodded. The questions were prosaic at first, mostly involving names, passports, police records if any, knowledge of the Cointreaux family, where met, under what circumstances, social contacts with the injured man, disputes if any, any marital jealousies, and so forth.

"Now," the short man said, "Mr. Cointreaux was taken to the clinic. He has lost much blood, but he will be, as you Americans say, okay. A few days' rest, all right. He made a short statement on operating table during sewing of neck. He says—" from time to time, he referred to the sheaf of papers before him—"that he cut himself."

Kay looked at Lon. Lon looked at Kay. Surprise was on both their faces. "He was shaving to go out this evening with you and his wife and he cut himself. You believe this?" Lon shrugged. "I have no reason to doubt the man's word," he said. "If he cut himself, he cut himself."

"Yes," the interrogator said. "Yes. But it is not easy to scoop out neck over here while shaving." He pointed to the far left side of his neck. "Mr. Cointreaux is right-handed. Maybe, if you are right-handed, you will show my inspector how you shave far left side of neck where no hairs grow?" Michaels made an involuntary motion to show how it could be done, and saw at once that it was ridiculous.

"Exactly," the fat one said. He held up an index finger. "Also difficult to cut deep as this finger and make round hole." Kay sat up. "He didn't cut himself?" she asked. "Then what happened?" The fat one nodded like a wise old Buddha. "Shot," he said. "Gun." Lon took a long breath, and slapped a hand against his waistband.

"Lose something?" the short one said. Kay saw the motion, and her fright returned. She said nothing. "No," Lon said. "I haven't lost anything." The stout one said something in Siamese. The short one said to Lon: "How much do you like Mrs. Cointreaux? You get along well together?"

The belligerence was back quickly. "If you mean what I think you mean," Lon said, "I love my wife. We were married about two weeks ago." He spoke so swiftly and angrily that the stenographer had trouble with the words. "If we had been married forty years, I would still not like Mrs. Cointreaux more than I like you right now."

"Does she like you deeply?" the short one asked. "No," Lon said. "I'm sure of it. She likes her husband. Deeply. Are you saying that I fired a shot at Cointreaux because of his wife?" The stout one spoke again. "We say nothing. You say."

"Now you listen to me," Kay said. "Whatever happened, my husband had nothing to do with it. If Mr. Cointreaux cut himself, or if he shot himself, or if someone else did it to him—my husband was with me every minute since we got here." The short one studied the notes. "You started to unpack?" Yes, she said, she had. "Before you unpack, you go to water closet maybe?" "Maybe," she said. "Husband go across hall, say he be back in a minute?" Kay thought. That was exactly what had happened. She had gone to the bathroom immediately after the bellboys dropped the valises in the room. Lon had gone across the hall to set up something for the evening—dinner or something. When she came out of the bathroom, he was back. She had asked him where they were going this evening and he had seemed vague. As though it had not been settled.

A moment ago, she had seen him slap at his waistband, the spot where he kept his tiny revolver pinned. It was obvious, even as she watched, that the gun was not there. She swallowed, and hoped she wasn't hanging him. "Yes," she said. "He went across the hall for a minute." Lon stared at her in frowning disapproval.

"Ah," said the little one. He turned to Lon again.

Lon leaned forward, elbows on knees, hands clasping and un-clasping. "I don't know," he said. "He seemed moody. Like a man who is interrupted in a thought. I think I said: 'What about to-night? What are we going to do?' And he said something like: 'Tonight? Oh, I don't care. Let's find a place where we can get some American food.' "

The little man asked what Mrs. Cointreaux was doing. Lon said he wasn't sure. "She was there," he said. "I'm sure of it. But I didn't particularly notice. She may have been unpacking."

"Tell me," said the short one, "did you shoot Mr. Cointreaux?" Lon got to his feet. The fat man also jumped up. "I've had enough of this," Lon said. "I'm sure that my country has an ambassador or a consulate here. I'd like to make a phone call." The fat man was not smiling. He was standing directly in front of Lon. "You will sit," he said. Lon thought about it, looked back at Kay, and sat.

"I did not shoot Cointreaux," he said to the stenographer slowly. "I did not—repeat, did not—shoot the man and I do not believe anybody did. He has a bad cut on his neck. He will live. If he says he did it while shaving, that's good enough for me. If it was done any other way, I know nothing about it. If I did it, why would he come in here and ask for help?"

The short one scratched his head. "That is your story. That is your wife's story. Cointreaux—" he again studied the papers— "says that he phoned the front desk of the hotel and asked for a doctor after he cut himself." Kay cut in. "Ask the telephone operator downstairs. She took the call from my husband." "Have asked," the fat one said. "No record of house call." "May I— may we talk to Mrs. Cointreaux?" Lon asked. The fat one shook his head no.

"You tell truth all the time?" he said. Lon shrugged. "I can't think of any reason for lying. I've done nothing wrong." The fat one dipped into his jacket pocket and came up with a grayish object between his fingers. "What is this, Mr. Michaels?" Lon reached for it, but the detective did not hand it over. He merely held it closer. "I don't know," Lon said. "It looks like a small-caliber bullet." The small one clapped his hands together. "Good. Very good," he said. "It is a twenty-two. From lady's gun. Who has lady's gun in your party?"

Lon shrugged. "Come now," he said. "You're not playing a little cat-and-mouse with me, are you?" The word play appeared to escape the big man. He looked at his assistant and repeated it. "No, no," the little one said. "We do not play. You play. What do you know about Cointreaux argument in New Delhi hotel?"

"Nothing," Kay said. "There was no trouble in our presence. On the plane this morning, I thought they did not speak to each other."

"As," the fat one said, "sometimes in marriage." "As sometimes in marriage," Kay said. The short one jerked his head toward Lon. "You have a permit for a gun?" Lon shook his head no. "In the United States," the man said, pursuing the same point, "a man must have one?" "Oh, sure." The little one held out his hand. "Then may I see your permit and your gun, please?"

"I have already told you—" Lon said. He glanced at Kay, who was pleading with her eyes. "I had a small twenty-two-caliber gun, yes. I never used it. In fact, I bought it for this trip." "Why?" the fat one asked. Lon smiled. "A tourist can be robbed in strange countries. It seemed like a good idea."

"It also seemed like a good idea to deny gun when you feel trousers?" the fat one asked. Lon nodded. "At the time, yes. I'm sorry, gentlemen." He folded the waistband of his trousers outward. "I usually keep it here. As you can see, the safety pin is still there. It was a small gun. This small. Now it is lost."

"Oh, no," the short one said. "It is not lost." He pulled a gun out of his jacket. "Can you identify this?" Lon gasped. So did

Kay. "Yes," Lon admitted. "This is mine. Where did you find it?"
The stenographer spoke for the first time. "Houseboy found it
in laundry." Kay said: "Whose laundry?" The stenographer nodded toward the door. "Other people," he said. The short man
waved him into silence.

"We have questioned Mrs. Cointreaux at some length," he said.
"We feel that we understand the truth. It is painful to everyone
when the truth is ignored. However," again he riffled through
the pages, "I will give you an idea of the story of the wife. You
will please correct if you hear an incorrectness." He looked up.
The Michaelses nodded.

"In India," he said, in the halting manner of a person who is
reading and translating at the same time, "Mrs. Cointreaux looked
for her husband, found him in shop at a hotel spelled A-s-h-o-k-a."
"Ashoka," Kay said. The short one kept on reading, or translating,
and the fat one was now leaning so that he too could read.

"He was busy with young woman clerk. Mrs. Cointreaux became angry. Mr. Cointreaux said she was spy. Looking all the time
for wrong. Both had big argument. She said she find him many
times busy with women. Very tired of this. He said he was trying
to exchange rupees with clerk—" "No," the big man said, pointing. "Dollars." "—American dollars for rupees. Cointreaux said
Mrs. Cointreaux spoiled chance to make three hundred American
on black market deal.

"Next day he have headache. He give money. Mrs. Cointreaux
go shopping." Kay interrupted: "That was the second day in
New Delhi. We went on a tour of old Delhi. Mrs. Cointreaux
went shopping." The short man appeared to be annoyed at the
interruption. "She claim come back in hour and slip into room.
Find Mr. Cointreaux in bed with lady clerk."

Kay and Lon looked at each other unbelievingly and whispered
a long "Wha-a-a-t?" together.

"Big argument. Mrs. Cointreaux hit lady clerk in bed; Mr. Cointreaux hit Mrs. Cointreaux to make her stop. Wife ready to tell

hotel. Get lady clerk sack. Mr. Cointreaux beg her please to forgive him, never to do this thing again.

"Mrs. Cointreaux do much weeping. She say all right. Before they leave on plane, she hurry into your room to ask Mrs. Michaels for something personal for women. Mr. Michaels in bathroom. Mrs. Michaels look in packed bags. Mrs. Cointreaux see small gun pinned to pants. She take it. Hide it."

Lon began to show shock. "I never missed the thing," he said. "How did she know I had a gun? I never told her." The fat man nodded at Kay. "She told Mrs. Cointreaux much worry about gun husband carry in trouser." Kay buried her face in her hands. "Oh God," she moaned, "what a dope. What a big dope."

"We knew," the little man said, "before we spoke to you that it was your gun. But Mrs. Cointreaux told us she aimed at husband and fired." Lon made a deprecating gesture. "I'm the dope," he said. "I should not be carrying a gun in the first place. I have my reasons, but I lied about that too. It's a personal matter. Is it against the law to carry a gun in Thailand?" The fat man said no.

"Then I am not in trouble?" "You are not. Better to speak truth first time." "You have my apology. I'm sorry. I feel sorry for the Cointreaux too." "I don't feel sorry for him," Kay said. "She should have killed him." The stout man smiled widely. "Man make big trouble," he said. Then slowly: "Pre-dict-able trouble. Women make no pre-dict-able."

"Mrs. Cointreaux is under arrest?" Lon asked. The short man said no. "Mr. Cointreaux insists it is shaving accident. So all right. We have statement from Mrs. Cointreaux. We also have bullet from wall in next room. We also have gun in Cointreaux laundry. But inspector says maybe it is shaving trouble. Why? Because it makes big trouble for police here, for courts, costs money, easier to wait one week, put both Cointreaux on airplane to somewhere else."

"I heard no shot," Lon said. Kay nodded. The fat one said:

"No shot. No gun. Just shaving cut in neck." "You mean I don't get my little gun back?" All three nodded. Lon was about to protest when Kay put her hand on his arm. "He didn't want it back, really. We had arguments over it." This struck the short man as very funny. "No arguments on honeymoon," he said. "Bad sign."

The fat one stood. "Talk to manager to permit you stay." "Oh, no," Lon said loudly. "We're getting out on the first plane. Glad to oblige." "We are not," Kay said. "I'm not going to have other people's troubles wreck my honeymoon. I'm going to see Bangkok and I'm going to see it with you." "You are?" he said.

"Mrs. Cointreaux wants room in hospital near husband," the stenographer said. "Maybe superintendent make necessary talk." Lon stood. He looked like a man in shock. "I never heard a shot," he said. "I never missed the damn gun either. Brother!" "Can we talk to Mrs. Cointreaux?" Kay asked. "I don't want her to think we've turned our backs —"

"Better to not," said the fat one. "Police helping her pack now. Take her to hospital. She cry for husband. First shoot. Then cry." His expression was Oriental disbelief. "Lucky she miss." "Almost," said his assistant.

- The roof garden at the Oriental Hotel had a glassed-in commanding view of Bangkok, and especially of the night river traffic. Lon and Kay sat at a window table, a small thing with a tiny shaded lamp. The menus were big, and in two languages. Lon's attention wandered between watching the dark river below and the busy atmosphere of the room, where waiters hurried from the kitchen with fresh salads in big bowls, and others swept trays of drinks from a dark bar and moved at a trot to the proper tables without spilling anything.

"Steaks," Lon said, pointing to the menu. "New York cut." Kay looked up and nodded, absent-mindedly. She wore a pale blue dress with a square neckline. The underlids of her eyes were puffed, as though she had been crying. The dress looked old-fashioned. The silk material kept sliding off one shoulder and she kept lifting it back into place. Lon seemed unconcerned about what had happened. He looked well-groomed and reasonably happy. It could have been the usual mask. She wasn't certain.

But Lon, despite his outward calm, knew that the honeymoon was close to an explosion. He did not want to precipitate it. The visit of the police had shaken him; the entrapment regarding his little gun had been accomplished so simply; the admission by Kay that she had told her fears about the gun to a practical stranger like Peg Cointreaux had shocked him; and the net effect of all this had rocked his confidence. He had thought of a honeymoon as glorious serenity; suppose Cointreaux had been killed? Suppose Peg had denied any knowledge of the gun—or, even better, suppose she had sneaked it back into his luggage with one shell missing?

"Eight o'clock," he said. "It is now eight A.M. in New York. Lucy is just leaving for school." Kay was sipping a sidecar. She looked up from it disinterestedly. "Then," she said, "we're about halfway around the world?"

"Almost," Lon said. "The halfway point is really on the next flight—somewhere over Indochina. We've been traveling east and we keep losing hours all the way to Tokyo. Between Japan and Hawaii we'll cross the international dateline and regain a whole day." "Interesting," Kay said, without understanding and without caring.

The conversation grew worse. It subsided to a please-pass-the-salt level. Kay ate well. Lon lost his appetite, and confined himself to pushing bits of steak back and forth across his dinner plate. After a while, he decided that the explosion was bound to occur, so he ordered drinks. Doubles. Kay surprised him by saying that she would like to order a few doubles, too.

When they left, Lon stopped at the bar and ordered a fifth of Scotch and a fifth of bourbon. The bartender had no bourbon, so Lon asked for Canadian whiskey instead. They rode down to their floor in silence and, when they got off, Lon yelled for Dong, who had a small alcove with a cot at the end of the hall. "You can ring the bell in the room," Kay said.

"I feel like yelling," he said. It was Wong, not Dong, who answered the summons. He came down the hall wiping sleep from his eyes. "Whichever one you are," Lon said with dignity, "bring some ice, please, and a few small bottles of soda." Wong bowed. "Ice and soda," he said, and went back up the hall.

At the door to their room, Lon had trouble finding his key. Kay glanced at the door on the opposite side, so silent now. "Larry and Peg were good fun," she said. Lon found the key. "I sent a message to the hospital," he said. "I told them they could count on us to do anything to help."

"That's nice," Kay said. In the room, she went up the short flight of stairs behind the curtain and sat on a bed. A forelock of blonde hair hung down over one eye. She kicked her shoes off and tried to blow the hair back up.

She was in the bathroom in bra, panties, garter belt and stockings when Wong left the ice. She bent over the basin and washed her face with cold water. It did nothing to dissipate the drunken feeling. She came out of the bathroom, saying: "The door locked? Is it all right to come out?" He locked the door, and sat looking out the window at the river. "May I fix you a drink?" he said.

Kay came down the steps slowly. Usually, she wore a faded blue silk robe, but tonight she had either forgotten to put it on, or didn't care. "How gallant," she said. "I'll fix one. How about you?" He kept staring out the window. The bottle of Scotch was on the floor beside the chair. He pointed to it. "I'm okay."

She sat watching him from the sofa, sipping her drink and looking at his back. He picked the bottle up, swung it to his lips,

and drank. "Wait," she said. "I'll get you some ice and soda."
"Don't bother," he said. "I'm trying to get good and drunk and
you're slowing me up."

As intoxication overtook them, Kay's tone of voice seemed
brighter, with more lilt and less rancor. His became more sullen,
more of a growl. "Must I stare at your back all night?" she said.
He said "Sorry," knowing that he wasn't, and that she would know
it. He turned the chair from the window and began to sing softly:
"A fine romance, my friend, this is; a fine romance, with no
kisses . . ."

"I thought of a good word to describe me," Kay said. The lock
of hair was down over her eye again. Her ankles were crossed and
resting on the coffee table. A small layer of snowy skin hung over
the garter belt. "Disenchanted," she said. He said nothing. "I am
Miss Disenchanted of Siam or something."

"You forget," he said. "You are also Miss Big Mouth of India."
Kay nodded sagely, her eyes a third closed. "Yes," she said. "I
forgot. I had to tell Peg about your gun. So I'm Miss Big Mouth
of India. I am also Miss Disappointment to you, dear husband.
Come to think of it, I'm a whole lot of misses."

He drank from the bottle and some of it got into the bronchia
and he bent double in a fit of coughing. His eyes were red and
teary. He stood and dropped his trousers to the floor and kicked
them out to the middle of the fiber rug. Then he dropped his
shorts, kicking them away. He was suffused with a feeling of well
being. He no longer worried about the accident. Everything and
everyone was under control. He drank the liquor slowly, taking one
swallow from the bottle at a time.

"Disenchanted," he said absent-mindedly. "That's what marriage
does to romance: it tears the lovely veil away." Kay fingered a
piece of ice in the bottom of her glass and got it into her mouth.
He could hear her break it with her teeth. "You," she said, sucking on the pieces, "are a lot smaller tonight than yesterday."

It was coming. He knew it. But he no longer worried about it. Kay had similar feelings, but she didn't pause to notice that she was starting the argument. "You were a very big man to me." she said. "Three times the size of any man I ever knew." "How many did you know, dear?" he said sarcastically. "Oh, shut up," she said loudly. That is, loudly for her. "Only a coward would lie about the gun."

He said nothing. He was thinking of how raw pure liquor feels to the throat and stomach on the first few rounds, and how mellow it is later. He wondered whether the mucus lining became accustomed to it or whether perhaps the sedative quality of alcohol dulled the nerve ends. "You were scared," Kay was saying, "shit scared." Lon pursed his mouth into a surprised O. "Such language," he said. "Scratch a lady and find a tramp." She started to speak and he held up his hand. "Just a moment," he said. "I know you're dying for a good rousing fight, full of accusations and counteraccusations. I don't want it, but if you do, let's go. I used to stage these three times a week with Elspeth."

"I wish the hell you were with her right now," Kay said. "I sure do wish it." "You mean," he said, "in the grave." She hesitated. The glass was refilled. "I don't know what I mean. I know I'm disgusted. You're just one more frightened man."

"Not frightened," he said softly. "Not really frightened, my pet. Not cowardly either. I told them I didn't have a gun because I did not know that a gun had anything to do with what happened to good old Larry. It seemed pointless to get myself in trouble when I had nothing to do with this thing." Kay glared at him. "You're a liar. You're a goddamn stinking liar. Not clever. Stupid."

"Admitted," he said. "That is precisely why I seldom lie. My mother caught me so many times that, by the time I was ten years old, I gave it up. So today I tried it once more." He shrugged. "Mother was right. She always said: 'This one isn't so smart, but he's truthful.' I walked into an Oriental trap."

Kay's head was rocking slightly. She unfastened the back catch of her brassiere and sighed a long sigh. "That isn't what makes me mad," she said. "That's not it at all. So okay. You goofed with the police. What bugs me is that you told them you had 'personal reasons' for carrying the gun. What personal reasons? You told me as protection against natives. Now all of sudden it's different. It's personal. What the hell kind of a marriage is it you keep secrets from me? What's so damn personal?"

He stood, and she giggled a little at the way he looked, with shirt-tails hanging around his thighs, a neatly knotted tie hanging in place with gold tie clasp, and a pair of black socks which were trying to roll down over the black shoes. "You're too drunk to understand," he said. "I'm going to bed."

"Oh, no you don't," she said, getting to her feet slowly, and weaving a little from side to side. "Oh, no. I've been eating my heart out all day waiting to hear the personal reason and I'm going to hear it or you're going home alone."

Lon didn't want to shout, but the growl was rising in volume. "Go home," he said. "If that's your pleasure, my friend, go home. I got along pretty well before I met you. I can still make it alone." She sagged back onto the couch and now the bra cups were up at her shoulders. Softly, she whispered: "Is that the way you feel, Lon? Truly?" He smiled. "Of course," he said, trying to find the short stairs. "Who the hell needs you?"

At once her head bowed toward her knees and the tears came. He was making his way up the steps and he could hear the sobs. They were real. He wondered what would happen if he went to bed and pulled the sheet over his head. Would she leave him alone? Or would she persist in the argument, sitting on the bed and yanking the sheet down to demand answers to questions? Or, worse, would she be drunk enough to open the door and walk down the hall undressed? Vaguely, he remembered what hysterical women sometimes did, or were capable of doing, in anger and intoxication.

Perhaps it would be better if he stayed awake for a while. At least until she fell off into sleep. It couldn't be too far off. She could hardly stand. He looked at his watch. Only eleven twenty P.M. Early. It seemed a long time since they had left the roof garden. Only eleven twenty. Incredible. It should be two or three A.M. at least. He shook the watch and listened. It was going. His eyes felt heavy-lidded and his knees rubbery. His fingers turned the watch over. He didn't need his glasses to read the inscription: "For you, forever. Elspeth."

He took it off and put it on the night table with extra care. Then he removed the tie and the shirt and dropped them beside the bed. The shoes came off easily. The socks remained on. He got to the stairs and went down them backwards, like a man on a ladder. When he reached the floor of the sitting room he tottered across it to the door, turned the key in the lock, took it, walked over to the window, opened it, and threw the key out.

"I don't like surprise endings," he said. "Two lies today. One to Charley Chan. One to you. I do need you, Miss Big Mouth. All the time, all the ways. You wanna know about that gun, hey? Okay. Stop crying. Blow your nose, kid." He was leaning across the back of a chair facing her. She began to wipe her eyes on her forearms. "You wanna really know about the gun. Personal reason? Okay." He made a cross on his chest. "Scout's honor. I bought it to shoot me."

She was trying to stifle her sobs but finding it difficult. As she looked up at him, her blue eyes were small and red; the bun above the back of her neck hung between her shoulders. One stocking was half down; one was still attached to the garter belt. She kept wiping her eyes and taking deep breaths to stop the sobs. "You?" she said. "Why for you?"

"In case," he said, "the marriage turned out bad. Silly?" He walked around to the front of the chair and sat. "Honey, I couldn't stand another lousy marriage. Just couldn't. Nobody knows how it's gonna turn out, Kay. Nobody but God, and he ain't speaking to me. So I figured I'd make out a will—" he made a big sweeping motion with his hands—"and it's all done and I'm leaving a good chunk of dough for you and a good chunk for poor Sonny and that's it. End of story. If it turned out bad, I was gonna pick a quick way. You can't expect a man to live through two of these damn things."

For just a moment, Kay seemed to sober. She wasn't, but the shock seemed to clear her head. "Let me get this," she said, slurring the tone so that the words kaleidoscoped into each other. "You wanted to commit suicide? Suicide? I don't believe you. Sorry, Lon. Itsa lousy plot story."

He got up from the chair, hands braced against the arms. "I'm too drunk to talk right," he said. "Going to bed. Opium den bed. The little old gun was for me. You'll find out." He tried to make the stairs by putting his shoulders back and aiming at them but fell to one side and knocked a floor lamp over. He straightened himself, looked accusingly at the lamp, and tried again. This time he made it and went up the little stairs and fell across the bed.

Kay tried to stand. By leaning on the glass of the coffee table, she was able to achieve an upright position. She turned halfway, so that she faced the drawn curtain at the head of the stairs. "Suicide?" she shouted. "You fulla bull, you are." There was no reply. The voice shrilled a little bit louder. "Big brave writer. Big brave at the typewriter, that's what you are. You probably going to shoot me. I know. I been living with this the whole damn trip. Funny honeymoon with a gun, hah?"

As she said "hah?" the effort was too much. She started to fall, recovered, and then slid between the coffee table and the sofa. She tried a few times to get off the floor, and subsided. A few minutes later, there was no sound in the room except deep breathing.

THE FOURTEENTH DAY

THE telephone rang in bursts of two. It was loud and imperative, but no one seemed to hear it. The strong light of morning came through the river window and painted a yellow block on the fiber rug. The ringing stopped. The only sound in the room was breathing. The telephone began again. This time the rings were protracted. There was no answer. No sign of life. When it stopped again, the breathing sounded rhythmic.

A few minutes later, there was a knock on the door. It too went unanswered. The knocking became a pounding. Then a voice said: "Me Dong, Missy. To answer, prease." Kay, on her back between sofa and coffee table, breathed with a petulant thrust of the lips. Suddenly, she grunted an unintelligible word, and turned over on her stomach. The fiber rug bit into her face,

"Prease. You be late. Me Dong." The voice was louder. The fists on the door were heavier. Up in the opium den, a pair of socks moved a little. The toes inside curled and uncurled. The pounding continued and, when Lon opened his eyes and squinted against the light, he thought the pulsing was inside his head. "Kay," he said. "Somebody at the door." There was no reply. He waited a moment, partly in the room and partly wherever he had been in his dream, and then consciousness came. He sat up.

"Just a minute," he yelled hoarsely. "Just a minute." He looked for a robe, and couldn't find one. He looked at the other bed and it was freshly made. The spread on top had no dents. "Kay!" he said. He found a pair of trousers and tried to step into them and almost fell. "Just a minute, damn it," he said.

Then he went down the stairs and tried to open the door. He couldn't. He asked who it was. It was Dong. Mr. Michaels had left a call for six A. M. to go to the Floating Market. Dong had breakfast on a tray. "Wait a minute," Lon said. "The key must be somewhere here." He looked around on the nearby tables and his eyes fell on the supine figure of his wife on the floor. His heart paused momentarily, then went on with a heavier beat. If Kay was dead, he had killed her. If she was dead, she had said something he couldn't abide and, in a drunken rage, he had killed the one lovable thing he had found after fifty years. If she was dead . . .

He tottered over to the sofa, sat heavily, and leaned down to touch Kay's cheek. It was warm. He saw her lips puff out as she breathed. He felt ill, very ill, but he almost burst into laughter. "Oh my God," he heard his voice say, "Oh my God. What a wild drunk that was." He placed one foot on his wife's round hips and rolled her back and forth. The middle part rolled; the rest remained motionless.

"Go away," she murmured. When he persisted, she said: "Not now. I'm tired." He kept the foot going, and she opened her eyes a little bit and saw the rug. Then she lifted her head, looked around wildly, and whispered: "Jesus, Mary and Joseph! What happened?" Lon tried to look well. "I just got out of bed and found you here. Dong is outside with the breakfast." Carefully she placed her head back on the rug. "Tell him to go away. Come back this afternoon or tonight."

"Darling," he said sweetly, "the man is waiting. I can't find our room key. Would you know—?" She moved her head from side to side on the floor. Her head hurt. She tried to thrust herself up on her hands and her brassiere fell off. Lon put both hands under her arms and half carried, half helped her up the little stairs. "My bra," she protested. "Get my bra first. It's on the floor." He helped her into the bathroom.

He went back to the door. Now his head was pulsing and so was his heart. He could see it trying to thump through his chest. "You have a key, Dong?" he said. "I must have put mine away." There was a sound of a key being inserted, and Lon pulled the upper bolt back.

Dong came in with a big tray of tea in pots with tea cozies, a couple of shirred eggs, some orange juice, and some toast with orange mamalade. He set them down on the coffee table. His nose was wrinkled and he giggled. "You seep good," he said. "Very good. Telephone ring. No answer." He laughed heartily. Lon tried to smile. He just couldn't. Dong stooped and picked up the brassiere. "Missy drop topside pants," he said. Then he withdrew discreetly. As he left, he said: "Man for froating market meet you downstairs. Seven. Okay?"

Lon nodded. He felt very old and very close to death and he had no intention of meeting anyone. He was standing there, looking at the breakfast, as Kay came down the steps clutching two aspirin. "Try these," she said. He downed them with orange juice. She sipped orange juice and rang for milk. Lon could not stand the sight of the eggs. He asked Dong to bring four more orange juices. He drank them all.

"I can't shower and shave in time to meet that man downstairs," he moaned. "I'm going back to bed." She shook her head negatively. Lon had to smile, looking at her. One side of her face was puffed red, probably from contact with the rug. Mascara had glued a black tear to each cheek. Her eyeballs were red; her lipstick faded in some spots, and still strong in others.

"You'll make it," she said. "You go in first. I'll stall the man downstairs. I'm not going to ruin our fun because we got drunk."

"Drunk?" he said in horror. "I think we started off drunk, but what did we do after that?" Kay smiled a sad smile. "Damned if I know. I've been thinking like crazy for fifteen minutes. My head hurts. My mouth is parched. My stomach is about to quit. My heart is beating somewhere in my neck, and all I can do is remember one word: disenchanted."

He started toward the bathroom, trying to light a cigarette with shaking hands. "What does it mean?" he asked. She shrugged. "It's all I remember. Oh, no. I also recall saying I was going home alone."

"That so?" he said, pausing on the steps. "What brought that on?" She suggested he take his bath. "We haven't got any time," she said. "And I'm going to this floating market if it kills both of us." "But why run away from me?" he said, going through the bathroom door and leaving it open. "I just don't know, Lon. People do crazy things when they drink. O my God!" she shrieked.

"What now?" he said from the bathroom. Kay moaned. "I just remembered poor Larry." "Poor Larry?" he yelled through the jet of water. She walked wearily up the steps and into the bathroom and pushed the lid of the seat down and sat. "Yes," she said. "He was shot yesterday. Remember?" From the shower there was silence, then "Jesus! I forgot." They did not speak for a while. She got up and peered into the medicine chest mirror and stuck her tongue out. "I guess," he yelled from the shower, "that's why we got good and drunk. Good God. Poor Peg."

Kay was brushing her teeth with vigor and trying to talk through brush and dental cream. "Some of it is coming back," she said. "The police. Larry. The hospital. She must be at the hospital. Remember the fat policeman said he wasn't going to press charges?" There was no answer from the shower. Lon was doing his own thinking, walking backward through a shower of Scotch, peering here and there through the previous night for clues. "We had quite a battle," he said.

"What?" she said. "A battle," he said. "It was a beaut but I can't remember what it was about. I think you called me some names." She washed her face in hot water, then in cold, then used a face cloth vigorously. "Oh, sure," she said. "It had to be me. It couldn't have been you. I think I drew a blank after we got back to the room. All I can remember is a dream I had." "What was it?" he asked. He stepped out of the shower with a big bath towel around him, his gray hair plastered straight down over his eyebrows.

"It seems that somebody was chasing me around a room. I was going around and around—" "Losing ground all the time," he said, as he dried himself. "—and then the man, or whoever it was, stopped chasing me and went to the door and locked it and took the key and threw it out a window."

"You see too many movies," he said. "May I have two more aspirin? My head is caving in. Would you like a hair of the dog—" She said no thanks. She hoped never again to see or taste liquor. "I abhor the cowardice in chewing on a hair of the hound," he said, "but I am in a weak and pregnant condition this morning and I am going to have one belt and then get dressed."

"Someday," Kay said, "I'm going to tell a psychiatrist about these dreams."

It was an old boat with a canopy flapping loosely over the white hull. The engine made rhythmic chugging sounds, sometimes syncopating the beat. Kay and Lon sat up on the bow, nervous and tense as they started across the Chao Phrya, but relaxing as the small craft moved up and down the narrow klongs of old Bangkok. The guide with the big flat feet sat aft and said nothing unless he was asked.

The day was still young and clear. Rickety old houses, porches heavy with green tropical plants, stood with their backs to tall jungle growth and beautiful flowers. Monkeys, scampering from branch to branch, froze in flight at the approach of the boat. The sun too seemed to flit from tree to tree, making deep blue shadows on parts of the water and sending hot shafts of light on others.

Small boats moved in a procession up the right side of the klongs, and others paraded slowly down the other side. Women in big floppy hats and loose white blouses and long purple skirts bunched at the sides manned sweep oars and moved by in lovely majesty. Kay noticed that many of the oarsmen held clasped hands, as if in prayer, under their lips. They did it as they passed the tourist boat, smiled, and rowed on.

"They're saying something," Kay said. Lon leaned back to ask the guide. His English was somewhat restricted. "They say herro," he said. "Morning greeting. *'So wat dee.'* Fingers under face. Like in New York: 'Hi, pal.'" Kay and Lon were entranced. They practiced holding their fingers under their chin and saying "So wat dee." A little later, a houseboat passed by. On the high stern, a Siamese man worked the long oar. At his side was a small woman and, in a tiny rope hammock, a young child.

"So wat dee!" the Michaelses said, almost in unison. At once, the man locked the oar in place, smiled, held fingers under chin, and repeated the greeting. So did his wife. The woman said something to the baby and it sat up in the hammock and grinned and repeated the hello. "That does it," Kay said. "This is just too beautiful. Can you imagine a place where everybody stops for a moment to say hello to strangers?"

"It looks genuine," Lon said. "This shocks me. The smiles. The hellos. They even stop work for a moment to say it to each other. They must be on some kind of pills." Kay had to smile. "That is so like you," she said. "It's the perfect observation for Lon Michaels. Me, I'm entranced. These are not only the politest people, they also seem to be the happiest. I have never seen so many massed smiles."

The guide was of little help, so, as they rode the bow of the boat, they consulted the guidebook. The only persons who did not seem to smile at strangers were women who manned small junks and had black streaks on their cheeks. The Michaelses learned that old Bangkok used charcoal as fuel and that these women sold it from their boats. Lon asked the guide why they appeared resentful. He didn't know. He pointed to other women manning small boats laden with garden-fresh vegetables, meats, coconuts, bananas, pots and pans, who appeared to be amiable. Kay said she thought she knew. She said that the sootiness of charcoal would be a blow to femininity and no female could enjoy working at a task which made her look and feel dirty all day.

Sometimes a boat went by with two men in bright orange robes. "Buddhist priests," said the guide, explaining that in Thailand the people were close to their religion because all males were expected to serve a few months as Buddhist priests just as, in other countries, young men enlisted in the armed forces. The little boat turned a bend in one of the klongs and came upon a great traffic jam. It looked as though all the sampans and dhows and houseboats and Chinese junks in the area were trying to negotiate the same narrow stream at the same time.

Little boats laden with green peppers, beans, romaine and radishes were jammed gunwale to gunwale against barges laden with neatly stacked bamboo poles. An old lady in a small boat passed by and Kay saw bananas. She said "So wat dee!", received a greeting in reply, passed over a one-baht note (about five cents), and received a full hand of ripe bananas. The crowded oarsmen had no room to sweep. They exchanged greetings and those with oars requested those with engines to move to one side, or pull ahead.

On some small boats, thin strips of red beef hung from limber poles. On others, little charcoal braziers cooked quick Siamese breakfasts of meat and fruit which were sold to oarsmen passing by. "This," said the guide, pointing, "is famous froating market

Everybody know Bangkok froating market. Every day seven o'crock right here." He grinned. "Rike Times Square?" he said. Lon and Kay, still sick and nervous, broke into laughter.

The traffic jam extended even to the banks of the klong. On it, Siamese women sold commodities to the women in the small boats who, in turn, hawked their wares up and down the canals to families living on houseboats or in houses along the banks. Kay's eyes encompassed all the bright colors of the scenes, the dewy fresh vegetables, the floppy hats and gathered skirts, the varnished boats. Lon's eyes saw no excitement among the merchants, no loud bargaining; the sweet pleasantries, even in another language, were monotonous. He saw an old lady, naked from the waist up, take a baby and walk into the jade waters of the canal for their morning baths.

Later, the guide took them to a big Buddhist temple, but Lon's mind was still on the happy people of Siam. To a man with a mental mosaic of life, with each tile in place, it was shocking to find that one did not fit. "This hangover," he said to Kay, "may have unhinged me. I swear I think these people would feed us if we were broke." Kay understood. "I don't find it difficult to believe that people can be this nice," she said. "All people are nice if you give them a chance."

"All people are not nice," he said. "Some are nice. Some are not. I have not given up on the human race. The astonishing thing to me is that there are so many sweet and lovely people in one place. It's like—like—well, like finding a boulder of pure gold stamped fourteen karat. Gold isn't found that way, hon. It is found mixed in with rock and sand, more rock and sand than gold."

They walked around the Temple of the Emerald Buddha, admiring the many red and yellow tile pagodas, the statues of old warrior-gods standing in silent stone for centuries, and Lon, who walked up the outside of the main temple, was surprised to find that the mottled blue effect was achieved, apparently, by breaking up colored crockery into small pieces and cementing them into the walls of the temple. When he came back down the steep steps, he said to Kay: "They must have taken four or five million old ash trays and busted them up to make the walls." The guide listened. "Aw brue brass," he said. "Yes-s-s-s."

The Siamese, Kay conjectured, were fascinated by the prang, a pointed object which seemed to top the headdress of statuary as well as the tops of temples. The guide showed them a low shed in which reposed all the royal barges, long slender shells with gilded dragons' heads as bows. "Forty-four men," said the guide, making a rowing motion with his arms.

"Please call at four thirty," Lon said. He sat at the telephone beside the bed, scratching and yawning. "Four thirty," he said slowly. "Yes. We are going to the fights at five thirty. One hour before fights be fine. Thank you." He hung up. "I'm beginning to talk pidgin English," he said, and flopped on the bed.

Kay was already on her bed. She was flat on her back, eyes firmly closed against the noon light, hands clasped across her stomach. Lon pulled the spread down off the pillow, punched a round hole in the middle, and turned on his stomach to court sleep. "You didn't tell me," she said, with eyes still closed, "why you had the gun." His head was sideways on the pillow and he hoped that this was not the start of another dispute.

"I told you last night," he said. Kay chuckled. "I don't remember much about last night." "Well," he said, "you were told." "Please tell me again." "No." "Come on." "I want to take a nap." "Never carried a gun in his life. Gets married. Needs a gun. Why?" "I'm sound asleep." "You are not." "I told you the whole story last night and I'm not going through it again." "Is that your final answer?" "Is that an ultimatum?" "No." "Then go to sleep."

"Who can sleep thinking?" "I'm trying to remember what happened after you put some ice in your mouth." "I did?" "It's a faint recollection." "All I remember is that I was mad about you lying to the police. You never lie." "I," he mumbled sleepily, "am a good boy." "Do you think," she said, "that if I went over to your bed we could take our nap together?" "No." "That's a blunt answer." "Go to sleep." "I won't." "All right. Let me." "I may get drunk again." Lon smiled into the pillow. "Be my guest," he said.

The telephone rang at four thirty. Lon awakened refreshed. He swung his feet over the side of the bed, glanced at his watch, lifted the receiver, and said, "Thanks." He slipped into his shoes, said, "Time, Kay," to the other bed, and went to the bathroom. He was halfway through the door and stopped. He turned and looked at Kay's bed. It was empty.

Oh, no, he said to himself. "If you're drinking," he said through the curtain, "you're going to be in lovely condition for the fights." There was no reply. He yanked the curtain back. The afternoon sun was strong through the bamboo shade covering the window. The room was empty. He walked through the room, lower and upper, looking for a note.

A press of the bell brought Dong. He had kicked off his slippers, and came into the room in white cotton jacket and trousers, giggling. Yes, he saw Missy. She walk to elevator with bag on arm. She say nothing, just walk to elevator. Missy she go by self. You ask front desk.

There was a deadly depressed feeling in Lon's chest. When a man of inordinate confidence is suffused with despair, it is a deep feeling whose direction is not easily changed. The emotional trip down is longer for the optimist, and Lon had been sure of Kay, sure of her love, sure of her feminine dependence on him, sure that she was happy in her role as his wife, even though there were disagreements and misunderstandings.

He knew that he could not abide her leaving him, even though she returned within an hour. As he washed, he recalled that she had said she had to go out and walk when she was in a dilemma or unhappy. He had once told her that only two things could break their love: one was if she fell out of love, or was unfaithful; the other was if either could not stand the child of the other. Now there was a third possibility—a wife walking out when she pleased, returning when she pleased.

He could not live with uncertainty. He would soon find himself in a situation where he would be afraid to disagree with her for fear that she might become so upset that she would dress while he slept and walk out.

He phoned the front desk. The clerk had not seen Mrs. Michaels leave nor had the lady left any message in the box. Could they ask the taxi drivers out front where she had gone? No, that would be impossible because the same drivers were not in the front park all day. While he was on the telephone, Lon asked if the newspapers had published any account of the "accident" to Mr. Cointreaux. No, the clerk said, nothing had been published because the police insisted that no crime had occurred. A man who cuts himself shaving is hardly worth publicity.

Lon got dressed. He was going to the fights. There was a telephone call from Pan American asking if the Michaelses and the Cointreaux planned to take Flight Two the day after tomorrow for Hong Kong. Lon said he was glad they called, because he and Mrs. Michaels planned to leave, but he thought that the others might stay in Bangkok a few days. Slyly, he asked if there were any other flights out of Bangkok in the afternoon going to the United States. No, there weren't.

He hung up, satisfied that she hadn't lost her sanity to the point of walking out on him and taking the first plane home. He was fixing a small drink for himself when he heard a key in the door. She looked happy. "You're up," she said. "I wondered if they'd call you." He sipped. "I'm up. Where the hell were you?"

"Oh," she said, peeling off white gloves and putting them on an end table, "I got to thinking about Peg and I couldn't go to sleep. You were snoring. There was no point in waking you up just to tell you I was going to the hospital—"

"I thought the police said to stay away."

She shrugged. "It's no longer a police case. You don't understand. I'd feel like an awful heel if I left here without even offering to help. So I went to the hospital."

He finished his drink and got to his feet. "What help did you offer?"

"Just help. No particular kind. I talked to Peg and she cried and said she thought she lost her mind and—"

"That's not my question," Lon said. "What particular help could you give? If you went there to offer something, what the hell was it?" She placed her bag beside the gloves, standing. "Nothing, I guess. Larry is doing okay. He's propped up in bed and allowed to read newspapers, but he isn't allowed to speak. They have a big dressing all around—"

"Here's your dressing," he said. "As long as you're my wife, don't ever walk out like that again. If I wanted a prima donna, I'd have married one." Kay's face showed surprise, then hurt and protest. But she was silent because, as Lon spoke, he gave her no chance to dilute his anger with explanations. "You have nothing to do," he said, "except as I tell you. You have no worries, no big decisions to make; in fact, when you get home, you won't even have to cook a meal. All you have to do is to be a good wife to me and a good mother to our kids. Any questions?" Before she could open her mouth, he was off again.

"Last night, I knew a fight was brewing long before the explosion. I hoped it would not happen, because I knew that no one was going to win it. But you had to have it. We got so damned

drunk I don't remember what we said or what was settled. Today, you run off in a strange city halfway around the world and—
and—" He looked at her stricken face and his anger collapsed.
He took her in his arms. She fought him, pushing him away in
the outrage that is the response to marital anger. He clung to
her and kissed her.

"All right," he said. "It's all right. You're back. That's the
big thing." She tried to speak and he kissed her into silence. "When
I'm hurt, I have the reaction of a rattlesnake," he said. "If you
knew what it meant to wake up and find you gone, if you understood the sagging feeling that goes with it—suppose you awakened
and I was gone? No note. No word."

Kay nodded. She understood. "You're sensitive," she said.
"Much more than I thought. You act callous but you're easily
hurt." He smiled and hugged her. "I just can't live in an emotional
storm," he said. "I've had it. I'm shell shocked. I had too many
years of battle. Whenever we're very happy, I keep reminding
myself that it can't last. It can't last. Why? Because it never lasted
before."

She broke away from him. "I should have left a note," she said.
"I'm the one who is wrong. As you say, if you walked out, I'd
be in hysterics. But, Lon—please, Lon—will you remember one
thing? I'm an adult human being. I can think and talk. Sometimes you're wonderful and then you become so demanding that
I suffocate. I have to have some rights of my own." He bowed
formally, elaborately. "I'll keep it in mind," he said. "But my
heart is still in my heels. I get sick when I think of this place
without you. Maybe when you walked in I should have put you
over my knee and spanked you."

Kay smiled. "I'm ready," she said.

The guide sat in the front seat. "We go Rajadamnoen Stadium,"
he said. "Go by way Chinatown. Very funny." He giggled. Lon

did not. He was dwelling on other matters. For a moment, he thought: "What's funny about Chinatown in a city of Orientals?" He wondered if the Thailanders considered themselves so different from others that they were amused by Chinese. It must be so. Otherwise, how could Bangkok be a great Oriental city and still segregate Chinese into an area apart from others? "Very funny," the guide said. He did not say "velly."

The taxi cost two dollars and fifty cents. The tickets came to five dollars a seat, front row ringside. The sun was still up when the fights began. To Occidental eyes and ears, it was a hilarious performance. The fighters fought to the accompaniment of an orchestra composed largely of loud cymbals. The orchestra sat on the west side of the stadium, making Chinese New Year's noise while the fighters were swinging, but lapsing into silence between rounds.

The Siamese are gentle people. Their idea of boxing, as a sport, was utterly mad, Lon decided. The fighters came into the ring, crouched on their knees and began a series of rhythmic supplications to Buddha. Their heads were in the rosin, their rears were aimed high, their gloved hands swept out slowly to full length, like the wings of a bird, then folded back under their foreheads. Then they stood, making jerky motions with their arms, pivoted slowly on the heel of one foot while holding the other leg out, bent at the knee, with the toes up.

It was slow, poetic and touching. When the bell rang, both fighters came out of their corners, punching, wrestling, kicking at chest and belly, jamming elbows in eyes and, in one case, dragging the referee to the floor with them. The kicking was more expert than the punching and, when the fight was done, the battlers bowed gravely to each other after mutual maiming. Kay enjoyed none of it.

Lon remained for three fights, and could not arouse himself from his depression. He nodded to the guide, who got to his feet, and led the way out. On the way back, it was dark and Chinatown became more apparent. The signs were bigger and brighter and merchants stood in the doorways of curio shops. Kay thought it looked like any other Chinatown she had ever seen. The guide was fascinated. "Do not rike Chinese in Thailand," he said. "They come few. Used to come many. Siamese keep them not here."

The Michaelses tried to get the same table at the roof garden. It was occupied. They took another, on the far side of the room facing the modern side of Bangkok. The room was large and busy and the headwaiter asked what they would like to drink. Both said: "Nothing, thank you," but decided to order a good-sized dinner: cream of asparagus soup, broiled pork chops, carrots, French peas, ice cream and coffee. Kay also ordered a fresh garden salad of tomatoes, romaine lettuce, sliced onions, inundated with olive oil and vinegar.

"You'll be sorry," Lon said. She shrugged. "I love a good salad," she said, "and this is a good one." He said he guessed it was safe, in a cosmopolitan restaurant like this. "But everyone warns tourists about uncooked vegetables," he said. "They lead to cramps known as the Trots, Travelers' Lumbago and the Oriental Two-Step."

"Please," she said. He said he was sorry. She asked if he had noticed the stacks of varnished boxes on Charoen Krung Road. "Yes," he said. "They're caskets. The people here are sensible about death. They shop for a box as you would browse for a bridal gown."

"I'm convinced," she said, "that people can always think of a tremendous reason for not wanting to go at this moment. Know why I think this? Because the thought of death crossed my mind the other night and I said a prayer to God, saying, 'Not now. I'm happily married at last. I'm in love. Let me stay for a little while longer.' "

"A nice dinner topic," he said. There was little conversation except recollections of the genuine friendliness of the Siamese a opposed to the aloof fatalism of the Hindus. As dessert was served, Lon said he had something important to say. Kay froze a little because she was always afraid it was something that would threaten their relationship. It wasn't.

"Some things," he said, spooning the ice cream, "are difficult to say. You may have noticed that we heard nothing further from Kate. This is a sort of code between her and me. It means that Sonny is under control. Well, not necessarily under control, but getting care, let us say."

"It occurred to me," Kay said. "I was going to ask you about it; in fact, I was going to ask if it would be all right to phone home and see if Sonny and Lucy were okay. I've never been away—"

"Sure," he said. "Call. You have to give the operator a few hours' notice, and you must remember that there is twelve hours' difference in time. Call at eight in the morning and you'll catch Lucy just before bedtime at home. But I wanted to tell you a little more about Sonny. He's a little more than an alcoholic."

"More?" "Yes. He's manic depressive." "What's that?" "It's a form of psychosis." Kay was torn between pity and fear. "He's insane?" she whispered. Lon smiled. "That's a harsh word, Kay. In fact, it is obsolete. To tell the truth, I didn't know anything about emotional illness until Sonny began to shout around the house and drink and talk like a Texas millionaire. That was two years ago and I have learned a lot and read a lot since."

The blue eyes widened, almost with accusation. "Why . . . didn't . . . you . . . tell . . . me . . . Lon? Why must I always wait until you think I'm properly primed? If that boy is sick, our place is there, not here. Besides, I happen to have an innocent child in that house." This was the blow he had expected. The "innocent child" matter was the reason Lon had not explained the illness earlier. It was a pitting of his son against her daughter and the inference was that Sonny might be a monster. He finished his coffee and asked for the check.

This was a dangerous subject. He knew it. He knew he was

defensive about his son. He loved the boy dearly, protectively; he felt vaguely responsible, perhaps guilty. He didn't like to discuss it with doctors, either, because he felt they had shattered all he had left. He had no desire ever to face Sonny squarely and look at him. The image he had was of a tall skinny boy with the dark eyes of his mother; a boy in tight jeans and loose sweaters who found life to be a combination of fun and laughter, and frustration and tears; a boy who was, in one instance, the life of the party and, in another, sat moodily for hours without speaking.

Lon paid the check and they took the elevator down to their floor. In the room, he removed his jacket and sat down. "Sit for a minute," he said, as she started up the steps. "I want to explain this to you. It won't take long." She sat down, smoothing her black crepe dress over her knees, unscrewing earrings and putting them in her lap as she listened.

"Manic depressives fall into types," he said. "I don't know enough to analyze all of it, but Sonny's kind is called manic. The others are called depressed, and circular. No one knows the cause; some doctors at Marlboro State Hospital think that the behavior of parents has something to do with it. If you had a mother or father who alternated between kissing you and beating you, it could predispose you toward manic depression.

"In any case, Sonny has it. How bad, I can't tell you. He was in Marlboro two years ago, and they said he was one of the youngest cases on the books. The way it works is this: usually the victim sets goals for himself that are too high. A boy who can't add, perhaps, wants to be a physicist. Nothing can drive the ambition out of his mind. The time we first knew that there was something wrong with Sonny—that is, Kate and I—was when he started to talk and we thought he'd never shut up. He talked and talked. He felt good. Everything was a joke. At the same time, he couldn't seem to sit for more than a minute. He kept jumping up and waving his arms and telling us how great everything was going to be. If I said that the lawn mower was busted, he'd say he would fix it. If I said my bank account was low, he was going to buy a service station and make a mint for me; everything was fine everywhere."

"Did he see things?" Kay asked. Lon lit a cigarette. "No delusions. No. But everything was out of kilter. If I said the Russians were going to drop a bomb on us, he'd laugh and say it wouldn't explode. He was in a sort of do-good mood, if you know what I mean."

Kay smiled a little. It was the first sign of sympathy. "Well," she said, "if you have to get something like that, I'd rather be the happy do-gooder than the wild maniac." Lon agreed. He looked at her and heaved a big, almost unconscious sigh. He began to feel that he was not going to lose her because of Sonny, and he wondered why he had been plagued with this worry from the start.

"There is no danger to anyone but Sonny," he said softly. "When the attack comes, it comes suddenly. One minute he is puttering around the house, getting his room in order, setting his books straight, using his phone to call a friend, and the next he is talking talking talking, and waving his arms, stealing liquor from the cellarette bar." He snapped his fingers. "That quick. He has no enemies; he loves everyone. He will probably promise Lucy the whole world and tell Kate to sit down, that he will make dinner tonight, and so forth. The danger is suicide. He has a definite tendency toward it. If it is going to happen, it will be when he slides down off the cloud."

"Don't you think we ought to go home?" He shook his head no. "He's in Marlboro right now. The last time, he was there six weeks. The first two weeks, they had him under restraint and this isn't pleasant to see. They put him in some kind of swirling baths for long periods. Then he gets a drug called chlorpromazine. When he starts to come down, the psychiatrist begins psychotherapy."

"What's that? Talking?" "You could call it that. Mainly, it consists of suggesting and listening. It isn't analysis. The doctor gets the patient to talk about himself. They establish an empathy. Incidentally, this part failed the last time. Sonny didn't like the doctor and told him nothing. It may work a little better this time.

"The one feature which surprises me—and hurts a little—is that most of these patients will recover by themselves if they are not treated. Just take them out of their homes, and put them somewhere else and, in a few weeks, the symptoms disappear. This leads to the belief that something in the home triggers the attack."

"This," she said sympathetically, "is what makes you think you're to blame?" He tried not to bristle. "No," he said. "I didn't say that. It is possible for someone in the house to be unhappy without anyone being to blame. I feel no guilt. If there is any, Elspeth can take a bow. She babied the kid, enslaved him, made him so dependent that if she went shopping he was in hysterics when she got home. Besides, she had the wild-swinging emotions the doctors talk about. It is possible, I suppose, that she was mildly manic depressive and we didn't know it."

"I feel better," Kay said. She fingered the earrings in her lap. "I feel much better. I felt all along that there was something wrong with Sonny—not just drinking—but I didn't know what it was." She looked at him accusingly. "You might have told me straight out. I'm your wife. I have to accept the bad with the good, just as you do."

The indictment was well placed. He knew it. He said he was sorry. He had always felt that it was something he had to fight alone and, when she came along, he was afraid to tell her. "Several times," he said, "I was on the verge. Then I'd ask myself 'Why risk everything? She'll find out soon enough.' "

"You think it will be all right to continue this trip?" she asked "It wouldn't bother me to go home tomorrow." No, he said. I would be wrong. In the first place, he hadn't been surprised in Paris to get the cable from Kate. The sudden marriage would upse the kid; he knew that. Sonny could have felt that, after his mother' death, he had nothing left except his father. Then a woman had come along and had taken him away. That could have triggered an attack.

"I don't see how you could leave if you thought these things," she said. "It sounds so selfish." Lon stood and began to undress. "No matter which way you go," he said, "in the matter of children, you are probably wrong. I spoke to the doctor at Marlboro before the wedding. I'm sorry I didn't tell you that, too. But his opinion was that my worries were meaningless. Sonny might feel resentment and he might not. If he did, it would precipitate another attack. If he didn't, he might embrace the new mother as a substitute for the one he lost. In any case, all the medical advice was: 'Get married. Go on your trip. Stop trying to walk a tightrope for your son.' "

He peeled his shirt off and Kay placed it with the soiled laundry in the bottom of the closet. "What a sad thing," she said. "I'm going to try to make it up to him when I get home. Now don't start fretting. I'm not going to use Elspeth's approach. My idea is to give him some genuine affection but, at the same time, to treat him as an adult—as one of us."

"Would you consult the doctor first?" Lon said. Certainly she would. She turned suddenly from the closet and wrapped her arms around her husband and buried her face in his shoulder. "Sometimes," she said, half crying, "I wish you didn't have that mask. You've been robbed blind by everybody. I'm going to call home in the morning."

THE FIFTEENTH DAY

THE morning was gray and damp. It was something that could be sensed in bed. When the telephone rang, Lon mumbled from the pillow: "Don't put me on unless it's important. You talk." For a moment, he was conscious that this was a telephone call from halfway around the world, then his breathing became deep and steady and he was back among the ugly people of dreams.

Later, when he awakened, he thought that Kay was still on the phone. "Kate want me?" he mumbled. Kay was down in the main room. She said she was typing. He sat up. "What's the news from home?" He floundered for a robe, found it, tried to brush his hair back with one sweep of the hand, and felt with his feet until he found his slippers. He found cigarettes and lit one. His shoulders hunched against the dampness of Bangkok, and he went down the steps.

Kay was using his portable typewriter. "Not much news," she said. "Though I thought you might have gotten up to say hello to Lucy." He grunted. "How is the child?" he asked. Kay kept tapping. It was a talent he did not have: an ability to write, and at the same time hold a conversation not related to the words on the machine. "Lucy misses me," she said. "The connection wasn't too good, but when she heard my voice, she started to cry."

"Understandable," Lon said. "She's still a little girl. That's one of the reasons why I didn't want to get on the phone. She thinks of me as the wicked witch who took her mother away." Kay said it was untrue. Lon disagreed. "I understand her. Give me time to do a little missionary work and I'll romance her."

"Sonny is in the hospital," Kay said. "I thought you'd like to know that he is doing all right." "It's what I expected." "You sound unfeeling." "Should I burst into tears? I'm thankful that he's doing well. But my main interest is in trying to stop the cycle or episodes or whatever the doctors call it." The typing continued. "Kate says she's having a little trouble with Lucy." He extinguished his cigarette. "Yes? That's something." "She complains that Lucy throws tantrums, refuses to take baths, and can't sleep at night."

This, they agreed, was the typical picture of a child who feels that her family has been broken, and who is rebelling against everybody. "Did you tell her we'll be home in two weeks?" he asked. She said yes, and that Lucy had always been high-strung. Lon said that his impression was that the child was not high-strung by nature, but felt betrayed. She was nervous and sleepless because she was being bounced to a lower rung all the time. "She started off with a father and mother—right? Okay. Every time you had a home and she became accustomed to it, your husband was transferred to another Army post. This meant a different and strange house, a different environment, a different playground, different children. Then her father was taken away permanently. Now she was moved to a smaller place in another town with but one parent.

"Then you got a job—right? So now she only saw her mommy in the morning, before school or whatever, and at night. She was shoved off to stay with paid baby sitters. She felt no love there either. Her whole world was falling apart. Her friends, her home, her school, even her parents were temporary. Nothing ever seemed to last forever."

"You draw a grim picture," Kay said. She stopped typing and drew a sheet of paper from the machine and glanced at it. "Not at all," he said. "You figured I was too lazy to get up and say hello to the child. I think this would have been a bad move. Isn't it difficult enough for her to try to understand why everyone has left her—including her mother—without having the reason for it get on the phone and say: 'Hello, dear. Are you happy?' Oh, no. I'm going to send a cable to Kate today and tell her to give Lucy a little more affection and fewer orders. Kate is old-fashioned. She forgets what it's like to be a little girl."

"You want to have breakfast in the room?" Kay asked. He nodded. The sleep had gone from his face. She rang the bell. "You think we did wrong in getting married?" she said, and there was something stricken in the tone. No. He thought not. He hoped she wasn't going to become emotional about it. He made his point: "Just because we're in love and we're happy doesn't mean that everyone around us is happy. Lucy isn't happy for the reasons I just outlined. Sonny isn't happy for similar reasons and has less ability to adjust to it than Lucy. Kate isn't happy because, for the first time, a young woman is going to be her boss and tell her where to sweep and what to cook. The dog isn't going to be allowed on the living room couch any more, and he's going to resent it. Hell, marriage is a big thing. It disrupts all sorts of situations around the bridal couple."

Dong came in. He took the breakfast order beaming as though he had just won a Shanghai lottery. He disappeared. Kay said: "I have cramps." Lon raised his brows. "Yes?" he said. "What kind?" She began to laugh. "Oh," she said, leaning on the back of a chair, "that's the best. What kind? And you know something? You're right. I just found out that there are two kinds. The one I have comes from food poisoning."

"That damned salad," he said. He walked over to the picture window and looked out at the river. The junks and sampans were running up and down the Chao Phrya, but something new had been added. There was a Chinese freighter anchored in midstream. It looked old, and it sagged in the middle. The one funnel appeared to be too tall, so did the fore and after masts. The bridge was square, and a Chinese officer leaned off the wing, gesticulating to a man in a small boat.

"If you must use the bathroom," Kay said, "please be brief. While you slept, I've been in and out. I also have perspiration." He smiled. "Those are the classical symptoms," he said, "of Montezuma's Revenge." He called the front desk. "Do you have some pills for dysentery?" he asked. "No. This is Mr. Michaels. In six o seven. Yes. Dysentery. Excuse me? No, I do not know another English word for it. Pains in stomach, run to bathroom alla time. Bathroom. W.C. Yes. Yes. Please send them right up."

In the afternoon, Kay felt better and they walked along the Charoen Krung, looking in the windows of scores of curio shops, seeing thousands of cheap bracelets, rings with synthetic stones and necklaces—all, it seemed, priced at forty bahts or less, which Kay learned was two dollars. Each shop along the avenue of tourists had a smiling, bowing clerk out front. A few spoke excellent English; most of them made up, with elaborate hand gestures, the welcome they failed to extend in comprehensible words.

Lon felt that shopping was a lady's prerogative, so he tagged along, agreeing to go into such shops as interested her, squinting through a fine drizzle and ignoring windows that did not capture her fancy. In most shops, the informal ceremony consisted of broad smiles from the manager, the assistant manager and the clerks. A clap of the hands sent a boy running for hot coffee or Coca-Cola. The shops had big front rooms, full of counters of silverware, crocodile skins, semiprecious stones, and wallets.

In most cases, there was a smaller room in the rear. This was brightly lighted and here were trays of real diamonds, emeralds, rubies from India, star sapphires, Mikimoto pearls and goldware. So far as Lon could see, these were legitimate businesses; in fact, most precious stones were priced below their value elsewhere. Here, American tourists laden with travelers' checks haggled with Siamese jewelers, threw up their hands, left, returned, bargained further, and finally bought the item or moved on.

Lon made one purchase: a world mercator map. He wanted to trace their trip in pencil, and show Kay where they were, and where they were going. Kay bought a few richly ornamented silver salad spoons, some small onyx-handled shrimp forks and, to Lon's surprise, a genuine crocodile briefcase for him.

He had been so busy looking in other showcases that he knew nothing of the purchase until she handed it to him. "From me to you," she said, and kissed him. The price tag said 2,200 bahts ($110), but Kay had bargained well and got it for $75. It was, he agreed, a most distinguished-looking briefcase, with the bumpy ridges of the crocodile's spine running down the middle of it.

The afternoon was wearing down when they began to walk back toward the Oriental Hotel. The skies cleared suddenly, and there were big holes of blue between clouds now magenta, now pink, now old rose. They dodged the small puddles and walked to the river's edge at the hotel. They watched a Siamese woman row two passengers to a landing next to the hotel, look around for passengers, and start to row to the other side. It was a broad river, and she made long sweeping strokes on her single oar, locked high in the stern of the little vessel, and gauging the tide so that she skirted the stern of the Chinese freighter at anchor.

"Let's go out tonight," he said. Kay thought it was a good idea. It would be their last night in Bangkok and, except for the memory of the Cointreaux episode, they agreed that they liked Bangkok and Beirut best. At the hotel desk, they stopped and asked for places to go at night. The clerk nodded wisely. He understood Americans.

"I would suggest," he said pontifically, "the Keyhole for dinner

and dancing and, later, a drink and some music here, in the Bamboo
Room. You been to Bamboo Room? No? Ah. Very good. I reserve
table for late. Okay? Okay. You tell taxi driver the Keyhole. He
take you and wait. Cost very little. Then you come here, table all
ready."

"You know," Lon said on their way up in the elevator, "I could
learn to talk like that. And like it too."

The Keyhole had a canopy over the sidewalk. The night was
bright with stars. Little girls stood near the club selling nosegays.
There was a doorman in uniform opening taxi doors and bowing
patrons in and out. The inside was early American Chinatown.
The big room was dimly lighted and had a bar in the shape of a
grand piano.

It was a busy place, a sort of sophisticated playpen for Siamese,
Chinese and Americans. The Michaelses watched steaming trays
of food move past their little table, and decided that they did not
want dinner. Both formed quick likes and dislikes in restaurants,
and, in the case of the Keyhole, they did not relish what they saw.
Kay settled for a bowl of soup and a Singapore gin sling. Lon
asked for a double Scotch on the rocks.

They listened to the music—jazzy and fast, and sometimes sentimental and slow—and watched the couples in tight embrace on the
small floor. To Kay, it was a romantic meeting of East and West;
she was surprised to find so much mixing of the races; perhaps
shocked too to find that the slit up the side of a flowered Chinese
gown sometimes went all the way to the top of the thigh.

The scene reminded Lon of a clip-joint in San Francisco, a plush
Chinese restaurant near Times Square, an Oriental night club on
Chicago's Loop. He saw no romance, only cheap customers. The
place might be all right, but the trade wasn't. An elderly
Chinese in a booth sat with a young girl. Her hands were busy
under the table. His sole interest centered on how many other

customers were watching. He smiled benignly at everyone who looked. On the dance floor, prosperous-looking American men danced with local girls; they danced vulgarly, not, one might guess, as they would with their own women.

The girls at the bar appeared to Lon to be Siamese, although they might have been Chinese or hybrid Malays. All of them were good looking, with dark shiny eyes and friendly smiles. Men customers who arrived without women stood in the doorway and examined the premises before deciding where they wanted to sit. It was indeed a true meeting of East and West on a level which can be called the common denominator.

Outside, Lon and Kay waited for a taxi. Lon watched two little girls selling white circlets of jasmine with a pendant orange flower. "For the lady's wrist?" Lon said. The children did not understand. They giggled. "How much?" he asked. One child with truly almond-shaped eyes held up two fingers. Two bahts. Ten cents. He held up two fingers, and bought one from each sister. Lon gave each one a five-baht note. The girls quickly ascertained that he did not expect any change and, at once, they ran down the dark sidewalk at top speed.

Lon put one on Kay's wrist. The other he held in his hand and sniffed. The odor was lovely and heady. The doorman found their taxi driver and they asked to go back to the Oriental. "I didn't come all the way to Bangkok," said Kay, "to go American." He agreed. In the cab, he held her hand and said he would always be grateful for her understanding.

"Of what?" she asked. He squeezed the hand. "You know of what," he said. "Oh," she said. "That. I'm his stepmother. I should understand." The subject died. Lon said he thought that, so far, she had given more to the marriage than he. Kay cocked her head, as though considering it. "You have a point," she said. He burst into laughter and released her hand.

"So sweet, so modest," he said. The taxi completed its bouncing and drew into the driveway behind the Oriental. He paid the driver and took Kay by the arm through the lobby and across the inner courtyard with its pretty flagstones and fountain. "I think," she said, half shyly, half hoping he would not take offense, "that almost all women put more into marriage than a man. And, before you start snorting flame, let me say that marriage is important to a man, but to a woman it's everything."

"I know," he said. He held open the door to the Bamboo Room and noticed that this one too was dimly lighted. "You know," she said, "only because you are reminded of it. You know it right now but you won't know it ten minutes from now. A woman studies her man as you study styles of writing. It's her life work."

A headwaiter took them to a corner table, where a small combination band played American music. "Don't sell the men short," he said. "A few months ago, I would have told anyone that I wouldn't remarry no matter what the circumstances. Now, I am ready to change my thinking, my way of life, anything to make my marriage flourish." She grinned and said, "Hmmmm."

She ordered another Singapore gin sling and Lon stuck to Scotch. The Bamboo Room was quieter, it seemed to them, than the Keyhole. There was nothing electrifying about it—a bar at the head of the room, a few Chinese waiters standing listlessly near the kitchen, a bartender who could speak in idiomatic English, a middle-aged couple at the next table speaking soft German, two young Englishmen drinking with Siamese girls and laughing uproariously through the music of *My Fair Lady,* a red-headed woman sitting alone and reading a newspaper.

"She wants to be picked up," Lon said. Kay shook her head. "There goes that mind again," she said. "The woman wants to read and listen to some music." "She's here to be picked up," Lon insisted. At the bar, a Thailander sipped his drink and studied the woman and the newspaper. He waited until she finished a page. As she flipped to the next one, her eyes roamed the room and, momentarily, locked with his.

He took another sip and slipped off the stool. At her table, he bent over and said something. She looked up, studied him as though surprised and then shrugged. In a moment, she was on her feet, tugging at her skirt and pulling her snug sweater down. She placed her arm around his neck and they danced to "Get Me to the Church on Time."

"You see?" he said mockingly. Kay had to admit that she was surprised. He looked at his watch. "We don't want to stay too long," he said. "We haven't eaten yet and we can get Dong or Wong to bring something to our room. Tomorrow, my pet, Hong Kong."

"How did you know about that woman?" Kay asked. He said he didn't; he just guessed that any woman who sat in a bar alone was asking for a male gambit. They paid their bill and went up to pack. Also to eat. When they got in the room, she tried to press the bell for the houseboy. Her husband stopped her.

"Just a minute," he said. He turned her around toward him. "I want to unhook your dress and help you into something more comfortable."

THE SIXTEENTH DAY

HONG KONG is a miasma of material-ism. It is a group of rocky coastal islands, but it is also a twenty-five-mile strip of Chinese land and is *owned by China.* No one is certain *which* China. (It was leased from a dowager empress, trans-ferred to Chiang Kai-shek's government, which later fled to Formosa. The new landlord is *Communist China.*) Hong Kong is peopled by three million Orientals and a cadre of British colonials. The little group rules the big one.

The British refer to it as a crown jewel, but it can neither feed nor support itself. Hong Kong is sampans and junks; it is rusty freighters at anchor and a paradise for bargain hunters; it is rick-shas and Cadillacs; an airport which is a strip of filled-in land ex-tending like a dirty finger into a bay; it is refugee squatters in bamboo shacks on hillsides and it is also garish mansions like the Haw Parr castle, built on the proceeds of an unguent called Tiger Balm; it is high tea at 4 P.M. and it is also a fatalistic philosophy about being swallowed overnight by Red China.

Hong Kong is crowded streets, curio shops, custom tailors, cheap cameras, duty-free perfumes and watches, water which comes from Red China and can be shut off at any time. It is big families living in one room, not because of poverty but because Chinese like to live crowded; it is floating restaurants and a little railroad bridge

at Lo Wu where the British stand watch on one side, and brown-
uniformed Communist soldiers stand on the other. The territory
is an economic and political liability—a place which no one can
afford but which nations would fight to keep.

Traffic policemen are shaded by white pagodas. Modern glass
office buildings stand shoulder-to-shoulder with little leaning shops
which sell warm rice wine. Barefooted children with pocked skin
beg in doorways; old Chinese scholars in long gray gowns and
black slippers pore over books on sidewalks; grandmothers carry
round tubs of water to sunny street corners to bathe babies.

There is a race track called Happy Valley. It is one of the few
in the world with a big ledge of rock in the backstretch, over which
horses must run and jump to the ground to continue the race. Hong
Kong is prostitutes, smugglers, a caste system, fishermen, spies,
remittance men, patience, lethargy, and strange names: Repulse
Bay, Dragon's Back, Big Wave Bay, Robin's Nest, Cloudy Hill,
Bride's Pool and Sunshine Island.

The mystical beauty of the colony is a backdrop for cheap labor.
Kay and Lon learned, between Kai Tak Airport and the Peninsula
Hotel, that there are porters to carry luggage, porters to open doors,
porters to help one into a taxi, servants who do nothing but twirl
a revolving door, others who open an elevator door which opens
automatically, floormen in hotel corridors with duties like snatching
the room key and running ahead of the guest to open his door,
fetching hot tea, shining shoes, turning down beds, lighting cigarettes, handing soiled laundry to other servants who wash it and
turn it over to others who iron it, and send it by a fourth man back
to the hotel where a package man receipts it, gives it to a bellboy,
who takes it to the proper floor, turns it over to the hallman, who
trots to the room to give it to the guest.

The Peninsula impressed them. It was an elegant, old-fashioned
place directly behind the docks of Kowloon, facing Hong Kong
across a mile of water. The lobby had old rosewood paneling and

little tables and sofas scattered among potted palms. Chinese in white cotton stood in the driveway, between the shafts of rickshas. In the shadows at dusk, Victoria Peak stood tall and jeweled with lights behind the freighters at anchor. Along the docks neon signs winked in Cantonese characters, advertising Japanese cameras.

The room was big and old-fashioned. The bed, the chairs, the vanity and the plumbing might have been fifty or seventy-five years old. The table radio was tuned to a local British station which was addicted to cheap American recordings. Lon tipped the two Chinese who were the last to carry the luggage and Kay kept reminding him that the Hong Kong dollar was worth about 20 cents. "Keep thinking five to the dollar," she said. He said he barely got accustomed to one country's coinage when he was confused by the next.

They unpacked, then undressed to take baths for dinner. "You first," he said, waving gallantly toward the bathroom. Kay went in, and was out in a minute. "No water," she said. Lon phoned the front desk and was told that water is turned on at certain hours of the day—8 A.M. to 10:30 A.M. and again from about 4 P.M. until 6.

Nothing becomes important until it is denied. The bath now became a cause. Lon demanded to speak to the manager and asked why the water was shut off. He was told that the British reservoir holds little fresh water. The amount that could be trapped in rain catchments on the mountainsides was even less. Most of the water came from Communist China and it was barely enough for the three million people in the Crown Colony.

"Why don't you publish this in your travel folders?" he asked. The manager said he thought it would be bloody stupid to advertise it. "All right," Lon said, "I'll advertise it for you." The manager said, "As you please." The floorman came in with ash trays and they spoke to him about the water situation. He said he could get them a few pitchers of water for "wash face." He made motions with his hands to show the face. They tipped him two Hong Kong dollars for two pitchers of cold water. He was a tall, grave-faced Chinese and he seemed to be overwhelmed with the tip. The Michaelses were overwhelmed with the water.

It was dark and the streets of Kowloon were bright. The rickshas moved slowly away from the hotel on the left side of the street. Kay rode the one in front, feeling that she was in a movie come to life. Lon watched the brawny Chinese between the shafts and could see the play of shoulder muscles as the man leaned forward to pull. Kay turned back, looking at her husband with the delight of a child.

"I wonder what would happen," she said over the street noises, "if I said chop-chop." She didn't have to say it. Her boy heard the word and broke into a trot and she slid against the back of the ricksha seat. Lon's boy broke into a trot too, and soon they were in the downtown section, bright with the lights of open shops and soft with the breezy warmth of a subtropical city.

They got out, paid the drivers, and couldn't get rid of them. Neither of the ricksha boys spoke English, but they made motions implying that they would follow the Michaelses from place to place, and, when they were finished buying, would take them back to the hotel. Lon kept saying no. This didn't seem to be understood. So he began to shake his head negatively. The two ricksha men understood this and looked sad. They spoke to each other in musical tones, which ranged rapidly between three notes. Then they nodded brightly and began to follow the couple from store to store.

The streets teemed with pedestrians. Chinese and foreign tourists made way for each other on the crowded sidewalks. Some walked in the streets and paid little attention to the honking of horns behind them. Little boys with leather straps over their shoulders and shoe-polish boxes hanging on their hips followed the Michaelses, saying: "Shine. Shine. You want good shine?" The word "no" meant nothing. The phrase "no, thank you" meant less. A shaking of the head caused the boys to precede the Michaelses, walking backward to face the customers, pleading: "Shine? Shine?"

"The best thing," Kay said, "is to say no and ignore these people." Lon was entranced with the exotic Oriental character of Hong Kong and the way diners looked out of second-story restaurants to watch the passers-by below. "How can you ignore ricksha boys who follow you?" he said, pointing behind. "What can you do with barefoot kids who can't be more than seven or eight years old when they are two steps in front of you, pleading?"

Kay was pleased to a point of glee by everything she saw. She went to Benny's and was fitted for custom-made shoes: one pair for walking; one for evening dress with seed pearls sewn all over; Lon watched the clerk place paper under each foot as Kay stood, and then trace each one separately. She was permitted to select any style of leather or cloth, any style of shoe with or without bows or straps; heels of any size; and any color at all.

He watched, and he kept thinking of a little girl in a shop full of beautiful talking dolls. Kay was so happy that it was transparent. She kept smiling to herself, and looking at him, and smiling, and selecting. The shoes averaged about eight or nine dollars a pair, cheaper than anything she could buy ready-made. Lon decided to buy a couple of pairs. He went through the foot tracing and selected a pair of cordovans with a strap, a pair of brown suede shoes and a pair of Italian black slip-ons.

They asked the clerk where they could shop for dresses and men's suits. He referred them to Frank Fong for women's wear, directly across the street, and to Jimmy Yen for men's clothes. The clerk said that all the shoes they had ordered would be made and ready to try on "tomorrow afternoon."

"Hong Kong," Kay said as they walked toward Yen's shop, "is a woman's paradise. I just can't get over those shoes—so beautiful, so specially made, so—so—" "Cheap." "No, not cheap. They're

dirt cheap, but that's not what I mean. Fantastic. That's the word."
They walked in the street and held hands. "I guess," Lon said, "it's
the greatest bargain center in the world. Take a Japanese camera.
It's cheap in Japan, but it's cheaper here. Why? Because in Tokyo,
the manufacturer must pay a tax to the government. Hong Kong is
duty-free, so the camera comes here at actual cost price plus a little
bit for shipping and a little bit for the merchant.

"But I don't think of Hong Kong as a shopping center. I think
of it as the mysterious East. I probably saw too many movies when
I was a boy, but every dark doorway, to me, leads to an opium den
where beautiful white girls are held as slaves. Every sampan in
the harbor is smuggling rifles or hand grenades. All the old Chinese
in gowns are scholars who are well versed in the death of a
thousand cuts. Crazy. Childish. But it's thrilling to me to keep
reminding myself that I'm in Hong Kong, just a step away from
mainland China."

Kay was amused by the difference in points of view. "I met some
stewardesses," she said, "who are mad to get to Hong Kong. They
do without things and save for the one trip to this city. Before we
left home, I met some women who said: 'Don't buy anything until
you get to Hong Kong.' You know something, Lon? They were
right. Such prices."

They went to Yen's Emporium. It was a small place with sofas
and wall mirrors and grinning clerks who offered cigarettes and
drinks and high-pitched laughter in return for business. Mr. Yen
came from behind a curtain and introduced himself. He was a tall
man with a streak of gray which seemed to have been dyed into
the black hair. He dressed in Western clothes and sat down with a
book of swatches. He spoke animatedly of patterns and focused
his attention on Kay, rather than Lon.

"These grays are popular," he said with a slight accent. "All of
them are deep, but not charcoal deep." Kay inclined her blonde
head to listen. Mr. Yen began to smile at her. "He would look

good in one of these," he said, pointing. "Not Italian style jacket. Just a nice drape." Lon took the book from him, flipped the pages, and picked out a pale gray and a navy blue. "I'll tell you how I want them made, Mr. Yen," he said. "You tell me the cost."

The proprietor seemed surprised at the abrupt attitude. "Okay, my friend," he said. "You pick. I make. When do you want the suits?" Lon figured. "Day after tomorrow at noon. Would that be all right?" Mr. Yen showed all of his teeth. "My tailors will sit up all night to sew them."

"That," said Lon, "brings up another point. I have heard that the suits here are fine, and the tailoring is great. But the sewing is poor. How about it?" Yen stood, still smiling, although now the smile was fixed and false. He displayed a book. "Look," he said. "These are names and addresses of American customers. All happy."

Kay took the book. Lon ignored it. He stood and said: "How much? I want superior sewing." "For you," said Yen, "Thirty-five dollars American. Now—we are friends?" "I'll be your customer," Lon said. The shop owner bowed. "Will you step into fitting room?" Kay began to frown at her husband. Lon saw it and paid no attention.

"How about shirts?" he said. A clerk stepped forward. "You like silk or broadcloth, please?" Broadcloth. The best grade, and white on white. The shirts sold for six dollars apiece. He ordered a dozen of them and removed his jacket as the clerk measured collar size, sleeve length, shoulder width and length from neck to shirttail bottom. He called the numbers in Chinese.

Another tailor, with the customary tape measure draped about his neck and the square of sharp chalk in his hand, led Lon into the fitting room. There he undressed to his shorts, and stared unhappily at the broad stumpy figure he saw. One tailor measured. One conversed softly in Chinese, repeating everything. Lon was never a shy person, but he was always embarrassed when the tailor put

one end of the tape on his heel and the other high into the crotch
to measure trouser length. None of them seemed to be able to do
it quickly.

When it was done, the clerk presented fashion clippings of styles
in men's suits, and Lon made his selection. The Chinese bowed out
of the room, and he was alone to dress. Outside, he could now
hear Mr. Yen talking.

"Of course my ancestors were all Chinese," he was saying, "but
I don't feel Chinese. Maybe I have too many American friends."
He laughed heartily. "If you know what I mean, Mrs. Michaels."
Kay said something, but it was so soft that Lon couldn't hear it.
"Oh, yes," he heard the Chinese say. "My wife is Cantonese. Very
fine woman. But Hong Kong spoils Chinese women. Makes them
act American. All day she is on phone with her friends, or out
playing mah-jongg."

Kay wanted to know if Mr. Yen had children. He said yes. His
tone became aggrieved and tinged with self-pity. "My family busy.
Always busy. Father spends time in the shop, making money for
phone calls and automobiles. At night, I close shop at ten, have
no place to go. Admire very much American woman. Would
offer Hong Kong to blonde American woman on a gold plate. A
man cannot make money all the hours. He must have romantic
interest—you understand?"

Lon was buttoning his shirt and swinging a knot into his tie.
He heard his wife say: "I understand. But what would Mrs. Yen
say?" This was followed by the laughter of the proprietor. "She
does not care. Not interested as long as money comes to her. You
and Mr. Michaels be here long time?" Just a few days, Kay said.
"Ah," said Mr. Yen, "maybe while Mr. Michaels be busy I can
show you interesting places in Hong Kong nobody sees." Kay said
thank you, but her husband had a list of places to see.

Lon was tucking the shirt into his trousers when Yen said: "He
will not show you the real Hong Kong. He must live here long time

to know Hong Kong. He take you to Aberdeen, floating restaurant, Victoria Peak, few restaurants for tourists, maybe racetrack and shops. Real Hong Kong is different. Have lunch maybe in Dragon Inn where only Chinese familes go." Well, she said, she'd see.

Lon put his jacket on and buttoned it. Then he came out of the fitting room and Mr. Yen, who was sitting so that his knees were touching Kay's, got to his feet and put on the broad smile. He looked at his wrist watch. "You see?" he said. "Quick. Fast service. Cheap price. You be very happy with suits."

"Do you want some money now?" Lon asked abruptly. Yen threw both hands into the air. "No, thank you. Money not important. You pay when happy. I will phone Peninsula for first fitting." Kay saw the cold dead glance in her husband's eyes and stood, ready to leave. "Good," Lon said, "and thank you for the offer to show my wife around. She's going to be too busy to go anywhere."

The radio was turned low, so that the music was audible. Kay undressed and opened one of the big windows, then closed the draperies over it. Lon typed a couple of postcards. He sat in an undershirt and a pair of bedroom slippers trying to think of something better to say than "having a fine time, wish . . ." There had been no conversation between them all evening except when Lon said that he had tried to place a phone call home and the operator said that all the telephone time to the United States had been reserved by others.

There was going to be a dispute. She knew it. He knew it. Neither of them wanted it, but Lon knew that he could not sleep until he had spoken his mind. Kay felt that he had been rude to Mr. Yen without reason. He kept staring at the next postcard, not writing anything and not able to think of the proper words. He would like to approach the dispute without rancor, but this was a contradiction in terms. A fight is a fight is a fight. If she wanted

to flirt with a Chinese merchant—even with innocent intention—
then she was cheap, hungry for the sexual aggression of men. He
could not accept this. He had heard what he had heard, and he
could play the conversation back in his mind and could find no
point at which she had put Mr. Yen in his place.

"Before you go to bed," Lon said slowly. "I want—" She sat on
the side of the bed, facing his desk. She wore a quilted blue robe
and her face was grim. "To talk," she said. "All right. Talk." He
thought for a moment, still studying the typewriter. Then he
turned her way. "Did you realize that Yen was making a play for
you?" Her lips thinned a little more. She took a long breath. "What
time is it?" she asked. He looked at his watch. He said it was
almost one A.M.

"I've been waiting since nine o'clock for you to ask that question. That's a hell of a long time to keep anyone on the torture
rack. The answer is no and yes. I thought he was being polite
when he directed the conversation to me. It wasn't until you went
into the dressing room or whatever they call it, the fitting room,
that he began to move a little closer and he made it pretty plain that
he would like to show me around the city."

"Oh, come now," he said. "I knew the story before that point.
I knew it when he brought the swatches and began to undress you
with his eyes. You knew it too." She stood and removed her robe.
She made a gesture of futility and slid naked between the sheets
and doubled the pillow under her head. "What's the use?" she
said. "No matter what I said, you wouldn't believe me."

He ripped the postcard out of the machine and set it on the
desk. "Don't quit on me," he said. "Don't try to go to sleep to
avoid this thing. We're going to talk because I need a few answers.
On my side, I'll be honest with you. I do not believe that you have
any interest in Yen or anyone else."

"Thanks," she said. "This is turning out to be a lovely honeymoon." He stood and removed his shirt and kicked off his slippers

and got into bed. "You got the cigarettes?" She handed one to him. "I heard the whole conversation in the fitting room," he said. "Or rather, not all of it. Just the part after the tailors walked out. That was enough."

She sat up. "Tell me," she said. "Tell me one thing I said to encourage that man." "Oh, no," he said. "Let's put it another way. Tell me one thing you said to discourage him." She lay back on the pillow and stared at the ceiling. "What should I have said? Shut up, Mr. Yen. I'm a married woman and I don't like affairs? And anyway, I'm afraid of Chinese?"

He lit his cigarette. "That would have done for a start," he said. "It would have established the fact that you are a lady. It is possible that he makes a game of fitting American men for suits while making a play for attractive wives. He may also have a little success along these lines."

"I doubt it," she said. "He's too obvious." Lon shook his head in mock bewilderment. "A moment ago you realized nothing. Now he's too obvious. I wish you'd make up your mind." She tried to speak, but he went on. "I have half a mind to let him make up the suits and shirts and not go back. I have signed nothing and I owe him nothing. However, that's a cheap way of doing things. I'll go back for the fittings without you, pay him, and be finished with the matter."

"Do you really think," she said, "that he wants to go to bed with me?" "Don't you?" "I will concede that he was fresh and needs to be told off, but I don't think he'd do anything wrong." Lon's anger came to the surface at once. "Don't be a horse's ass all your life. Of course he wanted to go to bed with you. Didn't he tell you he likes white women, especially blondes? Didn't he down-grade his wife to a stranger—you? Didn't he tell you how he'd give Hong Kong on a platter to the right woman? Didn't he offer to show you a Hong Kong you could never see with me?

"What does all that add up to? It's a proposition. I wouldn't care if you had never been propositioned before, but from all that you told me, most of the officers on Francis' post were trying to get you on the mattress. Am I right? Did you tell me this?" She whispered yes. "All right then," he said. "You must admit that you know men pretty well. You understand their motives. You know how they operate. Now you arrive in China and a total stranger, an Oriental, rubs knees with you and tells you what he wants in a woman, and he describes you and you don't think he means anything wrong."

"He did not rub knees with me." "You're a liar. I saw it when I came out of the fitting room. When he saw me he jumped to his feet. He doesn't know yet that I heard any of the conversation." "Yes, he does," she said, "because you told him that I would be too busy to go anywhere with him." "Okay," Lon said. "He knows that much. Do you want to go out with him?" She turned her head away and unfolded the pillow so that it was flat. "I don't have to answer insulting questions," she said.

This did not appease him. He had been hurt and he was going to hurt her. "Was it insulting when your husband's sergeant walked into your quarters and lifted you up and carried you into the bedroom?" Kay was silent a moment, then she sat up. Tears stood in her eyes. "When you proposed marriage, you asked that we be completely honest with each other. Now I'll hear that story for the rest of my life."

"Did he walk in and carry you into the bedroom?" Lon said, tauntingly. "Am I making it up or did it happen? You know damn well it did. He put your husband on guard duty and dropped in for a cup of coffee. Right? And may I ask one more question? If it was a mistake to be untrue to your husband, how come you told me it happened about twenty times?"

"Oh God," Kay moaned. "Oh God." Lon took another puff on the cigarette and leaned out of bed to stamp it out on the ash tray on the floor. "Don't 'Oh God' me," he said. "I told you every affair I ever had. I held back nothing. I wanted to start this marriage with a clean slate. But I have a long memory, and I think it was Ambrose Bierce who said it is easy to find a married woman who has never had an affair, but it is very difficult to find a wife who has had only one."

Kay wiped her eyes with the edge of the sheet. "I don't like Chinese and I wouldn't have an affair with one under any circumstances. I'll go a step further. I wouldn't have an affair with any man. Understand? Any man. I know now that I was never really in love until I met you. I don't give a goddamn what you believe, but that's the truth. For me, it's you or nobody. But how you can wait until now to bring up a thing I confessed to you just to straighten the record, I'll never know. I wish you were a mind reader so you'd know how often I've cursed myself, not only because of the sergeant, but because of Francis too. I wish I had never gone to bed with any man until we met. But what good is it? You think I'm some kind of prostitute."

"Untrue," he said. "Completely untrue. I'm not in the habit of marrying prostitutes or even consorting with them. I've made lots more mistakes than you have, but you are not going to play innocent with me at any time. I happen to know that at Fort Riley you were known as the flirt of the post. This isn't news to you. Your husband almost went out of his mind trying to keep an eye on you and attend to his duties at the same time."

"What did you do," she said softly, "run an F.B.I. check on me?" He flopped back on the pillow. "Twenty times," he said, half to himself. "And that's only your casual estimate of the number of times the guy carried you to bed." She was crushed. She felt that their marriage could not last as long as her affair with the sergeant remained in his mind.

"He only carried me the first time," she said. An interesting point, he observed. The rest of the time she must have been ready and waiting for him. "Yes," she shouted. "Yes, yes, yes. I was always waiting for him. I thought I was getting the love from him that I seldom got from my husband. Half the time I was already in bed so that we wouldn't waste time. I did everything he asked me to. I reveled in the filth of the whole thing. In my mind, he was terrific because I didn't know any better. He was rough and mean and cruel. I used to have to cover the bite marks with make-up before Francis came home. Now are you satisfied? Do you want more? I was a stupid immature child and he gave me a wedding ring and told me to hide it. He was going to run away with me when his hitch was up."

"Okay," Lon said quietly. "I'm sick enough. You don't have to tell me any more. And you don't have to scream." "Don't you want more details?" she said, still speaking shrilly, almost hysterically. "Keep quiet," Lon said. "You're going too far."

"Oh, no, I'm not," she said. "You started this thing. For once, I'm going to finish it. And please don't quote any writers to me about women. I was a virgin when I met Francis. I had one affair after Lucy was born. The sergeant. Nobody else. Nobody since. Nobody before. Just once. And I don't care what you believe or don't believe. I hope God strikes me dead right here if I've ever lied to you. I made one bad mistake and I made the mistake over and over. I didn't have to sink myself by telling you how many times, Lon. I could have said once. Just once. You'd never know the truth. But it doesn't pay to tell the truth. Now I have to justify my reaction to a Chinese who wants to make love to white women. No, sir. I'm not going to do it because I have no interest in him or anybody else but you. I just want you to get one thought in your head; I'm in love for the first time and I wish to hell I'd never seen a man until I met you, but I'm not going to defend myself every time a man looks crooked at me."

As her anger rose, his died. He was sorry he had made such an issue out of something in which, basically, she was blameless. "Okay," he said. "All right, Kay. I'll never mention it again. If I ever so much as hint at the subject, I hope you hit me with a vase. But there is one thing I'd like to get straightened out. One thing I'd like you to do, with no prompting from me. In the future, will you please—please—not be friendly to strange men?" She was not appeased. "You mean that if a man smiles at me, I'm supposed to turn away?" He smiled faintly. "No dear. Just act like a lady. Be slightly aloof. Remote. Men make passes through habit. Almost all of them do it, waiting for an echo. If one doesn't come, they're not too disappointed. Just don't be too amiable. Especially with men who are not in our circle of friends. I don't want a wife I have to watch."

"You haven't got one," she said. She turned over on her pillow as though to go to sleep. In a moment, she murmured: "I don't like to go to sleep angry. I'll admit I should have stopped that man cold. Abruptly. The way you talked to him. But a woman gets accustomed to men playing their little games and they don't seem important. I can see that it's important to you and it won't happen again."

He kissed the back of her neck. She felt sleepy, but she turned toward him and put both arms around his shoulders. "Kiss me good night," she said softly. "Slow."

THE SEVENTEENTH DAY

THERE was sleep and the sound of water. They ran together so that Lon was in a state of half dream, half wakefulness. He was conscious of being in bed, but too tired to arouse himself. Valiantly, he tried to drop off the edge of nothingness into deep sleep, but the consciousness of falling water drove him upward toward morning. Vaguely, he reached for Kay, who always slept with her back toward him in the shape of a V. He often wondered why, with her head and feet out of bed, she didn't fall.

She wasn't in bed. He opened his eyes, brushed the hair back from his forehead, and looked around. For a moment, he had no idea where he was, or where she was. Then he remembered Hong Kong and he also recalled the water problem. She was in the bathroom, filling the tub. He got out of bed like a man of seventy-five, his mind trying to distinguish between the real and the unreal.

Kay came out of the bathroom. "Good morning," she said. "Breakfast be up in minute chop-chop." The words were light, but the expression was dark. "You drawing a bath?" he asked. She nodded. "I'll be finished in a minute and there is still time for you to have one, also time to fill the tub again before the English turn everything off." "Excuse me," he said, and went into the bathroom.

Breakfast was coming in on a table when he emerged. Two waiters grinned, bowed and set the table and put out small eggs and black bacon. There was also a buttercup curl of butter, a small dish of marmalade, some toast, and a pot of coffee. "No orange juice?" Lon asked, but Kay had already gone into the bathroom. He looked at the more officious of the waiters. "You speak English?" he asked. The man made a rocking motion with his hand.

"We pay a hundred Hong Kong dollars a day for this room, and orange juice should go with it."

The waiters looked at each other. The bathroom door opened a crack. "I canceled the orange juice," Kay said. "It's all my fault. Like everything else." The door shut. Lon cinched the old bathrobe around him, signed the check and put a tip on it. The waiters left and he sat alone at the table, moving the eggs from one side of the plate to the other.

He tried a piece of bacon and it was salty. Marmalade he had never cared for, so he ate a piece of toast with butter. He had eaten breakfast alone for a number of years, and now he felt irritated because his wife was in the bathroom soaking herself. He didn't want to feel peeved. There had been enough of that last night. And yet, how was it that when she did something he thought was cheap the onset of tears made him feel apologetic?

He wanted his marriage to be idyllic. Common sense told him that it couldn't be, but he wanted it to be smooth and affectionate and eternal. He realized that, of the two of them, he would be the more difficult to live with. Kay was sweet and malleable and willing to overlook. His attitude was the opposite. He saw every slight disagreement as a challenge to his mastery, his manliness. He turned away from her in bed if she made the overtures. The man, he felt, should initiate love. The husband must win his wife anew each time. He knew that if love ever became a mechanical matter, his desire for Kay would die an agonizing death.

He was still sitting at the table when she came out wearing

a towel around her head. "I cleaned the tub and refilled it," she said. "Any time you're ready." He looked at her. Her face was still flat and expressionless. He crunched a piece of toast between his teeth and said: "Something on your mind?" She drew out a chair. "Lots of things," she said, sitting down. "And don't ask me about them."

"Last night?" She didn't answer. "These eggs are cold," she said. He got up from the table and went into the bathroom. "Sooner or later," he said through the open door, "you're going to have to learn that nothing cures itself. Talk helps." He stepped into the tub and almost fell.

—Mr. Fong was a man somewhat less than five feet tall. He was slender and pleasant and, when he smiled, his upper teeth hung over his lower lip. He had many brocaded mandarin jackets to show, most of them with sleeves wide enough to hide an extra child, but he had few dresses on display. "You tell me, please. I make it," he said. Kay and Lon took pencil and paper and began to draw sketches—bad sketches—and Mr. Fong brought out American fashion magazines and slowly flipped the pages.

Kay's summer-sky eyes began to sparkle. She liked so many, and the prices were so ridiculously small, that she didn't know what to say. She turned to Lon: "What should I do?" He shrugged. "This is not my department," he said. "Pick out what you like. Pick out as many as you like, within reason. The only thing I ask is that you dress like a thirtyish woman. I'm opposed to skin-tight toreador pants; I'm opposed—"

"I know what you're opposed to," she said. "The hemline should cover the knee. The neckline should not show cleavage." He said, "Right." She sighed. "Maybe if I bought a nun's habit you'd be happy." He started to leave the store. "That's enough," he said. "You're on your own." "No," she said. "Please. Don't go." He stopped. She looked contrite. "I'm sorry," she said softly, out of Fong's hearing. "Truly. I want to dress to please my husband."

"That," Lon said, "is the world's greatest fallacy. Every wife says she dresses to capture her husband's eye. It just isn't so. She dresses to capture the eyes of men she doesn't want. She has a need to know that she's still attractive, so she shows as much of her anatomy as possible. Don't tell me."

He came back into the main part of the shop. Mr. Fong began to look bewildered. "You want me to make measurements?" he said. Lon nodded. Mr. Fong bowed Kay into a dressing room. He turned to Lon. "You stay here, please."

"No," said Lon, "I'm going in there too." He followed. Mr. Fong shrugged. He said something in Chinese and two men came out of a back room and began to study Kay. She was standing in front of a triple mirror. She seemed pleased with herself. Lon drew a chair and sat. He was lounging, but in a moment he was sitting upright. The two Chinese tailors had tape measures. They measured his wife's bust line; they measured her hip line with suitable comments in Chinese; they measured from floor to knee with shoes on; then without shoes; they talked rapidly and musically and the taller of the two took his tape measure and placed it on the nipple of one breast and drew the tape across to the other, announcing the number as he proceeded.

"Is it like this in America?" Lon asked, almost in shock. His wife smiled. "No, dear. These are the gayest measurements I've ever known." He grunted. "Gay is hardly the word. No wonder they didn't want me to come in here." Mr. Fong smiled. "Must make exact for missy's figure," he said. "Material must be cut on bias to fit nice." He fluttered his hands down the side of his body. "Must be snug." "Not too snug," Lon said. "Give her room to breathe." This struck Mr. Fong as very funny. He laughed heartily. "Lady always find room to breathe no matter how tight."

"Tell him," Lon said, "that you don't want a tight dress."

Kay told him. He pinched a piece of Kay's dress at the waistline. "Leave a little bit room," he said. Lon made a face. "In case she coughs," he said.

When they left the shop, Kay had selected three dresses and a white mandarin coat with white brocading on it. "I'm on tiptoe," she said, beaming at him. "I never saw such beautiful clothes. I don't mean I never saw them, I mean I never had them. They're simply, simply gorgeous."

They went back to the shoe shop and got fittings on the shoes. The footgear looked bad with no covering over them, just the basic leather and soles and heels. They took a taxi to the Hong Kong ferry house and, in passing, Kay commented on the clothing of the Chinese girls. "I thought that the slits on the side were short. Look at that one. It's cut almost to the eyeballs." The slits were high and each stride displayed a great deal of thigh. Lon was surprised. "It must be the Western influence," he said. "The slits in Chinese skirts were always slight—until now."

He thought back to what he remembered of Chinese dress. The men, he said, at one time wore long gowns. Some of the old-timers still did, and, when a man and woman became very old, it was sometimes difficult to tell one from the other. Both had thin whiskers. "Chinese women used to wear black cotton pants with long loose blouses. I get the feeling that many of the Eastern nations are swinging away from the old ways, not only in dress, but in business and in social attitudes. Almost every place we've been to has night clubs. That's American. Or, let us say, European. A hundred years ago, both China and Japan were feudal nations. Now they trade with the world; they dress native style and Western. It's as though Asia, at this moment, were trying to face East and West at the same time. They have learned many things, including how to play power politics. Most of them have degenerated to neon signs and Coca-Cola."

Kay disagreed. The big cities appeared to be cosmopolitan, but she felt that the farm people and the natives of small towns lived according to the ancient customs. She mentioned the difference between New Delhi, where college girls in white saris waited for buses, and villages near Agra, where Hindus lay dying of malnutrition by the roadside as neighbors stepped over them on the way to the village well.

They boarded the Hong Kong ferry. Signs said: DO NOT SPIT and WATCH FOR PICKPOCKETS. There were few tourists aboard. Most of the passengers were Chinese. Some girls, in short skirts, crossed their knees and read the morning paper. A couple of coolies in floppy blue cotton stood amidships pointing to the many junks standing beside freighters. A few middle-aged women wore thick glasses and looked at the other passengers. One or two old men, wearing gray gowns, silently stroked hanging corn-silk mustaches.

On the Hong Kong side, the Michaelses studied the new city hall. Kay pointed to women in round black hats scrubbing flagstones on their hands and knees. The stones had been newly set before the city hall and the women were scraping surplus cement from between the cracks. Lon shook his head in disbelief. "Everywhere from the Middle East on," he said, "women dig ditches, pave roads, scrub streets and sidewalks, walk behind donkeys while their husbands ride. Women are as cheap as dirt."

They took a taxi to the hill area behind the Hong Kong wharfs, and walked through the Haw Parr mansion. The house and the grounds, by Western standards, were in excessively bad taste, splashed with clashing pinks and browns and blues and lavenders, complete with swimming pool and no water. Stone tigers and birds glared from behind trees and walls; Lon called it an "Oriental Disneyland."

He was more interested in the slatted shacks built on a steep hill. From a distance, they looked like dirty snowflakes. The refugees from mainland China lived in these shacks, he explained

to Kay, because there was no more room in the Crown Colony
and the British government was reluctant to build in a territory
that might be swallowed overnight by the People's Government
of China. The flow of refugees was so great that a new school
was being opened every eight days. At that point, the English
had joined the Red Chinese in trying to stop the one-way traffic.

Police boats patrolled the harbor; sampans and junks were
searched; guns were trained across the border at Lo Wu; the
weekly refugee train running between Canton and Hong Kong
was searched at the bridge, not only for Chinese with no means
of support, but for spies. The system was slow and expensive for
both sides, Lon said, and the British learned that the Chinese
were the finest people smugglers in the world. The population
had kept growing, and those with no means of support crept
through the streets at night stealing sticks of wood and building
orange crate shacks on the hillside at Tai Hang.

The police chased them. They found that the Chinese were
tractable intractables: they went, but, the moment vigilance was
relaxed, they returned. In 1961, a fire had started in one of the
orange-crate shacks at the foot of the steep hill and, in ten minutes,
the night breeze had fanned it to the top. The Hong Kong fire
brigade could not find any way to bring water to bear on the hill.
They stood and watched. In the ruddy glare, they could see the
peasants run from their tiny houses, screaming. But they could
not run up the precipice, and the flames were whipping upward
from the valley. There was nothing to do but stand and die.

"The shacks are still there," Lon said. "New shacks, I guess.
But look at them." After the fire, the Hong Kong government
forbade anyone to build on the steep hill, but the little crates could
be seen over and under every boulder. Lon said he thought it was
Franklin D. Roosevelt who said that one third of his nation was
ill-fed and ill-housed. In China, he guessed the figure would come
to more than two thirds.

On the way back across the ferry, he thought about his own good fortune. Many times, he had asked himself if it was possible to raise the common economic denominator so that the poor of the world could have sufficient food and housing and clothing, even if they had none of the luxuries of life. It was the dream of an economically naïve man, but it had occurred to him many times. He had an ability to steel himself against many kinds of vicissitudes, but mass poverty and chronic illness in children hurt deeply.

"The poor," said Kay softly, "ye shall always have with you." He came out of his reverie and smiled. "You're doing a mind-reading act," he said. "Maybe there will always be poor people; maybe it is right that the United States pays to store millions and millions of tons of grain to keep it off the market. Perhaps it is some immutable law that these people should claw and maim each other for a single bowl of rice. Little children by the millions—the scores of millions—die in India and China and the Middle East and Africa with their bellies swollen from malnutrition. It's the law of the jungle, I guess."

"All right, Schweitzer," Kay said. "What's the solution?" He shrugged. "None," he said. "Many people are too stupid to work, even if they could find it. If ignorance, let us say, is a lack of knowledge, then stupidity is an inability to absorb it. The world has many stupid people; it has misfits, it has cripples who cannot work; it has emotionally sick people who cannot hold a job; it has bums who have no desire to work; it has animalistic men who can fornicate and make babies, but who cannot support them. You'll get no solution from me, Kay. Better minds than mine have tried."

"I suppose," she said absent-mindedly. The ferry was drawing into the slip at Kowloon. Kay was in a reverie of her own. "You're such a contradictory man," she said. "I can tell by the way you talk that you're deeply affected by what happens to poor people or little children, and yet I've seen you so hard-boiled that I was sure—"

"—I had no feelings at all," he said. They watched the crew throw the lines over and, when the gangplank was lowered, they were among the first ashore. "I have lots of weaknesses," he said. "Callousness isn't one. I can tick them off to myself, but I'm not without compassion." They walked hand-in-hand toward the hotel, a block away. "I know," she said.

"I know you know," Lon replied. "You wouldn't have married a man who was without sensitivity. That isn't what I'm trying to say. What I'm trying to say is that I'm impatient. I cannot forgive mistakes in others. I can forgive my own, or attribute them to hard luck, or just erase them, but I cannot forgive them in others —especially in those I love. If you trip over a rug, I think you're stupid. If a stranger does the same thing, I think the rug should be fixed."

"You're a real man," she said. "But you're also a bastard."

They were on their way back to the room after dinner. "The waiter," Lon said, "was funny. You ordered bird's nest soup. Then you didn't like it. And he said: 'Bird is smawr bird. Come in springtime. Take nest. Boil nest. Velly good for stomach.' Your skin turned pastel green, my dear." Kay thought it was funny. "He made it worse," she said, "not better. I thought that bird's nest soup was the name of a soup. I didn't know it was a real nest. He didn't even tell me if the smawr bird was nest broken."

In the room, Lon said he wanted to type a diary entry. Kay used the time to shake out some dresses, and hang them in the bathroom so that they would catch the steam from the morning tub water. She also used a pitcher of precious water to shampoo her hair, cold.

Our marriage, Lon wrote, *is still in the adjusting stage. I guess it will be like this for a long time—maybe a year. Last night I permitted a burst of jealousy to come to the surface and brought* up Kay's past sex life. It isn't fair, but I did it before I could stop myself. If a husband doesn't know all about his wife's past, he worries about it. If she tells him everything, he eats his heart out worrying about mental comparisons. Either way, he cannot achieve sexual peace of mind, nor can she. The female has the amazing facility of feeling, when she is in love and newly married, that this particular man is the best. The past becomes dim, and she suppresses all memories of how good it was with somebody else.

At precisely the same time, he is beset by a suspicion that she may not have told all. How good was this other man? Or these other men? The husband frets. He is ashamed to mention it, but he looks at her and says to himself: "I wonder how many?" I will never forget the time I was in bed with a model. We were smoking cigarettes and looking at the ceiling and, just to make conversation, I asked her how many men she had slept with. It was a ridiculous question because it calls for a lying reply. She said: "I don't know. Forty or so. Maybe a few more." I almost fell out of bed. Like a true dumbkopf, I followed it with another question to cover my shock. I said: "Well, you never took money for it, I presume," and she said: "I never asked for money in my whole life. But now and then a man would leave a twenty-dollar bill on the table and I'd keep it."

Marriage, of course, is different. But, when two losers like Kay and me are mated, the past is on a different level. I believe my wife when she says she slept with no men except her husband and that goddamned sergeant who plagues me. What makes it worse is that the sergeant was among Francis's best friends. They played tennis together. They drank together. They had Friday night poker sessions together. And Francis suspected nothing. If he could be cold cuckolded, why not me? How can a second husband feel more immune than the first?

Why is sex so important? I understand the sex drive in the

male; he was made to pursue the female. Women, on the other hand, maintain that sex is not the paramount issue of courtship or marriage, but they never stop talking about it. Their favorite boast is "Who needs a man?" They talk about the requisites in a good husband: love, tenderness, respect, ambition, love of children, love of home, intelligence, sense of humor, etc. But not a word about sex. It is as though sex is to marriage what salt is to a good steak—it can be taken or dispensed with, without hurting the food.

I do not believe this. Sex, in my estimation, is most important. When I mention it, Kay says: "I know all about you and your women. Whenever I am introduced to a woman who knew you before I did, I ask myself: 'Her too?'"

She's wrong. She thinks she knows me, and she thinks I was a roué. I had affairs and I told her about them all. I skipped nothing. Still, deep down, she feels that there were more, and that I was a mangy tomcat. I know she feels this way because she told me so. In that case, she is sure that I didn't tell her everything. This makes me think that perhaps she didn't tell me everything. It wouldn't really make any difference because, when a man is as in love as I am, nothing out of the past could make him give her up. Nothing.

On the other hand, she never asks how our sex life compares with my past. She has never asked about Elspeth. Women have some kind of sense—false, indeed—that all women are alike in these matters. Techniques, they feel, are alike except insofar as the man initiates changes. In this they are in grievous error because women know nothing of the secret habits of other women. Also, they lie to each other freely and are suspicious of their sex. They trust not each other.

Naturally, I know my wife much better now. The intimacy of marriage is wholesome and beautiful and satisfying and creates its own hunger. So too does she know me. But the better I know her, the less I can understand two great things that happened to her. One is to marry a soldier simply because of a seduction. She says she was afraid that no one else would want to marry her if he learned that she was not a virgin. I cannot believe this. It is so naïve, so archaic, so little-girlish that it is out of character. Kay is, above all else, a sensitive woman and the story of her marriage could not surprise me more if she had told me that she had majored in weight-lifting.

One time, when we were at a bar near Sarasota, I asked her if she had ever truly loved Francis. Without a moment of thought she said no. Then how, I said, could you spend years living with him, keeping house, permitting him to make love to you, and bearing his child? She said she didn't know. She wished she knew. "He not only made love to me," she said candidly, "but I made love back. I kept telling myself marriage could be a lot worse. What I felt for Francis was respect. He was good. What I hated about him was his fanatic feeling for the U.S. Army. The Army never did a damned thing for him, but he loved the uniform, he loved being transferred from one post to another, and every time I blew up, he'd say: 'This is the time to be in the Army. Peacetime.' He wanted to stay in and get a pension. When Lucy was born, all my doubts about the marriage stopped. If I had walked out before I became pregnant, it would have been easy to start over. Now, with a red-headed little girl who looked just like her father, it was impossible.

She said she felt that she was in a rut. Before the baby was born, Block had paid little attention to her. He admired her, perhaps loved her in an abstract way. He seldom felt any desire for her, and so, in time, Kay became aggressive. It was she who made the initial moves. It was she who aroused him, despising what she was doing because she felt that he should arouse her. Then the sergeant walked in.

He must have come in on tiptoe. Kay said he used to knock at the back door in the middle of the day and ask if there was any coffee on the range. He made a big fuss over the baby. He wished he was married to a girl like Kay and had a baby like Lucy. Kay believed him. He was amiable and agreeable, a blond man with a thick shoe-brush mustache, and she sensed a deep manliness in him.

The coffee breaks went on for a long time. One day, as he was standing beside her, looking at the baby in the crib, he put a soft arm around her waist. She did not remove the arm. The sergeant didn't need to know any more. That was enough. The baby was asleep and the sergeant swung Kay around and kissed her hard on the mouth and pressed her to him and the embrace was so fierce that she lost her breath.

As she explained it to me, she suddenly felt no desire to resist the man; quite the opposite. "I kept telling myself, I hope he takes me. I hope he takes me." He did. He put one arm under her knees and another under her shoulders and lifted her and carried her into the bedroom. Kay thrilled to the thought of being overpowered, of being raped. She was not a party to it, she felt. She was being taken by force. For years, she had been the aggressor; it was she who had made all the moves. Now, virility was asserting itself and she felt more of a response to it than she had ever felt with Francis.

But when it was over, she knew at once that she had made a mistake bigger than the one she made in marrying Francis. The sergeant had turned out to be weak rather than virile, supplicating rather than demanding, easily affronted rather than dominating. She was dazed, shocked, frightened. He had been all male up to the moment she surrendered to him. Then he fell apart. She sensed the problem at once: this man didn't want to love her; he needed to be loved.

That evening, when Francis came in for supper, he appeared to be happy. "This morning," he said, "the Sarge gave me a real break. No work. He told me I could ride the ammo truck all the way to Plainsville and back. That's nine hours of riding on your tail. When I reported in tonight, he said he might let me go again next week."

"That's good," Kay had said with no feeling. She was sick. The sergeant had set the stage completely, and he had sent her husband to a place a hundred miles away so that there would be no interruption. She felt ill and nervous. Within two days, she was trying to philosophize about it, trying to tell herself that almost all women made a mistake or two like this one. Okay, she had made hers.

But, when the sergeant walked in the following week, he did it without knocking. He had sent her husband to Plainsville, and she knew that Francis had had the order the night before. So she was not surprised when the sergeant walked in. "How's the coffee?" he said casually and took her in his arms. She twisted away. "The coffee is cold," she said, "and there will be none of that." His face fell into a frown and he grabbed her roughly and said: "Don't talk to me like that. You may be married to him, but you belong to me." At first she fought him, almost violently as she told the story, but the same surrendering weakness came over her. The affair was as weak and unsatisfactory as the first time. It was as though anticipation was all and realization was anticlimactic. She wondered if that wasn't also true in her case.

The third time he arrived, he had a package. In it was a gold wedding band. "It's for you to hide," he had said, "until we can go away together. I only have seventeen months to go. Then I'm out with a pension and I'm going to open a radio shop in Philadelphia. After that, it's us and the baby." Kay told him he was crazy, insane, demented. She would not leave her husband for the best man who ever lived. At this, the sergeant smiled. "That's me," he had said. "All you have to do is do nothing and say nothing until my time is up. Francis isn't going to know anything until we're ready to walk out and leave a note."

Kay was impressed. She did not want this man. She was gradually becoming disgusted with him as a lover, and afraid of him as a person. But a wedding ring is a significant and symbolic item. With feet dragging, she went to bed with him again. And again. And again. Long before the affair ended, she realized that he never intended to marry her, or go away with her.

One afternoon when he showed up, Kay held the ring in her hand. "Take it," she said, "and go." He started to argue, then to demand, then to push her around. "Go," she said desperately, "because this time, I'm going to tell Francis and, even if it ruins my life, I'm going to tell the captain too. Now go while you're able to keep out of trouble." He wanted to know what he had done to offend her. She was breathing so hard she could hardly talk. "Just go," she said. "Go now. And don't ever come back. I want to hate myself alone."

The whole scene, as she told it to me in the bar outside of Sarasota, is so alive that I can re-create it at will. The quotations may not be exact, but they are close. The thing I cannot understand, or comprehend, is how she repeated what she knew was a sinful error. She repeated it again and again, in spite of the way this man pushed her around. This is beyond me; this is what plagues me when I think of that goddamned sergeant. And how do I know it will not happen again? How do I know that she didn't enjoy the little play she was getting from Jimmy Yen? Maybe she's insecure, and needs to know that all men want to drag her off to the cave. If so, this marriage isn't going to last beyond the honeymoon. I love her, and I cannot live without her, but if I suspect that she is encouraging men to flirt, to make a play for her, I will live without her. It's a choice of evils and I'll take the heartbreak of living alone.

Deep inside, I am certain that she made that one bad mistake and will not make another. That's my feeling. I don't want to be wrong, but I don't want to hypnotize myself into believing that I'm right. I saw a mutt of a man once whose wife used to say: "You're tired. I'll drive Joe home," and the husband knew why, but he was afraid to tell himself the truth. So he just nodded and said, "Okay." He was afraid to say that he was not tired, and he would drive Joe home. Later, the wife and Joe made no pretense about their relationship, and no excuses to the husband. In later years, he sat silent and brooding as his wife went off on vacations with Joe.

That kind of life is not for me.

Lon ripped the diary paper out of the typewriter and looked around. Kay was in bed. Sleeping. He hadn't even heard a good night.

THE EIGHTEENTH DAY

IT was almost noon and they were back at the hotel. The fittings had been done. The final fittings, Lon hoped. He was sitting on the side of the bed, filing his fingernails. Kay was at the window, looking out. "It's a lousy thing to say," she said, "but they look like ants down there. Millions and millions of them. On the sidewalks. In the streets. Everywhere but up the walls of the hotel.

"They have the same aimlessness as ants," she went on. "Inside the mass, they appear to be milling as though they're excited or panicked." "Or something," Lon said. Kay came back from the window. "They have beautiful mornings in Hong Kong. Bright and cool." He blew on the nail file and put it in a drawer. "We have to wait for a guide," he said. He looked at his watch. "Any minute." The manager, he explained, had sent word that a businessman of some distinction wanted to show the Michaelses around. The manager seemed to be impressed. So Lon had said okay. "I hope he has a car," Kay said. "What's his name?" Michaels glanced through some papers in his wallet. "Here it is. Sullivan. Mr. Walter Sullivan. Has an office on Nathan Road." "One of Jack Sullivan's cousins," Kay said. "Jack or Dorothy sent him."

"Not funny," Lon said. "This man is probably an Englishman or an—" The telephone rang. He pulled it off the hook.

252

"Yes," he said. "Yes. Thank you. Tell him we'll be right down. We'll meet at the front desk." He hung up. "He's here." Kay wondered if she should take a light coat. He didn't think so. She took it anyway, carrying it on her arm.

In the lobby, they met a little dandy of a man, a fortyish person who looked like David Niven if Niven had fallen into a tub of henna rinse. His name, he said extending his hand, was Walter Sullivan. Lon appreciated the fact that he did not say, "You can call me Walter." There was a dark young lady with him, more a flat-chested child in appearance than a woman. She was introduced as his business associate, Miss Irma McEvoy. "First," Lon said, "I want to express my appreciation of your kind offer, Mr. Sullivan. And secondly, if you don't mind, I'd like to ask why you made it."

They were standing near the registration desk. Sullivan pointed back over his shoulder. "The manager is somewhat of a friend. He tells me who is in town. Your name was mentioned, and I happen to be one of your addicts." Kay smiled. It always made her happy when she met someone who read her husband's work. "How nice," she said. She turned to the girl. "Have you lived here long?" "About seven months," Mr. Sullivan said. "She's a New Zealander."

Sullivan said his car was waiting outside. They walked around the potted palms, and around the ladies who always looked like tweedy English schoolteachers and who were always biting into bread and marmalade, and walked out into the sunshine. It was warm. Kay handed her coat to Lon. He made a face as they got into the car.

It was a good car and Mr. Sullivan sat up front with the chauffeur. He spoke, looking over his left shoulder, twisting in the seat to see his guests. The car drove onto the ferry and went across to Victoria and turned left on Connaught Road to go up into the hills and around the island. The trees along the highlands were bare, except in patches where little pink and white blossoms seemed to have been hit by a sudden frost and were petrified in the cool breeze.

The view of Kowloon was long and clear as the car climbed, and behind the New Territories the brown mountains of mainland China stood like stale pie crust. Along the stretches of harbor, there were places crowded with junks, gunwale to gunwale, and, at the north end, a British destroyer was making a low slow swing into the South China Sea.

Mr. Sullivan prattled. He was not a jolly man, but he knew the colony, and he seemed to know books. He was given to sudden flashes of error of the most painful kind. In one conversation he maintained that Harry Truman had preceded Franklin D. Roosevelt as President of the United States, and, in another, he told Lon that the best Michaels book was *Ballaboo*. Lon was prepared to let the matter rest there, but Kay said, "My husband didn't write that book." Mr. Sullivan was cheerful. "Of course he did," he said. "I have all of your husband's books."

Lon said that he must agree with Kay. *Ballaboo* was written by a rip-roaring imitator of Ernest Hemingway, a man who drank his way through African safaris leaning on an elephant gun. Mr. Sullivan smiled graciously. "I couldn't be wrong," he said, "but an author should know his books." It was embarrassing. It was also embarrassing when the car arrived at Repulse Bay. Mr. Sullivan seemed to be afflicted with spasms of candor.

He suggested that they stop for tea, or a drink, and the car pulled up before a long one-story country club fronted by a beautiful garden and urns of geraniums standing on white walls. Below was Repulse Bay, blue and dappled, and, off to the right, an old castle. They sat on the porch and the waiter brought Scotch, and pots of tea.

"She comes from New Zealand," Mr. Sullivan said, smiling at the young lady. "She has come to live with me, haven't you, dear?" The girl inclined her head a little, and smiled bravely. Yes, she said. Yes. "This is unique," Sullivan said, rubbing the tea from his mustache, "because we had never met before. That is, before seven months ago, when she arrived."

No one said anything. Kay and Lon began to look around at the flowers, and at the sparkling fountain just below the porch. They saw a waiter bring a lobster, set upright on a tiny wicker throne, to people at the next table. "I'm in the export business," Mr. Sullivan said, moving the wet bottom of his glass in circles over the table cloth. "I have agents in Auckland and I sent word that I would be very kind to any lady of breeding who would come to live with me. The only requirement was that she not expect anything of me except a good home and unlimited respect."

"You must feel homesick," Kay said. Miss McEvoy appeared to arouse herself for the first time. "Not at all," she said. "I'm —well, sensitive, I guess you'd call it—and the people of Auckland are quite insolent." Lon sipped the last of his Scotch and asked for another. "Insolent?" he said. "A whole city?"

"Have you ever been there?" Miss McEvoy asked. "No," he said. "Then you don't know," the child-woman said. "The people, practically all of them, I'd say, are very independent and insolent. They seem to be afraid that everybody else feels bigger." She shrugged. "It's hard to explain," she said. "A taxi driver won't take a passenger who wants to sit in the back."

"Intolerable," Mr. Sullivan said. "When Irma heard of my offer, and learned that I was bloody serious about it, she accepted. I sent the money and she came on." No one said anything. There didn't seem to be much to say. Sullivan tried some of the black tea and poured some for Miss McEvoy. "You know about this place?" he asked Lon.

"This restaurant?" Lon said. "No." "Oh, please," Miss McEvoy said. Mr. Sullivan smiled tolerantly. "The trouble with Americans," he said to Miss McEvoy, "is that they know no history except their own, and they distort that into cowboys and Indians. I'll bet you the Michaelses would like to know the history of this place." Kay nodded. Lon said sure. "You see?" Sullivan said.

"You do this on purpose," Miss McEvoy said. "Well, I don't have to listen. I'm off to the w.c." Sullivan reached across the table and caught her wrist. "It's not good manners to leave," he said softly. "You're hurting my lecture before I begin." Miss McEvoy relaxed.

"I'm sure," Mr. Sullivan said affably, "that you both know about the siege of Hong Kong. It happened at Christmas 1941, right after Pearl Harbor. We had some troops here and the general strategy was to fight a delaying action against the Japanese, starting at the Kowloon peninsula, opening the dams and scorching the good earth as we got our bloody heads knocked off. The Japanese had three full divisions to throw into the action, an overwhelming force against the British battalions, and they did a damned good job. They infiltrated our lines at night, drove wedges between units, and no one seemed to know where anyone else was so, every morning, our men ran faster toward the ferry. Well, they got over here to the Hong Kong side in fair condition, but there was never a chance of winning, never a chance of a stalemate."

"I remember now," Lon said. Sullivan nodded in appreciation. "The Japanese commander kept sending messages asking us to surrender, promising that our men would be treated according to the convention of The Hague, and our women and children would be permitted to stay in their homes without molestation and all that rot."

"May I leave for a moment?" Miss McEvoy said. "Not at all," Mr. Sullivan said, without interrupting his story. "Some of the units got back as far as this country club, except that it was a hospital." Kay looked around. "It was full of wounded, and the good sisters were running from bed to bed with plasma and bandages. The high command knew that there was no further place for retreat, so they backed up on the Stanley Peninsula," he pointed, "and left the hospital.

"The Japanese came in shouting and falling over each other. They went from bed to bed bayoneting the chaps, and in a few moments this was a screaming mess. They took the British sisters and the Chinese girls in the back and they raped them on the floor." Kay began to look away, toward the table where the lobster was now off the throne and on a plate. "An ugly story," Mr. Sullivan said, "but history as it is seldom written. They lined up in queues in the corridor waiting their turn for the women, and those who couldn't do anything voided on the sisters."

Lon didn't know what to say. His host was obviously sick on this subject, and his girl was even sicker. She folded her hands on the table edge, almost as though in prayer. She kept staring at her hands. "It is hard to believe all this," Lon said. "I mean, the setting today is so serene. Quite beautiful, as a matter of fact." Sullivan nodded with emphasis. "That's why I like to bring people out here. Especially intelligent tourists. They just don't realize what happened."

"So gorgeous," Kay murmured. "I can't even believe that this was once a hospital." Miss McEvoy looked up, as though asking Kay not to encourage the man. "Oh," Sullivan said, "but that isn't all. You see that dumpy-looking castle down there? Looks like an old fort? No? It's hanging off the edge of the cliff." Lon nodded, and pointed. "Well, the honorable Nipponese found a whole detachment of New Zealanders in there. They didn't bayonet those men. Oh, no. They took them one by one and tossed them over the cliff and down onto the rocks."

He smiled and tapped a cigarette on the back of his hand. "Have you ever heard men scream, Mr. Michaels? I mean, really scream, not with pain, but with terror? You would hardly believe it, but they sound almost exactly like women." Kay could feel herself becoming ill. She took Miss McEvoy by the hand without looking

at Mr. Sullivan. "Would you please show me to the w.c.?" she
said. "My husband can tell me the rest of the story later."

The men stood, and the women left. Lon smiled. "You can
hardly blame them," he said. "Their stomachs can't stand harsh
history." "But yours can," Mr. Sullivan said. "And that's good.
Irma has heard the story so often she's sick of it. She was sick of
it the first day, I guess, but it's the price she pays for staying with
me."

"If I'm not too bold," Michaels said, "why do you make such
a point of this story about sending to Auckland for a woman?"
"You're not bold," Sullivan said. "You're my guest. I cannot live
alone; I have a pretty good business; and I cannot marry." "Oh."
"No. I'm not married. I'm still single." Lon wanted to change
the subject again. "May I ask how you know those screams so
well?"

"Because I was here," Sullivan said. He puffed on the cigarette.
"Just another rag-tag New Zealand soldier wearing a big-brimmed
hat and fighting my guts out thinking I was saving the empire."
"Were you in that old castle?" "Indeed yes. Almost all of my
buddies died on those rocks below, and as long as I'm alive I'm
going to stay in Hong Kong and tell the story. Why the hell should
anyone be allowed to forget what happened to those poor bastards?
The Crown Colony doesn't put any tourist signs around here saying
that this was once a hospital. They want to forget the whole thing,
you know. We have Japanese tourists who come here with cameras.
They think it is 'ruvvery.' "

"What's that mean?" "It's their way of saying lovely." "How
did you escape?" "That's easy," Sullivan said, waving a hand for
the check. "I got on my bloody knees and begged for my life. I
begged so hard that one Japanese officer began to laugh. When
they finished killing everyone off, they stripped me." For the first
time, Mr. Sullivan appeared to be embarrassed. His pale brows
wrinkled, and he shrugged. "They threw me to the floor and took

turns treating me like a woman. You understand?" Lon swallowed. He stood as Sullivan paid the check. He looked for the women to return. "Then they castrated me and carried me back up here to the hospital. I lost much blood and almost died. Later, a doctor told me they did it because I was a coward. I fail to see . . ."

"The ladies," Lon said. The women had returned, talking casually and pointing out the beds of flowers around the fountain. Sullivan walked back to the car and held the rear door open until everyone was in. Then he got into the front seat and relaxed into a sort of beatific silence.

It was late and the room was quiet, except for the sound of Kay's typing. Lon was propped up in bed, with an English language newspaper in his hands. He wore white silk pajamas with black piping, black-rimmed glasses, and—unusual for him—was smoking a cigar.

Love Hong Kong, Kay wrote, *love it. Could spend a fortune in this glamorous, gorgeous place. Feel almost Chinesey at times. So picturesque. So busy. So mysterious, or is the word inscrutable? Husband is still very husbandish. Now feel that I know him a little better than he does. Silly feeling, but I have it. Such a perfectionist. Feel gleeful when he makes a blunder. He knows it too. Can't help it. He's so quick to point to mine.*

Every day, every hour, every minute I know more and more that Lon is for me. Lowest morale point on whole trip was when he asked about sergeant. Hate myself enough for knowing anything about other men without having it tossed into my face. That was a bad moment. Some questions are impossible to answer.

He made big mistake today. Took us off as guests of New Zealand expatriate. Man turned out to be sick. Maimed. Lon thought host was a big fan of his writings. After leaving Repulse Bay, gentle questioning brought replies showing the man knew little or nothing about the Michaels masterpieces. Had to smile. Much impressed with Aberdeen. Thousands of junks jammed together on muddy riverbed. Catwalks between rows of them. Children playing on dry land, develop into avaricious animals when coin is tossed.

Feel they would kill a tourist for a dime. Studied junks, no toilet facilities, nothing but mud under keels—thought of what one match and a breeze would do to scores of thousands of Chinese. Or two muscular germs.

Too fatigued to write more. Spent much time walking today and my feet are hot and pulsing.

THE NINETEENTH DAY

THERE is an instant in a day when a desert, a city, a sea, or a mountain is at its most beautiful. In Hong Kong, the moment is dusk. The setting, looking east from Kowloon across Victoria Harbor, builds in color and composition until a precise minute is reached, and the beauty begins to die in darkness. The Michaelses were leaving the hotel, turning up Chatham Road in a taxi, when Hong Kong became a breathlessly attractive place.

The sun was sitting on the edge of the mountains behind Deep Bay. The anchor lights of the ships were on. The water of the harbor was still, and took on the color of cheap wine. So did Mount Davis and Victoria Peak, so that the bay seemed to lift in two giant waves. There was a film of mist. It was caught by the sun and colored lavender so that the junks and the sampans assumed the same shade. Streetlights began to turn on along the hill roads on the far side, so that there was an illusion of yellow-lavender bulbs strung diagonally on a Christmas tree.

The sun set while the cab was moving up Chatham to Ma Tau Wei. The beauty was not obliterated; the colors deepened swiftly and the lights on the ships and up the sides of the hills grew brighter and brighter and night came to Hong Kong. Lon kept looking back, and talking to Kay at the same time. She looked regal. The bun was placed higher than usual on the back of her head and she wore a beige comb with rhinestones behind it. Her profile was cool and classical, tilt of her nose just right, her chin a bit too strong. She wore a white gown of Grecian cut with draped folds across the breast, and folds below the waist gathered on the right hip.

To Lon, she was always beautiful, even at that moment of morning awakening when all of a lady's artificial assets have deserted her. She was happy with the new dress, and the white shoes with the seed pearls. Kay's hands pulled the hem down, so that, as she sat, it hung straight out from the knees. "Think it's long enough?" she asked.

He shrugged. "It's out of my line," he said. "Mr. Fong says the fashion decree is for a certain length; the knee is supposed to peek at the man, or vice versa, as you sit. All I know is that I seem to have spent most of my life watching women yanking skirts down while sitting. They spend a lot of time wiggling and pulling. Their modesty is lost on me."

"But do you like it?" Kay said. Oh, he liked it all right. He thought it was beautiful and he also thought that only a statuesque woman like Kay could wear a Grecian gown. "It's not that," he said, "that makes me feel ugly. It's this damned dinner. I don't want it; I don't want to go; but I'm on my way."

"How could we say no?" Kay said. "Mr. Fong has been so nice." Lon sat back and adjusted his black bow tie. He was obviously at some pains to phrase what he wanted to say. "In the first place," he said, gesturing freely with his hands as he always did, "in the first place, Mr. Fong has not been nice to us. Mr. Fong is a nice person, but he is in business and he extracted from us whatever he wanted to show a profit.

"I just don't like deception. Mr. Fong got me out of a deep sleep this morning to ask if I would be his guest at a so-called real Chinese dinner. I told him I don't know what a *real* Chinese dinner is, and I don't know if I would like it. In the second place, I don't know Mr. Fong outside of his dress shop. Maybe I don't want to. Maybe I'm a little snobbish that way."

"Oh, stop it," she said. Lon grunted and, for a moment, subsided. Then he opened up again. "The barber was in the room when the second call came. I had a face full of lather and it was Mr. Fong again. 'Would we please come to dinner? Please?' So I said all right. Oh, boy, was he happy! He sounded like a child. 'Maybe six o'clock his place? Maybe six thirty?' Okay. Okay. I don't relish the notion of a real Chinese dinner, or even a phony one, but okay. I'll go. My wife will go.

"Then a message this afternoon when the dress is delivered. It's going to be a party for dinner. At the party, all of a sudden, are Mr. Walter Sullivan and his girl friend, and, of all people, Mr. Yen. Now I wonder how that happened? How is it that Mr. Fong invited us to a dinner I didn't want to eat, and I wind up with Sullivan and Yen? I don't like either of these people, and most particularly Yen."

"You imagine things," she said snappishly. Lon agreed that it was possible, but the way he felt about Yen it would be easier not to see him. "Who needs him?" he said. "And, by the way: how was your former husband in these matters? Was he jealous?"

Kay smiled. She had to smile. "He was just the opposite of you. He liked to show me off. He liked men to admire me." "You're kidding," Lon said. She wasn't. "In the matter of dress, he wanted the hemline higher and the neckline lower. 'Come on, honey,' he used to say. 'Show a little. I want my friends to eat their hearts out.' He used to bring his buddies home for card games and most of them always found an excuse for getting out into the kitchen to 'help me' with the drinks."

"Strange," Lon said. "The fool never knows enough to hide the rare gem he found. He must show it. I suppose the sergeant was a poker player too?"

Kay looked at her husband. "This has gone far enough," she said. "Just about far enough. Now look. I belong to you and no-body else, and I enjoy your jealousy; I like it; but, Lon, I know this game better than you do and nobody is going to make passes at me tonight."

"How do you stop it?" he said.

"I don't mean it that way. No woman can stop a man from staring at her, but she can stop any man by not encouraging it." The cab skidded to a stop, then backed up a few feet. They were in front of Fong's emporium near the airport. Mr. Yen, with black hair gleaming and slitted eyes burning, opened the door on Kay's side and stuck his hand in to assist her.

"Kay," Lon said abruptly, "we're getting out on this side." He greeted Yen curtly, got out and helped his wife out. "I thought this was Fong's dinner?" he said. "Where is he?"

"Inside," said Mr. Yen cheerfully. He could not have mis-understood Lon's attitude; it dripped with animosity, but obviously he had no intention of permitting it to upset him. "Mr. Sullivan too."

Momentarily, Lon noticed that Yen could pronounce the letter *L* correctly. He drew Kay's arm through his and walked past Yen, across the sidewalk, and into the shop. "Ah, yes," Fong said, com-ing through a door curtain to greet him. "We have nice dinner soon." Sullivan stood, extending his hand. "We seem to have mutual friends in Hong Kong," he said. Lon smiled. "Yes," he said. "It seems that everywhere I turn . . ." "How are you, this evening?" Kay said, addressing Sullivan's girl. Miss McEvoy, in a plain black chiffon dress with a small choker of pearls, looked like a little girl in mother's heels. She said she was hungry.

Fong got his coat and announced that they would go in two cars. "Where is Mrs. Fong?" asked Lon. Fong looked stunned, then grinned. "Chinese man does not take woman to dinner," he said. "Wife stay home." Lon stared at his wife. "Then we will not meet Mrs. Yen either?" "Oh," said Mr. Yen, laughing, "she's too busy. You know how women are." Lon nodded. "That's exactly what I was thinking."

They went out on the sidewalk. The night was full now, and the neon signs had assumed control. If it was Fong's dinner, which Lon doubted, now they would find out. The cars were at the curb. "Let's see who gives the orders," he whispered to Kay, "and in that way we'll find out who our host is." Kay just shook her head. She felt that he was carrying his jealousy of Yen down to the small decimal points.

"It isn't jealousy," he whispered, as though reading her mind. "It's disgust. No man makes a pass at a married woman unless he feels that she may be available."

Fong waved for the Michaelses to ride with him in the front car. Yen interrupted, and said something in rapid Chinese. Fong looked pained, then smiled. "Yen ride in front car with Michaels. He knows the roads, if you please. Irma ride up front too."

Kay was stunned. Lon grinned. She was stunned on several counts. The first was that her husband's assessment of Yen had turned out to be correct. The second was that they were being told with whom to ride, not asked. The third was that Miss McEvoy was ordered to ride with Yen. The fourth count was that Mr. Fong, as polite a man as one could find, called the girl "Irma."

Sullivan said nothing. He simply nodded to Yen and got into the second car with Fong. Mr. Yen was affable. "Confucius didn't say it," he said, "but Americans ride in car unlike Chinese family. Chinese family like to stay together." He opened the front door and motioned for Irma to sit up with the chauffeur.

Lon cut in at once, realizing that this would place Mr. Yen on the back seat with them, with Kay in the middle. "No, no," he said. "Let Miss McEvoy sit back with us, Mr. Yen. You sit up front with the driver. You know the roads, I understand." Yen bowed and put on the patent-leather smile he always wore when the game was against him. "Sure, sure," he said. "Make it any way you please."

The car started off, with the second one close behind. "How far is the restaurant?" Lon asked. A little way, Mr. Yen said vaguely. How little? He turned left, in the front seat, as Mr. Sullivan had done yesterday, so that he could see his guests. He talked to Lon, but the black little eyes were on Kay. "You know Hong Kong?" he said. "You go Prince Edward Road left, then right on Tai Po Road to Castle Peak Road. Follow straight out to Dragon Inn."

"Dragon Inn?" Kay said. "Is that the restaurant?" Mr. Yen said it was a very fine place for Chinese. "Not poor Chinese," he said. "Chinese businessmen and bankers, like that. Like fine steak in San Francisco," he said.

"You know San Francisco?" Lon asked. Mr. Yen looked at him briefly. "San Francisco, Los Angeles, Chicago—not much New York. I have many friends. Bunch of wise-guy newspapermen. They write big jokes in paper about Yen. Very popular." Miss McEvoy beamed at Mr. Yen. "He's not kidding," she said, and the brightness, the pleasantness of her tone—or perhaps the rarity of any speech from Miss McEvoy—made the Michaelses pay attention to her words.

"Jimmy knows many big people all over the world," she said. "You should see his scrapbooks." "That reminds me," Mr. Yen said, "I would be honored if you both would sign your names in my book. Autograph, it is called." He said the word autograph in separate syllables, as though this was a new one. "Happy to do it," Lon said, with no happiness in the tone. He turned to Miss McEvoy. "You know Mr. Yen?" he asked. Then, as an afterthought, "Pretty well?"

Kay glared at him. He paid no attention. Miss McEvoy seemed to give the question a little thought. "Yes," she said slowly, as Yen turned to whisper directions to the Chinese driver. "Pretty well." Again, she was looking at her fingers on her lap. "Yes," she said. "You see, Walter and Jimmy have some common business interests. Walter imports practically all of the woolens and silks that Jimmy uses." She smiled, again brightly. "It is more than business interests. They are good friends."

"That's nice," Kay said, not so much because it was nice as to say something before Lon could think of another question. The girl looked across Lon to his wife. "Walter likes to work in the evening," she said. "There's precious little a woman can do in Hong Kong alone. So sometimes he phones Jimmy and asks him to take me out to dinner, or a Chinese play."

"Oh," said Lon sarcastically. "That's not a bit gallant." He stared at Mr. Yen. "You have to be asked? I don't believe it." Yen was flattered. "First few times," he said, "Walter called me. After that, I called Irma. Right, Irma?" The girl smiled at him. "Right-o," she said.

Lon could not restrain a triumphant glance at his wife. "Not to change the subject, darling," he said, "but I was just thinking how you never liked to work on Chinese puzzles. The only part you enjoyed was putting the final few pieces in place." "Those," she said coldly, "were not Chinese puzzles, they happened to be jigsaws." "Oh," he said, "there's a difference?" Yen said it was strange, but he had never seen or worked a Chinese puzzle. "You should," Kay said, "you'd be good at them."

The car kept moving, and it seemed that they were on the road a long time. "We're heading toward the Bamboo Curtain," Lon said. "Aren't we?" Mr. Yen shook his head negatively. "Not quite," he said. "Lo Wu is west. Very west. We going southwest, south. When we passed Tsuen Wan back ten minutes, other cross-road goes to mainland China. We take left, go to Castle Peak."

"How far?" Kay said, then burst into laughter. "Don't answer that question." Lon said that the car had been on the road over half an hour, and there was still a little way to go. "It's worth it," Miss McEvoy said. "They have splendid food at the Dragon Inn."

"I hope so," Kay said. "I'm willing to try anything once." "Very interesting philosophy, don't you think?" Lon said to Yen. The man nodded politely. "How do you like the new suits?" he asked.

"I only got them this afternoon," said Lon. "I guess I should try them before we leave." "Oh," said Mr. Yen, "you're not leaving yet. Stay a few weeks." "Tomorrow evening," Lon said. Mr. Yen seemed to be genuinely surprised. He looked back directly at Kay. "So soon? You have not seen Hong Kong." Lon shook his head gravely. "The *real* Hong Kong," he said. "Exactly," said Mr. Yen.

Sometimes Mr. Yen seemed to lapse into slight pidgin English. This time Lon imitated him. "Want to see *real* children," he said. "Big boy, mine. Little girl, hers," he said, pointing. "Soon maybe new one—ours." The Chinese seemed to lose interest in the conversation. "Ah," he said. "Happy news." "No," Kay said quickly, "no happy news yet. My husband—" she seemed to be embarrassed, "is just hoping." Irma McEvoy, twining and untwining the fingers on her lap, parted her thumbs eloquently. "Better me than you," she said. "That would be bloody bright news in my case."

For a while, the car ran along the craggy edge of a bay, then turned right and up a hill. There were lights ahead and the driver slowed to turn into a driveway. He moved up toward a red-roofed building, a pagoda-like structure sitting on a rocky eminence over water. This was Dragon Inn. It was surrounded by small fountains and gardens. The car was parked and Mr. Yen said something to the driver, who hopped out and ran around to help the passengers.

The fountains could be heard as well as seen, and there was a sweet odor of jasmine on the night breeze. Still, there was an uneasy loneliness to the place, as though it had been set too far out from the crowded colony of Hong Kong. There were no other buildings near. Two waiters, in floppy white cotton and slapping slippers, trotted out of a back building holding trays up on the palms of their hands.

The second car came in a few minutes behind theirs, and Mr. Fong and Mr. Sullivan joined the group. "I feel so funny with all these men," Kay was saying to Miss McEvoy. "You and I are the only women. I didn't know that the others wouldn't bring their wives." Irma was tolerant. "Their wives," she said, "are not on the same social level as their husbands. The way they treat them—"

"Now we eat," Mr. Yen said, clapping his hands. He looked at Miss McEvoy. "Come. You and I will show the way." The others followed. "I think," said Kay to Lon, "you have a point." Softly, he said: "To go to a place you do not want to see, with people you do not respect, is more than a waste. It's a pain."

The Dragon Inn was broken up into several dining rooms. There were families at huge round tables, some dining with chopsticks out of a common bowl, others holding small bowls under their chins, and dipping into them with sticks. "You'll like this," Mr. Yen said to Kay. "It's a hide-away. A place to relax." His manner altered at this point. Once he reached the doorway of the big dining room, he became imperious. He spoke Cantonese to the waiters, and sent them trotting and scurrying. They sat at a table near a low squarish window. It was open and the perfume of jasmine filtered through the room. Mr. Yen selected a chair with its back to the window. He nodded to Miss McEvoy to sit on his right. Then to Fong. Then to Kay. Then to Lon, and to Sullivan.

Everyone sat. The waiters put big menus before each person. Also a bowl of water and a hot damp face cloth. Lon and Kay watched the others. The hot cloth was for cleaning the hands. Lon said: "The menu is in Chinese and English. I thought this place was for Chinese only." Mr. Yen chuckled and addressed Fong. "Boy," he said, "he's sharp." Then, more seriously—noting that

Lon did not laugh—he said: "Some British government officials come here. Also, some of the old families of Hong Kong. But mostly it is Chinese."

Lon and Kay read the English side of the menu together, pointing to items which, by name, amused them. There was a vegetable called Hairy Squash. There was another called Buds of Peas with Crabmeat ($6 HK) and a hot delicacy: Chicken Blood Soup ($2 HK). Everyone agreed that Fong should do the ordering for all. He laughed heartily, as though overwhelmed by the honor, and started with shark's fin soup. It arrived with shredded chicken and noodles.

All except Kay and Lon ate as though hunger must be fought with slurping gusto. The next course was "Fried Sliced Chicken Paper Wrapped." It arrived in small packages, wrapped in oil paper and placed on a centerpiece. A waiter snipped the end off each piece of paper and the diners picked select bits of chicken with chopsticks. "This," said Lon hopelessly, "is like trying to pick up a diamond with eyebrow tweezers." "In a dark coal mine," said Kay.

The next dish was Stewed Pigeon with Oyster Sauce. Kay and Lon said no thank you. They also excused themselves when the Ducks' Feet arrived. Kay glanced at it and said: "I'll eat the parts the Chinese throw away." Mr. Yen thought that this was very funny. He laughed heartily, looked at Kay, and laughed again. Between courses, he conversed animatedly. He spoke for a time about all that he had to undergo in humiliation every time he visited the United States. "When you come here," he said, "we say welcome. Happy to see you. When I go stateside there is searching of pants, jacket, wallet, everything. Also many questions. Also where is my ticket back to Hong Kong? Your government do not treat Chinese good at all. Very bad for friends."

The next course looked good and smelled good. "Whatever this may be," Kay said, "I'm having some." Mr. Fong heard her

"This grouper head," he said. "Just the head?" Lon asked. Fong nodded. The Michaelses put the ivory chopsticks beside their plates. "Well," Kay said softly, "I'll never knock hominy and grits again."

Lon began to distrust the nice appearance or nice odor of each course. He wanted to know what each one was. He skipped the Pig's Kidney and Bamboo Shoots. Fong apologized to Yen for not ordering the Braised Ox Tripe, but said it wasn't popular anyway. Yen kept asking the Michaelses: "Isn't it beautiful food? This real Chinese." The menu listed fifteen kinds of rice, or perhaps it was one kind of rice and fifteen ways of ruining it.

Behind the restaurant was a big aquarium. There, the customer could select a live fish, point to it and, in a half hour, eat it. Kay and Lon ate little. They tried to nerve themselves up to it, but managed only to push food from one side of a dinner plate to the other. As a dessert, Mr. Yen recommended Lotus Seed Cream, but, in this case, everyone declined. There was tea, of course—a choice of four kinds.

When the dinner was over, Lon said that he didn't like to rush matters, but there were some important things he had neglected, back at the hotel. The time was 10:30. Mr. Yen looked at his watch. "Tell you what," he said. "I have some business to discuss with some gentlemen in another room. Fong, you take them back to the hotel. No, better yet, I tell the driver to take Mr. and Mrs. Michaels to Peninsula Hotel."

Fong nodded. He didn't yet understand the plot, but he knew he would in a moment. "Irma," said Mr. Yen, "how about staying here with me for business? Walter can go back with Fong in second car." Miss McEvoy looked up quickly at Sullivan. He nodded his head abruptly. "All right," she said. "Be glad to." Lon stood, and helped Kay up. They thanked their hosts and shook hands all around three times. "Nice drinks here," Mr. Yen said, "if you want to stay."

No, they'd rather go now. It would require an hour to get back to the hotel and that was late enough. "But not too late, I hope," Yen said to Kay and laughed heartily. The Michaelses left and Yen stood in the doorway and spoke to the driver. The man held the back door open. As they moved toward the car, Lon said, "Want to bet one dollar Hong Kong he's stooped down at the little window looking at you?"

"No!" said Kay vehemently. "Okay," Lon said. "We'll both turn together. Now." They swung around. Yen was crouched behind the little square window in the dining room, watching. "I would think," Lon said as he helped his wife into the car, "that he is hardly interested in my back."

THE TWENTIETH DAY

A STRANGE man. He was slender and British and poised, in a vague way, and he talked incessantly but he said little. He had telephoned first, then he arrived in the lobby in the morning, and sat drinking beer. "The British Colonial Information Service," he said formally, "requires me to take you to the mainland border at Lo Wu." Then he relaxed, as though he had discharged half his duty, and said: "I'm Leslie Benson."

He impressed the Michaelses as an intelligent person who had come to many crossroads in life and, after considerable speculation, had always managed to pick the wrong turn. His hair was as black as Mr. Yen's, and he wore a thick close-cut mustache which seemed too big for his body. No thanks, he said, he wouldn't have coffee. Always drank beer in the morning. Warm beer, and more warm beer at one P.M.

"When do you eat?" Kay said. Beer was eating, he said. It had food value. He ate one true meal a day—dinner. The rest of the time, beer. Never tight, mind you. It wouldn't do for a member of Her Majesty's Service to walk around woofled. Never get a blasted bit of work done that way. Perfectly in order to get drunk at home, or in the club, but mustn't show the natives any weakness.

He must make it perfectly clear, Mr. Benson said, that he did not relish this assignment. Not that he had anything against Americans, mind you. Allies and cousins-under-the-skin and all that sort of rot, but the government of the Crown Colony liked to maintain a formal, peaceful atmosphere at the bridge—the so-called Bamboo Curtain—and kept everybody at least a mile away from the Sham Chun River. "Our desire," he said, "is to do nothing to antagonize Mao Tse-tung. It is hardly a place for tourists."

"Then we won't go," said Lon. "When I wrote to the British government, I asked—" "You," said Benson, "are an American writer and the Crown Colony has no desire to offend you. I am merely saying that we do not even permit our own people near the bridge. Except, of course, those whose duty requires their presence. Now, if you decline to go, I will be blamed."

"Oh," Lon said. Kay said he would go. That reminded Benson of another point: in the case of Mrs. Michaels, she would be left at the British Jockey Club, one mile inside the border. "Women are not permitted any closer," he said. She sipped her coffee. "It sounds dangerous," she observed. "No, not dangerous, truly. But risky. As though something *could* happen."

Benson finished his beer and nodded to a Chinese waiter. The morning sun was bright through the hotel entrance and it drew bright lines across the lobby rugs. "Not a blasted thing will happen," he continued absent-mindedly. "Nothing has happened at the bridge and nothing is going to happen; Her Majesty's Government has a determined policy on that. In fact, we get along pretty well with the Chinese."

"I know," Lon said. "You trade with them, you want them in the United Nations; you permit them to sneak merchandise through this colony which otherwise—" "Oh, now, just a moment," Benson objected. "Politics is not up for discussion, but we're the realists, old chap. Not you."

"Agreed," said Lon. "We're the idealists. But Britain has never been realistic about anything unless she had a stake in it. For ex ample, her whole empire has crumbled like a stale cookie in her hands, but she is eager to play footsie with the Communists just to keep this—well, crumb." Mr. Benson poured a glass from the fresh bottle and studied Kay. "You're a dashed sight prettier than he is," he said.

The shiny black car left the Jockey Club, and turned west. Kay had said she didn't mind waiting. She did, and Lon knew it, but the British Government was not to be moved by two people who did not want to be separated, even for an hour. He made certain that she was comfortable in a garden, and that the manager would see that she could have a drink, if she felt so disposed.

Benson ordered the driver to stop before a bridge marked, in English and Chinese: DANGER. There was a police box on the near side. Benson got out of the car to take his orders to the police, who would telephone ahead that an Information Services man was bringing an American to the bridge. Lon looked out of the car and noticed that most of the Chinese in the outpost area were women. They wore broad black hats with black veiling hanging off the brim about two inches, black pants and loose black blouses. Most of them carried big bundles of rushes tied to their backs. One or two led an ox, or a cow, by a ring placed in the nose, and a small tether rope.

It seemed quite a time, but probably wasn't, until Benson came back and said they could continue the final half mile to the bridge. The car moved forward, down the sandy convex road, and passed a railroad station with a sign LO WU. The driver slowed the car and, a hundred yards further, came to a small building. The tracks ran past it and onto a black iron bridge spanning a muddy river. On the far side was a small switch tower with a red star on it and over it a red flag.

"Follow me, please," Benson said. They went into the second room of the neat little building. A man in a brown sweater stood behind a desk. He removed the pipe from his mouth, asked if Michaels would like a spot of tea, and exchanged a few pleasantries with Benson. In a moment, he fastened the bottom button of his sweater and led them out onto the bridge.

"Just stay on this side," he said. He and Benson chatted, while Lon walked forward toward the middle of the bridge, and stood watching. As they had told him, there was nothing startling to see. Nor had he expected anything dramatic. It was the lack of drama that made the scene tense to him, because, at this bridge, as at the Brandenberg Tor, two ideologies stood toe to toe.

It was noon, and hot. The soldiers on the far side wore brown tunics and carried Bren guns across their backs. Some peasants sat in the small shadow of the iron bridge, carrying their possessions tied in fat white sheets. These would be the daily legal migrants to Hong Kong. The traffic moved both ways. Each group had to get off the train on its own side of the bridge and, after inspection, walk across to the train on the opposite side.

A sign near the refugees read: LONG LIVE THE GRAND UNION OF THE PEOPLES OF THE WORLD. The hills on the Communist side of the old iron bridge appeared to be as round and brown as those on the British side. The Sham Chun was hardly more than a creek, but it was muddy on both banks. The only restraint was a fence built on the British side. It ran along the edge of the river as far as Lon could see. He stood watching, thinking of how insignificant all of this was and of how yesterday it had been Greece versus Rome, Rome versus Carthage, versus Egypt, versus Gaul; it was Christianity versus paganism versus Judaism versus Mohammedanism versus Buddhism versus Shinto versus atheism; it was Rightists versus Leftists; Labor against the Conservatives; Republicans versus Democrats versus Socialism versus Fascism versus Liberalism; it was this language against that language; it was this province against this province; it was greed and fear and power versus power and fear and greed.

He stood on the track near the center and watched the Communist guards frisk the peasants and ask questions and study papers; then, as the group waited like patient animals for permission to cross, to go from a world which promised all and gave little, to a world which promised little and gave little, he turned to Benson and said he was ready to go.

"Did you see enough?" asked Benson facetiously. Lon nodded. "I think so," he said.

The messenger said, "We'll be boarding soon." The Michaelses were in the restaurant at Kai Tak Airport, Lon drinking Scotch mists, Kay working over a raspberry sherbet. "Time for a quick one," Lon suggested. Kay shook her head. She'd have a drink on the plane. She looked up at the clock. Five forty P.M. "Flight Two must be on time," she said.

"It's always on time," he said. "Almost." Kay laughed. "Now there is an ideal sentence." He admitted that he was partial because it was Flight Two Pan American that had brought them so far, so quickly and so safely. "You don't trust them with your typewriter," she said. Well, he said, he had trusted airline luggage people with typewriters before. Sometimes, they were returned bent. Now he made it a practice to carry the machine and the briefcase. "You wouldn't want me to trust them with this brand new crocodile briefcase, would you?"

He lifted it off the floor. "Indeed not," she said. He asked if she would like to return to Hong Kong sometime. "Yes," she said after a moment's thought, "I think so. I have three favorite places so far: Beirut, Bangkok and Hong Kong." Lon watched the stream of Chinese coming through a swinging door and another steady stream going out on the far side. "In a few years," he said quietly, "two out of three people on this earth will be Asiatic or African. A new world is coming up out of the ant hills. It is going to be theirs."

Kay looked around, disturbed. "There is one word," she said, "as far as the Chinese people are concerned: interminable. But I didn't know that Asia and Africa had us outnumbered that badly." He placed a bill on the table and reached for his gear. "They didn't worry when we outnumbered them. Or outgunned them, or whatever it was we did. Let's go."

Kay said she still had fifteen dollars Hong Kong. Lon said he had changed most of the foreign currency. They had already passed through customs, checked in their luggage, bought some magazines, had a drink or two, sent final postcards to friends—was there anything else? There was nothing else.

The sun was still up a little when they boarded the big Boeing 707 and found their places at seats 2A and 2B. The big Pratt and Whitney engines had barely started when night fell as though it had been dropped. There was no moment of precious beauty; no outrageous coloring of sky and water. One moment, the runway of filled-in land stretched out into the bay, the next moment, there was nothing out there but blackness and a double necklace of lights.

Kay fastened her seat belt. "We should send a thank-you note," Lon said, "for the Chinese dinner." "I already have," Kay said. "I sent it to Mr. Fong. After all, he was our host." "He was also a nice person," Lon said. The big ship stood poised at the head of the runway and the whine of the four engines worked slowly upward until they shrieked. Then the brakes were released and the big bird, with huge yellow eyes staring ahead, started down the runway, ran and ran forever, and then lifted gracefully off and into the darkness.

Lon looked at his watch. "I don't know whether you like geography as a subject," he said. She shook her head. "Well, instead of heading straight north for Tokyo, this flight will climb east to Taiwan, then northeast to Okinawa, then straight north to Tokyo. She'll run about 1,940 miles and," his voice began to trail off, "considering this and that, she should make it in less than three hours and a half."

"Is there a difference in time?" Kay asked. "That's the this and that I was just referring to. I don't know, but there should be an hour difference. Maybe two. In any case, by the time you finish dinner, we'll be coming down into Haneda Airport and, allowing for Japanese customs and so forth, we should be in our hotel room in Tokyo no later than midnight."

"Nice," she said, settling back. "What a wonderful world—even with all those Chinese marching and marching and marching."

THE TWENTY-FIRST DAY

KAY always looked a little puffy under the eyes in the creeping stage of the morning. She sat at breakfast speaking but not thinking, wondering vaguely if this was truly fried ham and eggs in truly Tokyo. Lon said little. He was looking at the pumpkin-shaped Japanese lantern hanging over the little tea table. It was saffron with black stripes. So far as he could see, this was the only Japanese touch in the Imperial Hotel. The rest of it was early Hilton—the automatic elevators, the busy lobby, the revolving doors, the doorman with his taxi whistle, the twin basins in the bathroom, the twin beds in the bedroom, the valet service, the view out the window of Hibiya Park with its big fountain and veil of falling water.

"It doesn't seem like Japan," he complained. She reached for a sweet bun. "Philadelphia," she said, "on Monday morning." Thought processes in the first forty minutes of wakefulness, he found, were abnormally slow and sporadic. The mind crept from one thing to another, without will or guidance. Sometimes, in the first half hour, he responded to questions with sensible answers but later in the day had no recollection of them. The door to the memory center was open only a crack.

"Philadelphia," he said absent-mindedly. She said nothing, her thoughts moving from Lucy, to last night, to school in Florida, to Lon's housekeeper, to a girl friend who had made a good marriage, to shopping, to how-many-days-before-we-arrive-home, to travelers' checks, to someone named Jones her husband was supposed to meet, to the new Grecian gown, to—

"You have to meet a man named Jones?" she said. "Huh?"

"Jones. He works for Pan American and he's going to show us Tokyo." Lon covered his mouth with his hand, and burped. "Sorry," he said. "Never heard of him."

"Do you remember a phone call this morning?" she asked.

He shook his head.

"You answered it. A Japanese told you that 'Sambawrr of Dina Crub' told him to call." Lon grinned. "Yeah," he said. "But that's a different call. He meant Sam Boal of the Diners Club. Jones— oh, you mean Davey Jones. Oh, that's different."

There was a night table between the beds. Lon got up and made a note to phone Jones. He turned the radio on. A little samisen music might put him in a Japanese mood. The sound came up and the song was American rock and roll sung by a Japanese boy. "What time is it?" Kay asked. He said ten. "The car and driver ought to be waiting." "What driver?" "The one you ordered when you came in last night. For ten A.M." "Oh." "You said he should speak English." "But not too well," Lon said.

He used the shower while she asked for someone to pick up the laundry left over from Hong Kong. Also, there were suits and dresses to be pressed and two ties to dry clean—what Lon called the debris of travel, collected at each new stop, set to rights, and converted into debris again. When he finished shaving, he came out with a towel cinched around his belly and Kay went in. If past performance meant anything, he thought with a grin, she would be out in forty-five minutes.

There was a knock on the door, and a pretty Japanese girl came in. She said good morning and seemed not to notice that he was standing surrounded by a small towel. It reminded him that these people enjoyed community bathing, but had a sensitive modesty about kissing. He went into a closet and put on shorts and a pair of dark slacks. The girl folded the leaves of the table, and pushed it out, still murmuring polite phrases which he could not understand.

Nikkada, unfortunately, had worked for the American occupation authorities for a number of years. He was a good driver, but the majors and colonels had turned him into a fast one. Fast, loose and laughing. Somewhere along the line he had learned that when one does not understand the words of a superior, one laughs uproariously. He no longer had a U.S. Army insignia on his automobile, but he was still in the habit of assuming that he had the right of way over all Japanese vehicles. He had a lean, almost Goya-esque face except for the almond lids and the raisin eyes. Some of his teeth were gold, and he could not—or would not—answer a question without laughing.

He drove off down the alley of the Imperial Annex as though, Lon remarked, General Douglas A. MacArthur were in the back and the general had to get to a bathroom. There was a cross-street at the end of the alley. Nikkada paid no attention to the possibilities; he approached it in high gear and flew across the intersection. Kay braced her shoes against the back of the front seat. Lon swallowed. "Nikkada," he said. "Slow down." The driver kept his eyes on the heavy traffic ahead. "Srow," he said. "Ha-ha."

But he didn't. He moved out of the downtown area, with its huge square buildings all looking like the home office of the Prudential Insurance Company, to the area of the palace grounds. Once, when Lon was frightened by a narrow escape, he tapped Nikkada on the shoulder. "Stop," he said. "Just plain stop." Nikkada laughed until his forehead almost touched the wheel. He wiped his eyes with the back of his sleeve. The car swung along the edge of a deep plaza, pulled to the curb, and stopped.

"Emperor," said Nikkada, pointing to a sloping wall.

"Okay," said Lon grimly. He leaned over the front seat and pointed to the foot brake. "Stop. Means stop." He pointed to the accelerator. "Means go. I say go, Nikkada, you go. I say stop, you stop. Savvy?" Nikkada laughed tentatively, as though this time he was not sure that his passenger was a comedian.

"I'll be a son-of-a-bitch," Lon said, "if you didn't scare the pants off me." At once, the tentative expression left Nikkada's face. "Yes-s-s-s," he breathed. "Son-of-a-bitch, bastard, fuck you, buddy." Then he laughed. Kay's eyes widened; she clapped both hands over her mouth. "No, no," said Lon. "Bad words. No good English. Speak nice words English." Nikkada stopped laughing again. "Emperor," he said, pointing.

They got out of the car and walked up the long incline toward the Imperial Palace. "We need a new driver," Lon said. Kay put a hand on his arm. "Give the poor man a chance," she said. "He doesn't know what those words mean." "Oh, I realize that. Some of our wisenheimers taught him all the bad words. I can break that. I'm worried about his driving." Kay grinned into the cold yellow sun of winter. "I almost broke something trying not to laugh." He smiled a little. "I guess it is funny when someone says it in innocence. But he's going to learn what one word means: stop. Good God, I thought the crazy bastard would kill us the first time out."

They approached a moat. The water below was green. In it the lazy gray carp swam. Behind the moat was a thick wall leaning inward. Somewhere behind that was the Imperial Palace of Hirohito.

"There isn't much to see," Kay said. She looked around. There were many Japanese coming up the long walk, not expecting to see the Emperor of course, nor even his palace from a distance, but rather to feel a closeness with a father image. The older women, Kay noticed, wore kimonos, some with the knapsack-like obi in the back. Some women wore Western-style street dresses. A few older men wore the Japanese sandals with the thong between the toes, and a kind of socks called *tabi*. The younger girls wore high Italian coiffures and tight dresses and loose, boxlike coats of hip length.

Many of the men had white gauze masks over their mouths. There seemed to be a difference of opinion about these, some maintaining that the masks were worn by people who had colds and did not want to spread the contagion; others that they were worn by hypochondriacs who did not want to risk catching a cold. In either case, many more men than women wore them.

Kay, who always carried a guidebook or two in her big white purse, opened one end, for her husband's edification, ran through some of the items of interest. This was one of the things that made her feel helpful. Sometimes she read the guidebooks on the plane, sometimes at night in bed, but always with a pencil to encircle the information she deemed important:

"All traffic keep to the left here . . . Take off shoes before entering private home or temple. . . . Japanese never use soap in bathtub; always wash thoroughly first, then slip into tub for soaking. . . . Currency is the yen, 360 to the dollar. . . . In eating habits, these people are dainty; like to make food look attractive; they eat seaweed and broiled eels, called *Kabayaki*—I may not be pronouncing it right.

"Sake you know about. It's a rice wine, but is also a liquor. Japanese beer is superior. . . . Major religions are Buddhism and Shinto. . . . Traditional theater is divided into Noh, Kabuki and puppets. Tourists favor Kabuki, in which even the female characters are portrayed by males. . . ."

"Get to the geisha girls," Lon said. "I'm cold." Kay continued, as though he had not spoken. "Time here is twenty hours later than New York. . . . Restaurants add tip to the bill. No tip to taxi drivers. . . . The guide says it is worth while to go to Kamakura to see the Great Buddha. . . . Tokyo is now the biggest city

in the world, close to ten million. . . . Main street is **Ginza**, derived
from the word *gin*, with a hard *g*, which means silver, and *za*,
which means foundry. . . . There are many trolleys and trains
here. . . . Small buses are called, in Japanese, pigeons. . . . Japanese are mad about pinball machines and baseball. . . ."

"Oh, for goodness' sake," Lon said, "the temperature now
averages forty-three degrees. . . . There are ninety-five million
Japanese and they live on five hundred and four islands. . . . The
women are so completely feminine that they make me feel masculine, and that's not in the guidebook.

"Also," said Lon, watching the traffic. "Much bicycles and
motorcycles. Come on, I'm hungry." They walked to the car swiftly,
and asked Nikkada to take them to a good place for lunch.
"Chinzan-so," he said, and took off so fast that they were pressed
back against their seat. "Slow down," Lon shouted. "Slow down."
Nikkada laughed, and slowed down.

"There," said Lon triumphantly. "You see?" "Maybe," said Kay,
unimpressed, "he's an old kamikaze pilot."

Chinzan-so was a black lacquered entrance inside an ugly parking lot. The name, Nikkada told them, meant mansion on the
camellia mountain. He parked the car, laughed happily, and
pointed to the young man bowing at the door. Kay and Lon, who
had never eaten Japanese food, were timid. They walked inside,
glanced at several rooms, and walked out in back. There, they
saw hills which rolled so gently that they both were certain that
they were artificial.

A captain of waiters joined them. "English?" he said. "No,"
said Lon. "American." "So sorry," the man said, bowing. "I meant
the language." Lon said that the front seemed unattractive, but
that the rear of the restaurant was beautiful. The man was cour-
teous and well informed. He said that the place had a history.
Originally, the back part had been discovered by Prince Aritomo

Yamagato. He found that the plot, in the heart of Tokyo, consisted of seventeen acres of rolling land and deep glens.

He bought it at once and built a house on it. His friend, the Emperor Meiji was invited to dinner. His Imperial Highness was so entranced that Chinzan-so became a favored place for relaxation and for informal conferences. This happened shortly after the time that Commodore Perry sailed four American ships into Tokyo Bay and opened the country to commerce and the struggle for modernity.

Later, the place was bought by Baron Fujita, who shipped a three-tiered pagoda all the way from the city of Hiroshima to adorn Chinzan-so. He also selected special small monuments and dwarf trees to grace the landscape. The pagoda was placed so that the center of the roof screened the late winter sun from the main house. The Baron told his friends that the estate had four moods: Fresh Green; Evening Fireflies; Russet Leaves; and Silent White.

The sentiment, Lon thought, was pretty. The Japanese, he began to feel, could impute grace and beauty to inanimate objects that had neither. They went into the rear dining room, a plain room with scores of small windows looking out onto the gardens, and sat on plush cushions at a low table. A waitress brought menus, but Kay waved hers away. "Bring something nice," she said. In the center of the table were inlaid iron ingots. Beneath them were hot coals.

The waitress cooked the meal at the table. She had more than average grace and she removed food from baskets with chopsticks (the Japanese call them *ohashi*) bit by bit. There were dewy fresh vegetables: bits of green pepper, slivers of onion, slices of mushroom. She laid these in neat rows. Also small pork chops, slices of beef and chicken. Kay, who had not felt hungry, smelled the pungent smoke rising from the table and smiled as the waitress assisted them into huge white butcher aprons.

It was food seduction. The Japanese, observed Lon, first assailed the senses and then satisfied the appetite they had awakened. They drank hot sake with the lunch, but thought little of it. "She is so gentle," said Kay, "so graceful, that I get the feeling that she's cooking flowers." Lon was happy. He had been afraid that there would be little of true beauty in Japan; his own interest was confined to the historical; and now Kay was saying: "These women will drive me crazy. Every gesture is poetry."

Later, she visited the rest room. "Oh," she said mysteriously, "you missed that one." Lon said he had no interest in rest rooms; most of the men's room he had been in had smelled like vats of ammonia. "These have fresh flowers hanging over each basin," Kay said, as they walked to the car. "There are two kinds of lavatories. One is with a seat in it. The other is a tile trough in the floor for ladies who like to remain standing."

Nikkado saw them coming. He jumped out, and held the door of the car open. "Good," he said. "Good?" They got in. "Very good, Nikkado," he said. "I thank you. I'm sorry I did not think to tell you to have lunch too." Again, Nikkado was amused. "Eat. Eat." He pointed to his chest. "Eat good. No sorry for you."

The night hides the vast ugliness of the city. The skyscrapers fade and the Downtown, U.S.A., atmosphere is transmuted into the gaiety of lights. One hundred thousand neon signs, in beautiful blending of color, put a gay and spurious make-up on the face of Tokyo. The Michaelses met Mr. and Mrs. Davey Jones in the lobby and, having nothing stronger than friends in common to bridge the gap between them, were a little formal for the first five or ten minutes.

Jones drove. Lon sat up front with him. Kay and Mrs. Jones— Virginia, she said—sat in back. She was tall and angular, a woman with sand-colored hair and glasses. She was animated, told stories well, and talked of her three sons as though they were part of the white woman's burden. Davey was short and dark, a man of motion and impish brown eyes behind a façade of solemnity. He was, Lon felt, the kind of a rouser who would shake hands with an electric buzzer in the palm.

They drove along the Ginza slowly. Like Broadway in New York; or the Kurfurstendamm in Berlin; or Sunset Strip in Los Angeles, it is more than an avenue. It is an area of revelry; like Montmartre in Paris, it caters to the pleasures of the senses with everything from opera to prostitution; from ballet to begging; from the most elegant dinner to pretzels sold on a stick; from the oldest crone sitting alone in an alley to a gorgeous show girl surrounded by admiring men. The rich, the titled, the bejeweled are crowded shoulder to shoulder with the pickpockets, the pimps, the shills and the hungry.

Kay said she had never seen so many lights. "Anywhere." It was true. The neon signs were multitudinous, but they were soft. They did not assault the eyes; instead, they seemed to light in stages of whites and greens and reds and blues and purples; some depicting a ravishing girl; others a spiral staircase; or an automobile; and all, of course, with Japanese characters below. The blending of many colors turned the Oriental faces of pedestrians to coppery tones and greens and brass.

The Ginza, in effect, is the clanking of old Samurai swords and rock and roll. Some of the prettier women on the street, mincing along on wooden clogs, their kimonos tight about them, flirt with service men who find out, in local hotels, that these are female impersonators. "First," said Jones, "we're going to take you to a Buddhist place." "Fine," said Lon. Virginia smiled. "You'll like it. It's not a real temple." Davey swung the car around in a narrow street. "Zen, sort of," he said.

He pulled the car to a curb. The building was a large theater built on a curve, so that it faced two streets. "It's a downstairs place," Jones said, "and there is only one rule. You must keep complete silence in the presence of the nuns." "We understand,"

Kay said. Lon said he didn't know that the Buddhists had nuns. They followed him down a flight of narrow steps. At the bottom was a narrow door. When it was opened, a flood of raucously loud American jazz assaulted the ears. A curtain hung across the doorway, and Jones held it aside.

Lon, whose pride was that he was slightly jaded, stood in the doorway with eyes and mouth wide open, and hands over ears. "My God!" he yelled to Kay, standing beside him. "What the hell is this?" She glanced around, and understood at once. Jones was passing his overcoat and hat to a hatcheck girl, and laughing at Lon. Virginia smiled a schoolteacherish smile and tried to say something, but she couldn't be heard.

The place was not a Buddhist temple, or Zen Buddhist. It had no connection with religion, unless the phallus is one. It was an oblong room with tables and booths in rows. On the left were jukeboxes, and someone had turned the volume high so that every note had a percussive effect on the brain. A few male customers sat at tables drinking. Near the entrance door was a small bar with a grinning Japanese behind it.

Around the room were about twenty teen-age Japanese girls. All had long hair in pony tails to their waists. Some of these were bleached pale blonde. All the girls were pretty; all wore skin-tight toreador pants in white. They all wore loose blouses with the shirred necklines at the level of the nipples. When they bent forward to serve a drink, the breasts often fell out.

The girls danced solo, when they weren't serving customers, or together, but always they laughed and shouted above the music. One girl took her long pony tail in her left hand, and waved it in circles to the music, and grabbed her pelvis with the right hand. A white man, somewhat intoxicated, called the girl over and held onto her pelvis while she danced without moving her feet. "I am silent," Kay shouted, "while the nuns are here."

Another young girl found two elderly men talking, or trying to talk, over cups of rice wine. One had his leg in the aisle. The girl straddled the leg and rode it like a cowboy. The man behind the bar came out, and turned the volume of the jukebox down from excessive shriek to plain loud. Kay and Virginia seemed to have more interest in the lascivious antics of the Japanese girls than their husbands. Davey was leaning across the table, telling Lon: "It's a crazy joint. Most Americans love it. They travel to see things they've never seen, and you're not going to find this in San Francisco or Salt Lake City."

Lon nodded. "These are not just entertainers," he said. "They go out with men?" Jones nodded. "From what I hear, yes. It's off-limits for American service men, but tourists can take any girl for the night—so they tell me—for thirteen dollars to twenty-eight dollars, depending on the market the girl has found." All the girls giggled immoderately; some came over and boldly examined Kay's hair with their fingers, discussing it amid laughter. Another girl stroked the fur on Kay's coat. "Murrican pussy," she said, and the other girls broke into laughter.

Zakuro is a quiet, almost formal restaurant across the street from the American Embassy in Tokyo. The party of four was escorted through the reception room to a room with translucent sliding panels—shoji. The hostess met them on her knees, bowing low. Jones spoke to her in Japanese. The shoji panels surrounded the room and the light seemed to come through them, suffusing the diners in a soft glow. There were three water colors, a foot-high hardwood table in the center, and cushions. Diners could kneel on these, leaning back on their heels, or sit tailor fashion.

Kay knelt. Lon sat tailor fashion. The customary damp hot towels were placed beside the diners. Dinner began with a brace of drinks all around.

Lon was happy to be out with the Joneses, not only because they were nice people, but because Jones had a background as a San

Francisco reporter and would therefore be able to answer the questions he wanted to ask. He was not surprised to learn, for example, that the Japanese are most particular about food. Not merely the eating of it, but the appearance of it and the serving of it. They are even interested in the type of conversation to accompany the eating.

The Japanese make an effort to dine in joy. The sight of the food must create a happiness of the stomach. The utensils must shine; the potables must be dainty; there must be flowers or the semblance of beauty in the room; the smiles of the diners are as important an ingredient as a sauce. The conversation is animated, and, except in the poorest of homes, one never sees a chipped cup or a pan that is not gleaming.

Kay was still astounded at the young girls in the juke joint. She talked to Virginia in a tone which said: I-shall-never-recover-from-what-I-have-seen. "But the sheer brazenness!" Kay said. She sipped her drink, still shaking her head slowly. "I'm no prude. But when you walk into a place and see that—"

"You haven't got time to be revolted," Virginia said. "Dave and I have been here six years, and the first time I saw that place I was too fascinated to be shocked." "Exactly," Kay said. "Although I noticed that my husband missed nothing." Lon shrugged. "I went there to miss nothing. I have a feeling that the only men who work up a subjective interest in those girls must be either very young or very old. Those are the only ones who will pay to see women degrade themselves."

"Oh-ho," said Jones. "You sound prudish." "No," Lon said softly. He was glad he went. It proved that the sex lure is the same everywhere. He said he once saw Egyptian belly dancers in Cairo and was surprised to find that they were all 180 pounds and over. When he asked a waiter why, he was told that Egyptian men are sexually attracted to stout women. In Havana, he said, women pad their behinds. The Cuban men must be partial to big hips. In Germany, the girl with big breasts seem to draw the most glances. In Japan, he said, "it must be faces, because those kimonos cover everything from the neck to the sandals, and that obi in the back gives the figure a distorted appearance. So it must be faces."

The first dish was a porcelain plate with bits of crabmeat, sliced smoked whitefish, and a slice of something that looked like avocado. It was all encircled in a dark ring of sauce. Kay and Lon were in a mood to try anything, and, in such a temper, everything tastes good. Next a big copper kettle was brought in. The inner ring of the pot was dry and held raw vegetables. The outer ring, which was narrow, held boiling water. Strips of pink beef, like the tongues of puppies, were on little plates. "This," said Jones, "is *shabu-shabu.*" The words meant nothing to the Michaelses. They took their *ohashi,* and managed to lift a piece of beef no bigger than a mouthful. They were told to dip it three times in the boiling water. The meat came out gray and cooked. It was then dipped lightly in a thick dark sauce and eaten.

When the beef was gone, the hostess took the raw vegetables and placed them in the water in which the beef had been dipped. She served little cups of sake, while she made soup. The hostess is, at all times, unobtrusive, Davey explained. Her efficiency is rated on her power to get the food before the guests without realization, on their part, that there is a stranger in the room.

Later, there was green translucent tea in bowls without handles, and huge fresh strawberries in serrated black bowls. These were served with heavy cream and sugar. The bill was paid. There were no tips. They were gravely bowed out of the restaurant by everyone.

"Thanks," Lon said to Davey. "I've enjoyed this. Now, back to the hotel." Davey chuckled. "Hotel? Not yet. You haven't finished your dinner." He turned to Virginia. "Listen to this guy—home. We're on our way to Yie-Lae-Shian, a Japanese coffee house. This one has a floor show."

It wasn't far. From outside, it looked like a three-story hotel. Inside, there was a lobby, with plush chairs, and a cashier's counter. Inside the counter were plastic replicas of desserts—everything from puddings and cakes to éclairs. "The idea," Virginia said, "is to point to what you want. The cashier will make out a check for it now, in addition to coffee or whatever drinks you want. You go upstairs, give the check to a waiter, and he will bring exactly what you ordered. In this case, you pay before you get the food."

They made their selections, and walked up a flight of stairs. The room there was very big and dimly lighted. The center was choked with tables. Around the perimeter were booths. It seemed to Kay to be a place for lovers, because, in the dimness, she detected all sorts of intimate attitudes. Some of the Japanese men, with an arm around a girl, looked up at the party and grinned at Kay and Virginia.

The drinks were being served when Lon heard music. Again it was American jazz, played fast and loud. It sounded as though it was getting louder. Lon looked at Kay. Kay looked at Davey, who pointed to an open space at the head of the room. It looked like an elevator shaft.

It was. An elevator approached the floor, moving so slowly that it barely inched upward. Over it were brightly colored lights. There were no doors on it. In the back was a fast Japanese combo of cello, xylophone, electric organ and drums. In the foreground, three Japanese girls in identical purple kimonos sang. "The Andrews sisters," said Lon. Kay nodded. "After too much tea," she said.

The elevator kept moving until it disappeared at the third floor level. It seemed never to stop, always moving up to the third floor and then back down past the second to the first. Then up again. Sometimes the girls harmonized on popular Japanese songs; sometimes they sang American favorites with Japanese lyrics. The singers held white ostrich fans, and waved them slowly against their skin. They wore rhinestone tiaras in high bouffant coiffures, and had long pony tails hanging down their backs.

After the drinks, the desserts were served and then Lon said: "This has been some evening, my friend. Now, back to the hotel." Davey looked at Kay in mock shock. "How do you possibly stand this man? How? Tokyo doesn't come to life until after midnight. We're off to Pacota." Lon smiled faintly. "Whatever that may be." "You'll find out," Davey said. "Just don't die on me right now. A lot of friends wrote and said to take care of you. Ginny and I can't take care of you unless you hold still." Lon pressed Kay's hand in his. "Tired?" Not unless he was, she assured him. "Okay," he said. "We go." They went. The car moved down narrow streets, threading through knots of revelers, passing little doorways where hawkers yelled the wares of the girls inside.

At midnight, more people thronged the Ginza area than at noon. "What is this place called?" Kay asked. Davey pulled to the side of the road—there was no curb—and tried to back his car close to the dark doorway of a bleak building. "Pacota," he said. "Don't ask me what it means. It is just a neighborhood bar."

Pacota turned out to be the most interesting part of the evening. It was reached through a dark and narrow hall. There was a room about fifteen feet by eighteen, with an irregularly shaped bar on the right, and about ten customers sitting in front. The bartender took orders—mostly for *birru*—and three young girls came through the drapery of a door behind the bar and sang. What they sang had sadness and gladness, but none of it was American.

They harmonized, not too well, but their Japanese folk songs held the customers to their seats. Some of the music, like the song about the interminable train trip from Tokyo to Osaka, was composed of many stanzas as the trained stopped, for example, while all the passengers got off to go swimming. The musical accompaniment was a ukulele. There was a sweet homelike quality about Pacota. The customers sang lustily with the girls, their heads swaying with the cadence.

Some of the songs were of unrequited love; in fact, no Japanese love song can become popular unless, in it, a woman is weeping over a man, or a young widow with children finds a man who loves her but not her babies, or a lovely woman smells flowers and finds no man. Kay and Lon were entranced; they did not want to leave. Davey explained, in Japanese, that the Michaelses were on a honeymoon; everyone cheered.

Kay went to the ladies' room and returned blushing. "What happened?" Lon asked. She lowered her eyes to the bar and whispered: "The can is co-educational." "You mean men are in there?" "Think nothing of it," said Davey. "The Japanese do not connect the baser functions of the body with sex." "Oh," said Lon. "There's a speech that has been made before." "It sure has," said Virginia. "Sooner or later, when we entertain friends from the States, the matter of the john comes up.

"Dave is right, of course. There is no connection between the business of the bathroom and sex. Kay is blushing because she had to go through the men's room to get to the ladies' room. The men stand there, doing whatever it is they do, and they may glance your way as you pass through, but they aren't fresh."

"That's nice," Lon said sarcastically. The four talked about it for a while, and about whole families greeting each other in the nude in public baths, bowing from the waist, but, as Lon said: "I'm sure we Americans are wrong in our thinking, but that's the way we were brought up." Virginia sighed. "It took a long time to get used to," she said, "but I must admit that these are modest people."

THE TWENTY-SECOND DAY

IT was a whisper. Mrs. Chiba stood inside the door, and bowed very low. The words sounded like a prayer. The woman before her was crouching, her head down close to the knees. She too whispered. They uttered the soft sibilances in staccato Japanese and then Mrs. Chiba turned to Mr. and Mrs. Michaels, smiled, and made a graceful motion for them to remove their shoes, and follow her upstairs.

Mrs. Chiba was the epitome of delicacy. She was tiny, a woman with the blackest hair piled up on top of her head with something like a small white bone thrust through it. Her skin was like pale molasses, her eyes pulled tight toward the temples, her kimono embroidered with rich pink flowers; she wore *geta*—wooden clogs on two runners. The rich mink wrap and the flawless English seemed out of key. She led the way upstairs in the geisha house on the Sumida River and, over her shoulder, explained the whispered words.

"Chinese," she said, "is a musical language. It is spoken on different tone levels and one can speak out without hurting the ear. But Japanese is, I am afraid, a monotonous language full of harsh sounds and is best spoken in whispers. The owner of this house made formal greetings, and I replied formally. Each of us knew the proper phrases, but we see no reason for shouting." She paused at the top of the highly varnished staircase, and laughed softly. "Only my husband shouts Japanese," she said.

Lon said they had been surprised at her invitation. Two girls in kimonos took the coats and Lon's hat. "I must tell you," Mrs. Chiba said, addressing herself to Kay, "that mutual friends of yours and mine asked me to telephone and invite you to a real geisha dinner. Or, rather, evening, because geisha implies more than food. So, against my will, I made the call as a stranger."

"We are the strangers," Kay said. Lon fidgeted. "Who are the mutual friends?" he asked. Mrs. Chiba smiled. "You will meet them in a moment. I am not to say a word about it. I promised. But let me tell you something about this place" The kimono girls brought hot face cloths, with which the three wiped their cold hands. "This is a geisha house," said Mrs. Chiba. "A real one. Not American style fun house with girls. Genuine.

"Geisha is, as you know, an art form. A geisha is trained from early childhood in the graces of entertainment—politeness, conversation, funny stories, samisen music, play-acting, parlor games, the use of fan and the art of ancient dances. It is not sex, as you might think. It is coquetry and how to please a man without becoming involved."

"I understand," Lon said. "I have always understood it this way." Mrs. Chiba handed the cloth to the girl without looking at her. "Then let me tell you further: there are perhaps three true geisha houses in Tokyo. Maybe three in all Japan these days. You will see true geisha tonight and the girls will perform and giggle and sit at your table, but I beg you to understand that though they will look young they are all grandmothers."

Kay showed surprise. "Yes," Mrs. Chiba said. "The twentieth century has come to Japan and no one trains new geishas, so we are left with a few, who will come out on special occasions. Tokyo has many places called geisha houses, but these are different. These are for—excuse me for being snobbish—tourists. Now, come. We must meet your friends."

They walked down a hall and, as they approached a room on the left, facing the river, the eggshell wall slid back. At the far end of the room was a low table. Beside it sat Larry and Peg Cointreaux. Kay and Lon stopped in the doorway.

"Surprise!" said Peg. She jutted her rhinestone cigarette holder high in the air. Larry stood. Lon could see the dressing on his neck. "Hi, pal!" he said, and he walked toward them with his hand out. They said hello faintly, as people will who are not only surprised, but not certain whether they appreciate the surprise. "Now," Larry said, "this party is on me and we figured we owe it to you and more. Peg and I asked Mrs. Chiba to call the Imperial and see if she could drag you out tonight. I do a little business with her husband getting Swiss movements to Tokyo."

"I must say—" Lon said, and he said no more. Kay swallowed and said: "You look good. Like your old self." "Oh, that," Larry said, touching the dressing on his neck. "The less we discuss it, the better I'll feel. Let me put it to you this way. Everything was finally straightened out; it cost a little moolah, if you know what I mean, but everything is okay. It never happened. The chief in Bangkok and I are now old friends. Peg and I are all straightened away—ain't we, Peg?—and let's say I needed the lesson."

Kay had never seen Lon so surprised that he could not master a situation with words. He just looked at Cointreaux. "Pinch me," Larry said, holding out his arm. "I'm no ghost. And if you're not too happy to see us, I can understand that too. As soon as I busted loose from the law, we hopped Pan American and came straight up here, skipping Hong Kong, just to see if we could find you and straighten it out." He slapped Lon on the shoulder. "I don't want to show up a year from now as a heavy in one of your books."

Cointreaux chuckled at his joke. Mrs. Chiba showed the way to the table. Lon was not happy; he felt Larry had resorted to deception in using Mrs. Chiba to arrange the meeting. He was scowling, but when he caught Kay's reproving expression, he hammered a smile onto his mouth and said he was glad to see that everything turned out all right.

"Couldn't be better," Larry said happily. "I have a present for you." He handed over a small silver gun. Then he pointed to the window. "If you'd take a tip from me, you'd throw it out the window." Lon put it in his jacket pocket. "Let's talk about something else."

"We have nothing to talk about," Peg said. "In fact, Larry and I have a pact. We're not going to discuss the accident with anybody back home, and we hope we can count on your discretion." Kay and Lon nodded. Mrs. Chiba seemed to have a sensitized antenna for delicate moments.

"How much of our country have you seen?" she asked Kay. The reply was a duet. Kay told some things. Lon told others. Drinks were served by petite waitresses who set small white cups without handles.

They had taken an automobile trip to Yokohama and Kamakura that day, going down through Kawasaki to Yokohama. Lon had wanted to see it because it was a great seaport town and the Americans had spent many bombers and a great number of men reducing it to impotence.

They drove out on a dock in time to see a Maru being helped out by a tugboat. The water was blue and calm; the wind was fresh and cold; and the sun was indecisive. They had looked around, and had seen no damage. Yokohama was as busy as ever. Freighters of many nations were moored there, and cranes whined as they unloaded and loaded the big hatches. There was an outer breakwater—a small sea wall with an opening for the passage of ships, and even this did not appear to have been hit.

The sight of a couple of policemen patrolling the docks had reminded Lon of a story he had heard, but one he was not pre-

pared to tell in mixed company. After the war, a certain American
major had been stationed at a U.S. Army office near a Yokohama
police station. The docks were off-limits to American soldiers because the Japanese dockworkers were big, belligerent and often
drunk. Still, day after day, the major watched small policemen
lead huge prisoners to the precinct station, using no more per-
suasion than a hand on the back of the dockworker's neck.

It seemed to the major that the prisoner, at any time, could have
turned, picked up the little policeman and dashed him against a
wall. It was never done; in truth, the prisoner always appeared
cowed. One day, the major, unable to restrain his curiosity any
longer, walked across the street and found a police officer who
spoke some English. He seemed to find the major's question
funny. He laughed heartily and explained that, in a dock arrest,
two policemen traveled together.

Each carried a gun and a coil of piano wire. One policeman
covered the prisoner; the other made him drop his trousers and
shorts. The piano wire was made into a noose; it was placed
around the testicles of the prisoner, and the end was pulled up
under his shirt to the top of his collar. The policeman then wound
that end several times around his finger as the prisoner pulled his
clothing up. The march to the station house proceeded. No
prisoners tried to run.

"The ride to Kamakura," Kay was saying, "was the most
interesting part. The countryside is low; there are many rice paddies; I saw women bent over in ankle-deep water and their heads
did not come up even when they heard a car pass; there were many
villages and lots of children. It's strange but, no matter where we
go, if you smile at children they will smile back and wave their
hands. Of course, this is my first long trip. I still maintain, though,
that there is a similarity in all children of all races. They laugh at
the same thing. Their normal disposition is to be friendly. They
don't appear to be shy, or strange, until they're about ten."

Kamakura lies on the shore of Sagami Bay and the southeast wind piles up huge green combers with high white feathers. The beaches were clean of debris, even in the cold weather, and the sand stretched tawny for miles. The little beach houses off the edge were on stilts and boarded up.

"Lunch first," Lon had said to Nikkada. "Then Daibutsu, you understand?" Nikkada said he would take them to a place near the temple. It was a modern restaurant with a sign out front in English reading: DE LUXE LAVATORY. They asked Nikkada to sit with them. The boy who took the order wore long sideburns, had his hair puffed up in front, and looked like an Oriental Elvis Presley.

Afterward, they walked across to the temple which, except for a gate and a ticket taker, appeared to be a piny woods. There were gravel walks and, on a small eminence in the distance, between the trees, stood the great Buddha. It is an enormous bronze with a headdress of bronze pearls and is so big that pilgrims are permitted to go inside the statue, where there is a stairway to the top. It was built in the twelfth century by the shoguns, who were trying to popularize Buddhism among the people.

The figure sits in bland serenity and perfect symmetry. The big hands touch each other on the lap, and the thumbs touch too. Kay and Lon had the impression that whoever designed it made one side of the statue and then reversed the mold. Originally, the statue was indoors but the temple was damaged by a storm in 1369 and, 126 years later, a tidal wave came up off the beach, smashed through Kamakura, and tore the temple from its foundations. Since that time, Amida, the Buddhist divinity, has sat forty-two feet six inches tall on a pedestal, completely composed in rain and snow and summer sun. On the grounds, shaven Buddhist priests strolled in colorful robes. Some watched a merchant who exhibited two birds in a cage.

When a coin was dropped in a box, the merchant rapped the

top of the cage with a stick. The birds shook their feathers peevishly, and one walked into another enclosure, picked a card with his bill, and brought it out. It was an old form of fortune telling and the priests watched eagerly. So did the Michaelses.

"Okay," said Larry, "did you have your fortune told?" Lon said no, he did not believe that a bird or a priest or even a pope could foretell the next minute, much less the tomorrows. "There are a few prerogatives," he said, "which I feel that God has reserved for himself." "Well," said Peg, "I guess that tells you off. Mrs. Chiba, if the food doesn't come soon, I'm going to be loaded."

Mrs. Chiba bowed her head and whispered. Almost at once, the sliding panels at the end of the room opened, and six geishas began to serve. The food courses were interminable, delectable and unpronounceable. The geishas crouched on their knees between guests, and drank sake with them. They bowed with hands on knees, giggled, uttered pleasantries in pidgin English, and Larry said: "Wait till I get home and somebody says: 'What's new?' "

The geishas performed ritualistic dances. Some played string instruments, others, with floury make-up on face and lacquered hair, danced in slow motion with graceful fans. Mrs. Chiba explained some things about the food to Kay, who said she loved to cook. There was *sashimi* (raw fish), lobster, a small salad of appetizers, seaweed, *chawan-mushi* (a hot custard soup). Almost all the food was dipped in a dark sauce called *shoyu,* composed of sugar, salt, sake and vinegar.

The geishas played games with matches, building them in delicate piles and asking the guests to keep adding one more without toppling the edifice. Another game consisted of placing a piece of rice paper over the top of a cup of sake; on it a coin was placed each guest and geisha then burned a cigarette hole in the paper The trick was to keep the coin from falling in. One girl took a cigarette, emptied the tobacco from it, then twisted the paper into the form of a ballet dancer with one leg arched, and arms akimbo. It was a delicate matter and, when she had completed the work, she stood the ballet dancer on the rim of a glass. Then she took a single drop of water and touched it to the head of the dancer. Slowly, the head turned, the arms moved, and the arched leg moved straight out behind the figure.

The dinner lasted all evening. It was late when Lon suggested that it was time to get back to the Imperial. "Well," said Peg, "I hope that this is not the end. A woman should be permitted to go off her nut once, and I did it." "Oh," Lon said deprecatingly, "forget it. We don't even think of it." This, Kay knew, was a lie. The man who never lied was lying in his teeth. He did think of it, and he was still shocked by it, and she doubted that he had any desire to cultivate the Cointreaux.

Still, in this case and in others like it, she would prefer that he lie politely. He could be so damned blunt at times. Ordinarily, it was a temptation to needle him when she caught him lying, but this time she would not. She could imagine his answer if she were to bring it up later. He would tell her that, from now on, no matter whom it hurt, he would tell people exactly how he felt. She didn't want this.

They said their formal good nights; their thank yous to Mrs. Chiba and the Cointreaux. Lon told Larry that they would not be able to meet tomorrow, because he had work to do. "Well," Larry said, "tomorrow is Saturday. My wife is looking to do some shopping, but how about Sunday?"

"Not sure," said Lon. "We're leaving Sunday night for Hawaii. Why don't you give us a buzz Sunday morning?" Cointreaux, usually a comic character, looked steadily into Lon's eyes. He wanted to know whether Michaels wanted him to phone, or whether this was a polite refusal.

"Okay," he said. "I'll call. We don't want to force ourselves on you people." "Not at all," Lon said. "If the time is open, we'll

make the rounds together. How long are you people staying here?"
Peg put on her Roosevelt grin. "We had no idea, until we heard
that you are leaving Sunday. Unless it's a private plane, we may
be aboard with you."

"Oh," said Lon. "Jolly."

They were in bed. Lon was making all the little overtures that
lead to love. Kay always sensed the signs long before the first
touch, the first kiss, the turning on of the small light beside the
bed. She was always quiescently ready for love, quickly responsive
at any time. If no overtures were made, she remained unexcited
sexually but happy. If a hand touched her in a tentative manner,
all of her senses became alert, and she felt something akin to a
wallop in the stomach and a trembling in the knees.

She felt this now. He had done nothing more than slide an arm
around her, touching the small of her back with his fingers. At
once, she was aroused. "Are you still angry at Peg and Larry?" she
asked. Lon kissed her on the mouth perfunctorily. "Good night,"
he said.

THE TWENTY-THIRD DAY

THIS is a good time to kill time. Kay is downstairs getting a shampoo and set. So, dear, neglected diary, this is as good a time as any for you to listen. I cannot understand why she must keep getting these shampoos and "sets," because all they do is straighten the deep waves in her hair. However, it's not my department. She spends hours and hours having these things done, then she asks me how I like it and I say not at all, and she says, "I do it to please you."

When she comes up, she wants me to accompany her through the annex of the Imperial Hotel where, I understand, there is an array of shops. She wants to buy "happy coats" for Lucy and Sonny and Kate, some junk earrings for relatives or friends and "something Japanesy" for herself. In the field of shopping, she is the damnedest "looker" I've ever seen. It drives me out of my mind watching her staring at things, and not buying. I average two suits of clothes a year and it takes twenty minutes to select the material and style, and another ten minutes for the tailor to chalk the jacket and trousers for alterations.

There is no point in making diary notes about the marriage, because there is nothing to report. Piggishly, I wish I had met her years ago. I think now, not only of my happiness, but of the happiness I missed; the irredeemable; the unreclaimable time. Hoggish.

Or, to put it in another light, I am resentful of the time she spent in the arms of other men. My possessiveness is overdone. I know it. If possible, I would breathe for Kay. A lovely sentiment, I guess, but it isn't healthy.

The inventory of love is three-sided: spiritual, mental and physical. Kay does not think of it in this manner. She thinks of love as "all." She does not want to define it, or analyze it. We are in love, therefore there is nothing to discuss. Sorry. My feelings are different. I must know the chemical components of the explosion. Her notions are better than mine because they move on faith alone. I have been burned before. I am painfully aware of what it is like to be in love and feel no echo. She only knows what it is like not to be in love and sense flattering echoes. There's a lot of difference. If anything, it emphasizes the less attractive side of Kay's character to have been able to stay with a marriage, and work at it, when she knew all along that she felt nothing for him except aggression.

In our marriage, I see a spiritual loss. It is not important at the moment, because physical ecstasy smothers it. But the fires will be banked in time, and then the spiritual side will assert itself. In the Roman Catholic Church, we now stand in the Limbo of chronic sinners. We are not eligible for sacraments or forgiveness. Unless, of course, we repent the sin of living together and promise to live as "brother and sister." This would be hypocrisy of a high order. Most Catholics who have traveled our path hope that, in time, they will be given an opportunity to be forgiven, to die in a state of grace. This is long-range hypocrisy because it implies that the sinner does not want to renounce the pleasures of love in good health; he's willing to wait until the curtain begins to fall. Then, and then only, will he fall to his knees.

Kay and I believe in our church, but it no longer embraces us. I don't feel vindictive. I never did anything for the church; never wrote a religious book, or a tract on a saint, or helped to rai.

*funds for a church or school, or even contributed to a Catholic
periodical. My life has been a secular one, where Mass is a duty,
not a joy. I am humble in the presence of the humble priest, but
the pompous one with big car and the ruddy, well-fed face is
anathema. The huge temples built in His name; the solemn proces-
sions with incense; the Cadillac funerals do not support my image
of Jesus, who said: "The least among ye shall be the greatest; the
greatest shall be the least."*

*So the spiritual side of this union is in bad health. It hurts Kay.
It hurts me too, but I do not wring my hands. I did that before
marriage. There was no spiritual innocence in me when I proposed.
I knew the consequences. There is always the possibility that there
will be no punishment because there is no God, but I cannot accept
it. The proofs, scientifically and historically, are too strong. It
would be easier for me to believe that the stars overhead are not
light years away, but only ten feet over the roof of the house,
supported by piano wires.*

*The mental—or emotional—side of the marriage is strong. The
only differences between Kay and me are the divergencies of
opinion one expects between a man and a woman. She has such a
pretty mind. It is full of dewy roses and cherubic babies and kisses
and delicious foods and extreme femininity and an insatiable desire
to spoil a husband. It is a breathless thing to watch; the prettiness
is inside as well as out. She admires other women if they dress well
and have good carriage.*

*Ironically, Kay has no fear of poverty. This is strange because
her standard of living has moved up considerably from Army life.
On a few occasions, I have said: "Well, suppose I am written out?
Suppose no one wants to buy my stuff? Suppose I have a stroke
and cannot write any more?" In each case, she shrugged. "So we'll
live in a furnished room if we must. I can get a job. I've worked
before. A bologna sandwich and a can of cold beer go pretty
well together."*

In a short courtship and an even shorter marriage, such as ours, it is surprising how much two people can learn about each other. I am not thinking in terms of sex, but rather in terms of emotion and lack of it; rationalization and fear; prejudices; sense of humor. My wife counts. She counts steps as she walks up them; she counts telegraph posts and gasoline stations. She doesn't know why. But then, I'm not immune to idiosyncrasies. I seldom go to the bathroom without muttering a prayer for everybody in the world. I don't even know why. Maybe when I was little someone listened while I was saying my prayers. Now I say them in bathrooms.

Also, I bristle at what I feel is lack of consideration. It is carried to extremes. If the car ahead of me does not move when the light turns green, I am certain that the driver is doing it on purpose, just to hold me back. I honk madly. If someone tries to push through a door ahead of me, he is belligerent. If a policeman answers a polite question in a surly tone, my impulse is to remind him that he is the servant of the law, not its master. When people whom I have not seen for years phone me, I know before the greetings are exchanged that there is a favor involved. If Kay moves my shaving cream to one side, especially if it is to make room for her lotions, my impulse is to drop her bottles on the bathroom floor.

She says that when we have a dispute she wants to put on her coat and take a walk and think things over. I told her that the first time she does it, to keep walking. Don't come back. She has no more right to walk out on a disagreement than I have to go to the neighborhood saloon and get drunk—which is none at all. We also disagree on the upbringing of children. She is opposed to discipline, and feels that overwhelming love will conquer all failings. I believe in the graduated form of punishment, starting with a half hour earlier to bed on first offense, then no television on the second, then cutting off spending money on the third, and good warming on the behind for the fourth.

This alarms her because she can see that Lucy, who is a sullen hysteric, is going to hate me. I think otherwise. Once Lucy understands that I love her, and that I do not want to deprive her of her father or their natural love for each other, she will gravitate to me. I don't feel this; I know it. She is a young colt and I am going to walk her gently around the corral and permit her to smell the fence. Once she understands these limits, I expect that she will feel more secure because she will know the limits beyond which she is not permitted to go. Kay thinks that a breach of discipline is cured by a hug and a warning, supplemented by a promise not to repeat it.

On the other hand, who am I to impose my thinking on the upbringing of her child? I didn't do well with my own. The normal courage with which I am endowed shrinks when I think of Sonny. Where, where the hell was the mistake made? Possibly, the kid felt my gradual divorce from Elspeth in the latter years. Children are sensitive to estrangements. But this can't be true because I've heard that if a child is to be warped psychologically it occurs before the age of five. At that time, Elspeth and I were happy.

Another weakness which Kay is going to have to put up with is intolerance of her opinions. I have never had a high regard for female opinions, except insofar as they bear on the home or the family. This is not to say that there are not women who understand much more than I of history, or current events, or the world of business. These, in my opinion, are the oddities. Most women think along lines unappreciated by men. For example, when I took Kay to the Fairfax Theater in Miami, she barely understood the plot. Her interest was in the private life of Elizabeth Taylor, or the attractiveness of Paul Newman. I went to the movie to see a picture.

Physically, our life is pluperfect. There is no union anywhere in the world to match this. It is incredible, unbelievable, unmatchable; it touches high happiness on the edge of madness. Satisfaction inflames desire which brings on a torrent of satisfaction which inflames desire which, in turn . . . I have never down-graded making love as an integral part of marriage. The physical is only slightly less important than the spiritual and the mental. The spiritual may be the mist of love, but the physical is the giant who walks through it.

Sex has become an enduring wonder. I must confess that this is the big surprise of the marriage because men in their fifties often think of sex only in terms of anecdotes, or sporadic excursions with teen-age girls, or as a monotonous act brought to life by a calendar. Elspeth, in anger, used to refer to me as "oversexed." This hurt, not only because it was untrue, but because she could make it sound like a hamper full of dirty linen.

Our love life—Kay's and mine—is inspirational. No written notices; no advance hints; no asking permission; no apologies; just the thousand and one spontaneous tendernesses which precede the frantic, interminable encounter so exquisitely exhausting, so close to death, so near to paradise. It is the crash of the big warm comber against the rock on the beach; it is a bird motionless in the sky; it is sunrise over an active volcano; it is a message in Braille; it is, more than anything else, the pleasing of someone other than self, and, in so doing, achieving an even greater joy.

She is exciting all the time. Not only at night; not only by day; not only when dressing or undressing or laughing or just looking through a window in silence; she is exciting to me in a crowd; she is exciting curled up in sound sleep with locks of hair over her face; she is exciting when we are at a table for two; she is overwhelming. Probably the most pleasant aspect of all is that, at this age, I am not deceived by the pleasures of the flesh. I do not subscribe to the erroneous aphorism that "If it is all right in bed, it's all right everywhere else."

In truth, I had a blunt talk with Kay about the sexual aspects of marriage before I became so involved that escape was impossible.

She is a woman in the prime of female life. Women are at their best in the thirties and early forties. Men in their fifties approach a male climacteric with a paunch and a swagger. They overemphasize their virility. They must prove—more to themselves than to the woman—that they are better men than they were at twenty. They exhaust themselves. If, on a solitary occasion, they are unable to perform, they commence to torture themselves with doubt. Doubt, even a furtive one, cannot be wed to desire, and desire will always die when it shares the same bed with doubt.

In this way, a momentary lapse becomes permanent. It requires all manner of patience and service on the part of a wife to restore vigor which is lost only in the mind. There was a chance, I told her, that this would happen to me. I know of friends, much younger, who had given up love-making and who now resorted to golf, fishing, bowling and gambling on a daily basis to display a maleness they no longer felt.

Kay would be taking a chance. She shrugged. "As long as your arms aren't paralyzed," she said, "I'll know I'm loved, and I don't need anything more." We sat in a parked car that night and I had to laugh. "It's a nice speech," I said, "but I don't believe it." She said: "Men feel that way. Women don't."

It was midnight. He turned the little radio down and dropped into bed with a book on Hawaii. The shopping trip had tired him. Kay had a list of relatives and friends and she had bought a few items in Bangkok, a few in Hong Kong, and she had completed the gift list in Tokyo. Lon called it murder. He said that the baggage would go far beyond the allotment of sixty-six pounds per person. It had to be done, she said. After a time, he had quit and had taken her bundles back to the hotel.

"You," he said, "are on your own." Kay was irritated. She derived so much pleasure from looking in windows and glass cases that she couldn't understand Lon's attitude. There wasn't much more to do, but she had done it alone and she had been cool to him all evening.

She went to her bed and fluffed her pillow. A sheet of paper fell out. She picked it up. It was really two sheets of paper. The top one was a note. "I love you," it said, "and I have never written a poem in my life, so please do not laugh when you read the attached." She sat on the side of the bed and read:

A Sentimental Cynic

I have been this high before,
And looked down
With a hand in mine
At the lonely mutes of the world below
Who do not understand.
I have been this high before
And the view is unchanged;
The hand is young and firm
And mine is old.
My hand is a wise hand;
It has traced words of solemn meaning
And has made mistakes.
It knows the contour of a breast
And the warm tear of a child.
A wise hand pays for its wisdom
And the rings gracing its fingers;
A wise hand can hush lips
Which were not meant to kiss.

I have been this high before,
Just once. We looked down
Into mists of enchantment—
Our fingers laced forever.
That was a long time ago
And now, with bursting heart
I have made the climb again;

The mists have gone, for me.
The hand is new; the grip is old
And the promises on the
Heights of love are promises
Which echo in mirthful mockery
Down the canyons of time.
Once, they were more than promises;
They were oaths sworn to
A sunny sky beyond stars unseen
To last a thousand light years;
They died in the echoes nearby.

I have been this high before
And should not have climbed again.
One love lives well in thin air
But not two.
Still, I shall not free your hand
Nor loose your glance from mine.
I shall not alter a promise
Even if the rocks split with laughter.
You shall not be betrayed
Nor deceived, nor left in solitude.
Let the oaths of love ring louder
This time, and travel further
To chill the distant stars
With their breath.
Stay with me, my pet.
Hold on tight
To my hand.
The journey down is lovely.

Kay wept.

THE TWENTY-FOURTH DAY

LON was looking out the hotel window across the roof of the old Imperial. It was Sunday and great crowds of families, dressed in their best, were walking the streets of Tokyo. He heard the laughter of Kay and the Japanese maid behind him, rising from giggles to hearty laughter to hysteria, and he paid no attention. Lon knew they were laughing about him. His wife had asked what he wanted for breakfast and he had circled every other item on the menu with pencil.

The maid took the order, and kept saying patiently: "For how many, prease?" This, to Kay, was cumulative humor. The more the maid said it, the louder she laughed. The more she laughed, the more the maid doubled forward, laughing. Lon concentrated on the people below. He was surprised—for what reason he didn't know—that the Japanese used Sunday as a day of rest. It had not occurred to him to wonder what day the non-Christian nations used as a nonworking day.

Another thing that impressed him was that Oriental adults had an ability, in the presence of children, to be as children. In parks or playgrounds, the parents were amused by the same things which amused the children, and it appeared genuine, not condescending. They were awed by the misty veils of water in tall fountains; they laughed uproariously at the antics of monkeys in cages; they pointed to tall office buildings and speculated excitedly with the little ones. He had noticed this in Bangkok, in Hong Kong and now in Tokyo. He felt envious.

Kay called him to breakfast and he cinched the belt around his blue bathrobe, and turned away from the window. He had learned a great deal on this trip; so much that, at times when sleep would not come, he would lie in the darkness recreating parts of the world and putting the people in place. Some of what he had seen fitted his preconception of what things would be like; other things he had seen augmented with new facets of information.

The one big lesson he had learned was something known to all historians and almost all schoolteachers: ignorance is the enemy of peace; knowledge breeds understanding. He was sure that if all people could meet all other people, they would feel a common kinship in their aspirations. Ignorance breeds suspicion; suspicion breeds belligerence; belligerence engenders counterbelligerence; counterbelligerence breeds war.

"Did you know," he said, holding a crisp slice of bacon in his fingers, "that Japanese industry has expanded about seventeen per cent in the past year?" Kay shook her head. "It's a dull subject," he said, "but Germany has made the same giant strides. The United States is trying to expand at the rate of five per cent per year and gets all kinds of government help to do it."

"So?" she said. So, he said, we won the war. So did Great Britain. The winners were struggling to keep their noses above water. The losers were prospering. Kay thought about it. "Most of the industry of the losers was destroyed," she said. "Aren't they sort of coming up off the floor?" Yes, Lon said. But that was only part of the story. The important thing was that the losers were competing for world markets, and winning. The reason, he felt, was that neither Germany nor Japan was burdened by heavy defense taxes.

"The winners tell you that you can't have an army, a navy or an air force," he said. "True, they have small defense forces, but

nothing like those supported by our country and the Soviet Union
and Great Britain. The world has reached a state in which the
winners are afraid of each other." He dipped an edge of toast into
the yolk of an egg. "Take the United States. Each American family
is going to have to pay about seven hundred dollars apiece just for
defense. Not for running the country, mind you. Just fear money.
Suppose we didn't need missiles and hydrogen bombs. Just suppose,
honey. Suppose Russia didn't need them. Can you imagine what
man could do with that kind of loose money? A father can pay off
a house at the rate of seven hundred dollars a year. Fifty billion
dollars out of a defense budget comes to a lot of scholarships and
roads and research. Our business would expand too. Everybody
would be living high on the hog. Think of medical research alone.
Think of the hundreds of millions of tons of wheat and corn and
butter and eggs we keep off the market. Think of the millions of
dollars it costs just to keep starving people from eating it—just
to store it."

"You sound like a Communist," she said. He grinned. "Sure.
I'm a fine Roman Catholic Communist. I'll tell you how much of
a Communist I am. If the Reds ever take over the United States,
your husband is going to be high on their list of writers to be
erased. No, seriously. I can't preach because I don't know the inner
depths of politics. All I really know is that it could be a fine world
if the men who build the tower of Babel realized that no one can
win an ideological war. Suppose the Soviet Union takes over the
world? How long will it last before a counterrevolution knocks
it over?"

"This part makes sense," she agreed, "because I majored in history and I know what happened to the Phoenicians, the Egyptians,
the Greeks, the Romans—all the world cultures of the past can be
seen for fifty cents on a guide-conducted tour." "Right," he said.
"And well said. Then, even if capitalism wins this struggle, it is
only a temporary victory. No ideology lasts long. So why struggle?

Why not permit little Thailand to live out its life in its own way; and big China to live according to its choice?"

"Do you know," she said, "that we leave here tonight and we have a lot to see?" He nodded, shut up, and addressed himself to his breakfast. "Do you also know," she said, "that you're practically living in that crumby bathrobe?" Yes, he said. He knew. He expected that when they got downstairs Nikkada would be so mad he would fall out of the car laughing.

Packing to leave was becoming simple. He had his valises; she had hers. They split the toilet articles between them, also the souvenirs. Soiled clothing went into one bag; it was a twenty-minute act with a two-bellboy finish. Counting the portable typewriter, they had six items. The last line was always the same: Lon patted his jacket and said: "Now where are the tickets?" Kay always had them in her purse, with the passports and whatever declarations of currency had to be turned in at customs.

Lon tipped the boys and the maids and stopped in the coffee shop with Kay. They sipped, looking at their watches now and then. "Strange thing," Lon said. "This afternoon we stood on a dock and looked out at Tokyo Bay." "Where the war ended," Kay said. "Yes," he said. "Where the war ended. Except for some small craft, it was just another blue bay. But on that water, the battleship Missouri squatted, waiting for the Japanese delegation to arrive in their top hats to surrender. Sunday. Tonight, en route to Hawaii, we'll cross the international date line and Sunday will begin all over again. Tomorrow morning—Sunday—we'll cross Pearl Harbor where the war started. The end and the beginning on the same day."

"Let's get started," she said. "I get nervous. It is amazing, now that you mention it. I hadn't thought of it that way. I still can't explain to myself how we spend all day Sunday in Tokyo and tomorrow we spend all day Sunday in Honolulu." "Well," said

Lon, as he followed her out, "you have been losing hours all the way from New York and you are now at a stage—" "Never mind," she said. "Let's look for Nikkada." They found him, with some of the valises in the trunk of the car and some up front beside him.

As always, he held his hat in his hand and grinned and bowed as he opened the door. "Go fry away. Nikkada sorry." Lon didn't feel sorry. Nor did Kay. She missed Lucy. They had telephoned home from Japan one night, but the conversation was clouded with a roar of sound, like a waxing and waning wind. Most of it was "I'm fine. How are you?" Or, "Everything is fine here. How are things there?" A waste of money, Lon said. Kay said not quite—just hearing Lucy's voice gave her confidence. Katie had tried to explain Sonny's condition to Lon, but the connection was bad and the German accent thick. Sonny would be home in the next few weeks, she said. The call, which exhilarated Kay, depressed Lon.

Was it guilt? Possibly. Perhaps, when he first heard in Paris that his only child was sick, he should have gone home. There was nothing he could have done to help him—that part would be medical—but he could have sat at the kid's side, held his hand, reassured him, made him understand that somebody cared. But he hadn't gone home. The matter was given fleeting consideration, and then he had continued his great affair with his great love.

Now, as they left Japan, it began to look like a selfish decision. He had done nothing for his son. Would it have been too much to send a telegram? Or a letter saying: "Say the word and we'll hurry home to you." It must have been a horror for the boy to come out of a sickening alcoholic stupor and find himself confined and restrained. To awaken and find himself in an ocean of white jackets and expressionless faces; to be questioned by psychiatrists who sat antiseptically behind patient pencils; to look around vainly for the one person in whom he had faith, and then to remember: "Oh him. He married a blonde and he went far away."

And the little girl? Did he feel guilty about her? She was left in a strange house with a strange housekeeper, a little girl whose sleep, and sometimes her waking moments, were disturbed by bad dreams. No, he didn't feel guilty. He felt sorry for any child who was in a chronic state of unhappiness, or, to put it another way, vacillating between misery and glee. He felt no guilt because her antagonism to him was so sharp.

"Why did you marry my Mommy?" "You know what? If it wasn't for you, my Mommy would still be with my Daddy." "What's a divorce?" "You don't like little girls, do you?" "Why do you tell me not to ask so many questions?" "Are you really my uncle?" "Where did my Daddy go? Is he going to get a divorce too?" "You're mad at me. I can tell." "Is Sonny my brother? Then why does he pull his head away when I kiss him?" "Mommy always sleeps with me. Where is *our* bed?" "You don't like my doll, do you?" "Sometimes when I say my prayers I ask God to make you go away so my Daddy will come back."

Lon wondered if a man over fifty could display true affection to a hysterical child. He had tried holding her, cuddling her in his arms, before the marriage, but he felt the slender figure stiffen. When he complimented her on her crayon drawings, she subverted the words and managed to make them sound spurious and hateful. Sometimes, especially when he noticed that she was staring at him, with lips compressed and eyes slitted, he felt compassion for her because she did not understand that, in time, matters were going to be all right; everything was going to be fine; he was prepared to put in time and love on this child so that she would stand a better chance than his child had had.

"A penny for your thoughts," Kay said. He looked out the car window. They were at Haneda Airport. "They're not worth a penny," he said. "My mind was wandering over all the places we've been, all the things we've seen, all we've learned, and a little bit about home." Kay got out and pulled her black gloves on. "That's funny," she said. "I was just thinking about Sonny and Lucy and Burge."

"Burge? What about Burge?" She said nothing special. He had crept into her consciousness and she wondered if he would like her. "It isn't necessary that he like you," Lon said. "I don't give a hoot whether he does or not; it's only important that he do as you tell him." Kay said it wasn't going to be easy for Burge. He was accustomed to fighting everything out with Lon.

"He's going to do as you tell him, or he's going to leave. I have enough problems without refereeing battles between my wife and the handyman." Kay said she anticipated no trouble. "That's funny," Lon said. "I do. I know this guy like I know myself. I'll bet he can't wait for you to come home so he can start a contest of wills. I'll bet that the first time you tell him to take the burlap screens from the rose bushes, he'll tell you that he's busy cleaning the cellar. If you tell him to straighten out the cellar, he'll say 'Not now. I have to take the burlap off the rose bushes.' This man is a real son-of-a-bitch, Kay, but he's a solid gold son-of-a-bitch."

The porters arrived and took the luggage, and Lon said: "Pan American desk," and gave them some yen notes. He tipped Nikkada well, shook hands with the old warrior, and gave him an extra envelope. "For the little grandchildren," he said. Nikkada took it and said nothing. He held the envelope in his hands and blinked his dark almond eyes. "Prease," he said, and all the laughter was gone from his tone. He tried to give the envelope back.

"Next time Tokyo," Lon said, "we write letter to you first." He made scribbling motions with his hand. In a moment, he was gone.

At one minute after midnight, Flight Two stood on the bay end of the runway in a rising shriek. From a distance, it was a silver monster with big bug eyes staring ahead. Then the brakes were released and slowly, steadily, it moved down the runway, rolling faster and ever faster, carrying 131 passengers and all their luggage, a crew of nine, and fifty-six tons of fuel. The speed kept inching up—eighty knots, ninety, one hundred ten, twenty . . . faster, faster, one forty, one fifty and, in a few seconds, Flight Two lifted off the long runway, tucked her wheels into her belly, and headed up into the night sky of Monday morning, turning eastward at 2,000 feet in a long climbing turn, and aimed her nose for Sunday and Honolulu, 3,900 miles and six hours and twenty minutes away.

"I'm going to have a late supper," Kay said, "and a long nap." Lon watched for the NO SMOKING sign to flick off. He looked below and saw the lights of Tokyo. "I know I'm going to hate myself in the morning," he said, "but I'm going to stay awake. I want to know when we cross from Monday morning back to Sunday, and I want to see Midway."

"Why Midway?" she asked. He shrugged. "An admiral named Nimitz sent two men named Fletcher and Spruance to ambush a Japanese fleet off Midway." She couldn't understand why he would want to see the island. "What's to see?" she said. "Nothing," he admitted. "I've seen aerial photos of it and it's just a little hunk of coral with a reef around it, but it's going to remind me of a squadron called Torpedo Eight, a cruiser named Mogami, a carrier named Yorktown—you wouldn't understand."

"I suppose not," she said. "But if you stay awake all night, you're going to be a wreck getting into Honolulu." Lon agreed. "But I must see the island," he said.

THE TWENTY-FIFTH DAY

"YOU don't mind?" he said. No, she
didn't mind. "Sure?" "Of course I'm sure. I need the sleep anyway. You go up and pilot the plane or whatever it is you do up
there. I'm going to doze. I wonder what happened to the Cointreaux?" "Please," he said. "I mean it," Kay insisted. "They may
be offended." "Ah," Lon said, "what a pity. The last word I got
out of Larry was that he might have to rush off to Switzerland on
a family matter." "I didn't hear that," she said. Lon got up. "I'll
be back later."

He walked toward the flight deck. The steward asked if he
wanted something to eat, and Lon told him he'd have coffee when
the crew had it. He opened the little door and stepped inside into a
world of darkness and radiant red dials. There were introductions
all around: Captain Harry Beyer, First Officer Herbert Platt,
Second Officer William Wakefield, Engineer William Newport.
They were voices, not faces. He saw the compass heading: 096.
Arcturus, almost dead ahead in the darkness, winked a saffron eye
at Flight Two.

The total weight of the plane on take-off turned out to be 170
tons. The four throttles had been set close to 90 per cent of full.
In the heavy air at Haneda Airport, Captain Beyer got 240 knots
out of the ship. But, as he climbed, resistance decreased, the air

became thinner, and, on the same throttle setting, the big plane was moving faster and faster. At 9,000 feet it was 290 knots. There were faint flashes of lightning on the left.

At 17,000 feet, it was 380 knots. Back in the passenger compartment, the purser and two stewardesses were offering midnight snacks, martinis, wine and coffee. The radar scope spun its little searchlight between the captain and the first officer. It showed big cloud masses on both sides of the craft. Beyer aimed between them. There was a little turbulence, less than one would experience on the front seat of a pick-up moving over a country road, and then smoothness. Beyer estimated Honolulu International Airport in six hours and thirty minutes. The engineer counted on using about 15,000 pounds of kerosene per hour, and informed the captain that the landing weight would be 45½ tons lighter than on take-off.

At 37,000 feet Flight Two was making 460 knots. Beyer leveled off and put the ship on automatic pilot. The crew homed in on a patrol vessel, and found that Flight Two, as expected, had edged into the eastbound jetstream. The stream was moving at 160 knots. This, in addition to the 460 knots, brought the true speed over the Pacific Ocean to about 620 miles per hour.

Beyer called for coffee all around. He was a dry humorist. "Estimating international date line in fifty-seven minutes," he said. "Check this because Mr. Michaels wants to take a picture of it." "That so?" Platt said. "Which side does he want?" "Give him the sunny side," said Newport. At three A.M. Tokyo time, the horizon of the ocean was pale green pastel ahead. Back in the cabin, some passengers slept under blankets, some read. "It is three A.M. Monday," said Newport, "but it will never reach four."

At 3:57, Flight Two moved back in time from Monday to Sunday. The rim of the world ahead was on fire. The captain and first officer placed green sunshades in place. Below were slate clouds in thick masses. "On the trip around the world," said Lon, "this is about the longest leg." Beyer nodded. He said it was about 350 miles further than the New York to Paris leg.

The sun came up in blinding light. It came up hot out of the cool Pacific and Flight Two was noisily suspended in space. The clouds had gone. Below was the blue of the sea; above was the same deep blue in the sky. The monster whined, but it stood still. The sun moved, but Flight Two hung like a dying moth in a spiderweb.

The sun is setting, Kay wrote. *He says that the typewriter will not disturb his sleep, but I will do this in longhand anyway. He says that the best way to write is in images. O.K. From what I saw of Hawaii today it is a five-cent postcard. Nothing more. It is pretty, and the weather is subtropical, but I'll take Florida or California, without the muu-muus. Lon would scorn this as an off-hand opinion. My only defense is that I must have expected more.*

The only happy surprise for me is that Peg and Larry are right here in Hilton's Hawaiian Village. They beat us by a day. I gather, from a talk with Peg, that Larry feels that Lon doesn't want his company. True, but I couldn't admit it. Lon is guilty of bad manners. When he is affronted, he becomes icy cold and contemptuous. He likes to think of himself as thick-skinned, but he is easily wounded.

En route from Tokyo, he wanted to see Midway Island. When we arrived here, I asked him if he saw it. He said yes; he seemed to be impressed, although how one can feel deeply about an atoll 7 miles straight down is beyond me. Most of the way, I slept, but when we arrived I felt as sleepy as when we left Tokyo. It isn't a good sleep anyway; sort of in and out. I was going to do some more when we got to the hotel, but he had other ideas. He and his "other ideas" are going to be the death of me.

We have a sitting room and bedroom on the 14th floor. Waikiki Beach is directly below; to the right is Diamond Head, a small lumpy mountain standing on the edge of the sea. I see dark-skinned boys balanced on surfboards riding the big green rollers in to the beach. This, to me, is Hawaii. It is unfair, I know, to think of it as commercial; almost everything is. The Hilton Village is commercial. So are Dole pineapples and the Henry J. Kaiser projects. Wherever the Americans go, the natives soon find themselves working for them.

Slept until 3, then Paul Kendall of Pan American public relations took us driving. He is tall, a crew-cut man in open sandals, and he was nice to us on his own time. It was a good drive, very pretty. We saw some beautiful homes in the hills behind Honolulu; gorgeous tropical flowers in orange and blue and fiery reds; lots of palm trees. The men seem to be addicted to outrageous silk sport shirts and bare feet with big veins and ugly toes; many of the women wear silk oriental prints; I saw a few muu-muus, but the faces in them came from Dubuque.

There are more tourists than natives. The tourists are middle-aged Americans; men who seem to spend most of their time reading newspapers and consulting their watches; women who are so busy studying the contents of windows and other women that they miss the scenery. It is possible that I'm fatigued and my mood is irritable, but, except for the backdrop, this is more like bacon-and-egg country than raw coconut and luau pits.

The drinks served at bars are tall and fruity. Lon got a shoe shine: 35 cents. This evening we are going to eat at Canlis. My husband sleeps through his first Hawaiian sunset. He needs it. He is such a nut for planes. Like a little boy watching choo-choos.

I know he is waiting for me to speak to him about the gun. It is never mentioned. I'm through talking about the danger of having that thing around. At least he might have learned something from what happened in Bangkok. But no. Some men hoard stubbornness as though their wives were trying to deprive them of it.

If I chose, I could take it now and throw it in the sea. But what good would it do? He'd blow up and there would be a scene that would last until we got home. Maybe longer. Then, if I read him correctly, he would go out and buy two big ones. No, it would be unwise to throw it away. Let him have his toy cannon. He says he never had one before our marriage. Then why? Is he going to shoot me if I turn out to be unsatisfactory? Shoot himself? One idea is as ridiculous as the other.

The only other thought is that he feels in danger from someone. Who? If he has any mortal enemies, he has not mentioned them. Come to think of it, we got on that subject one night in Florida at dinner, and he told me that there was only one man in the world whom he disliked sufficiently to mention: some editor in New York. Lon broke him into a job, or got it for him, or did something for this person and the man turned against him. Other than that, he said, he feels a mild dislike for some people, but not enough to work himself up to a pitch over it.

He has a philosophy about it. Says that hate, like love, requires emotional fuel and few people are worth hating. Still, I know that he dispenses contempt regularly. He finds it easy to disdain people who make common mistakes. A woman who blunders; a man who cannot distinguish between north and south; a child who is childish; all of them earn his mockery.

But I love him. He's mine. It's as simple as that.

THE TWENTY-SIXTH DAY

THE rain came down in a mist, as it does when it has no heart in its work. The sea was quiet under the dappled massage and the big rollers came in more slowly, standing tall in the shallows before crashing in exhaustion on the sand. The Michaelses were standing on the balcony. "It's a good morning for shopping," he said. She squinted her blue eyes against the mist and said, no, she had done enough. "They have a long row of shops off the lobby," he said. She had seen them; she didn't want to shop.

It seemed ironic to Lon that he, who dreaded the looking, the examining, the questioning and the buying, was pushing her toward a shopping tour. But he had noticed that she was slow to buy, slow to spend. She had bought silk bolt goods in India, and shoes in Paris, a few dresses and a gown and more shoes in Hong Kong, and gifts for relatives and friends, but, for a trip of this size, it was still small spending.

"Come on," he said. " I want to buy a couple of sport shirts anyway." Kay said that she would go, just to help him select some silk shirts. As always, Lon ran his fingers along a rack of shirts, picked this one, that one, and this one, and told the clerk to wrap them. Kay laughed at him: "You don't know how to shop." He nodded, and escorted her to the other stores, where she agreed to look around, "but only look around. I'm not spending any more money."

Lon knew she was not simply pretending to be thrifty in order to impress him. When he first started to date her, he had found that she was prone to base her dinner on whatever the supermarkets and food fairs had on sale that day. When she bought clothes, she always looked for the "slightly soiled," or "slightly damaged" items, examining them with care to make certain that she could make the dress or blouse look like new before deciding to buy it.

So now, when he caught her lingering over a pleated skirt for Lucy, or culottes for herself, he simply summoned a salesgirl and said: "We'll take this." Kay looked alarmed and shook her head. "No," she said. "A woman doesn't buy that way." He ignored her. "We'll take it," he said, smiling at the salesgirl. He kept pushing until they had purchased two more dresses, a bathing suit made in the form of a flowered sarong, white Japanese slippers, an Oriental blouse-and-slacks set, and a mahogany brush set for Sonny.

When they were back in their sitting room, Kay blew the hair off her forehead. "You are one crazy galoot," she said. "But I love it." She kissed him hard. "Some women," she said, "do not like to give. They prefer to be taken. I'm one of those." He looked at his watch. "We have a little time before I buckle down to a little work." She said don't work, and he said that he must.

"The diary?" No, he said. He had an idea for the next book. At once, Kay became excited. She phoned room service for two pots of coffee and some cinnamon toast and said: "Well, tell me. I'm dying." Lon rubbed his chin. "I'm sorry, honey," he said, "but I don't think it's your type of thing." Her happy smile died in mid-flight. "What is my type?" she asked. He figured that she would enjoy something romantic, something that Errol Flynn might have starred in years ago—"you know," he said sheepishly, "flashing swords and backing up the staircase toward the girl on top."

"Well," she said snappishly, "that proves a point. Indeed it does. It proves that if we got out of bed once in a while you'd learn that I also have a mind." "Sorry," he said. "I didn't mean to be insulting." "You were, though." "I'm sorry. You see, I'm accustomed to knowing that women do not buy my books. At least, that's what the publisher tells me. In any case, the plot is simple—" She held both palms over her ears. "I don't want to hear it," she said. "Oh, yes, you do," Lon said. "And I want your help too. This one will require a lot of research." She kept her hands over the ears for a moment or two, but it was obvious that she could hear every word.

"Remember we stopped at Byblos? That little town outside of Beirut? They call it something else now. But the part where the ruins are is ancient Byblos. I thought I would do a novel about the place; a novel, backed up, of course, with plenty of research."

Kay looked disappointed. Lon sat, elbows on knees, staring at her patiently. "You remember what the old Arab guide told us— that the Phoenicians had Byblos over seven thousand years ago. Remember the underground ruins on the edge of the sea? They died off, and sometime before the birth of Christ, the Romans took the place. The columns of their pagan temples still stand." She nodded. "Around 1150 A.D. the Crusaders stormed Byblos and took it. Their fort still stands facing the Mediterranean.

"Well, it doesn't sound like much of an idea, but I would like to do a book in three parts, using the same characters. The first would be the conquest by the Phoenicians, and how they lived and why they wanted the city, and how they did the first parchment writing in volumes. Then, four or five thousand years later, the Roman legions come in. Same characters. Maybe even the same slavegirl for the same conquering general." "Ha," said Kay. "Try that on Errol Flynn." "Oh, listen," he said peevishly. "In the twelfth century, we have the knights from France and Germany coming in to rescue Jerusalem from the infidels. Search for the

Holy Grail sort of thing. Same general, same slavegirl, same opposing characters inside the city." Kay thought about it.

"What," she asked, "is the point?" Lon nodded. "That's what I was afraid of. By using the same characters, we show that man never changes. He learns nothing from history. The spirit of conflict and conquest is always in his breast. He must fight and take something from someone. It's a dismal philosophy, but all his glorious victories are temporary. New generations are born; new generals, new armies, new battles, the same geography. It doesn't register? Okay. I wrote another poem for you."

She sat up. "You what?" she said loudly. "For me? Where? Quick." He had to smile. "Vanity," he murmured as he went looking for it, "thy name is Katherine Michaels." "Oh," she said, "say it again. It sounds so nice." He got the poem.

"Please," he said. "It's not real poetry because I'm not a real poet. It doesn't rhyme and it has no meter; it's just my feelings and the only reason I bother is to win your approval."

IF I COULD

Slice a second of time into a thousand parts
And my love for you is awake in all of them;
It is a ceaseless, sleepless, subdued ecstasy
Worn with pride, with pride.
Sometimes, your pretty face lights up a blank page
Unbidden; a shy smile wanting to be wanted,
And sometimes, it fades slowly and no magic
Of the mind can order it to stay, to stay.
The things I would give you in return for
Your giving are cheap and valueless—a coin,
A kiss, a grin of sheer delight, a heart
Which beats on tiptoe, for you, for you.

I would give—if I could—all the warm sands
On all the strands underfoot; all the high

Green combers curling white against the wind,
And years of yearning—if I could, if I could.
I would pull the night confetti from the sky
And spangle your hair; and save the solemn moon
To silhouette you standing in a warm breeze
Waiting for me—if I could, if I could.
I would fill you with happiness beyond happiness
And small sorrows, so that you could weigh
One against the other, and weep for joy;
I would make you a fulfilled woman—if I could, if I could.

A bark to take you to Rio on hyacinth-scented seas,
A silver bird for watching dawn from over the clouds;
Pink satin sheets for a pale and argent body; the laughter
Of old friends—these I would give, if I could, if I could.
A crystal goblet for madeira; sentimental music; the fruition
Of girlish dreams and eternal love and true peace;
A house with no locks, the rooms laden with flowers
These too, dear heart—if I could, if I could.
My poverty is of the soul and I must enrich it at your side
Spending a little of your goodness and hoarding the rest
Against the far-off time when I must be judged forever;
Then I would hold you to me again—if I could, if I could.

"It's lousy," he said apologetically, "but it comes close to the way I feel." Kay said nothing. She kept staring at the sheet. Then she looked up. He saw the tears and turned away, and walked out on the little balcony to see if the rain had stopped. "It's beautiful," Kay said. "Truly beautiful." He did not hear.

Kay was standing under the shower, tucking the bathing cap tight and speaking loudly against the the hiss of water. Lon was at the basin, brushing his teeth. They were talking about the dinner at Canlis Restaurant. The food had been good, "good old American," as Lon put it. The steak had been big and charcoal broiled; the baked potato was laden with sour cream and chives; the salad had been garden fresh and, in eating it, they didn't have to worry about dysentery; for dessert, there had been a fresh pineapple half filled with ice cream.

Lon was proud that Kay enjoyed food. She ate well, but she didn't seem to gain or lose weight. She liked food to look pretty on the plate; a little garnishing, a sprig of parsley; a leaf of lettuce under slices of banana with mayonnaise standing in a small hill on top; these were the things which made, or unmade, a dinner for her. "My mother always made food look attractive," she said. "There's no excuse for making dinner look messy."

He watched her step out of the shower, slender and dripping, the skin on her face scrubbed and ruddy, her body snowy and almost too pale, her feet big and ugly. She peeled the cap off and dug the bath towel into her ear, tilting her head as she did it. By this time he was shaving, a drudgery he preferred to undertake at night rather than in the morning.

"I've been thinking about Lucy," he said. Kay stopped toweling momentarily, as though she heard warning buzzers. "Yes?" she said. He made a grimace, as the razor scraped the white lather and the gray hairs off his chin. "I've got to be a hundred per cent father or nothing," he said. She looked at him, puzzled slightly, and then put a foot on a small white stool and started to dry her legs. "So?" she said.

"So," he said, stroking the clean face to see if he had skipped any whiskers, "it isn't an easy decision." He ran the warm water and doused his face in it several times. "It isn't easy because I don't think that men over fifty make good fathers for little girls." Gently, she said, "We've been over this before."

"I know. I know," he said. "But listen anyway. I've given it a lot of thought and if I'm wrong I want you to tell me." Kay finished drying herself and began to fluff her hair out. Their faces appeared in the same mirror; his, combing the gray hair; hers, tilting and turning from side to side as she dried the ends. "If it's bad news," she said. "I wish you'd get it over with."

Lon turned from the basin and took her in his arms. "With us," he said, "there is no such thing as bad news." He kissed her and released her. He went out into the sitting room, wrapped his naked body in his old robe, and sat down to smoke and have a nightcap of Scotch on the rocks. "Before I begin," he said, as she poured herself a hooker of rye and some ginger ale, "let me tell you that I've decided to follow your idea: be a one hundred per cent father." Kay's shoulders sagged, as she sat. "I'm glad of that," she said softly. "It takes a load off my mind."

He said that, in his opinion, Lucy was now the most important person in the family. "Sonny, for example, is sick. He needs medical attention and, whether I'm married or single, he is going to require treatment. I'm not downgrading the boy, but his relationship to you and to me is secondary at the moment. He will get well in time. I'm sure of it. The day will come when he's going to need you more than he will need me.

"When I was a little boy, I used to create imaginary situations and try to think of what I would do to get out of them. I'm still doing it, Kay. Only now they're not imaginary. I said that Lucy— contrary to what you may think—is now the most important member of the family. We can forget—well, not forget—but we can eliminate Sonny until he is well.

"That leaves us, and Lucy. We are happy people. We now have what we want out of life. If I never write another book, or live another day, I'm content. Now for goodness' sake, don't start crying. I want to put these cards on the table. I assume that you are happy. You have what you want. That leaves Lucy. The child hasn't got what she wants. She has neither happiness nor contentment. Unless I misunderstand the signs, she is in a sort of chronic misery.

"Something wrong has happened, but she isn't quite sure what.

She knows that she had a mommy and a daddy. To her, everything was fine. Then came an argument or whatever it was that precipitated your walkout, and suddenly her world cracked open. She is—how old?—eight? Okay. Whatever prayers the kid says at night I'm sure there's a special message to bring mommy and daddy back together again.

"To her, I'm an old man. No, don't shake your head at that, because she told me so. I know that at her age anybody over thirty is old. I'm old. She cannot visualize me playing ball with her on the nice days, or being patient with her homework, or mending a doll's head. She's right. I can't. Still, she needs a one hundred per cent father—a man with love and authority—and I'm it. Love means to stop my work when she's in tears and put an arm around her; it also means to romance her; to project a love I do not yet feel; shocked? I'm just trying to be honest with you. It means taking an interest in anything that interests her; it means reading stories to her; it means showing much more affection to her than she's willing to give me.

"Authority means that I'm going to be the boss in the household. Not only over her, but you and Katie too. Authority does not mean that I'm going to stalk around cracking a whip; it means that I will make the major decisions. Not us. Me. This also means spankings, if she's naughty. I know you are opposed to any corporal punishment, but I once saw you haul off and crack the child across the face. It was not because of what she'd done; it was because her tone was insolent. In other words, Kay, you were hurt and you got your revenge at once. I'm not that kind of person. When she told me that I was an old man, it hurt, hurt pretty deeply, but revenge didn't enter my mind because it wouldn't make me any younger in her eyes in any case. But when she does wrong things, either deliberately or repeatedly, she is going to be punished and I want no interference.

"Also, I am not going to permit her to split the two of us b using one against the other. You and I will have a solid front. If you say it is too damp to go out and play, I will not permit her to come to me for permission. I'll say: 'Have you asked Mommy? What does she say?' I want you to do as much for me. Love will come to Lucy and me in time. She will hate me less and less, and my apathy will change to interest and then to affection. It's bound to. I am not going to force this thing. It will come. Two people cannot share the same roof without getting to know each other.

"As far as her father is concerned, he is welcome. I mean, at our house. She will get to feel that she belongs in the house, and she will want him to see her room. If I feel any animosity toward him, or he toward me, that child will know it at once. And she isn't going to see any from this side, I can tell you."

Lon finished his drink. He stood. "I've said enough for tonight," he said, "unless you have something to add." Kay said no, she thought he had stated his side pretty well. She disagreed with some aspects, but— "What aspects?" Lon said. Kay said they didn't matter at the moment, but she did not favor Francis seeing the child too much, or being too welcome in the house, but these things would iron themselves out in time.

"Oh," he said. He led the way into the bedroom. "We'll be home Friday night and I think things should be discussed. I know that you have certain thoughts about Sonny, and I'll listen any time you're ready. But Lucy is just a child and—you know what I mean."

She did.

THE TWENTY-SEVENTH DAY

THE Navy driver was a quiet boy. He did his work and had little to say. He helped the Michaelses into the car, and then drove slowly away from the Hawaiian Village to Honolulu, through the city and out the far side to the bottom edge of the cloud-wrapped hills, and past the little monument to the old Regulus missile and onto the United States Navy Base at Pearl Harbor.

"We're packed," Lon said to the driver, "but we want to get back to the hotel by noon." The boy thought about it. "You'll make it, sir," he said. "It's only 0800." The car went through the gate, passes were supplied, and they went on down a long concrete storage dock to the outer edge. There, wearing a big smile and suntans, stood Commander J. W. S. Wandleigh, U.S.N. Public Relations. He was a man who forced himself to live in perpetual sunlight. No matter how bad the situation, he had a winning smile to oppose it.

This was a bad situation. The Navy had informed him that the Pentagon had invited a Mr. and Mrs. Lon Michaels to make a tour of Pearl Harbor. They were to be accorded the "A" treatment, which would mean a launch, two ratings to man the boat, an automobile tour of the facilities if they wanted it, lunch at the officers' club if that was in order, and, above all, he was not to

discuss anything classified. Michaels, he was told when the order
was cut, was a writer.

The commander dealt with writers—journalists, mostly—but he
didn't like them. They jeopardized his career; he had to appear to
be casual and friendly, and yet perpetually on his guard against
the wrong answer to the right question. He took a salute from the
driver, and introduced himself. "I suppose," he said jovially,
"this will be old-hat to you, Mr. Michaels."

Lon said no, it wouldn't. He had never seen Pearl Harbor before,
although his work as a war editor from 1942 to 1945 brought
him into close contact with events. "Frankly," he said, "I have
always thought that the Navy was sleeping off a hangover on the
morning of December seventh." The commander laughed heartily.
He was a tall skinny man with eyes which could show stark terror
through laughter. "Well," he said to Kay, "we can't fool this
man, can we?"

Kay supposed not. They got aboard the smartly rigged 26-footer.
At the wheel stood a rating in white cap and uniform. A second
sailor came aboard, smiled briefly at the three persons sitting
out along the stern, and turned on a loudspeaker. Between the
two was a high engine hatch and on it a map of Pearl Harbor, with
the battleships painted in beside Ford's Island. Little black crosses
represented Japanese dive bombers and torpedo planes coming in
to wreck the U.S. Pacific Fleet.

The commander decided to let the sailor do the talking. Perhaps if he paid strict attention, the Michaels might feel that this
was also *his* first trip around the battleground, and might leave
him alone. "I understand we're building a monument over the
Arizona," Lon said. The commander nodded. The boy at the
microphone kept talking, prefacing each statement of tragedy with,
"On your right is the anchorage of the battleship Nevada which . . ."
"On your left the first wave came over at high altitude seven
ty-five A.M. . . . . "

Lon was sickened, but he blamed himself because he knew before he accepted the invitation that only the primary shame for Pearl Harbor belonged to the Japanese. The secondary shame belonged to the American Navy, which was not ready for attack. Battleships had been moored in twos; the Army and the Navy had parked planes out in the open; week-end passes had been given as usual; it had crossed no military mind that the Japanese could send a task force to within 200 miles of Pearl Harbor while peace prevailed, and declare war as the first wave of bombers came in.

"The old Utah . . . " the boy said, and it occurred to Lon that the gallant Utah had been old before this boy was born. ". . . the Japanese made the mistake of leaving our repair shops intact." This, to Lon was almost too much. "That was no mistake," he said to the commander. "The strike was over; the Japanese had hit us with everything they had; they had sunk or damaged or killed anything that could move against them—unless I'm cockeyed, the sneak attack was a victory for Japan."

"Well," said the commander, and he began to smile. Lon waited for him to make a United States victory out of the battle, but he said no more. The sky was pale blue and the water of the bay had the indefinite quality of gray blue with the masts of long-dead ships sticking up silent and steady. "We have a right to remember our dead," the commander said.

The kid with the microphone announced that the monument built over the Arizona, was now abeam of the little boat. With disinterest, he told them that over a thousand men were still inside the old hulk, and that Old Glory was still raised at sunrise and lowered and folded tenderly at sunset. "Touching," Lon said. Kay glared at him. "The Navy let them down, so it builds monuments to their memory." He shook his head. "To its own lapse of memory."

The commander said: "Well, we can't win 'em all. How about a drink at the officers' club?" Lon apologized. He said he was sorry that he had come out, and he was sorry to have offended the commander with his remarks, but he had studied and restudied the events of December seventh, 1941, and he still could not forgive Admiral Husband E. Kimmel and General Short. They were the local commanders; they knew that peace between Japan and the United States hung on a tenuous thread; and they were not prepared for attack.

"The Japanese won the first battle," the commander said. "I know," Lon said. "We won the last. Tell that to all the kids floating around down there. Thanks for the offer of a drink, but we have to make the afternoon plane to the States." Kay added apologetically, "We have some packing to do too." They headed back for the dock and the gray car. On the drive back, Lon sat in moody silence.

They watched Flight Two Pan American come in from Tokyo and take off for San Francisco. In a way, they felt that they were watching an old friend. Flight One came in from the opposite direction, fueled up, and took off in a ripple of summer thunder for Tokyo. The air was hot and the sky was sunny. They bought magazines, last-minute souvenirs, had a fruit salad and tea, and left for the mainland and Los Angeles at 2:45 P.M.

This time, Lon did not go up on the flight deck. He sat beside Kay, sometimes holding her hand, sometimes dreaming through the window at fleets of caravel clouds, sometimes making notes on the tray before him. The voice of the captain came over the loudspeaker. "We're going to have a little of what we call turbulence," he said. "Just fasten your seat belts and relax. It is a natural thing for currents of air to move up and down, and it is natural for our ship to bounce a little passing through them. We're going to fly at 29,000 feet and we estimate Los Angeles in four hours and twenty minutes. However," the voice continued, "there is a jet ahead of us at 37,000. If he reports that the air is smoother there, we will ask for permission to go up."

"I think Los Angeles time is three hours later," Kay said. "I can look it up." He showed no interest in time. He said: "Four hours and twenty minutes . . . that's just about the same time as it takes to cross from L.A. to New York. And, about the same distance—twenty-four hundred miles. Just think, honey. A good ship requires five days to make this trip."

"I wish," she said wistfully, "that we were going directly home." Lon seemed surprised. "You're kidding," he said. She held his face in her hands and kissed it. "No, I'm not. And don't start accusing me of not enjoying the honeymoon. I'm good away from home for just so long, and then I want to hurry back, take a fast look around to see that everything is all right, and hop off again." Lon agreed that he often felt that way. "A quick check," he said, "and then hop the next plane out. I agree."

"I'm dead," Lon said. He was on the bed, still dressed. Kay finished unpacking. She said the trip was catching up with them. "I've been half dead for the past two days," she said, "but I didn't want to show the white feather. I'm honeymooned out, if that's the phrase." He said something, but it was undecipherable. Kay finished shaking out the clothes, and hanging them up. She looked at her watch. It was 11:05 P.M. Pacific Coast Time.

Lon was sleeping. She opened his portable and put it on a desk. She rolled a sheet of paper into the machine and, as always single-spaced it.

Last stop, she wrote. *The very last stop. It has been the most glorious, most wonderful honeymoon of all time. Beautiful, lovely, heavenly, adorable—there must be better adjectives. This is Tuesday night and we leave for home Friday morning. I'm not sorry that it is nearly over. I can't wait for the long regular life to begin. I'm a housekeeper at heart; I like to cook; I don't like making beds and dusting, but the rest of it isn't drudgery.*

I am full of new experiences—him and the world. Both are new and amazing to me. I am satisfied and more than. I saw everything, tried everything and I will never complain about being enclosed by four walls. Walls can be warm and encompassing, if they're your own. I will not be completely happy about the house at first; that's to be expected. I've seen it and no woman likes to take over where another one left off.

He has photos of Elspeth all over the place. I am counting on his good sense to take some of them down. Not all. But I don't want to live with a ghost, and I certainly don't want him to. Most especially him. I told him that I have no desire to replace somebody; I am sufficiently conscious that he had a previous wife, and that I had a previous husband and I wish to God neither of us had ever had anybody before this, but it can't be helped.

It may be a mistake counting on Lon's good sense, because, in spite of good intellect, he does not see as much as he thinks he does. Lots of little things escape him. I have seen women at various places making a play for him right in front of me, but he can't see it. He says that I am seeing things. Maybe. But I often feel that I'm the one who invented the game of casual flirtation and what he takes as casual conversational interest on the part of a woman is much more significant, in my eyes.

I'd kill myself if I lost him. I know I would. This isn't an idle phrase written into a diary to impress me. It's the truth. I'm too deeply committed to him. All of me wants all of him all the time. That's why I know I'd destroy myself if this marriage breaks up. It isn't the fact that this would be the second loss in a row; that's bad enough; it's that this is the first real marriage and I know now that I didn't know what marriage was when I was with Francis. I . . . just . . . didn't . . . know. . . .

As we get closer to home, I think more of home. He doesn't, I know. He lives each moment to the full; he drinks in scenery with the eyes of a poet; he sorts new people, discarding some quickly, hanging onto others. In many ways, he is sharp, discerning, but he is also lyrical and somewhat of a growling soft touch.

He thinks of himself as hard-boiled, so I do nothing to alter the portrait. If there was some way of finding out, I would bet that I know him better than he knows me. A woman will spend almost all of her time studying the man she loves; a man spends only the time he's with her in trying to understand her. Most men, in fact, weasel out of it by saying: "Who can understand a woman?" Lon thinks he knows women—and the little tidbits I got from his relatives, and from him, suggest that he has done pretty well with women over the years, but that isn't understanding.

That's charm. Conquest, perhaps. Certainly not understanding. Man, I guess, is always trying to assail the unassailable: a mountain, a sea, a woman, a career. I have his solemn promise that all other women in his life are out. I believe him because I have never known him to make a promise he did not keep. Also, he cannot fake the contentment he feels. He is happy and relaxed. I watch other women and I watch his reaction to them and they do not make a dent on his consciousness.

We are staying at the Beverly Hills Hotel, and Lon talked about it before our arrival as though it was a second home. He knows everybody here and he likes everybody. It is a gorgeous place. We arrived at night and the towers are lighted in blue. We entered under a long green and white striped canopy. The rooms are spacious and elegant. This one is done in green and off-white. The table lamps are bigger than most floor lamps. The rugs are thick and the bathroom has two basins. While Lon was registering, and shaking hands with old friends, I watched the traffic in and out of the lobby, and the ladies were dressed right to the gusset. Ordinary mink, in Beverly Hills, must be common, because most of the mink I saw was in varied mutations of color and style.

Some of the coats had sleeves big enough to make a wrap for me.

Lon says he will phone a few movie-star friends in the morning, and maybe we will see how a movie is made. I must say, after all these years of looking at them—and living through some of them as the queen bee—that I'm glad to be in Hollywood for a day or two, and I can't wait to see the inside of a studio. Most of all, I'd have liked to see my all-time favorite: Ronald Colman, but he's been gone a long time.

When we got off the plane, I made the mistake of asking Lon if he was now going to throw the gun away, because there were no more natives to worry about. Wrong question. I was told to stick to my knitting. This leads me to believe that the gun has some other reason for being on this trip. However, when we left Hawaii, he no longer carried it pinned to the inside of his trousers. It's in his briefcase. Even I know the answer to that: we passed our final customs search as we arrived in Hawaii. It's part of the U.S. and no one is going to rummage through our effects any more.

Sometimes I get so mad I could hit him with it.

THE TWENTY-EIGHTH DAY

THE day was sunny and cool. Three lanes of traffic poured through Beverly Hills, following the curves of Sunset Boulevard to Hollywood. Where once the measure of greatness was in the length and weight of the automobile, now it was in minuteness: the Jaguars, the Hillmans, Brewsters, M.G.'s and Corvettes. The producers, the stars, the idea men, the writers, the publicity agents, the directors—all those who earned bread with the crust chopped off in the empty temple of the Vista-vision eye—hurried on along the edge of the lofty hills as though time were of the essence; as though each of them had an idea for making a one-set picture which could be brought in under $2,000,000.

The warmth spread up through Coldwater Canyon and down into the San Fernando Valley where towns like Van Nuys, El Centro, Encino and Burbank steam in the sun. Hollywood wears gleaming teeth in a tight sunny smile. The fingers snap, the knuckles crack, the eyes are addicted to nervous ticks, but the smile is fixed. Like a retired policeman the movies live on an old reputation.

In Kay's eyes, Hollywood was grand and beautiful and exciting. On the Fox lot, Lon thought she looked like a little girl as she watched harem girls in filmy gowns eat sandwiches in the com-

344

missary with boys who were made up with gowns and fierce
beards as sheiks. Her mouth made pretty O's when she spotted
Peter Lorre and Billy Gilbert and Sir Cedric Hardwicke. She marveled at the lights, the interminable waiting, the sets like Baghdad
palaces built in the middle of huge barns.

In Lon's eyes, Hollywood had been dying for years of cancer
of the budget. The writers, the stars, the directors had devoured
the temple which gave them sustenance. On the Fox lot, where
once four or five expensive motion pictures would be on separate
sets, one scene of a television show was being filmed. Where
once there had been a cow town of the west, with hitching posts,
a bulldozer landscaped the earth for a housing development. Even
the oil well which had pumped crude oil out of the earth on the
movie lot for many years had now been moved. Down on Gower
Street, the Columbia lot appeared to be dead. Little weedy film-
processing laboratories grew around it, the place where once Rita
Hayworth and Dick Powell had lunched in Harry Cohn's private dining room. A block or two away, the newer, shinier temples
gleamed in the sun—N.B.C., C.B.S., A.B.C. Signs proclaimed
the presence, in person, of Lawrence Welk and Art Linkletter and
Bob Hope, in an area where frenzied women once fainted in the
presence of Rudolph Valentino and Clark Gable.

"This," said Kay, riding beside Lon, "is terrific. Imagine me in
Hollywood." He said the town could do worse. In Burbank, she
had seen Natalie Wood on the Warner lot ("She's so tiny and
so attractive") and Jack Lemmon ("I guess he can do about anything") and Bob Hope ("I couldn't help laughing when he said
hello") and Ethel Merman ("Good God, can that woman sing
loud!") and assorted directors and producers who were old friends
of her husband's.

She was interested in seeing Hollywood Boulevard and Vine
Street, a rough cut of yesterday's shooting of a movie at Warner
Brothers, the lot at Metro where Leo the Lion once lived, Republic

studios, built by a man who wanted to star his beloved, the new home of Glenn Ford in Beverly Hills, the gorgeous place inhabited by Ann Sothern and her daughter—every place, in fact, except Shadowlawn.

"I don't want to see that place," she said. "They bury movie stars there and the whole thing would depress me." So, late in the afternoon, they headed back to the Beverly Hills Hotel. Kay was interested in discussing what Hollywood was like to her; Lon was interested in getting his shoes off. "Let's eat in the room," he said. Kay was undressing. She stuck her head out between closet doors, smiled, and said, "Okay." He said that Hollywood at night was nothing: a few clubs, some good dining places, and drive-ins.

"At eleven o'clock, the place is dead," he went on, "except for neighborhood bars and high-school hangouts. This isn't a motion-picture capital anymore; it's a museum. You can see the place where Gloria Swanson left her footprints; where Cecil B. DeMille once rebuilt the pyramids, but you can't see much action today unless you want to watch the studios edit a film made somewhere else, or unless you want to see them shoot a television Western in three days.

"The old days of big mansions and tiger cubs beside the swimming pool are gone. Nobody bathes in champagne anymore. The city of Los Angeles is growing right across the body of Hollywood. Hollywood is now an assortment of garages and drugstores and quickie studios. Los Angeles is millions of people working at good wages in big plants and earning enough to drive out of the smog on week ends."

Kay laughed. "You're wonderful at painting dismal pictures," she said. "I find the place completely fascinating." She was down to a garter belt, stockings and shoes. "I find you fascinating too," he said softly, "but maybe you're not real either."

When the waiter knocked to take the table away, Kay clutched the bathrobe around her neck and hid in the bathroom. By the time he left, she was washing stockings. Lon watched, a thumb holding a place open in a book. Kay said she missed the children. The emphasis was on the word children. "Well," he said. "You can't miss Sonny. You hardly know him." She sensed danger in this lead, so she kept rinsing the stockings, then hung them over a towel on top of the shower stall.

He said: "How much latitude do I have in telling you what I don't like?" "In what way?" she asked. "In any way." "Well," she said, "that depends." "On what?" he wanted to know. "On how strongly I feel about it," she answered. "In that case," Lon said, "I'd better not say anything about anything for fear that you might feel strongly about it."

"Okay." She dried her hands and preceded him into the room. "What's on your mind?" "Neatness." She repeated the word as though she was sure she had misunderstood. "Neatness?" "Neatness." "Well, what?" "I have a passion for it. Everything in the house has a place." "You don't have to tell me. I know."

"I have a housekeeper with orders to put everything in its place." "So?" "So I don't think you're neat." "Oh, it finally comes out." "Yeah. It finally comes out." "How am I not neat?" "You don't want to know," Lon said. "Yes I do," she insisted. "Look at your shoes then," he said. "One in the middle of the rug, one under a chair—just where you kicked them." "What time of the morning do you and your housekeeper have inspection?" "That's enough." "No, I want to hear more."

"No, you don't." "Try me." "When you lived in Florida, I never saw you remove an empty glass from a table, or a greasy coffee cup." "Anything else?" "Isn't that enough?" "It sounds like small potatoes to me," Kay said resentfully. "I saw you put Lucy to bed with dirty feet." "Oh, now it's really coming to the surface." "You're dying to make a scene." "Let me tell you something, general. If you think that house is going to be run like West Point, you need another wife." "That a threat?" "No threat. I'm going to do my level best, and no more. When I move in, I take over." "Aren't you being fresh?" Lon asked coolly.

"You think it is all right for you to sit here and take me apart as a slob, or something, but when I disagree with you I'm being fresh." "I want a neat house," he said doggedly. "You're going to get one." "I already have it." "Well, it will continue that way. In ninety-nine cases out of hundred, I'm willing to defer to you, but that one time is now. You act as though everybody was raised in the gutter except you." "I wouldn't say that."

"Well," she said, "I would. And while we're on the subject, Lon Michaels, let me tell you something that your readers don't know—at times you are an all-purpose pain in the ass." He looked shocked for a moment, and then broke into laughter. He laughed harder and harder, until his face was contorted. He held his stomach and, in mid-anger, she looked at him in surprise. She waited until he was gasping. Then she said: "What's funny?"

"All-purpose," he said, and started to laugh again."All-purpose. Such a beautiful phrase." He wiped his eyes. "So apt. And you want to know something, Mrs. Michaels? You are one hundred per cent right. And, before you begin to back-track on me, let me say that I know it too. Neatness can be carried to an extreme, and that's the way it is with me. Or, let me put it another way: my father was neat. My mother was neat. When I dusted a living room for my mother, it not only had to be done completely, and stand inspection, but the pillows on the sofa had to be set, unwrinkled, in given positions. My attitude now is a hangover, I guess."

She didn't laugh. "Well, you're going to get over it. There will be no goose-stepping around the house while I'm running it. If I want to kick a shoe off, don't complain unless you fall over it." "At least," he said, "let's try to make Lucy neat." "She is neat." "The hell she is. Lots of times, while I waited for you to get ready to go on a date, I had talks with her. She is slovenly in her person, in her school work, in her way of scratching herself in front of people, in——"

"Oh," she said, "leave the child alone. She's only eight. Did it ever occur to you that maybe you were too strict with Sonny?" She was sorry she'd said it the moment she heard the words. "Lots of times," he said. "I have been back and forth over the history of that boy until I recall more about his life than mine. I went wrong somewhere; maybe I was too strict. Maybe if I had laid off lecturing, he might be a happy-go-lucky slob today."

She got up and walked toward her husband and, when she saw that he kept his hands clasped on his lap, she sat on the floor and used his knees as a prop for her back. "Why do we fight?" she said. "I love you too much for this." "We don't really fight," he said quietly. "Not really. I know what fights are like. We disagree; we needle each other, or rather, I needle you perhaps. But this is no real fight. The only real blow struck was the one you just landed."

"I felt like biting my tongue," she said, turning toward him. "Sonny should not be brought into these things. I said it to get even for what you said about Lucy's feet." "I'm afraid that Sonny is going to have to be brought into a lot of unpleasant conversations," he said. "I'm not complaining." "Lon," Kay said slowly, "don't wear Sonny like a cross."

"Want a cigarette?" "No thanks," she said. "A drink?" "No. You have one though." "I think I will have just one. I'm tired." "You're not angry?" she asked. He leaned forward and kissed her. "Not a bit," he said. "I have to smile because, when it's too late, I can see the fault on both sides. I'm too damned neat; you aren't neat enough. There has to be a halfway point——"

"No one ever complained about my lack of neatness before,"

she said. He shrugged, pushed her away from his knees, and stood. "Maybe your ex-husband was like you," he said. "Francis," she said angrily, "wasn't a bit like me. He was a soldier who was commended for his neatness." He poured the drink and raised his glass to his wife. You just hanged yourself," he said. "Now, if you please, the prosecution rests."

THE TWENTY-NINTH DAY

IT was late in the morning when the Michaelses walked out from under the hotel canopy and got into a car. The driver headed for Bea Busby's house in Bel-Air. "Strange," Lon said. "I knew her only for a short time, years ago. But she remembered." Kay gawked at the beautiful homes in the Rodeo section. "Maybe," she said, "you gave her something to remember." He thought this was funny. "Bea Busby?" he said. "She's a sexpot. I have never flirted with a sexpot, on the thesis that the competition is too much."

"Such modesty," she mocked. Lon talked about Bea Busby, how ambitious she was, and how determined to live in the glamourous manner of the old silent-motion-picture stars. "You know her pretty well," Kay observed. "Not really," Lon said. He had researched a hilarious story on Bea Busby when she first became prominent in Hollywood.

"She was always prominent," Kay said. "I used to call her the girl who never exhaled." He said that she had Bea all wrong; she was a shrewd woman who played sex until she became a satirical symbol of it, but it was all calculated; all contrived.

"Oh," said Kay. "Then I'm not going to find a sexy movie star after all. She'll be in the kitchen making hamburgers for the children?" "Well," he said, "not exactly." Bea Busby was hardly

351

the woman for hamburgers. The best way he could explain it was that one night, when they were on their way to Grauman's Chinese Theatre for a premiere, they had sat in the back of the car, talking about her career as a beautician in Tulsa in a calm, businesslike manner, when she suddenly saw the klieg lights. At once, she yanked the center of her neckline down, shrugged off one shoulder strap, and leaned forward so that her fans, held behind carpenter's horses on the sidewalk, could see her wave.

Kay shook her head. "She must be a bird. How did you come to pass it up?" "I just told you." "If this is some old flame—" "You flatter me. At the time I met her, she was having an affair with an old French actor and she was trying to drop him without hurting him, and he was trying to get away from her without paying ransom." "Was she married then?" "Not then. Not now." "I thought Bea Busby was married to somebody." "In her home town: Tulsa. She married an oil-well rigger when she was about sixteen. She couldn't have children, so they adopted two, a boy and a girl.

"Then she got this movie-star bug, and wheedled him into driving her and the children here. Once she got here on vacation, she arranged a big fight with him and he went home alone." "Nice girl." "Ambitious." "Sounds kind of doggy to me." "Well, we're not there yet. Hold your fire. Bea uses sex as a gangster uses a gun. It's the only thing she has. In another ten years, she won't have it and then the slide back to Tulsa will begin."

"Stop. I'm in tears." "Just remember. You wanted to see a sex symbol in Hollywood and this is it. This is it in spades. So please be nice." Kay saw the house before they arrived. It was on a hill and it reminded her, somehow, of the house shown at the opening of all David Selznick pictures. Or maybe it recalled Tara Hall in *Gone With the Wind*. She wasn't certain.

It was tall and white and had fluted columns facing the road. The electric gates opened noiselessly and the car crept up a curving driveway lined with white stones. At the top, the car stopped and a man in swallow tails and a wing collar came out of the center door. "Mr. and Mrs. Michaels?" he said. "I'm Jarvis. Miss Busby will be ready in a moment."

They followed him inside. There were two signs on the driveway. Both said No PARKING and were made in the shape of hearts. The house had a reception hall with a huge crystal chandelier—lit—dominating the entrance. The tiles were black and white and a reproduction of Michelangelo's David stood in a niche on one side and a replica of the Winged Victory on the other. "Please," said the butler, pointing to cordovan leather chairs. They sat down.

"I'm impressed," Kay whispered. "We can leave now." Lon ignored it. He was busy looking. "She used to have a small flat on Cayhuenga," he said. "This proves the power of the human mammary gland." "How vulgar," Kay said with a grin. They were still whispering when both became aware of a presence. They looked up and saw Bea Busby, in person and not a moving picture, standing over them.

She wore her hair in deep platinum waves to the shoulders. She also wore enough lipstick to make her mouth glisten when she smiled. She had on a loose jersey knit sweater which made the lack of undergarments apparent, and a pair of yellow toreador pants which were tight enough to be super-epidermis. "Lon!" she said, opening both arms. He stood and she kissed him and threw both arms around his neck. "Bea," he said, "I want you to meet Kay." "Oooh," said Bea. "Isn't she pretty!" She extended her hand. "Mrs. Michaels, I'm delighted. Welcome to the Jewel Box."

Kay tried to smile. "The what?" she said. "The Jewel Box," Bea said. "It's what I call the place. Come on," she said, leading the way. "Follow me. How about a little drinkee?" The visitors said no; it was a little early. "Ha!" said Bea. "I have a clock over the bar that says it's always five P.M."

They sat in a gorgeous breakfast room, done to match Bea's pants. She ordered coffee for all, and some toast and jelly, and spent a little time adjusting the sweater so that it hung over her breasts correctly. "Tell me about you," she said to Lon. "You're married, I know. Happy, I think. You have no right bringing competition this pretty so early in the day."

"Never mind me," Lon said. "I'm interested in you. What are you doing these days?" Miss Busby ran her tongue across the under edge of her upper lip. "Busy," she said. "Busy Busby. The studio gave me a fat part in *The Rose Died in June*. I play the part of the sister of the prostitute. We finished shooting last week." Lon asked if she thought it was a good picture. "Who the hell knows until those bastards in New York—especially the smart-alecks on *Time* magazine—take it apart? I think they're all good or I wouldn't be in them."

He wasn't hungry, but he began to eat wedges of toast laden with guava jelly. "You'd be in them if they stunk," he said. Bea laughed heartily, displaying her sharp little incisors. "He knows me," she said. "I'd be in pictures if they went back to D. W. Griffith. When I'm not in them, I'm looking at them. When we're finished here, I'll show you my projection room."

"Didn't you make a picture in Europe last year?" Kay asked. She wanted to assert her presence, and she was tiring of the way Bea Busby looked at her husband. "Two," said Bea happily. "I made *Napoli di Notta*—that means Naples by night—in Rome, and I made *The History of History* for Bronston in Spain." "Did you have fun?" Kay said.

Bea wrinkled her tiny nose impishly. "She doesn't know me, does she, Lon?" she said. "Did I have fun? I damned near married an Italian count in bed. He was an old bastard but his title is good." Kay swallowed coffee noisily. "He had a fever and said he was dying of pneumonia and if I would get into bed with him, he'd call a priest and we'd get married and he could go out—you know, fast."

Lon started to choke on the toast and Bea whacked him on the back. "But Rome is nothing," Bea said. "Statues, yes. But the men think that all they have to do is be introduced, and they're entitled to ask you right away. If you say no, they walk off mad. As though you hurt their feelings. Nuts." She put jelly on her finger and licked it off. "But Spain—now there's a thing. Spanish men ask for nothing and you give them everything. They have a politeness. They all act like you were a duchess or something. Ah, that Spain."

"How did you get any work done?" Lon said, looking at his wife. Bea shrugged. "I have bounce. I'm only twenty-six. I can drink all night and be had all night and still do a day's work. It's the goddamn waiting while they light the set that drives me crazy."

"*The History of History*," Kay murmured vaguely. Bea ran her fingers under her blonde hair and flipped it off her shoulders. "Christ, honey. Doesn't he ever take you to the movies? I'll bet you two are something alone." Kay began to blush in spite of mental warnings not to do it. "Your husband and I were never more than business, but I've heard stories. Always watch those gray-haired ones." Kay tried to shrug it off. "I'm just dying to see your house," she said.

"Come on, then," Bea said, getting up and pulling the toreador pants down a little. They followed her quickly. "I suppose he told you how I always wanted to live like a silent-movie star. You know, in the more or less grand manner. Frankly, I'm not making enough to maintain this. The studio says I'm whacky." As she walked ahead, Kay watched the muscles of the buttocks swing like small bar bells. "I'm up to three thousand a week on a seven-year contract, but if they can't use you more than twenty weeks a year, you're sort of dead, if you know what I mean. So I went to Italy and got $100,-000, and then to Bronston, who gave me $150,000 for playing

Mary Magdalene's sister. Honestly, I need the money. I go on
Skelton's show at $4,000 a copy just so he can look at me and
bust out laughing."

Once this girl starts talking, Kay decided, she doesn't stop. Bea
took them to a bathroom where the thick pile rug ran across
the floor, up the walls, and met itself in the middle of the ceiling.
"This is the guest bathroom," she said, standing in the doorway so
that they could enter and look. "I got the idea for the vases of
flowers abroad." She took them to a living room which, with its
arches and balconies and Belgian shirred drapes, might have come
out of a Moorish castle. There was a snow-white twelve-foot concert
grand piano, but Miss Busby said she couldn't play it and she didn't
know anyone who could.

There was a private theater downstairs with five rows of plush
seats and ash trays with "B-B" on them in gold. Kay said she
collected ashtrays. Bea said: "Help yourself, honey." There was a
kitchen with a middle-aged Negro woman working in it. "Here's
my baby," Bea said, and displayed a cage with a snarling animal in
it. "A small puma," she said. "In the old days, the silent-movie
stars used to have tigers sitting by the side of the swimming pool,
but I can never get one of these bastards to sit.

"They must all be born nervous. I had two others, but they
died. Just walked up and down in their cages, not eating, until
they died. I have one buried in the back, I'll show you. Now this
is the game room, but the games I play are not played here." The
room was huge. It had a billiard table, with old-fashioned orange
globe lights over it, old theater programs on the wall, two game
tables which, when the lids were lifted, held everything from
roulette to Old Maid. There was a bar made of black and white
diamond panels and the room had its own foyer, done in flame-
red wallpaper with black diamond inlay in the floor. The walls
of the little hall were covered with clippings of daring photos
of the owner. Every magazine; every cover, even the foreign

magazines, were displayed here. "In case I get blue," Bea said.

The dining room was large and tastefully done in old cherry-wood. Bea's bedroom was chintzy. It had a beautiful vanity with recessed lighting, some wing chairs, some books high on a wall, magazine racks, a white rug deep enough on which to sleep, and a circular bed big enough for four or six persons. "Look," she said. They looked up. The ceiling was a mural of all the love gods and goddesses from ancient pagan religions. Bea moved to the wall and pressed a button. "Keep looking," she said, and they kept looking. The murals parted in the middle and each side rolled back all the way to the wall, like heavy canvas shades. Exposed now was a huge pink mirror. "When I'm watching the action," she said casually, "I like to see it in pink. It's my favorite."

They looked at more bathrooms. More bedrooms. There was a study with an ornate desk, a mounted globe, and bookshelves with all the books bound in green, hand-tooled leather. "Come on downstairs," she said. "I want Lon to see the back." Kay glanced at him. They followed their hostess down and out a side entrance flanked by Grecian urns, and into the back. There, in a thirty-foot valley, was a huge swimming pool made in the shape of a heart. She pointed. On the bottom was a mosaic of Bea Busby nude, as though floating on her back.

Around the pool were dressing rooms, two cook-out grills, and a bar on rollers. A gardener walked through, lifted his hat in silence, and kept going. "Do you like to swim?" Bea said to Kay. No, Kay said, she couldn't swim. "Hell, I can't either," said Bea. "But I've been pushed in with my clothes on more times than I can count. I always manage to get out."

She took them to a small wall. "I make it a point," she said, "never to work with my hands. But right here I'm building a chapel. Yes, me. Once a week I try to get into the overalls. My man mixes the mortar and hands me the bricks. He just points. I do the actual work." Lon said he didn't know that Bea was

religious. "Religious?" she said. She burst into hoarse laughter.
"I'm the most truly religious son-of-a-bitch you'll meet out
here. Religious? When I was fourteen I taught Sunday school
in Tulsa."

"Ever hear from Johnny?" Lon said, studying the walls. "Once
a year or so," she said. "When he needs a couple of bucks, he
writes a letter and asks how the kids are. Otherwise, nothing. I had
to set him up in a dairy business, you know, just to cut loose. He
blew it, just like he blew everything else. But this chapel is
going to be nondenominational and I'm going to be the preacher
when it's finished."

"What are you going to preach?" Lon asked. "I mean, what
kind of preaching?" Miss Busby thought about it a moment.
"Well," she said, "I never got that far in my thinking. But I
know what I'd like to say. I'd like to tell everybody to believe
in all the good things and none of the bad things. There is a
heaven. There ain't no hell nowhere. Purgatory is just Serutan
spelled frontwards. There is a god and he's a great big wonderful
man just waiting to forgive all us sinners and take us to his
bosom. He thinks we're wonderful and we are wonderful. We
just lack confidence, that's all. He's going to give us confidence
and we'll all live in beautiful palaces with marble halls and we'll
be making love morning, noon and night because that's what
we're made for. To love one another the best we know how."
She paused a moment, then grinned. "And I know a few ways."

When they left, Kay said nothing for such a long time that Lon
asked her if anything was the matter. "Me?" Kay said. "I'm
speechless."

They packed too early. There was time, but the honeymoon
had run its course, and they yearned for home. "I'm going to
leave a good suit out," he said. "Black shoes, a dark tie and
one of Yen's striped shirts. In fact, if it sounds agreeable to you,

I'll dress in these things tonight and we'll have dinner in the Persian Room." She was reading. "Okay," Kay said. "Write a poem first." He said he was done with poems. "Write one for me," she said.

"It isn't nice," he said, "to ask me to do things I can't do." He wrote beautiful blank verse, she said. "Nuts," he said. "That's one of Bea's expressions," she said. "I heard her use it twice today." Lon smiled to himself. "Isn't she something?" he said. "Almost all movie stars are fake personalities. They have to work one up to support the parts they play, but Bea Busby is something dug up out of Shadowlawn."

Kay said she wasn't so sure. "I see her a little differently than I expected. I don't know what to think. She's sexy, for sure. She acts like she invented it. But a woman sees underneath a little bit. Your Bea is trying to surround herself with things to remind her that she's a movie star. Everybody believes it except Bea. As you say, when she loses that bust line, she's going to be seen less and less." He shrugged. "Maybe she's afraid of Tulsa."

"Maybe. But no woman is going around hopping in and out of bed with platoons of men unless she's out to buy something. This goes against everything inside the girl. All of them want complete possession of one man—right? Then why the Italian count, the Spaniards, the affairs she has had here with directors and producers and camera men and reporters—all the ones you told me about? Why? Because these are the people who can help her to think big, think star, be a star."

"That's parlor psychology," he said. Kay picked her book up, and poured a drink. "Write a poem," she said. He said no. "Please," she said. "I think of her as being gutter cheap," he continued. "She has no ability to act; the critics write funny lines about her; she can't sing a note; she can't dance, recite dialogue, understand script; she can't do anything except hop out of bed, excusing herself as she does it, and run off to the studio hairdresser at six A.M. Between the bed and the camera, she hopes to remain Bea Busby, the last of the silent-movie stars."

"Please write a poem," Kay said. "Even a nasty one will do." He chuckled and dropped a dram of Scotch on his ice. "I can't write a good one," he said, "but maybe I can write a nasty one. No, not truly nasty, but bluesy; you know, the other side of the coin." She dropped the book. "It's only six," she said. "You'd make me so happy if you'd write just one more. I won't ask again."

He went to the typewriter, scratching the back of his head. "I'll do it instead of a diary entry," he said. "Why should I quarrel with the fact that you don't know good poetry from junk? This stuff pleases your vanity, not your intellect." "Just write," she pleaded. "Don't analyze."

Lon was slower this time. He made many changes and, when he had retyped it, he turned to present it to her and she was sleeping, with the book on her lap.

A BLUE EVENING

Free me, spring the lock
Take me back a short time
To where we had not met.
Let me walk alone under the stars,
Bare feet in wet sand, the stinging salt
Of the sea on an insolent breeze.
Make it so that I know you not
So that I can dwell with pleasure
On simple things: a hill of ants,
A gull in silhouette against the sun,
A little girl concentrating on shoelaces.

Until I met you, the world was me—
A universe of backdrops; percale snow

Plastered on one side of black oaks;
It was me, with coconut palms leaning
Drunkenly against an east wind;
It was me, in a dark bar laughing
At the stories of faceless friends.
It was me in an empty room, a sock half on,
Sleep edging eyes which watched the
Sinuous dance of cigarette smoke.
It was me immersed in music which
Bathed the body in warm harmonics.

I set a trap for you, and watched
With the instinct of the hunter as you
Walked toward it. Your head was high, your expression
Noble as you fell. Your world became one of
Spinning darkness as you dropped into emptiness.
The hunter has no pity; he watches the fall,
Hears the cry of pain; he pulls the net closed.
For him, the game is over. The sport is done.
He must not draw close to look at his prey.
I did. I saw you in the pit, the blue eyes
Searching upward for light; the mouth helpless
And trembling. I stayed too long. I leaned too far.

Now we are in the pit together and I trace the tears
Across a face dim in cool darkness; I beg to leave
The prison and my shouts loose tiny pebbles which fall
Like grains of rice on a forsaken bride.
I hold you tight because my world has been reduced
To two hearts which can be heard
In the dark silence. There is no way out,
My love, for you or me; and I would not go
If the old gods lowered ropes of apple blossoms.
Rather would I suffocate eagerly in the
Perfume of your breath. Now I hear the strains

Of strings which no musician plays; I hold you
To me and stare up at the indecipherable
Code of the night stars—and I swear, through
Constricted throat, that I will be with you forever.

Across the bottom, Lon scrawled: "This one writ wrotten by
Gnash, Ogden, who is without honor among sleepy brides. . . ."

THE THIRTIETH DAY

THE Michaelses were still buttering rolls as the bellboys were carrying the luggage out. "Take your time," Lon said. "It's only seven A.M." Kay was eating fast. She looked funny, gulping coffee with a hat on, watching the bags go out, keeping one hand on her gloves. "I'm going to carry my heavy coat," she said. "It's going to be cold in New York." She had been talking about her father, talking as though she remembered him well and fondly.

"Do I remind you of him?" Lon asked. She smiled. "You're asking me if I married you because you're a father image?" "Stop anticipating the plot," he said. "Am I like him?" Kay shook her head. "He was tall and very slender, an easy-going man." "He was your idol," Lon said. Kay nodded and finished her coffee. "The only thing he had in common with you," she said, "is that he was all male." "Most men are all male," he said.

"You mean sexually," she said, picking up coat and gloves. "That's not enough. The female is responsive to many signs of maleness: pitch of voice, a man's walk, his gestures, his attitudes about things. Some men are more male than others."

Lon stood, brushed the crumbs from his jacket, and put his hat on. "I sent a couple of wires while you were washing." Kay raised her eyebrows. "One to Katie, saying that we would be

363

home about seven and to ask Burge to pick us up at four o'clock
at Idlewild. The other was to Dr. Robertson, telling him I would
stop by his office before seven."

"Doctor who?" she said. "Robertson. He's my doctor in Spring
Lake." She looked alarmed. "Something wrong?" she asked. "Not
a thing," he said. "I had a thorough examination just before
we left, and he owes me some reports." He tipped the maid and,
under the canopy, the bellboys and the doorman. Everybody said,
"Come back soon." The taxi was jammed with suitcases. They got
in, and started for Los Angeles International, fifteen miles away.

The morning was clear and warm and United Airlines Flight
Eight Fourteen made a scamper getaway. Kay asked Lon if he
was going "up front." He said no. He was going to sit the final
leg out with her. He had completed a log of the trip, if she
wanted to see it. Kay was interested. He reached down and pulled
a sheet of paper from the briefcase. The gun shone silvery in the
morning light.

He made a final notation. "The captain says that we will be
in New York in four hours and thirty minutes. Now, here it is,
fairly complete."

FLIGHT	TIME	MILES
New York—Paris	6:30	3,661
Paris—Beirut	4:30	2,243
Beirut—Jerusalem round trip	2:15	600
Beirut—New Delhi	5:00	2,578
New Delhi—Bangkok	3:05	1,836
Bangkok—Hong Kong	2:13	1,167
Hong Kong—Tokyo	3:17	1,940
Tokyo—Honolulu	6:20	3,900
Honolulu—Los Angeles	4:26	2,400
Los Angeles—New York	4:30	2,450
STOPS: 10	TIME: 42:06	MILES:22,775

Kay studied the chart with more interest than he had expected. "It's incredible," she said. "Out of thirty days, we were in the air less than two." It was really less than that, he said. "The total reads forty-two hours and six minutes. But that's counting the side trip to Jerusalem and back." He figured rapidly with a pencil on the edge of the sheet of paper. "It really comes to thirty-nine hours and fifty-one minutes around the world, and twenty-two thousand, one hundred and seventy-five miles."

A stewardess asked what they would like for breakfast. They said coffee only. For a while, Kay stared out the window at the changing views. First the Santa Barbara mountains, then the desert, then bigger mountains followed by more desert. "Oh," she exclaimed, pointing. Lon bent across her to see. Four jet fighters were crossing above the United DC-8. They weren't close, but they left four straight white lines across the deep blue sky.

"What did you like best about the whole trip?" Lon asked her. "You," she said. He insisted: "What did you like—" "Beirut," she said. "It's fascinating to me. The meeting of the Moslem world and the Christian world. How about you?" "Bangkok," he said. "I enjoyed all of them, but Bangkok is so friendly, so uncomplicated." "I liked Bangkok too. Almost as much as Beirut. What's least on your list?" "Paris," he said. She nodded in agreement. "Too commercial for me. I love the city, the beauty, the parks, but the people do not love me." "The people of Paris," Lon said, "do not even love other French people. They are in love with themselves."

They sipped their coffee and thought their separate thoughts. The big plane sat high and still; even the edge of sunlight coming through the window seemed to remain fixed on the tip of the curtain. "Home," he said nostalgically. "I can't say I'm sorry." "Me either." "A honeymoon is such a beautiful thing—even with disagreements it has the same fascination as a portrait in shadows." "I regard a honeymoon as part of the marriage itself," she said.

"No. I mean, part of the wedding ceremony. Beginning tonight, we start a married life."

They dreamed on a while. "I'm happy," he said. "And I can't say how happy. I want the house to be yours as much as mine; all I ask is that you do not disturb the office. You may not like the way you find it, but leave it that way." She said they should call the Murrays when they got in. Also the Sullivans in Spring Lake. "We can have dinner there," Lon said. "Did I tell you that they once made a trip around the world with a writer. An insufferable chap. Knew everything about everything. One of those—what is your phrase again—all purpose pains. . . ."

She pointed to a blue lake. He consulted a chart and looked at his watch. "That town," he said, "should be Claremore, Oklahoma. Will Rogers was born there. Funny, we're two hours out of Idlewild. That means that Burge has already left the house for the airport." "It takes two hours?" she asked. A little more, he said. "Tell me," Kay asked. "Does Burge have any trouble getting a driver's license?" "On account of the missing leg? No. He has a plastic one with stainless-steel hinges."

"Are you going to write a book on Byblos?" she asked later. He said he didn't think so. It had sounded good at first, but her lack of enthusiasm made him think readers might not like it. "Don't go by my opinions," she said. "God, I'm the poorest . . ." Quite the contrary, he said. The idea of three separate civilizations with the same set of characters in all three seemed sound to him but he regarded her as an average reader and, if she didn't like it lots of readers wouldn't. "Please," she said. "I'm sorry I had anything to say—"

"Forget it," he said. "Don't ever feel guilty about your opinions. The final decision on books is always mine. If someone else writes that book, and it becomes a best-seller, believe me, the fault is mine, not yours. We'll be coming down soon. How about one drink for the world's most magnificent honeymoon?" "Ah, she said. "I'll drink a double to that."

They toasted each other. "To you," he said, "if you were ten years older, and to me, if I were ten younger." "To us," she said, "as we are." They drank. The captain's voice came on. "We are over Sunbury, Pennsylvania," he said, "and we will start down soon. There will be a little turbulence because the New York area is cloudy. The temperature at Idlewild is thirty-eight and snow is even promised for tonight."

"Oh," Lon said sarcastically, "we're home all right. Stick some stamps on my forehead and mail me to Bangkok." She took his hand in hers. "Cold or hot," she said, "it's home."

Traffic was slow all the way through New York. A long line waited two abreast to get through the Lincoln Tunnel. "Commuters going home," Burge said in the front seat. Lon sat in back, holding Kay's hand. "It's also Friday," he said. "I don't care, as long as you keep the heater going." Burge chuckled. "I can blast you out of the back seat," he said.

He had asked how the trip went, and he had asked it perfunctorily, as though he didn't care for a reply. Kay thought that Burge was resentful, jealous, but Lon knew that he was always like this. "Does Lucy get along with Kate?" Kay asked. Burge looked over his shoulder at her. "As well as anyone can," he said. "In fact, I detect a softness in the old bag since Lucy arrived. You see, underneath that tough German shell lies a Gestapo agent. And under that is a soft mother. Lucy is there."

"I don't suppose you heard anything about Sonny?" Lon said. "I mean, medically." Burge moved down into the tunnel, a few feet at a time. It was like squeezing toothpaste back into a tube. "I met Robertson one day at the A & P. He says the kid may be home in a few weeks. He would advise you to stay away for a while. They're doing same kind of psychotherapy. He tried to commit suicide, you know."

Lon's heart dropped. He hated the way Burge tossed bad news into conversation. If the greenhouse burned down, he would start by talking about the seedlings. "I got no message," Lon said. Kay held his hand more tightly. "It wasn't much," Burge said. "Robertson said it was a bluff to get attention. He tied his shirt in knots and hung it over a steam pipe." Lon emitted a long sigh. "Anything else?" he asked softly.

"About what?" Burge said. Lon's voice rose a little. "About anything." Burge thought about the question. "Not a thing. The septic tank had to be pumped out. Katie had a virus while you were away. Gone now. And, let me see—we almost ran out of oil for the heater." "Did Sonny start drinking the same day we left?" Kay asked. Burge nodded.

"When that kid decides to go, he goes," he said. "You left Idlewild early in the evening, didn't you? Well, you didn't clear Long Island before he was frazzled." "Do you think," Kay said anxiously, "that perhaps if we hadn't gone—" "Burge isn't a psychiatrist," Lon said, "yet. His opinion is worth no more than yours. Even Dr. Robertson isn't a psychiatrist. When I want an opinion, I'll ask Sonny's doctor."

"Did you say you want to stop at Robertson's first?" Burge asked. Lon said yes. The car got through the tunnel and onto the Garden State Parkway. There wasn't much conversation after that. Lon asked himself why he had never discharged this quietly insolent man. "There goes me. . . ." he murmured. "What did you say?" Kay asked. He shook his head. "I was just thinking that the air here is more polluted than ever; it is cold and damp all winter; the sky is amber and gray on a clear day—it's lousy."

"You don't talk like that," Burge said, "when you're sailing out of Manasquan Inlet on a summer morning." Lon had to smile. "Right," he said. "Maybe that's the hold this part of the country has on me." "Plus the fact," Kay said, "that you were born and raised here. All your friends are here." "Yours aren't," he said.

"My work could be done in Florida as easily as in Point Pleasant."
"Lucy likes the school," Burge said. "She's been in it only
three weeks and she got her first report card." Kay leaned forward,
excitement in her face. "She likes it? Funny, she never liked any
school before." "Mad about it," Burge said, stopping to pay a
toll. "She likes the teacher. In fact, that old piano may be put
to use. She told the teacher she likes music, and the teacher says
she'll teach her piano if you okay it." "Of course we'll okay it,"
Lon said. "Why the hell do you always hold back the good news
until after the scourging?" Burge shrugged, and pulled down past
Victory Bridge and over through South Amboy. "I don't even
know what a scourging is," he said. Kay cut in. "She really, really
likes it?" she persisted. Burge nodded. "Haven't I just said it?
The kid can't wait to go to school in the morning. I already
told you she melted Katie down."

"So you have," Lon said. "Any news from Dale Yacht Works?"
"Forgot," Burge said. "You got practically no compression on
cylinders three and seven in the starboard engine. They think it
needs a ring job." "Okay," Lon said. "I'll call Hahn and have
it done." There was little traffic now, and the car sped on through
the early-evening twilight, and soon the first fat snowflakes rushed
toward the windshield, to be pinned against it and shoved down-
ward by the wiper.

By the time they passed Asbury Park, the snow was thick and
swirling. "Hungry?" Lon asked. Kay said a little bit. "There's
a place on the highway where we can stop." "Oh no," she protested. "I'm dying to get home. I've been waiting forever and I'm
not going to stop now." Forever? A mere thirty days. Still, thirty
days could be forever if one was anxious. Unless, of course, one
had the unique ability to shunt aside anticipatory fears. Lon could
do this. He could be aware of fear about Sonny, but he could—
if necessary—derail the ugly chain of thoughts and concentrate
completely on matters that he had the power to control.

Burge drove off on Exit 96 and went down through the little towns of the Jersey Shore until he reached Spring Lake. The wheels of the car scarred the smooth white cotton on the road with black ribbons. He turned off onto Third Street and pulled up in front of a house with a light on the porch. A sign on the lawn said T. W. ROBERTSON, M.D.

"Want me to go in with you?" Lon shook his head. She watched him get out and she felt that she was watching a wounded animal who wanted to sneak off into the brush alone. She didn't know why she felt that way. It wasn't sensible. But there was something in his silence, something in the way he left without a glance. Going up the walk, his posture was a little too straight, the shoulders a bit too square. Still, it was probably her imagination. Everything was so wonderful, so happy, so enduring that she was looking for dark clouds in an azure sky.

In a moment, he was out again. He bounded down the steps, his head cocked against the falling snow, and got into the back seat of the car and threw both arms around Kay. He kissed her so hard she felt her teeth cut into her lip. "My God!" she said. He sat back in silence. Burge started the car, staring into the rear-view mirror and looking puzzled. "What is the matter, dear?" Kay asked, but Lon didn't answer. He seemed to be in a reverie. Then he glanced at her, smiled, and kissed her tenderly.

"We slew the dragon dead," he said. "Burge, take us over the Manasquan Bridge." Burge turned almost all the way around "There is no other way," he said, "unless you want to go over the railroad bridge." "Don't argue with me," Lon said, still smiling, "just go. And go slow. Keep in the right-hand lane." He was impish, happy-crazy. "And turn that rear-view mirror aside so that I can make love to my bride without watching you watch me."

Burge turned the mirror. His head was shaking sadly. Lon cupped Kay's face in his hands, and squeezed it until her lip protruded. "My Ubangi," he murmured, and kissed her again. "If you have lost your mind," she said, "I wish you'd lose it more often." He pushed away and took a deep breath. "All this time," he murmured. "I'm going to kill that doctor." The car started up the bridge. Kay began to smile. "I don't know what it is, but it must be something good."

"Good?" he said. "Good? An understatement. Use a Hollywood word—terrific, sensational, fantastic. You see this?" He held out a piece of paper. "No, you can't see it in the dark. Wait a minute." They were nearing the center of the bridge. He reached into his briefcase and yanked the little gun out. Then he rolled down the back window and heaved mightily and the gun disappeared into the snow. They didn't even hear it when it hit the surface of the river. "There," he said. "Is that a good start?" Kay shook her head in wonderment. "I wish—" she said.

"In good time," he said. "I'm so damned excited I think I'm going to have a heart attack. You know what that son-of-a-bitch did? Could you guess?" Kay coughed politely. "What son-of-a-bitch, darling?" "The doctor, of course. I told you I had an examination before I left. Remember? Well, right behind the palate he found a small mound of something. It was so important that he called another doctor in to have a look."

"You never said a word," Kay said. "I know. I know," he said. "How can two people go on a honeymoon thinking cancer? Bad enough for one. So he took a specimen and did a biopsy. Did you ever sweat out one of those things? Well, don't. You feel good except that some pathologist you never met has a shred of you and he is going to tell you whether you will live or die. And tomorrow is the wedding day." He became serious for a time. The mood had swung all the way. "I just didn't have the heart to tell you. I asked Robertson for the low-down, no smiling evasions. He said that if it turned out bad, it was inoperable." He opened his mouth wide and pointed, although she could see nothing. "Inoperable. The back of the throat, right next to the spine.

"So I said 'Please, please let me know as soon as you can.' I gave our itinerary to his secretary. 'Just cable Okay, or Not okay,' I said. Would you believe it, the girl mislaid the itinerary and Robertson said 'It will keep until he gets home. He's okay.' It was negative. He knew it, honey, but I didn't. I couldn't tell you. So, the morning I met you to get married, I did two things: I made out a will leaving seventy per cent of everything to you and Lucy, and thirty per cent to Sonny."

"Nothing for me?" Burge said. Lon grinned again. "Not a dime, my friend. I think there's a clause that says: 'My friend Burge took care of himself in my lifetime,' so you get nothing when I go. Anyway, I made out the will and got the little gadget you just saw me throw into the river." "Oh God!" Kay whispered. "What you must have been through!"

"So I was sure it was bad news as we pulled up to Robertson's house. The bastard hasn't even got the decency to be home. He left a note, said he was sorry I hadn't been told, but that the mound, or whatever he called it, turned out to be proud flesh from an old cut or something." He looked into her eyes as they passed the streetlights of Point Pleasant and turned up toward Clark's Landing.

"I had myself dead," he said. "I'm not kidding. All the way around the world I kept telling myself: 'Have fun. Drink it all in. This is the last time for you.' I even faked the idea of the book just to keep the bad thoughts out of my mind. Sometimes it worked. Sometimes, when I was mean and sarcastic, the gloom was on me and I couldn't shake it."

"We're almost there," Burge said. Kay sighed. "May I say something?" she said. "I'm swamped with words. Let the bride say two words before we get home. Thank God for everything." "That's four," said Lon and Burge together. "Okay," she said. "I'll stick to the first two."